Sweet Offerings

by
Chan Ling Yap

Pen Press

First published in Great Britain by Pen Press

Pen Press is an imprint of Indepenpress Publishing Limited
25 Eastern Place
Brighton BN2 1GJ

ISBN: 978-1-906710-98-9

Cover design by Jacqueline Abromeit

Acknowledgements

I am indebted to my husband for the encouragement and help he has given me. I wish also to thank Dr. Margaret Walters for her valuable comments on my first draft and all those other kind individuals who have looked at the manuscript in its various stages, including my son Lee and daughter Hsu Min. Thanks also go to the Bodleian Library where I spent many happy hours of research.

Prologue

Commanding the Straits of Malacca, a historic and strategic trade route, the Peninsula of Malaya has long been a meeting place of people from all over the world. In the second and third centuries, traders and adventurers arrived from India and exerted a strong influence for some 1000 years. Later came new influences. Chief amongst these were people from Sumatra, the adjacent island to the west. Malacca was founded by a Sumatran exile, Prince Parameswara, later known as Sultan Iskandar Shah. Through him strong links were established with the Ming dynasty in China and Malacca became effectively a Chinese protectorate. Trade flourished in the city and the influx of traders from all over Asia, as well as from the Middle East, grew. By the 1430s, Malacca was the commercial entrepôt for South East Asia as well as an Islamic religious centre.

Foreign influences were not confined to those from the East. In 1511, the Portuguese captured Malacca. They were followed in 1641 by the Dutch. By then, however, Malacca's importance had declined. New areas in the Peninsula came into prominence. The Buginese from the island of Celebes established the sultanates of Selangor and Johore during the 18th century. In the 19th century, the British arrived. They brought in many Chinese, mainly as indentured labour, to open up the Straits Settlements and for tin mining.

By 1941, Malaya (which then included Singapore) had a rich mix of races. The Malays made up the bulk of the population; Chinese, representing some 40 percent of the total, came a close second; Indians and Tamils from Sri Lanka (then Ceylon) made up most of the rest.

Inter-marriage was generally limited. Differences in religion, language, geographical distribution and even occupation, were all important dividing forces. Ethnic Malays were Moslems and spoke Malay. The Indians were generally Hindus from South India and spoke Tamil. The Chinese, mainly from southeastern China, spoke Hokkien, Cantonese or Hakka. They were Buddhists, Taoists or Christians, but, regardless of their religious belief, Confucianism was the prevalent force in their way of life.

For the most part the three principal ethnic groups lived in harmony. 'Give and take' was practised as a matter of course, and differences in culture were generally accepted and respected. Most people spoke Malay or at least some kind of 'market Malay'. English became the *lingua franca* following the growth of English missionary schools. It was the language of the judiciary, public administration and business. Running parallel to the English infrastructure were the Chinese schools. The priority given to education by the Chinese, with their Confucianist tradition of learning, helped maintain this separate system of education.

This largely harmonious co-existence of the different racial groups was already well established in the late 1930s when this story begins, and gave Malaya its unique character and cultural environment.

Mei Yin

Chapter 1

Mei Yin hitched her school satchel higher up her back, struggling at the same time with a large rattan basket that she carried balanced in the crook of her arm. Filled with cakes, the basket was threatening to tilt and spill its contents onto the ground.

"I'll be in big trouble if I drop the cakes," she muttered under her breath, "worse still, I'll be late for school again."

She hurried along the dirt track, through the paddy fields and coconut groves, her sandals dragging on the rough earth. They were loose and her toes kept snagging on the straps.

It was early dawn but already the sun was shining fiercely. The dew that had sparkled on the sharp blades of wild *lalang* grass had already evaporated and the humid air was dense with the green scent of plants. Beads of sweat formed on her forehead. She hitched up the satchel again before turning, with some relief, into the dusty market square where traders were setting up stalls and laying out their wares. Trays of fresh vegetables lay next to each other, some on the ground, some on trestle tables, their bright colours of red, green, yellow and white, competing for attention: fat white turnips, mounds of pointed red chillies and bunches of long beans. At the far corner of the open square stood the fish stall. Fish of all shapes, sizes and hue lay inert on slabs of ice. Next to it, an old woman bustled around cages of squawking hens and ducks, her arms busy wrestling with the birds, sending clouds of feathers flying, before finally pulling out the one chosen by a customer.

A chorus of greetings in Malay and Chinese heralded Mei Yin's arrival. The little girl, though barely 12, was popular among the market people. "What have you got for us today?" Aminah, the Malay cake vendor, and Ah Sam, the Chinese vegetable seller, called out to her.

Mei Yin placed her basket carefully on the ground. She lifted the cloth cover, releasing a sweet fragrance of freshly steamed dough. She took out the first layer of cakes – *kueh talam*, a Malay sweet flavoured with bright green, aromatic juice from the *pandan* leaf, and topped with coconut cream. Next came a tray of steamed glutinous rice cakes, grainy white with sprinklings of bright blue juice from the Morning Glory flower, and topped with a baked conserve of egg custard, coconut and sugar. Finally she took out the bottom tray, a cake consisting of thin alternating layers of pink, white and yellow sweet rice pudding cut into diamond wedges. The layers, nine in all, were so delicate that each one would peel into a separate sheet of sweetness in the mouth.

Standing back from her display, she announced proudly, "Mamah made these cakes this morning. They're still warm."

Her mother, Sook Ping, had warned her that Ah Sam would want to be sure that the layer cakes were freshly made. They were for the wedding of her neighbour's daughter. The nine layers are symbols of longevity. If the cakes were to turn rancid, it would be a very bad omen. Sure enough, Ah Sam was already lifting the tray to her nose and placing a finger gently on each cake to test their consistency. Soon people gathered around them, attracted by the sweet aroma of the cakes and friendly banter.

"Mmm ... *wangi*! *Bagus*!" They sniffed and nodded appreciatively to each other.

But Mei Yin was impatient to be on her way. She shifted her weight from one leg to the other. She hopped in exasperation. Still they talked, filling the air with musical chatter, the two languages clashing then mingling into one. Her mother had taught her to raise the subject of payment with delicacy, but she was running out of time. Finally, she could contain herself no longer. She hesitated before blurting out, "Please can I have the money? I'm late for school."

"Yes, yes, of course!" Ah Sam pressed an extra coin into Mei Yin's hands. Aminah, not to be outdone, gave her a piece of *kueh talam*.

Mei Yin barely paused to thank them. She grabbed the empty basket and broke into a run. The school was ten minutes away and the school bell could ring any moment. She had already arrived after the bell twice that week because she had left home late. But how could she explain to the teacher that she was late because the coconut cream had not set? This was always a problem when the cream came from young coconuts. Mahmud, who supplied the coconuts, had run out of old ones, but her mother did not want to buy from anyone else. Mahmud depended on his small grove of coconut palms to feed his entire family. It seemed such an unlikely explanation, even though it was true. Ah Sam or Aminah would have understood, not Miss Kung, her teacher. She did not look like someone who did much cooking.

As she approached the school gate, Mei Yin slowed down and wiped her face and arms with a little square of towelling that she kept tucked in her pocket. Her legs were dusty, her uniform crumpled, but at least she was not late. Heaving a sigh of relief, she joined the queue of girls waiting to go into the main hall of Chung Kun School for Girls.

* * * * *

Mid-day. The sound of the school bell rang out across the playground. Long, orderly processions of girls dressed in black and white uniforms marched out of the classrooms, their arms and legs moving with almost military precision. The orderliness was short-lived. The minute they emerged from the schoolhouse, they scrambled for the tuck shop, elbows jostling, in their effort to be first in line. The teacher's admonishment to behave, forgotten.

The tuck shop was a plain wooden shack, but to the girls, it was a magic place. Jars of sweets, prawn crackers, pickled ginger, and sweet and sour dried plums filled the shelves. To the front stood a wooden trestle. In one section of this long counter lay banana-leaved parcels of rice cooked in coconut cream with a spicy *sambal* and fried rice noodles. Tall glasses of rose syrup, sugar-cane juice and barley water came next. But, best of all, at the far end, stood an ice crusher that churned out balls of grated ice filled with sweetened maize and red bean paste.

Mei Yin did not join in the scramble for the tuck shop. Instead, clutching her purse in one hand and the rice cake Aminah had given her in the other, she made her way to a bench in the shade of a mango tree. She unwrapped the cake and ate slowly, making each mouthful last.

"Should I buy an ice-ball?" she wondered, her eyes lingering on a girl sucking on the ice, cheeks drawn in with the effort, eyes closed in apparent bliss. It would take nearly all the money Ah Sam had given her for herself and she needed to save to buy her exercise books. But thoughts of the sweet ice melting on her tongue kept tempting her. She could almost feel the cold ice touching her lips when she was awoken from her reverie by the voice of Siew Lin, her best friend.

"Come on Mei Yin, come and join us. We're going to play hop scotch." Siew Lin turned in the direction of Mei Yin's gaze and grinned. "I know what you want," she teased. "You've been staring at the ice ball for ages. Get one. They're really good."

Mei Yin blushed. She shook her head. "I can't," she replied. Immediately Siew Lin realised she had embarrassed her friend. Quickly covering up her blunder, Siew Lin added, "I'm going to get another. We can share it."

With a grateful glance, Mei Yin clambered down from the bench and the two friends hurried, hand in hand, towards the tuck shop.

* * * * *

Siew Lin's family, the Tans, had moved into the big three-storey mansion on Tai Peng Road, not far from where Mei Yin lived, six years earlier. White with tall columns flanking the marble steps that led to its entrance, the mansion stood in stark contrast to the wooden huts resting on stilts that dotted the surrounding landscape. It had taken months to build and had caused major consternation amongst the villagers.

When Siew Lin's family finally moved in, they held a big feast for the entire village. "This is to thank the people and get them to accept us," Mr Tan had told his family. Mei Yin and her mother Sook Ping were among the scores of villagers who were invited. Chain after chain of firecrackers were let off to bring future prosperity and to frighten away evil spirits. The ground was littered with the red cases of the firecrackers for days after.

The feast took place mainly in the garden courtyard. Makeshift barbecue stands were set up in one corner; flames blazed in the pots of glowing charcoal over which metal grids had been placed. Sticks of *satay*, thinly sliced chicken or goat meat marinated in turmeric, lemon grass, coconut cream and sugar and threaded on to bamboo sticks, lay sizzling on the grids. Every now and then, the cook would dip a bunch of lemon grass into coconut oil and shake it over the meat, fanning the fire vigorously with his other hand. The leaping flames turned the meat golden brown and the dense night air became suffused with a blend of aromatic scents, of cooking spices and caramelised meats. Now and then voices, punctured by sighs of appreciation, rose above the sound of crackling fire as the village guests tucked into the sticks of *satay* and bowls of spicy peanut sauce. People spoke in hushed tones, overawed by the grandeur of their surroundings.

"Do you think they will fit into our humble community?" one of the villagers asked.

"No!" another replied. "They are not like us. They don't dress like us, they don't eat the same food, they don't even speak Malay. They are from Hong Kong. See there, behind the palm leaves, the entire family is eating their meal away from us." He scowled. "So much for all that big talk about wanting to meet the villagers!"

Heads craned, bodies shifted as the villagers tried to get a good view of the large round table behind the huge fronds of the palm trees. Servants in black and white were laying dish after dish on the table.

"You are Chinese so why do you think you are one of us and not one of them?" one villager, a Malay, asked the speaker.

"How could you ask? How long have you known me? I am a *Baba*. It is true my family came from China, yes, there is no doubt about that. But that was centuries ago. We have lived here for generations now and we married your women. You should know what *Baba* means, Straits-born Chinese."

"Inter-marry? Not any more you don't," the other retorted.

"Yes, yes, I admit, it's different now. We have to keep to our Confucianist belief. It's difficult to juggle two beliefs. We can't all become Moslems. But we certainly like the same food as you. We speak like you. We even dress like you," he continued pointing to the colourful ankle-length batik *sarong* and tight-fitting top of his wife.

"I don't really care what they eat, but I still think they are stand-offish, rude even, to invite us and then not eat with us," commented another. "But we should enjoy ourselves and not waste good food." Taking a stick of *satay*, he held it in front of little Mei Yin, trying to entice her to come out of hiding.

Mei Yin, then six years old, responded by burying herself even more deeply in the folds of her mother's *sarong*. Bewildered by the crowd, nothing could persuade her to budge from her refuge. Not, that is, until she spied a little girl of her age, dressed in a traditional Chinese *sam foo* with its silk top and high-buttoned mandarin collar and matching silk trousers running towards her. The little girl smiled brightly at Mei Yin, her mischievous grin revealing pearly white teeth.

"Go Mei Yin, go! Play with her," said her mother. Encouraged, she relinquished her mother's skirt and held out her hands to the girl.

An elderly maid, complete with pigtail and dressed in a starched cotton *sam foo*, came rushing over, hands raised to stop Mei Yin. "Oh, no, no, you must not touch our little Miss Siew Lin." She wagged her finger in admonishment at Mei Yin. "You," she continued rudely, "sit over there! Our little mistress only plays with her own kind. You could get her dirty and untidy."

Under the baleful glare of the maid, Mei Yin retreated once more to the folds of Sook Ping's *sarong* while Siew Lin was hustled back into the house to join the formal banquet being held by the Tans.

Chapter 2

Two days after the feast, Sook Ping received a message from Mrs Tan inviting her to the big house. She was asked to bring Mei Yin along with her. Curious about the invitation, Sook Ping rushed through the morning's housework and then set about getting Mei Yin ready.

"Come on, time to wash and dress." Sook Ping marched Mei Yin to the bathhouse, an outbuilding near the well. Small and made of concrete, the bathhouse had a raised stone tub fed by a pipe that connected to a hand pump at the well. She stood the little girl in front of the tub. In and out went Sook Ping's bucket, each time barely missing the carp that was kept there to stop the water becoming a breeding ground for mosquitoes. "Look, look," shouted Mei Yin, jumping to keep warm and pointing at the carp, swimming wildly, its golden body flashing, dodging the bucket. The water was cold.

"Stay still," her mother scolded, sluicing water over Mei Yin. "Here and here," she said as she vigorously applied homemade soap on Mei Yin. Then more rinsing and, finally, after a vigorous rub-down with a towel Mei Yin was pronounced clean. Her skin glowed pink. Her mother combed, parted and plaited her hair. Once in her best dress, a hand-down from her sister, she was ready.

The Tan's house was only a short walk away. Mei Yin recognised immediately the maid who came to the door and shrank instinctively behind her mother. She was the person who had stopped her playing with the little girl. There was no finger wagging this time, but there was not much of a welcome either. She led them into a large, austere room with a marble floor. Four straight-backed ceremonial chairs of lacquered ebony stood against one wall. Each pair shared a high side table. A long, low settee flanked by two armchairs graced the centre of the room, their soft upholstery incongruous in a room that was otherwise formal and severe. Further to the side was a screen with four panels painted with gold leaf. Beyond this lay a smaller area, with a square table and four chairs at its centre. Mei Yin and her mother were directed there.

"Please take a seat. Mistress will join you in a moment," the maid announced curtly, turning away with a swirl of her pigtail to leave the room even before she had finished her words.

Mei Yin and her mother sat down, feeling more than a little self-conscious and uncomfortable. Soon afterwards, Mrs Tan entered the room. "So good of you to come, so good," she greeted.

Mrs Tan sat down, arranging and re-arranging her skirt and patting the topknot she had tied so tightly that her eyes were pulled like wings to the side. She had invited Sook Ping on impulse and had been fretting about it ever since. She had not consulted her husband or her mother-in-law and was afraid now that they might disapprove. Her fingers clutched nervously at the pendant hanging around her neck. She struggled to begin. An awkward silence followed. Mother and daughter sat waiting, their eyes fixed on the dithering Mrs Tan.

Finally, Mrs Tan said, "It's about my daughter, Siew Lin. She is my only child. When she was a little baby, I took her to Hong Kong to see *Nai-nai*. My mother-in-law fell in love with her and out of filial respect I had to leave Siew Lin with her."

"Oh no, poor you!" Sook Ping exclaimed, completely forgetting the strangeness of her surroundings and her early fears of Mrs Tan.

"It broke my heart," Mrs Tan admitted, her mouth quivering as she recalled the event, the harsh words when she tried to refuse and the unequivocal demand of her mother-in-law that was satisfied only by her complete capitulation.

"But is she still with your mother-in-law? Didn't I see her at the party the other night." Sook Ping was confused.

"Yes, Siew Lin is back with us now. She stayed in Hong Kong until she turned four. Then my mother-in-law joined us in Kuala Lumpur and so Siew Lin came back to us." Mrs Tan turned and looked nervously behind the screen, almost as though she expected to see her mother-in-law standing there, before continuing in the same hushed voice. "Siew Lin was with us in Kuala Lumpur for only two years, barely long enough to make friends, before we had to move here. These changes, especially the last move, have really unsettled her. She has no playmates here. We . . . we seem unable to make many friends in Malacca."

She paused, afraid she might have blundered with the last confession. What would her *nai-nai* say, she wondered. She looked hesitantly around and then, encouraged by Sook Ping's sympathetic expression, continued.

"Siew Lin is going to start school soon. *Nai-nai* wants her to attend a Chinese school. She wants her to learn the traditions of Chinese culture. I am afraid my mother-in-law still clings to the old beliefs, and what she wants goes. Girls, she says, must learn to obey the family. She is afraid that an English school will spoil her attitude because she believes that the missionaries who run these schools have values that are different from Confucianism."

Sook Ping grew apprehensive, wondering where all this was leading. Too polite to interrupt, she nodded again encouragingly.

"When Siew Lin saw Mei Yin the other evening," continued Mrs Tan, "she took an instant liking to her. So if you agree, I would like Mei Yin to come to visit us and play with Siew Lin."

Sook Ping's bewilderment changed to surprise then consternation. All kinds of obstacle came to mind. What would Mrs Tan's *nai-nai* say? Visions of the maid's disdain and rudeness as she snatched Siew Lin away from Mei Yin haunted her. Her face clouded over.

"Please don't refuse. It would help me very much and it would be wonderful for Siew Lin," coaxed Mrs Tan, sensing her unease. "If things work out, we could take it a stage further," she continued.

"What do you mean, a stage further?" Sook Ping's voice wavered. She had a sudden fear that Mrs Tan was going to suggest that she sell Mei Yin to serve as companion to Siew Lin. She knew of at least two cases in the village where poverty had forced mothers to sell their daughters. Why else had the two of them been summoned to the Tan mansion? She pulled her daughter closer to her.

"I mean, if the girls get on well, I would like them to attend school together. I will pay Mei Yin's fees," Mrs Tan replied, anticipating that Sook Ping's reluctance must stem from financial worries. "And if you have problems in meeting the other expenses, you have only to let me know."

Sook Ping's face brightened with relief. At last she was beginning to understand why Mrs Tan had told her about the schooling that was intended for Siew Lin. She had always hoped to send Mei Yin to school, but it had been nothing more than a dream; that was, until now.

"Thank you," she said, overwhelmed by the generous offer and not a little embarrassed at her earlier fears. "If you are willing to pay Mei Yin's school fees, I will do everything I can to pay any other bills. You are already being most generous." To cover up the surge of emotion that made her almost breathless, she pushed Mei Yin forward and asked her to thank Mrs Tan for her kindness. Mei Yin bowed and clasped both hands together as she had been taught.

"So it is settled. If you could leave Mei Yin here this afternoon, I will see she is well cared for. She can have lunch with Siew Lin and get to know her. After tea, the driver will bring your daughter home. I have friends coming over for lunch and *mahjong* this afternoon, but I will make sure the children are alright." With a gentle squeeze of Sook Ping's hands, Mrs Tan took her leave ushering Mei Yin before her, pleased with the day's progress.

Sook Ping nodded her farewell, unable to speak. She sat alone in the room listening to the sound of the receding footsteps of Mrs Tan and Mei Yin. As they faded so too did her initial joy. Sadness washed over her as she reflected on how eager her daughter had been to go to Siew Lin. She had left with no more than a glance and quick goodbye. What if mixing with the wealthy Tans were to turn her head and she no longer felt at home with her own family?

Sook Ping shook herself. "I must not think like this. What's wrong with me? I should be happy." And, with quickening steps, she left the mansion and headed home.

* * * * *

Mei Yin's schooling and friendship with Siew Lin affected Sook Ping more than she had expected. Mei Yin was the youngest in the family. Sook Ping had hoped not to have any more children when she found herself pregnant again. Of the eight children she had borne, only five survived. Four of them were from her first marriage. Widowed at a young age and left impoverished, life had been hard. To keep the family supplied with essentials, she had taken in laundry and sewing. Clothes and shoes were passed on from one child to the next, patched and re-patched. So when the village matchmaker approached her on behalf of Sung, the blacksmith, Sook Ping readily agreed to marry him. Mei Yin was Sung's only child.

With Mei Yin attending school, Sook Ping took on more work to provide the extras for her schooling; she did not want to be totally dependent on Mrs Tan. Each morning after Mei Yin left for school, she would gather up two large rattan baskets and trudge down to the nearby beach. There she waited, crouched in the shade of a coconut palm, until the fishing boats returned. When the catch was good, she would buy fish cheaply, usually *kembong*, a tropical mackerel. What she sought most, however, were the salted and semi-dried anchovies brought in by the purse-seiners. The anchovies were less than three inches long. If she could buy them cheaply, she would clean, gut and re-dry them and then sell them to local merchants.

Mei Yin knew things were hard at home. Although her schooling was paid for, books, pencils and uniform still had to be bought. Her mother was proud. She refused to ask for more when so much was already so generously provided by Mrs Tan. The household's tight budget had to be juggled for even the smallest purchase. Father Sung did what he could. As a blacksmith, he had earned little enough, but now with advancing years, his occasional cough had become incessant and his eyesight was failing.

Mei Yin's job after the evening meal was to work the large stone mortar to produce rice flour. Holding its wooden handle, she would walk round and round the mortar to grind the rice, stopping from time to time to add water and more grains. At times Mei Yin felt she ought to give up school and help her mother more, but she would have none of it. "Learning will give you a better life and your friendship with Siew Lin is a good thing. You are learning things that you would never learn at home or working in the market. All I want you to do is study hard and help me when you can," her mother would say.

Mei Yin would hug her mother in silence, unable to express what she felt. All she could do was gather up her schoolbooks, sit by the kerosene lamp and study as hard as she could to make her mother happy. As the family settled down and darkness fell, a silence would descend on the household, interrupted only by the coughing of her father, the hum of insects whirling around the kerosene lamp and the chatter of the geckoes clinging to the walls and ceiling. This was the part of the day that Mei Yin enjoyed most: to have her mother and father close by and to have time to study. She knew she was privileged to go to school. Her brothers and sisters had not had the chance. Her brothers had been sent off to work the moment they were old enough to find a job. Her sisters had fared no better. They were faced with only two choices: to work as domestic helps or to marry a local man.

Chapter 3

2 January 1941, Mei Yin was almost 14. The morning sun blazed hot and bright, its heat relieved only by a slight breeze rippling through the leaves of the trees that lined the footpath. Mei Yin had delivered cakes to the market and like many times before had only just managed to reach school on time. The class was already assembled and standing to attention, straight-backed and serious, waiting for Miss Cheng to come into the classroom. Mei Yin rushed to her allotted space and stood on tiptoe in search of Siew Lin. She was surprised not to see her. She turned to the girl next to her. "Have you seen Siew Lin?" The girl just shrugged, placing a finger to her mouth signing Mei Yin to keep silent. "She doesn't usually miss school," continued Mei Yin. "Are you sure?" The girl shook her head vigorously and gave her a hefty nudge to silence her.

Mei Yin peeped out of the door. She could see Miss Cheng, grim-faced, walking purposefully towards the classroom. Behind her was Siew Lin, running. She passed Miss Cheng and practically leapt into the classroom, just managing to arrive ahead of the teacher.

Without bothering to put her satchel away, she quickly turned to Mei Yin. "I've got to talk to you," she whispered. Her face was pale and her eyes red and swollen.

"Stop talking! Siew Lin! Sit down!" Miss Cheng's voice thundered across the room. "You are late as it is. We will begin our lesson. I do not want to hear another word from you until I say so." Tough and stern, Miss Cheng, who had trained in China, was known for her orthodox interpretation of Confucianism. To challenge her, even to ask a question, was not a thing her students would ever contemplate. Self-expression did not feature in the school's ethos.

The two girls bowed their heads, quickly turning to the pages of the book set before them. They tried hard to concentrate, but failed.

The words were just a blur. "Something must be badly wrong," thought Mei Yin, casting a surreptitious glance at her friend, aware of her continuing distress. The time dragged until, at last, the lunch bell rang. Both girls hurried out of the classroom and headed for their favourite place under the mango tree.

Siew Lin sat down on the grass, folding her legs under her. She looked up at Mei Yin and then down. Keeping her eyes firmly fixed on Mei Yin's shoes, her voice faltering and broken, she confided, "We are leaving Malacca. We are going back to Hong Kong. Mother and Grandmother have already begun to pack. It's awful. Mother was crying and Grandmother was scolding everyone. The servants were in tears. People were rushing in and out of the house."

"What about school? You can't just stop school!"

"It has all been decided. I will go to school in Hong Kong. Father is moving his business headquarters back there."

"Why?" asked Mei Yin.

"Because our relatives have asked us to and Grandmother has agreed," she sobbed, abandoning her resolve not to cry. "Last night, Father got a telegram. His family in Hong Kong is worried about what's happening in China, Japan and South East Asia."

"I still don't understand! Why do you have to leave?"

"Remember Teacher telling us about Japan's attack on China in 1937, how lots of Chinese were killed? It has still not ended and it isn't just Japan that is involved. Father says other countries are just standing by and letting it happen. Even worse, he says, the Chinese are fighting amongst themselves."

"Are you sure it's that serious? That you have to leave? I know the teacher has talked about the fighting between the Nationalists and the Communists. But I always think of it as, well, a story, not real!"

"No, no it's real enough. When I asked my mother, she said that people in Hong Kong are really worried. Refugees are arriving from China every day. My father's relatives think that the family should stick together. We have to go back to Hong Kong straight away."

Mei Yin listened to her friend in disbelief. Could this be happening? She felt numb. For a while, little was said. What was there to say. Everything had been decided. Gradually, however, the enormity of the change began to dawn on them. Their plans of going together to high school and later to university would have to be set aside. Just a week ago, they had even planned for Siew Lin to ask her mother if they could learn English together.

"What can we do?" Mei Yin asked.

"Ma-mah wants to meet your mother. I think she has some ideas. She asked if your mum would come to see her this evening?

"I will ask her as soon as I get home."

Placing her hand in Siew Lin's, Mei Yin stared unseeing at the familiar scene: girls playfully pushing each other, vying to be the first at the tuck shop, others playing hopscotch or kicking little tied bunches of frangipani flowers. Shouts of joy and jeers floated across the playground: familiar comforting sounds that would soon, it seemed, no longer be a part of their lives.

* * * * *

For Mei Yin, the road home had never seemed so long as on that day. It was three o'clock in the afternoon. The sun had turned the dirt road into a shimmering snake of red heat. Each step churned up dust. The plants by the wayside were covered with fine red powder. Flies buzzed. Flowers and leaves that had looked so fresh and beautiful in the morning now seemed tired, drooping under the heat. People turned to stare at Mei Yin as she hurried past, her eyes brimming with tears, curious as to why she looked so unhappy.

The road was busy at this time of day. Hawkers returning from the market bobbed down the road, their shoulders weighed down by thick bamboo poles with rattan baskets dangling at each end. Food vendors were going in the opposite direction pushing wooden carts laid out with kerosene stoves and cooking utensils. In a few hours, workers leaving their offices would stop for a quick meal before their journey home. The vendors needed to be at the market ready for business. Most of the traders knew Mei Yin, but none of them had much to say other than to mutter words of comfort, as much to themselves as to her, "Never mind, never mind. Things will be all right. *Tai see bin siew see, siew see bin mo see.*" For them, fate determined everything: big problems became small problems, and small problems eventually became no problem.

Mei Yin pushed past the gate and crossed the dirt courtyard to the house. Perched on stilts to protect against floods, the house was made of wood. It had a sloping roof, graceful wide eaves and carved archways typical of Malaccan houses, the style of which had changed little from the dwellings of the Sumatran Minangkabau settlers of the early 1400s. A central stairway at the front led up to the living quarters on the first floor. These consisted of a kitchen and three partitioned areas that served as small bedrooms, each furnished simply with rolled grass mattresses for beds and baskets for belongings. A verandah skirted the house. Stained dark brown with age and wear, its planks were covered with a dusting of fine sand. Warm moist sea air blew in all day long, bringing an endless supply from the nearby beach. At ground level beneath the house, a roughly cemented floor opened onto the courtyard. This was where Sook Ping did most of her work. Mei Yin headed straight there.

Bamboo and rattan baskets, some filled with dried fish and others with rice flour, were lined in neat rows on either side of the steps leading up to the verandah. There was no sign of her mother. This was strange. Normally she would be bustling around the baskets, sorting the fish, splitting them open and patiently extracting the tiny bones. Or she would be busy feeding the chickens or washing clothes. The clothes were still hanging on the line. The chickens were pecking and scratching the ground in search of food. Her mother was nowhere to be seen.

Mei Yin turned, back-tracked to the steps and was about to run up them when she caught sight of her mother seated behind one of the wooden pillars that supported the house. Sook Ping was slumped down cradling her head in her hands, her elbows propped on the rice mortar. Next to her stood the makeshift ironing board, bound and lined with old bed sheets. A pile of washed and dried clothes lay untouched in a basket beside it; the old smoothing iron was cold on its stand.

Mei Yin rushed over to her. "Are you alright?"

Sook Ping raised her head, her eyes looked tired, despondent. "Have you heard the terrible news about the Tan family?"

"Who told you?" asked Mei Yin. "I rushed home to give you the news. Siew Lin said her mother would like to meet you this evening."

Wearily Sook Ping replied, "I know because Mrs Tan was here, shortly after lunch. She said she could not wait until this evening. She wanted to discuss your future urgently. They are leaving for Hong Kong."

"I know, Siew Lin told me."

"The Tans have been very good to us. I shall miss them."

"Me too!"

"It means great changes for us, I'm afraid. We cannot afford to send you to high school." Distress was evident in her face.

It was now Mei Yin who comforted her mother. "It's alright," she repeated over and over again, gently patting her mother's back.

Sook Ping looked at her daughter and gazed deep into her eyes, "Mrs Tan has come up with a proposal."

"What is it?" asked Mei Yin, thinking that anything would be better than the way things seemed to be at present. Even without her mother saying it, she had realised that she would have to leave school. Her mother could not take on more work; every minute of her day was already spoken for. Certain she would have to leave school, she hoped her benefactor's offer would involve some kind of job for her. Almost 14 she was willing to work.

"Mrs Tan says that the only way forward is for you to marry a rich man. If you remember, when Mrs Tan first came to Malaya from Hong Kong, she lived in Kuala Lumpur. She still has a good friend there. She learnt from her friend that her mother is looking for a wife for her only son. Her mother is the second wife of a well-known businessman, Ong Siew Loong. The son is 24 years old. You could become Mrs Ong's ward and companion, and continue your education until you marry."

Mei Yin turned pale. She opened her mouth to speak, but nothing came out other than "Oh!"

Mindful of the frightened look on her daughter's face, Sook Ping continued gently, "I am not sure this is a very good solution to our problems. I do not like the idea of you going to live with a family totally unknown to us. And to marry! You are far too young!"

She stopped to reconsider what she had just said. For a few minutes, Sook Ping became completely lost in her own thoughts. Then, as if concluding her silent debate, she corrected herself, "Of course, you are not too young to be considering marriage. What am I saying? Your sisters were already engaged at your age and so was I."

Yet, this was not the future she had wanted for Mei Yin. She shook her head as though to dispel her previous thoughts and counter what she had just said. "I would like you to have an independence that neither I nor your sisters have had or could possibly have expected. And what if they do not treat you well? But what alternatives do we have?"

So Sook Ping argued with herself, sometimes aloud, sometimes *sotto voce*, sometimes in her thoughts. She owed so much to Mrs Tan who had insisted that this was the best solution. It would guarantee some continuity in Mei Yin's education. What was more, it would make them financially secure.

Mei Yin stood stock still, shocked! Her sisters had all married young but, until then, her mother had never talked about marriage for her. She had said that she wanted Mei Yin to concentrate on her studies and make good on her own. Was this all to be brushed aside? Mei Yin closed her eyes tightly and prayed fervently that somehow this nightmare would disappear.

The minutes passed with Sook Ping pacing up and down talking to herself and Mei Yin trying to follow and muster her thoughts.

She could not; there was too much to absorb, too many things were happening at the same time. Before she could say anything, a loud noise came from the front of the house.

Shouts of "Is anyone in?" followed by the thumping of wheels on the dirt greeted mother and daughter as they emerged from under the porch into the full glare of the sun.

"Ah, there you are. I thought for a moment no one was in," grumbled a tiny woman. Her skin was darkened to almost mahogany brown by the sun. Wrinkles radiated out from a pair of slanted eyes. Suddenly her face lit up with a broad smile when she saw Mei Yin standing behind Sook Ping, "Don't come out here, get back into the shade. I'm going to put my barrow under the tree and then I will join you," she continued all in one breath. Without much effort, she pushed the wooden barrow, which was loaded with an assortment of empty bottles, towards the papaya tree.

Sung Ji was Sook Ping's cousin. She collected empty bottles and sold them to a nearby bottling plant. Kind-hearted, loud and pushy, Sung Ji loved all her cousin's children, but Mei Yin was her favourite; 45 years old and childless, she had long given up any hope of having children and treated Mei Yin as her own. Wiping her dark, lined brow with a large flannel, she hitched up her black trousers and squatted down beside Sook Ping.

"I visited your patron, Mrs Tan," said Sung Ji. She looked closely at Sook Ping to see what effect this news had on her, but Sook Ping gave nothing away. Sung Ji continued, "I chatted with the servants. They told me the Tans are leaving. They also told me Mrs Tan has found a husband for Mei Yin. Is it true?"

Sook Ping nodded. She did not really want to discuss the matter. Not with Sung Ji. She had still to tell Mei Yin's father and her own mind was in such a muddle. Sometimes, she felt that the proposal opened up great possibilities for Mei Yin. But the thought of Mei Yin leaving home filled her with dread.

Sung Ji was not put off by Sook Ping's silence. She repeated her question.

Wearily Sook Ping replied, "It is the Ong family from Kuala Lumpur. Nothing has been decided; it is too early. We need time. Their only son, I don't even know his name, is looking for a wife. Well, truth be told, his mother is looking for a wife for him and she has been told about Mei Yin."

"Why, that is very good news. Mei Yin will not get a chance like that here, especially without Mrs Tan's patronage. There are few prospects in the village. I don't understand why you are hesitating. It will solve your financial problems and Mei Yin's future will be secure. You can devote more time to your husband. He needs extra care now that he can hardly see. Don't worry, I am sure Mei Yin will come back to visit regularly. I too will miss Mei Yin, but you should be thinking of her, not yourself."

"I know, I know. But he is ten years older than Mei Yin. And what if Mei Yin doesn't like him?" countered Sook Ping.

Frowning, Sung Ji retorted, slapping her thighs to reinforce her views. "*Ai yah!* Ten years, that's not much. My neighbour's daughter was married off as second wife to a rice merchant 20 years older than her. At least Mei Yin will not be a concubine. It may well be that Mei Yin will not mind. How can we know whether or not she will like him if she doesn't get a chance to meet him?"

Chapter 4

That evening the entire family gathered on the verandah to discuss Mei Yin's future. Mei Yin's *Kah-cheh,* elder sister, was there with her baby swathed in a *sarong* wound tightly around her shoulder. Mei Yin's brothers, their wives and children were also present. Sung Ji had also been invited. Everyone spoke; they all wanted to have a say. Only Mei Yin's father, seemingly, had little to contribute. He sat in a corner, apart from everyone, drawing deeply on his water pipe. Loud gurgling noises came from it as his cheeks alternately swelled and sunk with the effort. His nervousness was reflected in the crescendo of gurgles. So great was his effort, deep frowns, like two vertical ruts, formed between his eyebrows. No one spoke to him nor he to them.

The loud chatter subsided when Mrs Tan arrived. Concerned about Mei Yin's future, Mrs Tan had come again instead of waiting for their response. It was more convenient for everyone and time was precious, she explained. In reality, she had come in an effort to influence the family's deliberations.

No sooner had the obligatory cup of tea been served to Mrs Tan than everyone began talking all at once.

"Please, please, let Mrs Tan speak first," pleaded Sook Ping.

Clearing her throat, Mrs Tan leaned forward to look at her audience and began, in the directionless, meandering manner Sook Ping had come to accept was her way. "I hope you do not think of me as an interfering woman."

She was immediately interrupted by Sung Ji, a wide grin on her face, "Of course not! We would not think that of you."

"Hush," Sook Ping admonished, "let Mrs Tan go on."

Mrs Tan smiled, pleased at Sook Ping's encouragement. "I have thought a lot about Mei Yin. She is pretty, well behaved and obedient, and she has done so well in school. It would be such a pity to let all this go to waste."

"I agree, I agree," interjected Sung Ji. She too had thought a lot about the matter and was keen to help secure what she considered a desirable outcome for Mei Yin. Sook Ping tried to catch her cousin's eye to stop her from interrupting. Failing, she grabbed her hand and squeezed it hard, willing her to be silent.

"I have a friend, Kai Hing. We first met in Hong Kong but she is from Malaya and has been a good friend during my years here. She has often talked to me about her family. I have met them. They are really nice people. When I told her about Mei Yin, she contacted her mother. They are interested in having Mei Yin as her mother's companion."

"Just like that!" exclaimed Sung Ji. "She has not met Mei Yin."

"Of course, not just like that," replied Mrs Tan, mimicking Sung Ji. She was irritated. "She, Mrs Ong that is, has first to meet Mei Yin before she can decide. I am only jumping a few steps ahead. You don't need me to draw out every detail, *wak toh chut cheong*, do you?"

The children, who had meantime rejoined the gathering, giggled and clutched their little bellies. *Wak toh chut cheong* meant literally drawing out the entrails to illustrate the anatomy of the belly. Their loud laughter and playful miming of the process brought a smile even to Sook Ping's face, banishing just for a moment the furrows on her brow.

"If she decides to take Mei Yin as her companion," continued Mrs Tan, ignoring the commotion, "Mei Yin will be able to continue her education and all expenses will be met by them. The idea is to give her son, Ming Kong, enough time to get to know Mei Yin. If he likes Mei Yin, arrangements will be made for them to marry. It's really a very modern form of arranged marriage. She has come up with this idea because she knows her son will not have it any other way."

"This is very good. In my day," said Sung Ji, "children had no say. You might not see your future husband until the wedding day." Then turning to Sook Ping, "See, I told you, it will be fine."

"It is not all good-heartedness on the part of Mrs Ong. She has no choice. Ming Kong, I am told, is very independent," explained Mrs Tan. "He has been brought up by the first wife. Unlike his blood mother, his adopted mother is a *Nyonya*, a Straits-born Chinese, just like you, Sook Ping. You will have something in common with her and that's a good thing, isn't it?" she asked, puzzled at Sook Ping's silence. So far, she had said very little and Mrs Tan was beginning to worry that she might be having doubts about her proposal.

Intent on persuading her audience of the tremendous advantages of the match, Mrs Tan continued. "The first wife was born in Malaya and her ideas on how to educate Ming Kong were very different from those of his real mother. He has been educated in English while his own sisters under his mother's care have been taught in Chinese. It is too complicated a story to tell in one go!"

Her voice and manner changed abruptly. She was exasperated as much with her audience, none of whom seemed to understand what she was driving at, as she was with herself. She realised that, once again, she was meandering. She heaved a big sigh. "What I'm trying to say is that Mei Yin can, in fact has to, learn English. Ming Kong does not write Chinese or speak it all that well. This means she will get to fulfil one of her ambitions in life, to study English! Siew Lin was telling me all last week just how much Mei Yin wants to do this."

She continued with her efforts to gain support for the proposal. "To get back to the main point, this arrangement will give Mei Yin so many opportunities. What will happen if she stays here? Who can she meet except hawkers and traders?" She looked around, daring anyone to contradict her, before concluding, "And we all know that times are hard. With the chaos in China, Mei Yin's school is bound to close. And when it does, bang goes her education."

Nine pairs of eyes stared at her. Mrs Tan reached for her cup of tea, took a sip and waited for their reactions. She was pleased with herself. Her audience looked at each other.

Kah-cheh spoke first, hesitatingly but firmly, "I think it is a good idea and worth considering." She believed what Mrs Tan said was true. She was herself a typical example of what lay ahead for her younger sister if she stayed at home. Toil and poverty had taken its toll on her. With two very young children, one left at home with the father and the other in her arms, and with yet another on the way, her life was a continuous round of work and struggle to make ends meet.

While the men had little to say, all of the women supported Mrs Tan's proposal. They agreed in their hearts that, given the same chance, they would have been better off. No one, except Sook Ping, had asked Mei Yin what she thought. Mei Yin herself was carried along by the enthusiasm shown for the proposal. She had little understanding of what was really involved. She was sad at the prospect of leaving home and her parents, sad too that she would not see Siew Lin any more, and she would miss her brothers and sisters. Yet, underlying the sadness, she felt excited at the prospect of a new life in Kuala Lumpur. In the absence of objections, Mrs Tan concluded that an agreement had been reached and the discussion switched to how and when Mei Yin would be taken to meet Mrs Ong.

Ming Kong

Chapter 5

Dark and well built, Ming Kong stood at least half a head taller than most of his fellow men. Charismatic, his presence was never ignored. People invariably felt drawn to him. When he spoke, they listened, charmed by the deep timbre of his voice as much as by his words. All this he took in his stride. He was neither proud nor vain, but completely comfortable with himself, a confidence that had been instilled in him from his earliest days.

The first wife Mrs Ong Suet Ping arranged the marriage of Ming Kong's mother to his father. Following the birth of her second daughter, she decided she would have to look elsewhere for a male child to ensure the continuation of the family dynasty. With the help of a matchmaker, she found Su Hei, a Cantonese girl whose family came from Kwangtung. As part of the agreement, Su Hei's parents agreed that her first male child would be 'adopted' by Mrs Ong as her own. In return, Su Hei would have her own separate household.

The arrangement suited Mrs Ong. When questioned about the wisdom of her decision, she would reply, "I can share my husband with another woman as long as I do not know all the details. In fact, the less I know, the better." In private, she acknowledged to herself it was not entirely magnanimity that had prompted this concession. She knew she was already sharing her husband with others. Adding Su Hei, especially when she had a say in the matter, was less troubling to her pride. "It will be good so long as I have the first-born son."

Ming Kong grew up in two households. Both mothers adored him. During the week, he lived with his first mother in a large house

situated in what was later to become the central district of modern
Kuala Lumpur. The front of the house faced a busy road that eventually became the main thoroughfare connecting the city with the
north. The rear of the house backed onto a Malay village, Kampong
Hijau.

The Ong house was very different from other buildings in the
area. The main road was lined with terraces of ramshackle shop-
houses, two-storey buildings with commercial premises on the
ground floor and accommodation above. Away from the road, just as
in Kampong Hijau, there were clusters of *attap* houses – small
wooden buildings on stilts, with roofs thatched with palm-leaves.
Built in the early 1900s, the mansion remained the main residence
of the Ongs even when other buildings and shops rose around it.
Unlike the surrounding properties, it had a big garden complete with
coconut palms, banana, papaya, rambutan, chiku and mango trees.
The garden provided the household with fruit and Ming Kong,
when he was young, with an adventure playground.

The living quarters were on the first floor. The rooms were large
with rosewood and teak furniture. Skirting all sides of the living
quarters was a wide verandah. Mrs Ong enjoyed sitting on the back
verandah in the late afternoon. She would spend hours there with
Ming Kong, telling him stories, listening to his adventures,
ambitions and reports on life at school. She watched him scramble
up the trees, play with visiting school friends or harvest green
mangoes for the kitchen using a catapult. Each weekend, however, he
would return to his biological mother.

Su Hei's house was only 30 minutes' walk away. To reach it, Ming
Kong had to go through Kampong Hijau towards the market. From
there, the road connected with another settlement, Sun Chuen (new
village), which was predominantly Chinese. The surroundings
changed abruptly on entering this settlement. There were few trees
and fewer plants. Every available space was built upon. Unlike in
Kampong Hijau, the houses were all set at ground level and made
either of wood with zinc roofs or brick with tiled roofs. Little

attention was paid to style or proportion; bits were added on to the houses as families expanded. Dirt paths, some just wide enough for trishaws, wound through the jumbled maze of buildings. So popular was the trishaw, essentially a two-wheeled rickshaw with a cycle attached to the front, that the paths in the village were often jammed with them. At times, their bells could be heard miles away. The settlement throbbed with activity; children playing, mothers washing, vendors selling wares, people going about their business hurrying to and fro.

Sun Chuen was not affluent. Its residents were small traders or low-ranking, white-collar workers who were employed in office blocks that had sprung up on the other side of the river Klang from the settlement. These buildings housed some of the most important tin mining and rubber companies of the time: Sime Darby, Harrisons and Crossfield, The Orient and the Great Eastern Company all had offices there.

Su Hei lived in a bungalow situated in a cul-de-sac in Sun Chuen. A modest brick building, it had a small backyard but no garden. At the front there was a large terrace shaded by a wooden pergola that was densely covered with sweet white jasmine. The front door opened onto a modest-sized sitting room that led, in turn, to a corridor with two bedrooms on each side. Further back was the dining room and then the kitchen. The bathroom, toilets and servant quarters were at the rear. Amongst the jumble of makeshift houses in Sun Chuen, her home stood out in its pristine order.

Su Hei had lived there for 13 years. She moved in shortly after the birth of her last child. Her marriage, welcomed by her parents and which had brought her much happiness in the beginning, had slowly deteriorated. Ong Siew Loong's business took him away often. His absences became longer and longer. By the time Ming Kong was 20 years old, Su Hei rarely saw her husband. The only real evidence of her marriage was the monthly allowance that kept the family in comfort and style. Su Hei was bitter at this neglect and even more bitter that she had been obliged to give up her son, a sacrifice that meant she would be on her own once all her daughters were married and had joined their husband's families.

As a defence against such times, she immersed herself in Chinese traditions and culture, drumming into her children the importance of 'filial piety'. Story time inevitably revolved around the famous 24 tales of filial piety. Every tale tells how children sacrificed themselves to save their parents. Su Hei longed to gain her son's undivided love and become an important part of his life.

Ming Kong felt the conflict created in him by his affection for his first mother and strong desire to please his natural one. When he was small, Ah Keng, his first mother 's maid, generally brought him each weekend to Sun Chuen in a trishaw. She would leave him at Su Hei's house in the morning and collect him the following evening. "Ma-mah, I'm here," he would shout as he clambered out of the trishaw. Hugging her, he would talk incessantly to fend off questions about his first mother. Even as a young child he knew that speaking of his other home made his mother unbearably sad. As the years passed, however, the nagging guilt he felt during the weekly visits gradually diminished. He grew closer to his first mother.

Chapter 6

Ming Kong swung his leg over his motorbike, a gleaming Royal Enfield, and kick-started the engine. Waving cheerily to Nelly Fong, his girlfriend, he roared off to work. It took him just ten minutes to reach his office at The Orient. Like many overseas mining companies in Malaya, The Orient had progressed from tin mining to general trading, with a particular interest in rubber estates. Pushing through the swing doors, he walked briskly across the open-plan office with its wooden desks, piled with folders and files, towards his own office.

"Any messages?" he asked once inside his private office.

Foong Yee, his assistant and secretary, placed a wad of correspondence in his in-tray and a pile of letters for signature in front of him before venturing, "Your mother phoned. She asked you to give her a call when you have a moment."

Ming Kong gave a non-committal shrug, but his eyes clouded over and his carefree expression gave way to a frown.

"Would you like a coffee? The boy will be around to take orders any time now," asked Foong Yee, intent on being discreet, but aware of his boss's feelings. There had been many such calls of late.

Ming Kong forced a smile. "Yes, please. I'd better call my mother and get it over with. I'm sure she wants to know why I didn't go to see her at the weekend."

Ming Kong was a junior manager at The Orient. He was one of a select group of locals assigned to oversee the company's activities on the west coast of the Peninsula, especially in the tin mining and rubber planting states of Selangor, Perak and Pahang. He had joined the company after leaving school at 18. Unlike his school friends, he did not go on from school to Britain for further education, the usual destiny of children from wealthy families. He recalled his father's words shortly after finishing school, as he saw school friends preparing to go overseas. "Your place is here, with me! You will fare much better learning all you need in life through practice and experience. I have reached an agreement with the management of The Orient." His eyes were stern and unwavering. "You will start at the bottom and go from department to department learning all the skills needed to run a company. Eventually you will be ready to run my business. Don't fail me," he had warned. "You'll not have privileges because you are my son. And I won't bail you out if you do wrong. I have given my word you will work hard and do a good job."

Ong Siew Loong had no qualms whatsoever in having his son start on the bottom rung in order to gain experience. It was in keeping with family tradition. His own father had set him on a similar path and his father's father before him. Now, at the age of 24, with six years' experience and a successful career in The Orient behind him, Ming Kong was expected to resign and join his father's company. His father saw little point in him staying on.

"Make sure that Ming Kong knows it is time for him to start taking over from me," he told his wives whenever the opportunity arose. "There is no point in him staying with the Orient. He has no future there. And it was never my intention for him to stay. He should know by now that the British companies here almost always recruit senior managers from among their own. He might have had some chance if he'd been educated at one of their top public schools and gone on to Oxford or Cambridge. But the way things stand now, he has no chance at all!"

As he sat in his office, Ming Kong's thoughts kept switching from the recent conversation he had had with his father and the difficult visit he was bound to have with his mother that evening. He tried to push aside these worries to concentrate on his latest assignment. He turned again to the minutes of the previous day's Board meeting. He had been instructed to start planning for an expansion of the company's office in Seremban. Located just north of Kuala Lumpur, Seremban was expected to become the hub for the expansion of rubber plantations in the state of Negri Sembilan.

But his mind kept straying. "Seremban! What luck! If only I can stay on with the company and be posted there. Perhaps Father could be persuaded to change his mind. It would be an ideal place to set up home with Nelly. It is far enough from Kuala Lumpur to avoid any confrontation with my family, yet near enough for me to visit my mothers." No one in the family had met Nelly although his youngest sister had seen them together by chance. He could not introduce Nelly to the family; they would not consider her respectable and were unlikely to accept her. Already, he could anticipate his birth mother's reaction should she ever find out.

Foong Yee came in with more files and papers for him. Reluctantly, Ming Kong forced his attention back to the job at hand. He worked fast. He barely touched the bowl of noodles that had been delivered earlier to his office. By the end of the day, the first draft of the project was ready to be typed.

* * * * *

Ming Kong pulled his motorbike onto its stand and strode into the house. "Mother, I'm home." Almost immediately, Su Hei burst into the room, her face glowing with happiness. She had been waiting for him and, alerted by the distinctive roar of the approaching motorbike, had rushed into the living room.

"Come, sit down, you must be tired. Ah Jee will get you a cup of tea and a hot towel." She touched his arm, patting it as if he were still a little boy. "Ah Jee spent the whole day preparing your favourite dishes when she heard you were coming this evening. You must stay for dinner. We have so much to talk about."

Ming Kong was surprised and pleased at the absence of accusations in her welcome. He broke into a broad smile and sat down. "Great!" he responded before being struck afresh by the gloominess of his mother's home. It never failed to amaze him. Everything in the room was sombre. Just like his mother's severe and uncompromising outlook, he concluded. His eyes strayed to the large altar stood against the wall. On it were incense and joss sticks, offerings to the ancestors. The smouldering ashes emitted a heavy and sweet scent. Plaques with inscriptions of respect for the dead were placed side by side, together with a small statue of Kuan Yin, the goddess of mercy.

He knew his mother's ritual each morning and evening included at least an hour of prayer. Guarding the entrance of the house were still more joss sticks, this time to ward away evil. The kitchen had another, smaller altar. This was for Tsao Chun, the kitchen god. She believed this god observed all that happened in a household and then ascended to heaven once a year to make his report. To ensure a favourable account of her household, she presented him with gifts of appeasement: rice wine, boiled chicken, roast pork, mandarins, joss sticks and incense. He shook his head in wonder at her beliefs.

Su Hei believed the gods had different ranks and needs, as did the dead. In this way she combined a mixture of worship borrowed from Buddhism, Taoism and Confucianism. She plied the gods with gifts and prayers to grant her a place in the rigid hierarchy of 'heaven and earth'. This was, he knew, how she dealt with the sorrow of being abandoned by her husband and losing her son to another woman.

Ming Kong did not share her beliefs but went along with what she did more out of pity than anything. He had been educated at a Catholic school. His father was an atheist and his first mother did not press any religious dogma on him. The first Mrs Ong also believed in respect for elders, but she was liberal in her views. Now, seated beside Su Hei, he was made even more aware of her increasing religious fervour. Though just 49, she dressed like an older woman with her hair tied at the back in a tight bun. Prayer beads were held, ever ready, in her hand. A familiar sense of foreboding began to stir in him as he waited patiently for the inevitable question.

"Have you seen your father?"

"No, not this week. We went shooting last week." Feigning a cheerfulness he did not feel, he went on brightly, "Father has found good hunting grounds for wild boar near Tanjong Malim. He is thinking of getting a friend in the village to rear some hunting dogs.

That way we won't have to take them all the way from Kuala Lumpur. I will be helping him to select the dogs this weekend."

"Good, I am happy you are keeping in close touch with him. He has not been to see us for some time. Your sisters don't get much chance to talk with him. I know that Kai Hing is married and has long left home but poor Kai Min. What about her? I wish he would visit. Has he asked after us?"

He had little to say in reply. Much as he tried to get his father to visit her, the answer was always an emphatic "No". He felt a great relief when Ah Jee came in to announce dinner. He was even more pleased when his youngest sister, Kai Min, joined them.

"My you have grown. You must be eating my share of the food to have grown six inches in two weeks," he teased.

Kai Min gave him a playful punch. "You talk nonsense. I have not grown six inches. You say it every time you visit. You have grown six inches and it's all round your waist! See here, and here and here," she replied with a wide smile, pinching his waist.

His mother interrupted, "Kai Min, behave! Ah Jee will be bringing the food any time now. Remember your manners."

Kai Min sat down still holding on to her brother's hand. He winked at her. Being the youngest, all the family favoured her. Ming Kong was her own particular favourite.

Once everyone was seated at the table and the food laid out, Kai Min began the ritual of inviting her elders to eat. Ming Kong then followed suit, inviting his mother to eat. The simple ceremony completed, Su Hei picked up her chopsticks and the meal began.

Ah Jee hovered behind, anxious that everything was to their taste. Steaming hot rice was heaped into their bowls. Everyone then helped themselves to the dishes placed on a lazy daisy in the centre of the table. A dish of steamed chicken in rice wine with ginger, red prunes and Chinese mushrooms took pride of place. It was surrounded by a braised carp in soya sauce; bean curd cooked in a clay pot; and two kinds of leafy green vegetables, *pak choy* and *kai lan*, tossed fresh out of the steamer, in a dressing of soya sauce and fried garlic.

"I know you like the wing." Ming Kong helped his mother to the food, intent on observing the rules of a good son. "Have some red prunes. They're delicious. I remember you saying they are good for the circulation."

"Ah Jee, this is wonderful," he said, gesturing to the dishes laid before him. "When I'm away, all I can think of is your wonderful cooking. The chicken is perfect, succulent and tasty. Mmm . . . and the fish is absolutely smashing, so smooth and moist." He licked his lips in appreciation.

"Thank you, Master. I fear I may have over-cooked the fish and made it dry." She had been full of trepidation before dinner. Pleased by his words, she gave him a grateful smile, but her relief was short-lived.

"Yes, the fish was cooked longer than need be; it is dry," said Su Hei. "And Ah Jee," she went on, "you should have a lighter hand with the salt. The *pak choy* is far too salty." She pointed a finger at the guilty dish, waving it away.

So the meal continued. Each dish was analysed and discussed. Poor Ah Jee nodded and agreed to whatever opinion was expressed. She knew better than to object.

"If you remember, Mother," Ming Kong began cautiously, "I mentioned some time ago that The Orient is setting up an office in Seremban. I have been given the job of drawing up the project. The company wants to decentralise to improve the management of the estates and mines."

"Why do people always want to change things? What's wrong with the way things are done now?"

"Nothing. The Board feels that decentralisation would help in case of war."

"War? What war?" Su Hei, dropped her chopsticks in alarm.

"I'm not saying there will be war, only that the company feels it should be ready for one. Just in case Japan wants to establish a stronghold in South East Asia. It has already done it in China. If Japan invades Malaya, the whole country will be disrupted. We rely on the rail network to link the major towns and cities on both coasts through Kuala Lumpur. If war breaks out, the railway will be affected and the head office might not be able to keep in touch with its plantations and mines."

He paused. The conversation was taking a course that he had not planned. He did not wish to talk 'politics' with his mother. He tried to steer the conversation back to the news he intended to break to her. "The office in Seremban will need an experienced manager, someone local on the spot, to take care of things or, at the very least, keep them ticking over until the situation returns to normal."

"No, I cannot believe there will be war. We are such a small country. Why would the Japanese be interested in us?" Su Hei seemed oblivious to what he was saying.

Exasperated, he could not help retorting, "We may be small, but we are important. Capturing the country, especially Singapore, would give the Japanese a base from which to control South East Asia. See what is happening in China. Imagine this in South East Asia. Don't forget, we are a valuable source of raw materials for the industries in Britain."

"Your company should make better use of its time than indulge in this war-mongering. If you must draw up a project, do so. Your involvement should end there."

"That is what I am trying to tell you. I might have a chance of being posted to Seremban."

Her jaw dropped. Shock and alarm were followed by dismay.

Seeing her distress, Ming Kong quickly explained, "You don't need to worry yourself about it. I will be near enough to KL to visit you often. This is an opportunity for me to get a promotion beyond junior management."

Su Hei got up abruptly from the table, crashing her chair. "No, I will not hear of this. Why do you need a promotion?" She headed for the sitting room, her face tight with tension and anger. Ah Jee, quietly but hurriedly, shooed Kai Min from the table and asked her to go to her room so that her mother and brother could talk.

"Mistress, shall I serve tea and fruits in the sitting room?" she asked.

"Yes, yes," Su Hei replied testily.

Once settled in her armchair, she pressed both hands to her temple. "This talk upsets me; it is giving me a headache." She looked up at her son, who stood hovering above her with concern. "Before you tell me about Seremban, let me say what I have been planning to tell you all day."

Ming Kong sat down facing her. "What is it? Are you ill?"

"It really has nothing to do with me. It has everything to do with you. Your father's plans are for you to take over his business. This was the understanding right from the start. You could jeopardise your future if you delay joining the firm. Your father might change his mind."

"No! I'm not ready yet."

"You would be if you had a family. A family gives a man responsibilities. You should settle down."

"No!" He jumped up from his seat, scarcely able to conceal his anger at the prospect.

"Sit down!" she ordered with a wave of her hand; the expression on her face invited no discussion.

"I have found a very pretty girl from Malacca. She is young and well taught, but comes from a poor family. This need not be a bad thing. I came from a poor family. She's young enough to be taught to be a good wife, mother and daughter-in-law. I shall be able to judge better whether she has the necessary qualities when I meet her tomorrow. If she is not suitable, we will drop the matter. If she is what I have been led to expect, I would like you to marry her."

"Never! I cannot marry someone I do not know. I have my own life to lead. Mother, I will do a lot to meet your wishes, but not this."

"Hear me out," she said sharply. But his face was unflinching. She changed her tactic; she softened her approach. Her voice became reasonable and cajoling, "This will not be a forced marriage. Only if all goes well. First, I will send for her and she will stay here with me.

She will study under a tutor and you can meet her as often as you wish. She is still young, she will be14 this May, so there is plenty of time for both of you to get to know each other."

He did not reply and looked away. He could not bear to look at her and to see the plea in her eyes.

"It is so difficult to find a good girl any more," Su Hei continued. "Times have changed. If after, say, two years, you still do not wish to marry her, I will adopt her as my god-daughter. You might change your mind. Give it a try; do this for me."

"I'm not sure I want to be part of this," he replied.

"Her name is Mei Yin. Please give it a try. Where's the harm? She is not being forced into anything. I will give my word to her mother. If Mei Yin does not wish to marry you, she does not have to. So it is not only your decision; she has to agree as well."

"Give me a chance," she continued. "This way you will have a good wife and I a good daughter-in-law. Such a hard thing to come by these days. I was a perfect daughter-in-law myself. I served my mother-in-law well into her 70s. Surely, I deserve a good daughter-in-law, especially in my present circumstances. Your father's neglect is breaking my heart. He has not come to see me for weeks." Tears welled up in Su Hei's eyes as she reflected on the injustices she had suffered.

Ming Kong sighed. "Alright, alright, let's leave it like this and we will see." He felt weighed down by the proposal. A girl not quite 14! And what about Nelly? He could not tell her that he would have to leave her, not after all she had been through. Yet he knew it would be futile to argue with his mother at this moment.

Mei Yin

Chapter 7

On 23 January 1941, five days before the spring festival, the start of the Chinese New Year, Sook Ping and Mei Yin travelled by bus from Malacca to Kuala Lumpur.

After the relative calm of Malacca, Kuala Lumpur came as a shock. People seemed to be rushing around aimlessly. The streets were congested with lorries, loading and unloading; coolies in wide woven hats balanced baskets of wares on bamboo poles, calling out at the top of their voices to likely customers; buses, belching clouds of black fumes, stopped to pick up and disgorge passengers; and everywhere a babble of voices, a rainbow of colours and costumes, and a mélange of smells - pungent, spicy and musty.

Sook Ping wanted to ask the way to Sun Chuen. She could not get anybody's attention. People pushed by intent on their business. Eventually, she succeeded in getting an elderly gentleman to stop and listen. "Please, could you tell me how to get to this address at Sun Chuen?" She thrust in front of him a piece of paper on which Mrs Tan had written the address (in Chinese, English and Malay to be on the safe side); Sook Ping could neither read nor write.

"Sun Chuen is on the other side of the river Klang. If you walk over there," he pointed to a bus stand, "you should be able to find a bus that goes in that direction."

He looked at her doubtfully, noting her agitation. "On second thought, you will probably get lost if you try to get there by bus. You look new to the city and you have to change buses twice. A trishaw would be better. See here, cross over to that corner shop and then turn right. You will find some trishaws parked outside a coffee shop. Remember to bargain. Knock 20 percent off whatever they ask. They always put their prices up because they expect people to bargain."

"Thank you. You've been most kind." Holding Mei Yin's hand tightly she crossed the busy street and, just as the man had said, found a string of trishaws, their owners dozing in the passenger seats. After a great deal of haggling Sook Ping eventually found a man who asked a price she could afford.

"Please get us to the address as quickly as possible. We have to be there by noon."

"Get in, get in. I will try. My legs can only do so much. You want a good price and you want to travel fast. Typical." Speaking to himself, as though Sook Ping and Mei Yin did not exist, the trishaw man grumbled, "Country bumpkins are the worst; so tight with their money. *Ai yah*, it's hard to earn any money from them."

Despite his ill humour, he was a good navigator. Still, it was past noon when Sook Ping and Mei Yin finally arrived outside the house at Sun Chuen. They were slightly late. Sook Ping hoped Mrs Ong Su Hei would understand. This was their first time in Kuala Lumpur. Everything took longer than she had thought.

The gate was open. Sook Ping and Mei Yin walked in, crossed the porch under the trellis of trailing jasmine and sighed with relief. The sweet smell of the flowers and the shade provided a welcome contrast to the noise and dust of the trishaw journey. Sook Ping stopped to check that Mei Yin was neat, brushing away strands of hair from her face. Taking a handkerchief, she dabbed at her daughter's nose.

"That's better. You'll be okay, just be yourself." She knocked on the door, a slow hesitant tap, tap, tap, that seemed, to her ears, unnecessarily loud. Her stomach churned with apprehension.

The door opened.

"Good afternoon, you must be Mrs Sung and Mei Yin. Second Mistress is expecting you. Please come in."

Leading them to the sitting room, the maid indicated where Sook Ping and Mei Yin should sit.

"I will let Madam know you are here. Would you like some tea? We have Jasmine tea. Or would you prefer Chrysanthemum tea? It might be best on such a hot day."

Before the maid could continue, Su Hei made her appearance. It was now almost 15 minutes past the appointed time for the meeting with Sook Ping and Mei Yin. She had waited with some anxiety for the whole of the morning; a little longer and her anxiety would have turned to anger. She did not like to be kept waiting. However, good manners dictating, she favoured the new arrivals with a smile as she entered the room.

Waving Ah Jee away, she said, "Don't fuss. I am sure Mrs Sung will appreciate whatever you serve." Turning to her guests, she explained, "Ah Jee is always trying to serve us cooling drinks and warming drinks to balance our *yin* and *yang*. When it is hot, we have to have more *yin* and when we are cold, more *yang*."

Taking a seat, she motioned her guests to make themselves comfortable. "I hope you had a good journey."

"Yes, thank you. I am sorry we are a little late. We had some difficulty finding our way here."

Su Hei looked at Mei Yin and was pleased with what she saw. "Such a pretty girl, promising," she thought, indicating with a wave of her hand and a smile that their lateness was of no concern.

"Have you eaten? Would you like something to eat before we begin our discussions?" While Su Hei was anxious to get on with the interview, there were customary pleasantries to be observed.

"Thank you. We have already eaten a snack we brought with us. So we are all right. We will have to go back this evening to Malacca, so it might be better to begin our discussion." She added, "That is, if you do not mind."

Sook Ping was embarrassed. She sounded, even to herself, that she was in a hurry to leave. The truth was the journey had already exhausted her savings. She could not afford to rent a room for the night. Hotels within their means, they had been advised back home, were likely to be disreputable.

Su Hei could have had little idea of what was involved in preparing for their journey. Money meant for food had been used instead to buy the bus tickets. Mrs Tan, with her usual kindness, had helped. She had bought a new pair of shoes for Mei Yin and provided Sook Ping with a new set of clothes. Now, dressed in a dark blue shantung Chinese *sam foo* instead of the shabby *sarong* she normally wore, Sook Ping looked, in the words of Mrs Tan, "very presentable".

"It is important to look smart," Mrs Tan had said. "Mrs Ong knows your circumstances. There is no need to remind her. It is better for you and Mei Yin if she does not look down on you."

Su Hei looked at mother and daughter appraisingly. Preoccupied with her own thoughts, she had not thought of inviting them to stay. "How impolite of me," she said to make up for the negligence. "You must stay with us. You should not take the bus back to Malacca this evening. It would be too tiring. Stay. It will give us a better chance to get to know each other."

Su Hei was not heartless, but her mind was focused on having a daughter-in-law who could win her son back, someone she could mould in the way she wanted. She had given little thought to anything else. Brushing aside a twinge of guilt, she beckoned Mei Yin to come to her.

She studied her closely, thinking, "So this is Mei Yin. Pretty! Good intelligent forehead, high but not overly so. Intelligence is useful, but for a girl, a good nature is even more important. Big almond eyes, a straight nose and a lovely mouth. Ming Kong would approve."

Turning to Sook Ping, she smiled her approval. "I like Mei Yin's mouth. The shape and size of the mouth is very important you know. A girl with a big mouth creates poverty in the family. A big mouth signifies the squandering of wealth. Mei Yin's is about right, not too small, not too big."

"What is less pleasing, Mrs Sung, is Mei Yin's skin. She is really brown. Why do you let your daughter go out in the sun so much? At her age, the skin should be the colour of ivory and as smooth as silk."

"Mei Yin helps with household chores and delivers cakes to the market. She is in the sun a lot, I am afraid," Sook Ping explained.

"And her hands! They are so rough, like sand paper. Never mind, we will see that she stays in the shade and does not play in the sun too much. Not a big problem."

Patting Mei Yin's hands, she added, "I have asked Ah Kew to join us for tea later this afternoon. Ah Kew is our local matchmaker. She is well versed in the Chinese almanac. I have asked her to make sure that Mei Yin's character and fortune are compatible with my son. She will need some details about Mei Yin such as the time, date and year of her birth. All I can say is that I hope she is not born in the year of the tiger. If she is then our discussion need not go any further. Tiger women bring only sorrow to their husband's family."

For Su Hei the almanac would be of great importance in deciding whether Mei Yin would be suitable for her son. A wife must not undermine her husband, and Mei Yin's future must not out-shine her husband's; her role must be to serve him and boost his importance.

Sook Ping was aghast. "Is it necessary to use the almanac?"

"Of course! I consult it on everything."

Sook Ping neither used nor believed in the almanac. Uncomfortable with the concept, she was also surprised by the speed at which Su Hei was pushing matters forward. She had hardly been given a chance to utter a word; Su Hei seemed to have taken over completely. Where was the discussion they were supposed to have? Whether the engagement went through seemed to depend entirely on Su Hei and the results of Ah Kew's interpretation of the almanac: she and her daughter, it seemed, had little say in the matter. They had not met or even seen a photograph of Ming Kong. She felt uneasy. She had expected the Ong family, one that had been in Malaya for generations and had strong connections with the western world, to be more 'modern'. She was apprehensive that Su Hei's attachment to old-fashioned propriety and class could make life hard for her daughter.

"Mrs Ong, please can we discuss what you have in mind before we decide? After hearing your proposal, I would like to see what Mei Yin thinks about it." Sook Ping tried to regain some control over the situation.

Su Hei's eyebrows lifted in consternation, visibly taken back although she kept her thoughts to herself. "See what her daughter thinks! Her daughter should do as she is told. If there is a need for consultation, it should be the young seeking advice from their elders. It is like saying that heaven is below and the earth above. What can this woman be thinking of? She is spoiling the child."

"What would you like to know?" she asked out loud. Hard as she tried, her face could not disguise her disapproval.

"I only know what Mrs Tan has told us," replied Sook Ping, undeterred by Su Hei's look and determined to press her point. "She said you are looking for a bride for your son and you are interested in considering Mei Yin. She said there would be no pressure on either your son or my daughter to marry and that Mei Yin would be given time to continue her education, perhaps study English, and get to know him. There is, I believe, quite a big age difference between them. She advised, however, that I clarify these points with you to be absolutely sure."

"What you say is correct," replied Su Hei softening her stance slightly, realising that, despite her lowly status, this woman might prove difficult. "I don't see a need to rush into the marriage. I propose that Mei Yin comes to stay with me, providing Ah Kew finds no incompatibility between the two of them. While she is here I will teach her etiquette. It is important that she prepares properly for her future role as the first wife in an important family."

"Mrs Tan said that Mei Yin will be able to continue her studies and will be taught English," pressed Sook Ping.

"Yes, yes, she may continue her studies if she wishes. But the most important part of a girl's education is how to be a good wife."

"Will she be allowed to attend school?"

"A wife should be an asset to the family," Su Hei continued as though she had not heard. "If everything goes to plan in a couple of years' time we will make the wedding arrangements."

"Can we wait for a little longer? We would need time to prepare the trousseau." Sook Ping was hoping for more time for Mei Yin to complete her schooling.

"I will not expect you to provide a wedding trousseau. I understand your circumstances. We will pay for everything, including the dinner and ceremony. If the morning following the wedding night, the nuptial sheets show red, arrangements will be made on the third day for the return wedding procession of the bride. The bridegroom will bring gifts."

Mei Yin tried to follow the conversation. She could not grasp fully what was being said, but she could see that her mother was troubled.

Her mother protested; Mrs Ong insisted.

"Please don't shake your head," said Su Hei. "It is the traditional way of saying thank you for bringing up a virtuous maid. You could tell me now what you would like to have and we will see if this can be done."

"No, no, it will not be necessary. We are poor, but we manage. Our only concern is for Mei Yin's future. I have, however, one important request. I would like to visit my daughter and have her visit me frequently. I need to be sure she is happy." Sook Ping felt overwhelmed, reminded by the likely imminent separation from her daughter; she could not stop tears from trickling down her cheeks.

Moved by this display of emotion, Su Hei hastened to reassure Sook Ping, "Don't distress yourself, it will be as you wish. Look, Ah Jee has brought in some refreshments. Drink and eat something. Afterwards we will show you to your bedroom and you can refresh yourselves. We will talk again later. A short break will give both of you time to think over what has been said."

The conversation now turned to more mundane matters. Mei Yin remained silent, except when spoken to, which was not very often. She realised she was being keenly observed and felt uncomfortable. She did not know what to expect. Since the agreement to go along with Mrs Tan's proposal, there had been little time to think. Everything had happened so quickly and she had allowed herself to be swept along.

Looking around the room, she saw many photographs in ornate frames. There was a picture of Su Hei with an elderly gentlemen and three young children, two girls and a boy. Further on, a picture of a young man was prominently displayed on the dresser. Curious, she leaned forward to have a closer look.

"Yes, that is Ming Kong. A picture taken last year," said Su Hei.

Blushing, Mei Yin retreated.

"Don't be shy. You will meet him soon. It will not be today. We have much to discuss and Ming Kong does not live here. Instead, you will meet my youngest daughter who, no doubt, will give you all the family gossip. Wander around and look at the photos if you like while I talk with your mother."

So saying, she turned back to Sook Ping. She wanted to make her position clear. Already, she regretted her earlier impulsive agreement to Sook Ping's request to see her daughter regularly both here in Kuala Lumpur and in Malacca.

She returned to the subject. "I can understand your wish to see your daughter often." She smiled affably to soften her next words. "And I have no objections to this at the start, but a time will come when your visits might not be helpful. Your daughter needs to grow up and not cling to you. Now she is a child, but over the coming years she must mature fast if she is to attract my son. As you have said, there is a big age difference between them, not important in the future but, for now, it is. In fact at this moment, I can safely say he will not be interested in her as a woman. However, by the time Mei Yin is 16 and as pretty as I expect her to be, it will be a very different story."

Chapter 8

It was evening before Sook Ping and Mei Yin finished their interview with the matchmaker, Ah Kew. Both mother and daughter were exhausted by her endless questions. She wanted to know much more than just the date, time and year of Mei Yin's birth. She asked about her moles; examined her face, fingers and palms; and consulted the almanac at every opportunity. She turned Mei Yin this way and that so she could better examine her hips, muttering all the while about their importance for child bearing.

At last, alone in the bedroom, mother and daughter fell into a fit of nervous giggles; the pent up tension, anxiety and emotions of what had proved an exhausting day spilling out in uncontrollable laughter. It was some time before Sook Ping calmed down sufficiently to ask, "Will you be alright on your own with Mrs Ong?"

"I don't know. She's scary, always staring at me. But I like her daughter. I saw her peeping in and she waved. She might become a good friend. That would help."

Mei Yin cheered up visibly at the thought of finding a new friend. Seeing her mother's distress, she quickly added, "But, of course, I will miss you and Father."

"You don't have to stay, you know. The thing is you will definitely have a better chance of an education here. We will not be able to keep you at school in Malacca. We just can't afford it."

"Will I be staying then?"

"I don't know," her mother confessed. "Let's wait until we have met the rest of the family before deciding. If you do stay, I will come to see you often, at least in the first few months. You should know by then whether you like it here and want to stay. Really, we cannot make a decision now; we have still not met the most important person in this, Ming Kong."

* * * * *

At dinner Sook Ping and Mei Yin were introduced to Kai Min. Boisterous and out-going, she was the only one, it seemed, who could get around Su Hei. In fact, she paid little heed to what her mother said. "In one ear and out the other" was how her mother described her. After dinner, Kai Min wasted no time in telling Mei Yin about the family. Taking her hand, she took her on a guided tour of the house and the family pictures.

"This is the most recent photograph of my brother. He's my favourite person; he makes me laugh. I wish he would come here more often but he stays with *Tai-mah-ma*, First Mother. You'll like him," she assured Mei Yin.

"Why?" asked Mei Yin.

Kai Min's eyes opened wide. What a question! "Because all the girls in my school like him. When he came to collect me from school one day, all my friends wanted to meet him. They were so envious that I had such a good-looking brother." She looked around for her mother and, seeing she was out of earshot, whispered. "I suppose I shouldn't tell you. He has lots of girlfriends. Please, please, keep it a secret. Promise? Otherwise, I'll get into trouble."

Mei Yin nodded solemnly. She looked with renewed interest at the photograph. "He looks old," she thought. "I wonder what Siew Lin would think. If only she were here. Anyway, it doesn't really matter. I don't have to marry him if I don't want to."

Comforted by this thought, she chatted happily with Kai Min.

"Mother has arranged for the seamstress to come tomorrow. That means everything has gone well with the interview. Ah Jee told me that Ah Kew said nice things about you. We will have to go shopping. I love new clothes. I want to come with you. Tomorrow is Saturday, so I don't have school."

Looking over her shoulder, she whispered mischievously, "Ming Kong will join us for lunch or tea. You will see what I mean. You'll like him."

Sook Ping was having quite a different conversation with Su Hei. With dinner over, both women had adjourned to the sitting room.

"Mrs Ong, I appreciate that you wish Mei Yin to have a new wardrobe. But can't this wait until after we have met your son? I do not want you to go to unnecessary expense. Suppose the two of them do not get along."

"Don't worry. I intend to get only basic items. Mei Yin needs a change of clothes. She can't possibly wear the same ones for the entire stay here. And, of course, I would like my son to form a good impression of her. Please let me do this. Don't worry about the cost."

Buoyed by Ah Kew's good report, Su Hei was convinced that Mei Yin would be an ideal daughter-in-law and wife. "Born in the year of the rabbit, a good companion for the snake," she had been told.

She was excited at the prospect of having Ming Kong visit more often. It would allow her to build a new relationship with him. Already she saw a renewal of her importance to her husband. In time, she hoped to be surrounded by grandchildren, especially grandsons. A grandson would give her the status she lacked at present. She did not recall any agreement with the first wife to relinquish her grandchildren as well as her first son.

In the midst of these comforting thoughts, a niggling irritation with Sook Ping was beginning to form in Su Hei's mind. She could not understand the woman's hesitance. "One would think the silly woman is not interested," she thought. "She does not seem to understand how lucky Mei Yin is to be chosen as a wife for the heir to the Ong fortune. Many girls would give their eye-teeth for the chance."

Chapter 9

Mei Yin awoke to clear blue skies and the soothing, throaty gurgles of pigeons. It was Saturday. Looking out of the window, she could see Kai Min, dressed in floral silk, bent over the ground mimicking their sound. Every now and then, she dipped her hand into a blue enamel bowl to pull out bits of bread and scatter them on the ground, cooing and gurgling all the while.

"*Yee Siew cheh*! Second Young Mistress, please come in. Breakfast will be served any minute. I am sure your mother would like to see you seated like a lady before she joins you for breakfast. Miss Mei Yin is waiting for you," called Ah Jee.

Kai Min did not reply. Instead, she squatted, her bottom barely skimming the ground, to retrieve the uneaten pieces of bread she had thrown down earlier.

"*Ai yah*," mourned Ah Jee, "you will get your clothes dirty. That is your favourite dress. Please don't blame me or throw tantrums if you have to change. Quick, come in. Mei Yin is waiting," she repeated.

"Don't tell fibs. I can see her looking down right now from the bedroom window."

She waved to Mei Yin. "Hurry up, get dressed and join me. You have 15 minutes," she shouted.

"I'm coming. Give me a minute."

Mei Yin pulled on her clothes, reached into the basin of water that had been left in their room and splashed some on her face.

"Mei Yin, that is not a wash!" her mother admonished. "Wash properly. First let me braid your hair." She brushed her daughter's hair until it shone, parted it at the back and began braiding, weaving and pulling until she had produced two perfectly-formed coils of hair.

"I see you've found a friend, but remember why you are here," Sook Ping cautioned. "Don't forget. You are older than her and you are to be engaged to her brother. You should behave like a young lady and set a good example. Mrs Ong will expect it."

Mei Yin stopped mid-track. Up until then, she had been bouncing up and down eager to sprint off. "I am sorry," she said. "I forget sometimes. I wish I could just go to school and not bother about anything else."

* * * * *

It was dusk. Su Hei, Sook Ping, Mei Yin and Kai Min were gathered around the coffee table awaiting the arrival of Ming Kong. The day had been a great success. After breakfast, they had driven to the central shopping district of Kuala Lumpur to buy fabrics, shoes, bags and buttons, in fact, everything needed for a new wardrobe.

Young and impressionable, Mei Yin was enthralled with the colours and bustle of the city. In China town, they had shopped for brocades for the *cheongsams* and short jackets, silk and cotton for *sam foos* and western dresses. Everything had to be bought, from underwear to pyjamas. The colours and range of fabrics in the shops took Mei Yin's breath away. Never before had she been faced with so much choice. Burying her hands in the soft silk in one shop that they visited, she secretly agreed with Kai Min that shopping was really fun.

Su Hei proved to be the perfect hostess. Charming and amiable, she pointed out the different places of interest, while Kai Min kept up a steady stream of anecdotes she had been told by her school friends, some of whom lived in streets that they visited. Sook Ping and Mei Yin began to relax and enjoy themselves. Now, waiting for Ming Kong to arrive, both mother and daughter conceded that Su Hei was perhaps less formidable than they had first thought.

As the conversation turned to the things they had purchased and what still needed to be done, they heard the sound of a motorbike.

"He's here!" Su Hei's face brightened visibly. She turned to Ah Jee. "Open the door for First Master. Then fetch another cup of tea and a hot towel for him." And to Mei Yin and Sook Ping, she continued, almost in the same breath, "I am sure you will like him."

"Like who? I hope my mother has not been singing my praise. She is always embarrassing me like that. None of what she says about me is true, I promise you. Ah, you must be Mrs Sung and you must be Mei Yin. I am very pleased to meet you," said Ming Kong as he strode into the room.

"How did you get in? Ah Jee has hardly left the room."

"With my keys, of course," replied Ming Kong, amused at his mother's surprise. "I seldom get the chance to use them. Somehow Ah Jee always manages to be at the door when I arrive."

"I apologise for my son," Su Hei said, turning to Sook Ping. "He has no manners and does not wait to be properly introduced. He always barges in; he is too westernised and First Mother does nothing to correct his bad manners."

Despite the criticism, Su Hei's face was suffused with pride.

To avoid any discussion of why Mei Yin was there, Ming Kong turned to his customary teasing of Kai Min. He was intent on keeping up a normal front, but his mind was busy. He stole a glance at Mei Yin again. "Surely Mother must be joking," he thought. "This girl is nothing more than a pretty child and a very shy one at that. She hasn't said a word or even looked at me. Her mother also seems very quiet."

"Stop teasing your sister. We are here so that you can meet Mei Yin." Su Hei caught hold of his sleeve and tugged it. "Talk to her," she whispered urgently.

A pin drop would have been heard in the ensuing silence. Sook Ping pretended she had not noticed and looked out of the window.

"Ma-mah, please leave me alone!" Ming Kong was embarrassed. Desperate to find something to say, he said the first thing that came to his head. "I understand you might be staying with my mother and will probably go to the same school as my sister. If you need any help, just ask. I often help Kai Min with her homework. I would be happy to help you too."

He saw his mother looking anxiously at him, willing him to say more. She nodded her head in the direction of Mei Yin and mimed, "Go on! Go on!" The others were also looking at him expectantly. It was awkward. The preparations he had made earlier for the meeting had vanished. "Keep to generalities," an inner voice urged. He found himself saying, rather lamely, "Kuala Lumpur must seem strange to you after the quiet of Malacca."

Mei Yin nodded, but she continued to stare at the floor.

"There is a lot to see. I take Kai Min to the Lake Gardens quite often. You could come along as well."

Blushing, Mei Yin raised her head for the first time and replied, "Thank you. I would like that."

Beaming, Su Hei nodded her approval. At last a response. She was pleased, the encounter was beginning to go well. She glanced at Sook Ping. She looked less worried. "Yes," thought Su Hei, "this is not a time to force the pace. I will let things take their course."

* * * * *

The following morning, Sook Ping returned to Malacca, alone. Tears streamed down her face as she clasped Mei Yin close to her to say goodbye.

"I will come to see you as soon as I can," she assured Mei Yin. Then, turning to Su Hei, "Please look after Mei Yin. I beg you to let her come to visit us; she will want to see her father and the rest of the family."

Sook Ping was filled with anguish. It was just minutes before the bus for Malacca was due and her mind was already filled with doubts about her decision to leave Mei Yin behind. What had seemed so right the previous night now seemed hasty and flawed.

Chapter 10

Three months on, Mei Yin was strolling in the little backyard of the house. It was twilight and she had an hour before dinner. Her thoughts kept returning to the first days in Kuala Lumpur when her mother was with her. She missed her terribly. Her heart felt heavy. It was difficult to explain to anyone the sense of loss she felt. She could not tell Kai Min and certainly not Su Hei. She needed desperately to talk to her mother. Her only means of contact was through letters and even that was difficult. Because her mother could not read or write, her letters had to be sent through someone who could read them to her. This made it difficult for Mei Yin to express her thoughts freely. In two weeks' time, she would be 14 and her mother had promised to visit. She willed the days to go faster.

So far, Su Hei had been unwilling to let her visit her family in Malacca. Every time she broached the subject, she would reply that it was too soon. "It is for your own good. You need to get over home-sickness, once and for all. If you go back now, it will just unsettle you."

After the initial excitement of being introduced to the city, her daily life had settled into a pattern. She attended a Chinese school with Kai Min in the morning. Afternoons brought a round of different activities. A private tutor taught the girls English. Su Hei kept her word on that. The rest of the day, however, was spent mainly with Su Hei. Each day she had to listen to how Su Hei had served her mother-in-law. The stories of the 24 episodes of filial piety were her bedside reading.

Kai Min provided some light relief. Snatching the book from Mei Yin, she would often read aloud the stories in a tone that showed comic disbelief. "And the son cut his own flesh to cook for his mother when he had no money to buy meat to feed his ailing parent!" She grinned and rolled her eyes. "So chop, chop! Ouch! Ouch! Nothing left! Who would believe this?" she asked. In this way both girls spent many an evening huddled together giggling over the stories.

Su Hei also gave her a list of duties that she would be expected to perform after she married Ming Kong. As the wife of the first son, she would look after the family altar and be responsible for all the ceremonial rites attached to it. She had to memorise the important festive dates when offerings are made to ancestors. Annual prayers at the cemetery during Ching-ming, the festival of the ghosts, had to be organized to appease the spirits of the dead when they returned to earth. She would also be responsible for maintaining the family burial plot. Then came the list of responsibilities on special occasions such as engagements, marriages, births and birthdays. They ranged from invitations and seating arrangements of the elders down to the auspicious foods that should form part of the menu, and foods that had to be avoided at all cost. Her duties to the immediate family went on and on. She was constantly reminded that a daughter-in-law had to obey her mother-in-law. Permission had to be sought for everything; she would have to have permission to visit her parents and even to go out with her husband. Looking after her mother-in-law would be her main task. It could involve anything from massaging her head to getting her tea, cooking special food and carrying messages.

Ah Jee showed her the rudiments of Cantonese cooking. "We Chinese," the cook told her, "live to eat. *Sik hai fook!* To eat is happiness!" Ming Kong was proof of this, she learned. In addition to Cantonese food, he liked spicy hot food. He had acquired this taste, partly from his first mother and partly through contact with Tamil workers in the rubber plantations. On visits to the plantations, his diet was the inevitable curry and rice. Mei Yin was told she would be given lessons on Indian and Singhalese spices, how to select the best ones, how to combine and grind them to make pastes for the various curries and then how to prepare the different dishes.

"You have a lot to learn," Ah Jee assured her. "Not only in cook-ing, but in the art of massage. *Mui Chai* will show you how to do that."

Mui Chai had been with the family for her entire 19 years. She was sold as a baby to the family. She had no name; *Mui Chai* means, literally, slave girl. Among her many duties was to give Su Hei a massage before she retired to bed. Most evenings would find her rubbing Su Hei's head and shoulders, sometimes applying tiger balm, nutmeg oil and other unguents, working them deep into the muscles to relieve aches and pains.

Her diligence was soon to be rewarded. Su Hei had agreed to let her marry the owner of the herbal store down the road. This would release her from her bond. Until someone else could be employed, Mei Yin was to take over *Mui Chai*'s duty. The art of massage, she was informed, was an essential skill for a wife. "In the old days," said Su Hei, "a good wife would massage her husband's head, shoulders, arms, legs and feet in the evenings to relax him after a hard day's work. You would do well to do the same."

Mei Yin nodded and agreed at each and every turn. By the end of the day, she was exhausted. She found it hard to absorb all the details and impossible to disagree. She had no one to turn to. Kai Min encouraged her to rebel, but Mei Yin found it difficult to emulate her. She turned to Ming Kong, the only one she believed would understand. He came every weekend to help them with their homework and give them a chance to practise English. He took them for short outings and during these he tried to dispel Mei Yin's increasingly sombre mood. He treated her like a sister, but was gentler with her because he knew how difficult his mother could be. His frequent visits pleased Su Hei and, believing they were the result of Mei Yin's presence, she was pleased with her too.

* * * * *

Just five days before her 14th birthday, Ming Kong brought Mei Yin and Kai Min to the Malay bazaar in Kampong Hijau. It was a Friday night. Every Friday evening, the villagers set up a market. Stalls selling local handicrafts, batiks, food, woven baskets of all shapes and size, food covers, kites, dolls and carvings lined the far end of the village. The entire village turned out. It was a chance to chat with friends and neighbours as well as to buy or admire the wares on display. It was a festive occasion. Kerosene lamps cast a yellow glow around the stalls, people sat on benches beside low tables eating, drinking and talking; children scrambled and played around the adults; dogs barked, excited by the moving shadows of their play.

Kampong Hijau was not far from the house of Ming Kong's first mother. She often sent the maid there to buy fruits and cakes. He had explained to his first mother the plans that Su Hei had for him and Mei Yin, and she expressed a desire to meet Mei Yin. Not wishing to anger Su Hei, he conspired for them to meet, as if by chance, during a visit to the night market. He was determined to find a way out of the arranged marriage without hurting anyone. He knew his sister would let the secret out if he were to bring them to visit his first mother. This would be safer. As it was, he had great difficulty persuading Su Hei to let the girls visit a Malay *pasar malam*. She was not pleased. A resounding "No!" had been her first response. "You cannot take the girls out at night. It's not safe. All kinds of people go to that market. Goodness knows who you might meet. Hooligans, no doubt, will be there with their tight trousers and bad manners."

"Please, please, we promise to be good," Kai Min had pleaded.

"I'll make sure they behave and we will not stay long," Ming Kong had promised. "We'll keep to the brightly lit parts if that will make you happier."

"No! I know Kai Min. She is a handful."

"Please, please I won't. I promise to do whatever Ming Kong asks. If I don't then you can punish me and cancel all my pocket money."

Su Hei had looked uncertainly at her children. Ming Kong had smiled his encouragement and mouthed a silent "Please".

"Alright, just this once. Make sure you are back early."

The girls were delighted. Kai Min, whooping for joy, had jumped up and down in her excitement. Mei Yin had held on to her hand, a broad smile on her lips, a smile that lasted all the way to the market.

The market reminded Mei Yin of Malacca. Everyone seemed to be talking at the same time. She was familiar with the soft cadence of Malay mingled with the singsong tones of different Chinese dialects. Now and then even some English would be heard, but not that of the colonial rulers, this had an ethnic slant, "What-*lah*! Yes-man!"

"*Goreng pisang!* Would you like some?" Ming Kong asked as they threaded their way through the crowd. "This stall sells the best fried bananas in town. See how many different kinds of banana there are. Choose what you want; he will fry them for you."

Kai Min was not interested. Her attention was elsewhere. She broke free, ran a few yards ahead, then ran back. Her face stretched in a mischievous grin.

"I've seen her."

"Who?"

"Your girlfriend. She has seen us too. Let's go over and you can introduce Mei Yin to her."

Her brother looked nonplussed.

"Don't worry. I have told Mei Yin about Nelly and made her swear not to tell Ma-mah. Come, come."

She tugged his hands and frog-marched him forward.

Ming Kong was embarrassed. He had never thought that Kai Min might tell Mei Yin about Nelly. He turned to look at Mei Yin. She did not seem bothered. The expression was just one of curiosity as she stared at the long-haired, beautiful young woman approaching them.

Nelly's face was wreathed in smiles. She had not expected to see Ming Kong. He had called from the office to tell her he would be late and that she need not wait for him. He explained that he had to deal with urgent family matters.

She knew Kai Min was his sister, but she had not seen Mei Yin before. Her first thought was that this pretty girl must be a cousin or niece of Ming Kong. She found it strange to see him at a banana fritter stall with these two young girls when he had told her that he had urgent family matters to settle. She weaved deftly through the crowd towards them. "You must be Kai Min. Ming Kong has talked a lot about you, but I do not know this young lady. Can you introduce us?" Nelly offered a hand in greeting as she spoke.

Mei Yin, round-eyed, took her hand and answered solemnly, "I'm Mei Yin."

"Yes, sorry, this is Mei Yin, Kai Min's friend," blurted Ming Kong in confusion. "She is from Malacca and is staying with my mother. She goes to school with Kai Min." After a moment's hesitation, he added, "I am teaching them English. That is why, that is . . . ah..."

"That is not quite everything," interrupted Kai Min. "You have not mentioned the real reason why Mei Yin is here."

Kai Min would have revealed all if Ming Kong had not quickly covered her mouth with his hand, almost gagging his excited sister in his anxiety to silence her. "Big mouth," he hissed as he bent over her. "Don't say anything more or I will never take you out again."

Puzzled by Ming Kong's reaction, Nelly could only try to calm him down. "What a fuss! You are choking your sister." But Ming Kong made no move to release her, aware that she might easily tell Nelly in defiance. Kai Min tried to bite his hand. He held her even harder.

"Stop it! Stop it!" demanded Nelly, wresting them apart.

"I am sorry. Did he hurt you?" She turned to Ming Kong, "What a way to behave. You should treat us all to fried bananas as a penalty for losing your temper," she said in mock anger.

She invited the two girls to sit, settling herself alongside them on the bench. "I'm glad to see you here. I've been wanting to meet you and other members of the family for some time," she continued, more for the benefit of Ming Kong than the two young girls. "Whenever I mention it to your brother, he says he is busy. I was beginning to think he was ashamed of me. Has he mentioned me?"

Kai Min answered by shaking her head and, using her thumb and index finger, drew a line along her lips to indicate they were sealed.

Amused and slightly exasperated, Nelly turned to Mei Yin. "So tell me what brought you to KL?"

Mei Yin took her cue from Kai Min and indicated that her lips too were sealed.

Nelly realised that she was not going to get anything from the girls. She turned to Ming Kong. "Why didn't you tell me you were coming to this market? I was more or less reconciled to an evening alone at home after you told me you would not be back. It is good that I decided to take a stroll here."

"Is Ming Kong staying with you?" asked Kai Min. "I thought he was living with *Tai-mah*." Her eyes were bright with mischief.

Embarrassed, Nelly looked to Ming Kong for an answer. He rolled his eyes, pulled a face, but said nothing. What a mess. He should not have tried to be so clever. He stood up and excused himself. The fritters were ready and he needed to pay for them. As he walked towards the stall, he saw his first mother, Suet Ping, and her maid. With a sigh of relief, he hurried towards them.

"I'm in trouble. A girlfriend, Nelly, has turned up unexpectedly. Please help me out. They are asking each other too many questions and, of course, Kai Min is all ears."

His first mother nodded, patted his arm and went over to the group. Suet Ping was a diplomatic woman. Long a confidante to her adopted son's mixed and confused emotions concerning his natural mother, and sympathetic to his dilemma, she was always willing to cover up his failings. This time was no different.

Kai Min stood up immediately on her approach. "Good evening *Tai-mah*. My mother sends you her good wishes." She had been taught to give her mother's greeting to First Mother whenever she met her.

Mrs Ong exclaimed, "How you have grown since I last saw you. This must be Mei Yin and Nelly. Ming Kong has mentioned both of you. He was planning to arrange a lunch party for all of us, but he has been so busy with his new project at the office."

She directed questions at Kai Min about her school; she asked Nelly about her work; she talked about Malacca with Mei Yin. She sent the two younger girls with Ah Keng to buy fruits. The evening passed smoothly. Kai Min was on her best behaviour and made no other indiscreet remarks.

* * * * *

At the end of the evening, a much-relieved Ming Kong said farewell to his *tai-mah* before taking Kai Min and Mei Yin home. As he left, he whispered to Nelly that he would see her later. Nelly went her separate way home to her apartment.

Situated above a shop-house, the apartment was tiny. A little kitchen, a living/dining room, a bathroom and a small bedroom made up its entire accommodation. Except for potted plants on the table and shelves, and brightly coloured cushions strewn on the sofa, there was little else in the living room. But Nelly loved it. She worked in a nearby beauty salon where she doubled as the manicurist and assistant hairdresser. Ming Kong had found her the job through a colleague. The work gave her a sense of independence and self-esteem. It also kept her occupied during the day. Ming Kong was not always with her; he still lived part of the time with his first mother.

"I enjoyed meeting your family this evening," she said when Ming Kong finally let himself into the flat.

"Good," he replied without much enthusiasm.

He had hoped to avoid discussing the evening's events. He should have known that Nelly would mention it the moment he stepped through the door. He stood there looking sheepish, having little more to add. The effect of this was to encourage Nelly to continue with a question.

"You should not have been so rough with your sister. Why did you treat her like that?"

"We were just fooling around. She is a handful. Just play really."

"And did you notice how her friend, Mei Yin, watched me. Her eyes followed my every movement the entire evening. Very strange."

"She was probably admiring you. Come here. I didn't come back to talk about my family," replied Ming Kong trying to divert the discussion to safer ground. He put his arms around her. Nelly did not respond. She felt uneasy. Mei Yin's close observation of her, Kai Min's banter, their silence when she questioned them and most of all Ming Kong's behaviour had sparked off a train of thought. All manner of suspicions came to her mind. She wanted answers to the questions that had bothered her all the way home.

In the beauty salon she heard all sorts of gossip. Generally she took little notice. When asked what she thought, she would nod politely and give non-committal replies. Neither did she venture any information about herself. Three days ago, however, one of the clients, a Mrs Saraswathy, had attracted her attention when she began talking about a family called Ong. Mrs Saraswathy said she had been giving English lessons to the daughter of Mrs Ong, but in recent months she had had two students instead of one, the daughter and a daughter-in-law to be. "A pretty girl, but very, very young", she had exclaimed. At the time, Nelly had not really taken much notice. There were many Ongs in Kuala Lumpur.

Nelly had few friends and no relatives in Kuala Lumpur so she knew very little about Ming Kong or his family other than what he had told her. He had mentioned his first mother and explained that his natural mother was the second wife. She knew his natural mother was old-fashioned and might be reluctant to accept her. This knowledge had made it easier for her to understand why he had not introduced her to his family. She realised her circumstances were such that many a mother in search of a wife for a son would be reluctant to consider her.

But the strange behaviour of everyone that evening had troubled her. Something was not right. Could Ming Kong's family be the one her client had gossiped about? Could this child, Mei Yin, be the young girl? What was Kai Min trying to tell her? The more she thought about the matter, the more plausible it seemed. Why else would Ming Kong behave so strangely?

Trying to keep calm, she broke away from Ming Kong's embrace and busied herself gathering the glasses and cups on the table. It was difficult. Her mind churned with unwelcome thoughts. Finally, unable to contain herself any longer she asked the question that was troubling her most, "Who is Mei Yin?"

"I told you. She is from Malacca and is staying for the present with my mother and sister."

Unconvinced, she walked back to him and looked straight into his eyes. "Anything else?" she asked.

"What else should there be?" he replied with a shrug.

It was the shrug that did it. Too nonchalant, it contradicted the anxiety in his eyes. She decided he had to deny or confirm her suspicion. She would have no peace until she knew. She prayed he would deny it even as she said, "You tell me. I have heard in the salon your mother has her future daughter-in-law living with her."

It was not strictly true, it was her own conjecture, but what else could she do? She pressed on. "I took little notice. Now, I'm not so sure. There was such a lot of awkwardness this evening that I could not help wondering. The girl is just a child!"

"Precisely. That is why you shouldn't worry."

"You mean it is true?" asked Nelly, aghast. It was not the answer she wanted. She held a cushion to her body, clutching it tightly. She swallowed quickly, nausea welling up inside her.

Cornered, Ming Kong nodded. "Look, I am only going along with it for the moment because I feel sorry for Mei Yin. You have no idea. You have not met my mother." He had not intended to deceive her. He had postponed telling her about Mei Yin in the hope that somehow the nightmarish situation would go away.

Ming Kong had not intended to have a lasting relationship with Nelly, but it had developed. He had always known deep down that marriage was out of the question, but he did not want to lose her. Clasping her hands, he spoke gently. "I wanted to tell you about this mess; I just couldn't bring myself to do it. This crazy situation has nothing to do with me. My mother arranged it. And, with luck, it will come to nothing. Like you say, she's just a child. Don't cry. I don't want anyone to be hurt. If the project at the office goes well, we can still be together. We can set up on our own in Seremban."

Nelly did not reply. What could she say? She was totally dependent on him.

Nelly

Chapter 11

Nelly was born in Singapore. Her real name was Tze Min. Her father had been among the thousands of labourers brought there from Southern China in the early 1900s under what was known as a credit-ticket system. He was given a ticket to travel to Singapore and in return he had to work for a low wage, most of which went to repaying the fare. He toiled more than seven years before he was finally free of debt.

Then, in the 1930s, came the Great Depression. He lost his job. Stony-faced, his employers told him he could return to Fukien, his home province in China, if he wished. The company would pay part of his fare, but it offered nothing towards the travel costs of his wife and family. "If you return to Fukien, don't even think of returning. It will not be possible. The new Immigration Restriction Ordinance will not allow it," they warned.

With few opportunities in Singapore, Tze Min's father sought work on the mainland of Malaya. Day in and day out, he crossed over the causeway from Singapore to the mainland and joined the long queues of people desperate for work. But none was to be found. With little prospect of work and five hungry children, Tze Min's parents were forced to turn to their daughter for succour. And at just 15 years of age she was married off to a wealthy Chinese businessman Woo Pik Soo as his second wife.

Nelly would never forget that day in 1931. For the first time that she could remember, she was not expected to get up early and prepare the family's usual breakfast of thin rice gruel. Nor did she have to draw water from the well or bathe and dress her little brothers and sisters in the communal backyard. Instead, she had the luxury of eating a breakfast prepared by her mother. By nine o'clock, the little two-bedroomed, zinc-roofed house began to fill with people. Relatives, neighbours and children crowded into the tiny space that doubled as both living room and kitchen. In the tiny bedroom she shared with her four brothers and sisters, Tze Min was being dressed by her mother, helped by her aunt, Li.

"Do what you are told and it will be alright," Aunty Li advised.

"Remember you have to serve and obey your husband and his first wife," added her mother as she brushed her daughter's long black hair and arranged it in a shiny loose coil at the nape of her neck. "You are a lucky girl. You are starting a new life. Mr Woo has been very kind. He is going to see to the schooling of your brothers and sisters, and he has agreed to provide us with a monthly allowance. What more can we ask for? So don't let us down."

But behind the stern and blustery advice, Tze Min could see that the two ladies were anxious and uncomfortable.

"Have you told her what marriage is about? Is she prepared for tonight?" whispered Aunty Li. When her mother did not reply, she sighed, "Well, someone should."

Nelly's mother shook her head. "I can't!"

"If you won't, then I will!" Aunty Li cleared her throat and prepared to broach the subject of sex and marriage. No sooner did she start, she faltered. Her face turned crimson, she coughed and spluttered before blurting out, "Your mother should not have left it till now, little more than an hour before your marriage, to explain the facts of life to you. All I can say is that the wedding night is not very pleasant, but all women go through it. What to do? It's just something we have to put up with. Think! In return, you will have beautiful children and that will be your reward."

Embarrassed and unable to elaborate further, she cleared away the breakfast things, clattering the dishes energetically into a pile and hurried out of the room.

"Mother, what was Aunty Li trying to say?"

"Nothing. Don't worry."

"I don't want to leave home. I will work and earn money for the family." Desperately, she grabbed both her mother's hands. "Please don't send me away. Please, please I don't want to marry Mr Woo. Please don't make me."

"It's too late, too late." All her mother could do was hold and comfort her, repeating over and over, "Everything will be alright".

By mid-morning, preparations for the wedding were complete. Dressed in a dark red silk top and skirt embroidered with the traditional phoenix and dragon, and with her hair adorned with gardenias, Tze Min was ready, but her tears would not stop.

Over and over again, her mother had to wipe them away, Finally, just minutes away from the arrival of the wedding sedan, she placed a silk veil over her daughter's face and rearranged the gold filigree necklace round her neck. Mr Woo had been generous. His prenuptial gifts to his bride were the wedding trousseau and gold bracelets, earrings and necklace, and a jade ring set in gold.

Aunty Li whispered, eyes dark in anger and full of accusation, "You are selling your daughter."

Tze Min's mother nodded and began to cry. "What can I do?" she sobbed, gathering the other children to her. "It's one life for four."

* * * * *

The wedding sedan, balanced between two poles shouldered by four men, arrived at Tze Min's home. Mr Woo believed in doing things in style. He had hired a traditional sedan chair, richly decorated with peonies, dragons and phoenixes, and painted in gold and red. It was, in his view, the best way to show off his beautiful second wife.

Tze Min, her face shielded with the silk veil, was helped into the sedan. Tears streamed down her face. There was no going back. Her mother had already accepted the gift of money, delivered in a red envelope, and drawn on it to settle the family's debts.

Tze Min could hardly see. Her body felt numb, insensitive to the sharp jolt of the carriage when the men hoisted it onto their shoulders. The procession began. People gathered to watch and to gossip. To Tze Min, their chatter and laughter seemed to mock her grief and she was filled with shame. It was not until the sedan had left the narrow alleys of the Chinese settlement and reached the wider roads that the crowd thinned out. Slowly, the sedan swung its way into a tree-lined road and onto the pavement. Only then did the tearful young girl raise her head to peer out from beneath the veil.

Angsana trees with their brilliant yellow flowers alternating with the fiery red blooms of the flame of the forest trees lined each side of the wide avenue. Behind the trees were high walls and beyond them the palatial homes of the rich. Even here Tze Min could not entirely escape the stares of curious passers-by. Passing cars slowed down to allow the occupants to catch a glimpse of the elaborately painted sedan and its veiled occupant.

Tze Min was not taken directly to her new home. Her first stop was at the official residence of Mr Woo and his first wife. When the sweating and tired bearers came to a halt, Mr Woo himself was on hand to help her out of the sedan. Once she had stepped out, he gave her a cursory inspection, nodded in satisfaction and strode hurriedly back into the house. He stopped only to speak briefly to a sturdy-looking woman.

Moments later the woman came forward. "I'm Ah Kuk. We are to wait in the hallway until the master and mistress are ready to receive you. Come with me, this way, this way," she repeated as she went up the steps to the main entrance of the house.

The minutes dragged by until a tinkling bell signalled that all was ready. "They are waiting for you," Ah Kuk said softly. "Here, take this handkerchief and dry your tears. It will not do to cry during the marriage rite. I will help you and show you what to do."

Ah Kuk led the young bride through a half-moon doorway into the drawing room. All eyes turned toward the bride. A sudden silence descended in the room. Mr and Mrs Woo, flanked by maids and relatives, were seated on ceremonial high chairs in the centre of the room. A side table had been set with a porcelain teapot, little cups and saucers, and a bowl of lotus seed and *longan* fruit.

Gently, Ah Kuk indicated that Tze Min should kneel. "Make sure that you bow low. See the silk cushion placed before the couple, that is your headrest. Don't look up until asked. I'll fetch the specially-brewed tea, infused with sweet *longan* and lotus seed and you, in turn, must offer the drink to Mrs Woo. The tea symbolises a gift of sweetness so try to smile," she encouraged.

Trembling, Tze Min approached Mrs Woo, knelt and waited. She could see very little because of her veil. All she saw was the lady's feet encased in embroidered and beaded slippers next to Mr Woo's shiny black, patent leather shoes. The room was silent except for the sound of pouring tea, followed by the soft footfall of Ah Kuk as she delivered the cup to the kneeling bride. Holding the cup in both hands, head still bowed, Tze Min offered the sweet tea to Mrs Woo.

"So this is to be your second wife," Mrs Woo said quietly as she bent closer to Tze Min. "Welcome to my house."

"May I look at your bride?" she asked, turning to her husband. Seeing his nod of assent, she leaned forward and gently lifted the veil. She placed a finger under Tze Min's chin and tilted her head up.

"You are, indeed, a beautiful young woman. I wish you well and I hope you will bless us with many sons." Reaching into a pocket in her Mandarin jacket, she brought out a box and a red envelope.

"This is for you. Open the box."

Tze Min looked up to find a pair of soft brown eyes full of compassion gazing at her. Mrs Woo was not at all what Tze Min had expected. Her face was serene. Only barely perceptible fine lines radiating from the corner of her eyes and silver-lined hair hinted at her age. Whispering her thanks, Tze Min bowed and opened the box. Inside was a gold chain with an emerald jade pendant of two fish intertwined.

"Let me help you to put it on," she said softly. She unclasped the chain and placed it around Tze Min's neck. Her husband looked on and for the first time a smile appeared on his broad flat face. He was pleased that things were going smoothly. When Tze Min offered him tea, he took it with relish, drank noisily and then stood up.

"We will take our leave," he said impatiently, turning to his wife. "You go ahead with the dinner for our relatives. Tze Min and I will be on our way to the new house."

With nothing more than a cursory farewell, he strode out of the room, leaving the guests aghast at his bad manners. No one spoke, but the expression on their faces said it all. Tze Min could only murmur her apologies and thank Mrs Woo again before she too left, assisted by Ah Kuk.

When they were well away from her mistress, Ah Kuk whispered, "My lady is very kind. We all love her. I have been given the job of carrying messages between your household and this one, so I will see you again. Mrs Woo said that if you need help to let me know." She hesitated before adding, "Be careful, I wish you luck."

The warning puzzled Tze Min. "What was she trying to say? Why is she whispering in such a secretive manner?" Already exhausted from crying and a fear of the unknown, Tze Min allowed herself to be escorted to the sedan to continue the journey to her new home. Mr Woo had gone on ahead in his limousine.

* * * * *

Tze Min stepped into the hallway of her new home. She could see through the archway that it led into a drawing room with French windows framed by a riotous growth of purple-hued bougainvillea. They in turn opened onto a terrace and garden. All the windows and doors were open and a flood of late afternoon sunshine turned the vast expanse of marble floor into a glimmering pool. On the left of the hallway, a carpeted staircase led to an upper floor.

"So here you are," said her husband appearing seemingly out of nowhere. She had not seen him when she entered. He stood before her, smiling. He had already changed to an open-neck shirt. "The guests are here. We are waiting for you. Go upstairs." Motioning to a woman at his side, "Ah Siew will help you change. Then come down to the dining room. I have invited some close associates to celebrate with us. Go along and be quick about it."

The maid led Tze Min to a bedroom. Once inside the room, she hurried towards a wardrobe that lined an entire wall of the room. She opened a door to reveal a long row of dresses, all neat and new. "Master had your dresses made and delivered. He particularly wants you wear the red *cheongsam*." With a deft movement, she removed the dress from the rack and laid it out on the bed. The silk shimmered in the light.

Tze Min stared at the clusters of pearl beads embroidered on the bodice of the dress and then at the woman. She wanted to say to her, "Please help me," but nothing came out, the words remained stifled like a lump lodged deep in her throat.

The woman continued brightly, seemingly unaware of Tze Min's plight. "Once you have refreshed, I will help you dress. I will be by the door. Call me if you need me. Best to hurry; the master does not like to be kept waiting."

Left to herself at last, Tze Min slumped down on the bed, drained of all emotion. She moved mechanically, following the maid's instructions. She undressed, washed and put on the *cheongsam*. Once dressed, she sat down again, unsure whether she should call. There was no need. Ah Siew was already knocking on the door.

"Ah! Beautiful!" exclaimed Ah Siew, nodding her head with approval as she stepped into the room. "I will brush your hair. Master has instructed that you are to leave it loose. But how pale and wan you look!" A fleeting look of concern passed over her face and then as though it had never taken place, she smiled and continued, "I have brought you a cup of tea and some pastries from the kitchen. Try to eat. You must. However little. From my experience of Master's dinner parties, you may not have much chance later." She brushed Tze Min's hair with long firm strokes until it glistened. "Poor girl, she is little more than a child," she thought.

* * * * *

The sound of loud raucous laughter came from the dining room. When Tze Min entered, heads turned to look at her. The room was packed with people. Men and women, drinking, toasting and making merry. "*Gan bei*" they called, goading each other to drink. No one wished to look a loser in the contest. All looked the worst for drink.

The men were business associates of Pik Soo. Almost all had come with mistresses or girlfriends. They were not the kind of people he could invite to his first wife's home; since his mother's death, he had grown apart from his relatives and his first wife's immediate family. As the night went on and the drink flowed, the atmosphere became ever more rowdy. The number of empty bottles of VSOP brandy grew on the sideboard. Tze Min's head began to ache and her stomach protested with hunger. She felt ill.

The dining room clock chimed midnight. As if planned, the guests began to clap and chant, "Time for bed, time for bed."

With much jostling, they pushed the couple up the stairs, following them to the bedroom. Turning around in panic to look for Ah Siew, Tze Min's face burned with shame. All she could see were leering faces and the vulgar signs some guests were making to each other. Stood at the bottom of the staircase, Ah Siew looked on in horror.

"Come on, old man, get on with it," they shouted. More laughter and exhortations to Pik Soo to show his prowess. Finally, someone said, "Let's leave them to it." Tired with teasing the couple, the unruly guests began to disperse, staggering back down the stairs. At last Tze Min was alone with her husband in the bedroom.

The door closed. Fearful, Tze Min retreated to the far corner of the room. She could smell the drink. Disgust made her feel ill. He lurched after her, frantically shedding his clothes, his steps unsteady.

"Where are you going? Come here." His words were slurred. "You're not going to turn shy on me, are you? It's not like before, you know, now you belong to me."

He took another step forward and tripped. Grabbing hold of the bed, he steadied himself before lunging forward again. With a violent kick, he got rid of the remaining trouser leg that had caught round his ankle.

His face was flushed. Impatiently, he pulled the frightened Tze Min to him. He ran his fingers down one side of her face until he reached the Mandarin collar of her *cheongsam*. He hooked them inside it and yanked. He pulled so hard the buttons holding the collar snapped and scattered. The dress, from the collar and down one side of the tight-fitting bodice, split open. In vain, Tze Min tried to cover herself. The more she struggled, the more inflamed Pik Soo became.

Whack! He slapped her so hard her head jerked backwards. He forced her down onto the bed and fell on top of her. He tried to pull her hand towards him, but she resisted. He hit her. When she cried out in pain, he became even more aggressive and excited. Far stronger than Tze Min, he succeeded in forcing her legs apart and cruelly pushed inside her. He began thrusting into the sobbing girl. He paid little heed to the sounds of merriment still coming from downstairs; he cared even less about her pleas for him to stop. There were no soft words of comfort, no gentleness of touch. Just rasping breath and grasping hands. The perfumed sheets became soiled and sodden with sweat. Finally, exhausted by his drunken assault, Pik Soo collapsed over her and then, still panting, rolled away, sated. Soon he began to snore.

Tze Min eased herself from the bed and moved gingerly to the bathroom. Bruised and bloody, she sank slowly to the floor and wept. So this was what Aunty Li had meant. She wept until her eyelids, swollen and bruised, could hardly open. Then she stood up, undressed and washed. She flushed away the smears of blood and semen from her thighs and then scrubbed and scrubbed her body in a desperate effort to become clean again.

* * * * *

Woo Pik Soo was not always so cruel. Certainly Tze Min's life became more comfortable and secure. She lacked for nothing. Her own family also benefited from the union. Her brothers and sisters were able to go to high school and Pik Soo, as promised, supported her parents. In the course of time she had two beautiful children, a boy and a girl. Mr Woo's first wife, Mary, was delighted and treated the children as her own. With Tze Min, she was supportive and gentle.

Through their servants, Ah Siew and Ah Kuk, the two wives kept in close contact and became good friends. Tze Min found she could talk with Mary about things she could not discuss with anyone in her own family. She found it particularly difficult to talk with her mother. Tortured by guilt at having forced Tze Min into the marriage and apprehensive of Pik Soo, her mother rarely came to visit.

After the birth of the children, the marriage fell apart. Pik Soo's violent tantrums and erratic behaviour grew steadily worse. The carousing with his friends became ever more intemperate, his mood more unpredictable. Often, after a night out, he would return home and force himself on her, re-awakening the horror of the wedding night. He beat her frequently and brutally. When she retreated from his cruelty, he would rail and shout. "I can be with anyone I choose, but I come back here. And all I get is an ice maiden."

At other times, he would be contrite and buy her presents to make amends. By the fifth year of the marriage, however, the beatings had increased to a point where it became apparent, even to Pik Soo himself, that his pleas for forgiveness no longer rang true.

* * * * *

One morning, Tze Min awoke to loud banging on her bedroom door and the calls of Ah Siew. "Wake up. Hurry, hurry! We have to dress the children. We have to leave immediately for the first mistress. Call the driver. Master has just left her and he is on his way here. Ah Kuk called to warn us. She said he is in a terrible mood."

"Why?" asked Tze Min clambering out of the bed.

"He lost his temper because First Mistress refused to accept a third wife into the household. He smashed his way around the house, turning over furniture and breaking ornaments. He only just stopped short of hitting Mistress herself."

"Is she alright?"

"Yes, yes," she nodded vigorously in reply, her hands busy thrusting clothes into a bag. "He would never dare lay a finger on her. She owns most of his company."

Seeing the surprise on Tze Min's face, she explained. "When the master started, he didn't have much money. It was First Mistress's family who financed him. He might have forgotten just how much he owes her, but I am sure he has not forgotten completely. He must still remember where his rice bowl is."

"Quickly, get dressed. We have to leave before he gets here. We can shelter with First Mistress until things calm down."

Tze Min rushed to the children's bedroom. She woke them up and began taking off their nightclothes. Her heart was beating fast, she felt breathless. Usually her husband's tantrums were late at night or in the early hours of the morning when he returned from one of his outings. At least then she could avoid involving the children; she would hate them to see how he treated her. As it was, she had difficulty explaining the bruises.

Roughly awoken, the children were fractious. "Mummy, I want to sleep," complained Chai-chai. Mei-mei began to cry, burying her face into Tze Min's breast. Upset by the commotion, she was completely uncooperative and clung to her mother. It was impossible to dress her.

"Mei-mei, please help Mummy. We have to dress quickly. We are going to *Tai-mah*. She appealed to Chai-chai. "Help Mummy. Do as Ah Siew says. We have no time to spare."

Before she could say any more, they heard a car roar into the driveway and screech to a halt. A door slammed, followed by the thud of footsteps coming up the stairs. Turning to her distraught maid, she gave quick instructions, "Take the children. Hide them downstairs."

"What about you?" Ah Siew asked anxiously.

"Don't worry about me. Look after the children. I don't want them to see this," pleaded Tze Min.

Alone, trembling, she waited. Pik Soo crashed open the door. "You bitch! What have you been saying to Mary? She has refused my request for a third wife. You have put her up to this. She said you were different. She accepted you because there was a good reason. There were no children from our marriage. Now you have given me a boy and girl, she thinks I should be satisfied."

He advanced towards her, his face contorted with rage. "You must have given her this idea. She did not refuse before. Understand this," he shouted, "I do not marry to have children. I am tired of you. Your coldness bores me. It is no fun making love to a log. What pleasure do I get except this?" he shouted, slapping her cheek.

He pushed her to the floor and punched and kicked her. "Answer me, stupid bitch."

Clutching her side, Tze Min struggled to crawl away. "Please, I have never put any idea into her head. You can have as many women as you want. I don't mind."

"What! Are you trying to insult me. You have no objection? Who asked you for your views? I bought you. I paid your parents. You have no say. You are no better than a slave." Pik Soo pulled her up roughly and pushed her on to the bed. "Let me show you who is the master." Kneeling over her, he opened his trousers and hitched up her dress.

"Mummy, Mummy, is Daddy hurting you?"

Tze Min opened her eyes to see the children at the door. Ah Siew was frantically trying to stop them from looking by covering their faces with one arm and trying to close the door with her other hand.

Tze Min stayed lifeless on the bed. Overcome with shame, she made no effort to defend herself from the punches and slaps. The shame of being seen by her children was the final humiliation.

Completely passive, she lay back, unseeing, unfeeling until, mercifully, blackness came.

* * * * *

It was almost noon before Ah Siew came into the bedroom. "Master has left," she said, gently helping her mistress to sit up. "The children are frightened, but they are fine. I have fed them and they are playing in the garden. They will be having their afternoon nap soon. Let me help you clean up. Once you have bathed, I will put hot compresses on the bruises. Then we will put some of this *theet tar yeok* on them. They use this ointment in martial arts to heal bruises. It gets rid of blood clots."

She busied herself helping Tze Min to undress.

"Thank you Ah Siew, I have to wash him off me."

She shed no tears, she just patiently washed and scrubbed as she had done countless times before, willing herself to feel clean once again. This time, as she sponged and sluiced the warm water over her body, a deep, burgeoning anger replaced her usual sense of helplessness.

"*Yam kong*, for pity's sake, your eyes are a mess," the maid exclaimed when Tze Min returned to the bedroom. "And look at your lips, all cut and bruised. Even your stomach. Oh Mistress, how can you put up with this?"

Tze Min looked down at her body. New bruises, an angry red and purple, were mixed with old ones that had turned a sickly yellow-green. Her body ached and the wounds tingled and smarted under Ah Siew's diligent application of the ointment. She could hardly see through her swollen eyelids; she could hardly move her swollen lips.

"Ah Siew is right," she thought. "How much more can I take?"

* * * * *

Tze Min went to Mary. "It is now or never," she thought. Tze Min looked intently at Mary, her friend and confidante, the woman who had first claim on her husband, but who, in all respects, was like a mother to her. "I have thought long and hard," she began, "I can no longer take the beatings, the humiliation." She stopped. Her voice became muffled, "I have to leave. This is as much for the children as for me. It is not right for them to witness such violence. But I can't leave without your help."

"But what can I do?"

"Will you look after the children as your own? I can't take them with me. With you, they will be safe." Eyes glinting with tears, Tze Min continued, "I have to leave Singapore. I must go where he cannot possibly find me."

"Oh my poor child. Of course I will take the children, that goes without saying. But can you bear to leave them? Once you go, there can be no return. You must know that."

"I do, I do, but I cannot think of any other way. The beatings I can try to bear, but not the humiliation. I just cannot stand the thought of him touching me. Please, please help me."

Mary tenderly stroked Tze Min's battered face. She thought for a moment. "The only way I can think of is to get you out of Singapore by taxi and over to Johore Bahru. Ah Kuk's brother-in-law drives a taxi. I am sure he would be willing to help. From Johore Bahru you would need to take a train north to Butterworth. From there you could take the ferry over to Penang. That is about as far away as you can easily go without leaving the country completely. And Penang, from what I hear, is expanding. You should have a good chance of finding work there."

At this, Mary stood up and left the room. She returned holding a box. She took out a wad of money and gave it to Tze Min. "You will need this to live on while you find a job. It should be enough to help you make a start. I cannot give you more without drawing it from the bank and that might arouse suspicion. The money in this box is what I set aside from time to time. Pik Soo doesn't know about it."

Tze Min was overwhelmed. She took both of Mary's hands and placed them against her cheeks. Her heart felt full. She felt indebted to Mary; she owed her life to her and, more importantly, the future of her children.

"Take the money, but don't make up your mind now, Tze Min," begged Mary. "It is such a drastic decision. He will never let you see the children again if you leave."

"I know, but I am sure this is the best, in fact, only solution."

"I do not know whether I am doing the right thing by helping you."

But Tze Min's mind was made up. "I will not come back to visit you or the children, nor will I make contact. I promise. I have thought about it all day. Staying in touch will just confuse the children. It is better that they forget me and think of you as their mother. Please speak well of me. Tell them anything you see fit to explain my absence. You could say that I was called away urgently and met with a fatal accident. Anything. It is better this way. Please do not think badly of me. There is no other way."

Chapter 12

It was evening. Mary, Ah Kuk and Ah Siew wept silently as Tze Min bid a quiet farewell to her children as they slept. She hugged and cuddled them, crooning soft lullabies. She caressed their hair. She studied every detail of their faces, burning the images into her memory. She buried her face in their necks, smelling their sweet baby scent. She wanted to take their smell and warmth with her. Her face, throughout, remained a pale forlorn mask. There were no tears in her eyes, just pain, and resignation to an unkind fate. Yet beneath her agony lay a steely determination; a determination to start again.

Finally, she announced she was ready. A small carpetbag held her clothes. Mary's gift was safely hidden in a little pouch tucked under her blouse. With her hair hidden under a triangular headscarf of the kind worn by women bricklayers, she left the house alone and got into the waiting taxi that would take her to Johore Bahru.

That same evening, Tze Min was on the train, starting the long journey northwest to the port of Butterworth. Huddled in her seat, she sat as quiet as a dormouse. Outside the night was pitch black. Exhausted, she fell into a disturbed sleep. Luckily no one was there to witness her start and twist in her seat as she struggled to ward off the blows. The train chugged slowly northward, oblivious of the anguish and fears of the lone passenger in one of its carriages.

When Tze Min awoke early the next day, it was still dark. Startled by the abrupt jolting and screeching of the train as it came to a halt in Malacca, she opened her eyes. Through the soot-clouded window she saw people milling about, some waiting to climb aboard, others meeting passengers leaving the train; urchins with baskets of food ran alongside the carriages, hawking their wares. Hunger gripped her; remembering the flask of tea and steamed buns Ah Siew had carefully packed for her, she reached into her bag for the food and began to eat.

By the time the train pulled out of Malacca, the sun was up. The carriage was crowded now. At one corner a woman sat holding two huge rattan baskets containing ducklings. Opposite her was a gentleman, reading his papers and steadfastly ignoring attempts by the woman to engage him in conversation. On the other seat were two little boys with their mother. Half asleep, they were slumped on either side of her, swaying in unison with the moving train. Tze Min turned away quickly, not wanting to be reminded of her own children. Behind a couple were busy arguing, their every gesture a sign of dissent, they made no effort to disguise their mutual anger.

She turned her attention to the window and the scene rushing past her. Tze Min had never travelled on a train before. It was also the first time that she had been on the Malay Peninsula.

Some minutes into the journey, the outskirts of Malacca town gave way to a patchwork of paddy fields with their glistening sheen of water and confetti of green tufts. Already panicles of rice grains were forming. In a month's time, the plants would be heavy with the swollen grains. Women, with *sarongs* hitched high, or with pyjama-like trousers rolled up to their knees, stood in the fields. Some carried babies in hammock-like pouches slung on their back; many wore wide-rimmed hats woven from *bangkuang*, the local straw; all of them were stooped over, weeding and hoeing.

As the train headed further north, the paddy fields gave way to plantations. Mile upon mile of rubber trees planted in straight rows dotted the landscape. Then without warning, the plantations gave way to massive excavations, many filled with water, the remaining scars of what had once been tin mines. Then came more settlements and market gardens before the train finally arrived at Kuala Lumpur.

The train slowed as it approached a building complete with spires, minarets and keyhole arches of the kind seen in mosques. Once inside, the train finally came to a halt with a sudden release of clouds of steam from the engine.

She must have looked puzzled because the lady with the two boys leaned over and said by way of explanation, "Is this the first time you've been to Kuala Lumpur? This is the railway station. Beautiful, isn't it?"

Tze Min remained silent, embarrassed, staring at the letters on the notice board, letters she could not read.

"You look lost. Is anyone meeting you? I can point you in the right direction if you need help."

"Thank you, but I am staying on the train."

"The train will not leave for at least half an hour, perhaps more. Ask the guard. You should get out and stretch out your legs. You've been on the train longer than me."

During the journey the woman had noticed the bruises on Tze Min's face and arms. Her attention was drawn to them once again. Tze Min followed her gaze and tugged at her sleeves to cover them.

"Thank you. I think I will," Tze Min replied, getting up from her seat. "Here, let me help you with your bags. You need both hands free for your little boys. They are waking up."

As she helped her newfound acquaintance down from the train, Tze Min explained she was going on to Penang.

"Do you know Penang? I am looking for a place to stay. I cannot afford much. I don't have much money."

"Are you in trouble?" the woman asked, looking concerned, mesmerised by the bruises on Tze Min's arms.

Tze Min shook her head.

"You should do something about those," the woman advised, nodding in the direction of Tze Min's arms and face. She stood still, holding the hands of her two children, uncertain. Her husband had frequently chided her for talking too much. He had warned her not to give her name and address to strangers. The last time she had done so their house was burgled. "I'm not familiar with hotels," she went on hesitantly. "I've never stayed in one. It's not safe for a woman to stay in a hotel on her own. It's better to have lodgings with a family."

"I don't know anyone," Tze Min explained. Fatigue and pain were taking their toll. She swayed unsteadily on her feet.

Seeing her obvious distress removed what remained of the woman's uncertainty. "I have a relative who might be able to help."

She dipped into her bag and took out a pencil and paper. "This is her address. Mention my name, Sik Wan, to her. My husband will kill me if he knows I am doing this. I just hope my faith in you is justified. So don't let me down. And good luck! You look as if you need it."

* * * * *

By the time Tze Min arrived in Butterworth, she was train-weary. She felt the grime in every pore. Her body, already sore from the beating, throbbed with pain and discomfort from the long hours cramped in the hot compartment. The distraction of the changing scenery had long worn off, giving way to a deep sense of foreboding. Every time she dozed off during the journey, she saw her children, their eyes accusing her of betrayal. Wearily she gathered up her belongings, descended from the train and went in search of the ferry that would carry her to Penang.

It was nightfall again when Tze Min found the address given to her in Kuala Lumpur by Sik Wan. She knocked on the door and waited, hungry and weary. Soon she heard footsteps approaching; there was a clatter of bolts and the door opened.

"Yes, what do you want?" a man's voice demanded gruffly. "Go away! It is too late to try to sell me things and we do not give to beggars." The man stepped back to shut the door.

"Please. I got your address from Sik Wan. She said you might help."

"Sik Wan?" The question was followed by a moment's hesitation. "Come in. I will call my wife."

Shaking his head in disapproval, he shouted, "*Loh-poh*! Old woman! Come here. Sik Wan has sent someone to us." He grumbled, "Sik Wan is always sending us people in need. The last time it was a young boy who had run away from home. Why doesn't she send waifs and strays to her own parents."

Up till then his body had shielded Tze Min from the light behind him. Now as he moved aside and invited Tze Min in, he saw for the first time the bruises and cuts on her face and lips.

"Goodness!" Turning away from Tze Min, he shouted, "Hurry up, you're needed. Urgently!" Then, taking Tze Min gently by the elbow, he led her to a rattan armchair. "Sit down. What happened?"

By then, a short, plump, middle-aged woman had joined them. She was wiping her hands on a white cotton towel decorated with an inscription "Good Morning" in bright red Chinese characters. It was just like the towel used by Ah Siew, Ah Kuk and her mother, and probably most Chinese households in Singapore.

Tze Min stared at the inscription for a moment and then broke into a hysterical giggle. She could not stop, she laughed mirthlessly and then began to cry. Chest heaving, she sobbed. Tears long-stifled during the journey flooded down her cheeks, trickling down her neck, splattering her top. Eventually, holding the cup of hot tea that had been pressed into her trembling hands, she calmed down sufficiently to tell her story.

The man, Fook Yuen, and his wife, Fook Soh, listened attentively, visibly moved as her story unfolded. They were silent for some time after Tze Min had finished.

Fook Soh slowly wiped her eyes and bent forward to touch Tze Min's bruised face. "You can stay here tonight. You will be safe with us. Let's eat now: you must be very hungry. After dinner we will see what we can do to help. Here, take this towel and wipe your eyes. It's clean."

Taking the towel, Tze Min said, "I am sorry for my outburst. I don't know what came over me. When I saw the towel, something just snapped. It brought back memories of home, my previous life. It was as though I cannot escape from the past. It is silly of me, I know. These towels are sold everywhere. I'm so sorry."

"Please don't worry, we understand," came the comforting reply.

The three of them moved into a narrow room facing the backyard. On one side was the sink with a little draining board. On the right of the sink was a concrete shelf with three little stoves. Embers of charcoal glowed in all three, warming little clay pots that sat on them. A small table with four stools was pushed against the opposite wall. A wooden store cupboard, its front enmeshed with chicken wires and its four metal-tipped legs standing in china saucers filled with water, stood next to the table.

Beckoning Tze Min, Fook Soh said, "Come and sit down. We don't have much, just plain boiled rice, some *do fu* and vegetables. But it will fill a hole in the stomach."

Few words were spoken as they ate. The meal over, they took their stools into the backyard. Outside, away from the hot stoves and confined space of the kitchen, and with a gentle sea breeze, the evening air was quite pleasant.

"I teach at the local primary school and my wife takes in laundry to earn a little extra," explained Fook Yuen. "Our two young boys are visiting their grandparents so you can stay in their room. I am afraid we do not have a room that we can offer you on a permanent basis. They will be back tomorrow." Seeing the alarm on Tze Min's face, he added quickly, "We have a friend in the next street. She lives alone. We can ask her if she will take in a lodger. You would be company for her."

He paused, his expression thoughtful. Exchanging glances with his wife, he continued. "From what you told us, your husband seems to be an influential man. He might send someone to look for you. We do not want any trouble and we would not want to cause our friend any problems if she agrees to take you in. It might be best to change your name to one that will not be recognised."

Before Tze Min could reply, he suggested, "How about Nelly, pronounced Nei Li, like Mei Li which means beautiful." Smiling encouragingly, he continued, "I've just read a book where the heroine has that name. If you agree, we shall introduce you to our friend as Nelly and the name Tze Min will become just a memory."

"Yes. It's a good idea to adopt a new name. It will make it more difficult for your husband to find you," his wife agreed.

* * * * *

From that day on, Tze Min was known as Nelly. She moved into a house in the neighbouring street, which was very similar to where the Fooks lived. All the houses in the neighbourhood were single-storey, wooden-plank buildings, each with a tiny backyard for a clothesline or chicken pen. Her landlady, Mrs Yen, or Yen-*mah* (Mother Yen) as she liked to be called, was 60 years old, a kind but cantankerous soul.

From her lodgings Nelly made daily expeditions to the city in search of work. Armed with a list of addresses and possible vacancies extracted by Fook Yuen from the Chinese newspapers, she started each day with optimism only to end it in frustration. It was becoming increasingly evident that the lists of "honourable" jobs that he carefully picked were not within her reach. Inevitably she was asked for her qualifications and work experience. She had none. Late one afternoon, after five weeks of futile searching, Nelly returned to Yen-*mah*'s house once again with a heavy heart.

Yen-*mah* was sitting just outside the front door, crouched on a wooden stool that stood no higher than four inches. She loved to sit there in the evening, fan in hand, feet tucked in and knees chest high, watching people pass by or the children playing badminton or kicking a ball on the little patch of waste land opposite. Their shouts and chatter kept her company.

Nelly sank down on the doorstep beside the old lady and laid her head wearily against the doorframe.

"Any luck?" Yen-*mah* asked.

"No! I have failed yet again. No one is interested in employing me. I just don't know what to do."

"It takes time. You don't speak English and all the foreign firms, big or small, want English-speaking staff. You have no qualifications, you have no work experience and you are not strong enough for manual labour. And, of course, Fook Yuen's idea of an honourable job requires some, if not all, of these things."

Tze Min knew all this. They sat in companionable silence broken only by the sound of children playing and the high-pitched tittering of the swallows as they performed their aerobatics above the house. Several times, Tze Min sensed Yen-*mah* looking at her quizzically, but when she tried to return her gaze, the old lady turned away furtively. Yen-*mah* was in deep thought.

"Let me tell you a secret," she said at last. "You must promise never to repeat it to anyone."

"Yes, I promise."

"I'm only telling you because I was in a position similar to yours when I was young. After my little girl was born, I was left on my own. I don't want to go into the reason why. It's too painful. Anyway, I needed money. I tried for months to find a job. In the end, I had to take what Fook Yuen would consider a dishonourable job to support my child and myself. I worked as a hostess in a gambling den. I scraped and saved. Once I had enough money stashed away I quit the job, moved here and enrolled in a handicraft centre where I learned how to weave baskets and make things. With these skills I was able to begin a new life. The job as a hostess saved my little one and me. It would have been impossible for me to learn a craft without some savings to live on."

"Thank you for trusting me with your secret, Yen-*mah*, but, even if I am to follow your example, I have no idea where to start."

"Fook Yuen will not take it kindly if I interfere. All I want to point out is that high ideals are fine, but sometimes you have to come down to reality."

"Do you know of any job like that? I don't mind hard work or long hours."

"Well, while I was in the market yesterday, I heard from a friend that her daughter is working in a new dance hall called the Lucky Night in Tanjong Tokong, just outside Georgetown. She is a dance hostess there. They are still recruiting. Working as a dance hostess is not the sort of thing that Fook Yuen would approve of and I know that a dance hall is not an ideal place to work in. Still, providing you stick to just dancing and nothing more, I don't see why you should come to any harm."

Chapter 13

It was while working in the Lucky Night that Nelly met Ming Kong. It was a mid-June evening and it had been raining all day. The southwest monsoon winds seemed to have delivered a month's rain in a day. Much of Penang's Chinatown was flooded. The roads were difficult for cars and impossible for trishaws.

Getting to the nightclub had been a problem. By the time Nelly arrived, she was soaked to the skin. Her umbrella had offered little protection from the pelting rain; the gusting wind kept turning it inside out. To make the final stretch to the club, she had to roll up her *sam foo* trousers and paddle through the water. Several times she stumbled. Oozing mud sucked and pulled at her flip-flops, making it almost impossible to lift her feet without losing them. Her wet hair clung to her face and neck like seaweed to a rock.

The manager was waiting at the entrance of the club. "Look at you! Get into the dressing room and clean up."

"I'm sorry I am late. I . . . I . . . the bus . . . I walked," she finished lamely.

"You're lucky. Business will be slow with this rain. No one is going to arrive until the storm has blown over." He looked anxiously at the sky. "So make the most of it."

Inside the dressing room, a buzz of excited chatter filled the air. Many of the girls were, like Nelly, wet and cold. Although the rain was warm and the night air humid, the draught from the swirling ceiling fans gave Nelly goose bumps. She began to shiver. Someone came in with a big enamel teapot.

"Hot tea! Bless the manager. Sometimes he acts like a human being." The girls drank the warm brew and passed the pot around.

Annie reminded Nelly that they had each been given a bucket of hot water, which stood waiting in the bathroom. "Take a quick sluice before you finish your drink," she advised, "or you will find your water gone. You will still have time to dry your hair," she advised.

Annie very rarely danced and then only with her own established clients. She was more of an assistant to the manager, helping him out with some of the personnel problems. Some of the girls said she had managed to stay on only because she was his mistress. They even hinted that her child might be his, but Nelly ignored the gossip. Annie had always been kind and helpful to her.

"Why is everyone so excited? Is there something I should know about?" Nelly asked as they made their way to the bathroom.

"We had a rush of cancelled bookings. Then, out of the blue, we received a call from The Orient. It is having a staff conference and because the company has been doing well, all the people at the meeting are being treated to a night out. It was to have been a dinner, but most, if not all, of the women have apparently opted out because of the weather. And, typically, the men have decided to change the venue from a restaurant to the Lucky Night. Lucky for us," explained Annie. "It's a big company and there will be people from all over the country."

Washed, dressed and feeling much warmer, Nelly felt herself being caught up in the excitement. By the time she had put on her make-up, the first batch of Orient people were arriving.

"Come on girls. Hurry, you should be out front, not in here," chided Annie.

Nelly stepped out of the dressing room and instantly collided with a young man who was hurrying down the corridor. Wet, dripping with rain, he looked lost and embarrassed.

"I am so sorry. I have made you wet."

Taking a large handkerchief from his pocket, he went to mop up a large wet patch that had appeared on Nelly's blouse. She stepped back abruptly as his hands reached out. Realising immediately the rashness of his action, he turned crimson. "Now I'm making things worse. I was looking for the gents and was told it is in this direction. I'm sorry. I wasn't paying attention."

Before he could continue, another young man interrupted him. "Come on, Ming Kong, the girls are here. You said you've never been to a real night club so why are you wasting your time blabbing?"

Ming Kong ignored him. He felt a need to explain, to say something. He was entranced. He just could not take his eyes off Nelly.

"I'm with The Orient," he said. He found himself stuttering, "I got wet while directing the coach in the car park. I thought it best that I dry off. Look what I have done instead. Will you be able to get dry? Are you with someone?"

"I work here," she replied. At that moment, she wished more than anything that she did not, but there was no point trying to conceal it. "Don't worry, I'll be fine. We keep spare clothing in the dressing room."

"I will wait here to escort you out. I should feel greatly honoured if you would join our party tonight."

This was the start of Nelly's friendship with Ming Kong. He visited the Lucky Night almost every evening throughout his five months of training in Penang. When the dance hall closed, he would wait to accompany her back to her lodgings. Normally impatient, he showed a patience that he never dreamed he had. With time, he learned about Nelly's story and developed a deep compassion for her. He was not sure if it was love, but she was beautiful and her sadness made him want to protect her.

* * * * *

It was the week before Ming Kong was due to return to Kuala Lumpur. He had waited for Nelly as usual and walked her home. They sat down on a wooden bench in the small park opposite her lodgings. The balmy night air enfolded them in a moist, dark cocoon. They held hands, not saying a word. Nelly felt a sense of belonging.

The minutes passed. He moved, bending slightly away from her. Then he gently turned her face towards his. "This is not the sort of life for you, Nelly. Come with me to Kuala Lumpur." He had broached the subject before. And he had been relentless in pressing the point. "You don't need to worry about money. I will rent a small apartment for us. Think about it." But she remained uncertain even though she dreaded his departure.

She had consulted with Annie. "You would be silly not to go," she said. "He seems a nice young man and comes from a wealthy family. If I had a chance like that when I was younger, I would have certainly taken it. I assume he has proposed marriage?"

"No. I believe it would be difficult. His mother would not approve."

Annie quickly revised her earlier view, "Then, you should think carefully before committing yourself." Nelly, however, could think about nothing else than this chance to restart her life. The past five months with Ming Kong had shown her that not all men were like her former husband. She was able to talk, laugh and do things with him that she had never done before. She believed he would stand by her and she loved him unreservedly.

Two weeks after Ming Kong's departure from Penang, she travelled south to join him in Kuala Lumpur.

The Japanese Occupation

Chapter 14

Mei Yin stood desolate as the bus carrying her mother disappeared into the distance. Sook Ping had been to stay with Mei Yin to celebrate her 14th birthday. Mei Yin had kept cheerful throughout her mother's stay. She did not confide in her about Nelly and what Kai Min had told her. Mei Yin had learned that her father's health was failing rapidly. Her mother had enough worries without having to fret about gossip that might prove to be exaggerated. As the last of the dust settled behind the departing bus, she made her way back to the house.

A big meeting was to be held in the house, one of many that had been held recently. Many of the villagers would be there. Ming Kong was also expected. His visits had become more and more frequent. She detected a growing sense of urgency in the meetings. All the talk seemed to be about the war in Europe, the Japanese pillage of China and the threat that it might spill over onto their doorstep. As she approached the house, Mei Yin quickened her steps. Ming Kong's motorbike was already parked in the lay-by. The house thronged with people. She pushed her way in with the help of Ah Jee. She saw people crowded around Ming Kong, who was struggling to keep some order and calm. It was no use. Everyone seemed to be talking at once, but some voices could be heard above the general hubbub.

"The Japs are here! They've landed. There has been no resistance to speak of. Soon we'll be swamped. We have to do something!"

"Yes! Yes! If we don't, the Japanese atrocities in mainland China will be repeated all over again in Malaya, especially on us Chinese. I say we join ranks with the MPAJA. It might be called a Malayan People's Anti-Japanese Army but it is mainly a Chinese movement and will have our concerns at heart. No one else will. We have to defend ourselves."

"What about the British Administration?"

"They have enough to do defending their own country. They don't have time for us nor the manpower. But, from what I hear, they will provide arms and even training if we join up with the MPAJA."

"I . . . I'm not sure. The MPAJA is a guerrilla movement."

"What hope have we if we don't?"

"No! No!" Ming Kong's voice finally rose above the sounds of dissent and agreement. "I do not think it would be a good idea at all to join the MPAJA. It is only a short term solution with possibly serious repercussions."

"Then Ming Kong, you must take the lead, organise something. You and your father are the only people in the village who have weapons. If you refuse to join forces with the MPAJA, surely you cannot refuse to help protect the women of the village!" demanded one of the villagers.

"Yes," said another, "not only the women but the children as well. We have to hide them. You have women in your family. Remember what they did to our women in China. What about a hideout in the jungle. You are the only one here who knows the jungle."

"I can't. There are just too many. I do not know where to house them. And there is food to think of. I can't do everything on my own and to involve my father is out of the question. He is too old. And the more people who are involved in any scheme, the more difficult it is to keep secret and the more dangerous it will become."

"Then why not ask the MPAJA for help? Some of us have sons in it and we could talk to them," asked a villager.

Ming Kong shook his head. "No! I don't want any dealings with the MPAJA. I am not sure what they aim to do. They have a political agenda that might not be quite what it seems. Also, I have to think of the company I work for."

Despite his misgivings, the villagers continued to argue that he was their only hope. They would not take no for an answer. Slowly the germ of a possible plan began to develop in Ming Kong's mind. "Alright, I will try to come up with a plan. If you agree, I will try to find a safe place nearby for those women least able to journey from the city while those who are fit and able would be moved out to the countryside. As for you men," he said, "I am afraid you will have to take care of yourselves and stay in Sun Chuen to protect your possessions from being ransacked. We just do not have enough resources to look after everyone. As we are all agreed here that women, especially young girls, have the most to fear from the Japanese, we must concentrate on protecting them."

* * * * *

Ten girls, aged between 12 and 16, were chosen to be moved out of the city. Kai Min and Mei Yin were included in this group. All had their hair cropped short like boys and their chests bound tightly. Dressed in loose, long-sleeved shirts and coolie trousers, they were bundled into one of the company's trucks and taken to the new Seremban estate that Ming Kong was to have managed.

Situated at the edge of the jungle, the estate had residential blocks for staff. With the outbreak of war, the project had been suspended and the buildings, although ready for use, remained empty. "They are perfect for the girls," he thought, "and the caves in the mountains behind provide a place to retreat to if the Japanese find the camp." Over thousands of years, running water had eroded the limestone rock of the mountains creating numerous caves. Some of them had once been places of worship. Abandoned and covered by dense jungle, the shrines' only visitors now were bats, birds and flying foxes.

Once the girls arrived and settled in at the estate, they were paired off and assigned work. Mei Yin and Kai Min were to look after two small pigs contributed by the people of Sun Chuen. Ming Kong had already stocked up with supplies of rice, oil, salt and salted fish.

To supervise the girls, Ming Kong enrolled the help of Mr and Mrs Wong, a middle-aged couple, from the village. Reluctantly, he also enlisted the help of the estate foreman, Ali, and his assistant and friend, Ahmed. He had not wanted to involve them, aware of the budding friction between the Chinese and the Malays, but he needed their local knowledge. They were posted in an estate adjacent to Seremban, and he kept them there, well away from the hideouts. He made the two men responsible for reporting any unusual movements of people. His excuse for their assignments was that the Company needed to safeguard the machinery and supplies in the newly built offices. They did not know of the hideout in the caves nor were they told of the presence of the girls on the estate.

The very young and the older women presented a more serious problem. Disguising the older women as boys was impractical and he could not separate mothers from their infants and babies. In desperation, he went to his old school and discussed the problem with the Catholic Brothers. They, in turn, consulted the Sisters who ran an adjacent school. The Sisters agreed to conceal the women in the convent and church. Built into a hill, the convent had a labyrinth of passageways and cells. He persuaded Nelly to join this group together with Su Hei. It was difficult for his mother; she did not wish to hide in a Catholic establishment, but she had little choice. The alternative was to join her husband and his first wife and she knew she was not wanted there.

Su Hei was not happy at the convent. She had no one with whom she could relate. She hated the cramped conditions. The incessant chatter of the other women taxed her patience sorely. She had little affinity with the prayers and hymns. She detested the meals of plain, boiled rice congee with a sprinkling of soya sauce, day in and day out. Ming Kong was not there; Kai Min was with Mei Yin; and her older daughter was in Hong Kong. Ah Jee had been left behind to watch over the house. Su Hei grew despondent.

Ming Kong introduced Nelly to his mother as a good friend. He had asked Nelly to watch over his mother, warning her of his mother's asperity. He made excuses for her sharpness of tongue, attributing it to her aches, pains and unhappy background. Nelly went out of her way to make Su Hei comfortable, fetching and carrying for the embittered old lady.

* * * * *

It was a particularly hot, muggy day. The heat was made worse by the need to keep all the doors and windows in the convent shut. A storm was brewing outside but, despite hours of threatening dark clouds and incessant wind, no rain fell. Nelly was helping out in the kitchen. They had very little food to cook. The ration of rice had got smaller; only half the normal amount had been delivered that morning. All she had were vegetables left from the previous night, which she minced as a base for a watery soup.

"Many farmers are holding on to their stocks in case they run out too," a Sister explained as she foraged in the basket she had earlier hauled in from the backyard. "There is nothing in the market. Traders don't want to risk ambush in the countryside trying to get food. The delivery man said that he has given up sending people to scout for food after losing one of his men."

The Sister gave Nelly two tapioca roots from the basket. They were shrivelled and grey, but she handled them with reverence. "We will have to eat tapioca this evening; we don't have enough rice for two meals a day. Soon, we might not even have tapioca."

That evening when Nelly brought Su Hei her small ration of tapioca, she tried to explain why there was no rice. "We must not complain," she added, hoping to pacify her. "Some people do not even have tapioca or sweet potatoes to eat."

"Speak for yourself," retorted Su Hei.

Su Hei was wary of Nelly; she suspected she was more than a good friend to her son. But she was on her own and needed someone to talk to. The other women avoided her. Gradually, over the weeks, Nelly's patience won through.

One morning, after a particularly restless night, she went to Nelly. "I am in agony. It's my back," she complained. "Sleeping on these camp beds is not good for it. Ever since the children, I've had problems."

"Would you like me to rub your back for you?" asked Nelly. "I have a small amount of ointment for bruises. It might help."

"There's no need for ointment, I don't have bruises. But if you would just rub here," she indicated her lower back, "it will help."

Su Hei closed her eyes and sighed, responding to Nelly's ministrations. "You have good hands." She turned to look more closely at Nelly. "Ming Kong says he has known you for over a year. How did you meet? He never mentioned you before."

It was a question she had wanted to ask for some time. When Nelly did not reply, she became convinced her suspicion that they were more than friends was right. "You have to be careful with my son; he is a breaker of hearts. All the girls love him."

Nelly was too taken aback to make light of the comment or to answer with any convincing flippant remark. "What do you mean? He loves them and leaves them?" she asked hesitantly.

Su Hei sensed her anxiety. "The poor girl is far-gone," she thought to herself and then replied, "Oh no! In fact, the problem is he does not leave them, even after love is long gone. He finds it difficult to end a relationship. He is kind and often confuses infatuation with love."

Thinking it best for Nelly to know the worst, she continued, "It could be just part of growing up, the folly of youth. The men in the Ong family tend to have many wives and mistresses. His father is no different. Nor was his grandfather or even his great grandfather for that matter. Why, the story goes that when one of his forebears came to Malaya in the early 1800s to mine for tin, he was given a license to recruit workers from China. He also imported Chinese women to keep the men happy. With each consignment, he would also acquire a woman for himself. By the time he died, he had over 10 concubines."

"Surely, Ming Kong is different."

"Yes and no, but the result can be the same. You see, while he has inherited his father's tendency to philander, he has also a deep compassion for women. He knows from me how they suffer so he keeps his women rather than discard them."

Nelly said nothing. She did not want to hear any more, but there was no stopping Su Hei.

"I remember when he was 17, he fell in love with a Eurasian girl. Of course none of us knew about it. She was half Portuguese, a quarter Indian and a quarter Malay. He was still at school. She was three years older and worked in the hospital, I'm not sure what she did. One day she went to First Mother and demanded a lot of money. She said she was bearing Ming Kong's child. She had been pressing for marriage, but he knew we would never approve. He was right. After all, he is the sole heir to the Ong fortune. We do not countenance mixed marriages; a quarter here and a quarter there! Bah! Totally unsuitable!" She shuddered to show her disapproval.

By this time, Nelly felt ill. Forcing herself to continue with her ministrations to Su Hei's back, she asked weakly, "What happened?" She did not want to know, yet she could not stop herself from asking.

"First Mother consulted me. We agreed not to involve his father. We got a detective and had her checked out and followed. Sure enough, it was as we had suspected, she had other men. So we told Ming Kong of this and her threats. Then we went to her, demanded that she leave him alone or we would expose her loose behaviour and blackmail attempt to the hospital authorities; her reputation would be ruined and they would certainly have fired her. Even a girl like that needs some vestige of respectability to survive. And that was that. We did not hear from her again."

"But," continued Su Hei, her eyes shining with delight, "I think I have found the ideal solution." She looked at Nelly, conspiratorially, "I have found a beautiful young girl for him. She is ten years younger than him, but that won't matter in years to come. Women age faster than men. Ming Kong has promised to give the arrangement a chance. I cannot see how it can fail. She is beautiful and, in the short time she has been with us, she has grown even more so. I am sure he will fall in love with her. He is with her all the time. He is with her even now."

Su Hei turned and grabbed Nelly's hands, excited by an idea that was fast taking root in her mind. "In fact, I could probably persuade everyone involved to bring the marriage forward. The war has changed everything. They should be married as soon as possible. We cannot wait two years, leaving the two of them on their own."

Nelly paled at the news. Her whole world had been turned topsy-turvy. Her new life was ending before it had really begun. She had herself partly to blame. How could she have let Ming Kong persuade her that everything would be alright; how could she have believed his mother would eventually come around to his argument that Mei Yin was far too young for him. Just as previously she felt that things would turn out right, she now became equally convinced they would not.

Her mouth felt dry, her heart heavy, as she continued to massage Su Hei's back. She could not contemplate a life without Ming Kong. Whatever his mother might say of him, she had received only consideration and love. His follies were when he was in his teens, he could have changed and matured. She wavered, switching between uncertainty about her future with him and a conviction that he would stand by her. She realised the biggest obstacle was his mother. It would be difficult, most likely impossible, for Su Hei to accept her as an official daughter-in-law once she learned about her background.

* * * * *

Mei Yin blossomed. Away from Su Hei and with the newfound freedom of life on the rubber estate, she gained confidence. Looking after the pigs involved gathering and cutting banana stems from a deserted plantation near by. Kai Min was supposed to help, but she could not cope with the hard work of slashing the old banana stems and chopping them up to make the pigswill. The first time she had to handle the coarse fibres of the stems, her hands bled and she cried herself to sleep. Neither did she like working in the pigpen. It was muddy, smelly and dirty. Without any prompting, Mei Yin became the leader. She was used to hard work. So a system developed where Mei Yin would slash, gather and lug the heavy stems back to the camp, cut them with Kai Min and then leave her to feed the animals.

Three months into their stay, Mei Yin had lost the soft plumpness that came from a life of comparative idleness in Su Hei's household. She looked taller, slimmer and was again as brown as a berry. Her body took on the curves of a young woman that were difficult to conceal. Her soft brown eyes shone with health. Mr and Mrs Wong, the guardians of the girls, had taken to teasing her that somehow her mother must have got the wrong baby. "There must have been a mix-up in the hospital," they would tease. "You are not Chinese. Your eyes are too big and lashes too long. And look at your skin. It's brown!"

One day following a bout of teasing, Mei Yin ran out of the communal kitchen to sit on a log under a mangosteen tree, shouting defiantly, "You don't know what you are saying." She sat there for some time, smarting from the teasing, but she stayed there long after the hurt had passed. There was a reason.

For two months now, Ming Kong had taken to visiting the estate around this hour. On each visit he would find Mei Yin waiting for him. He would sit and chat with her. She was one of the older girls in his care. One of the few he could have a near adult conversation with. These were her happiest hours. She loved to listen to his tales of hunting and fishing. "Will you take me with you when the war is over?" she would ask. "I would love to come. I would not mind picking up the pigeons and snipes. My mother used to rear chickens so I am not at all squeamish. I could even pluck them if you wanted," she offered as a further inducement for him to accept.

Now waiting for his arrival, she felt anxious. "What if he doesn't come today," she asked herself. She got up and paced up and down the patch of grass round the tree waiting for signs of him. She wiped her cheeks. Her eyes were still damp. Worried they might be swollen and red, she ran back to the dormitory. She snatched a hairbrush to tidy her hair and sponged her face with a flannel. Her hair had grown and it would have to be cut. Today, however, she was happy it was longer and that she looked less like a boy.

She heard his truck turn into the dirt path of the compound. Her heart lurched. She was not sure whether to run to greet him or wait for him until he came over. She hid her indecision by calling for Kai Min. "Your brother is here. Let's go to meet him."

"You go. I'll join you. I am washing my hair," Kai Min called back. But before she could go out, Ming Kong came into the building. He had with him the other girls and the Wongs.

"We have to leave. I am told by Ahmed that Japanese soldiers are heading this way. They were fighting guerrillas about 20 miles south of Tanjong Malim yesterday and are now giving chase. They lost some men and are taking it out on any village that lies in their path. Houses have been pillaged, women raped, men beaten." He did not elaborate further, but Ahmed had spoken of the corpses he had seen and how women, both young and old, had been rounded up and assaulted.

"Gather up what you can. Don't leave any evidence that you have been staying here. We must make for the caves. Be as quiet and quick as you can. We have practised this before."

He turned apologetically to the Wongs. "Wong-*mah* will come with us, but you, Wong-*sook*, must stay. It is not possible to pretend that these buildings have been completely unoccupied. We must give an impression that they have been used as a half-way house for staff." Mr Wong had his complete trust. He would never give the girls away. He had too much at stake. His wife and daughter were amongst those about to leave.

He left the couple to say their goodbyes. Turning to Mei Yin, he asked, "Where is Kai Min."

"Washing her hair."

"Quick, come with me." Taking her by the hand, he rushed to collect Kai Min. He hugged his sister, then, turning to Mei Yin, hugged and kissed her as well. "Let's go."

Mei Yin blushed; she felt deliriously happy, despite the bad news and the danger.

Unaware, Ming Kong turned to Wong-*sook*. "Could you use a siphon to empty the truck's petrol tank? If the Japanese find the vehicle, they are sure to requisition it. So we must hide it and leave the petrol tank nearly empty as an extra precaution. We will carry the petrol up to the hideout. And, please, whatever happens, do not reveal to them the existence of the girls or the hideout. Remember, they will still torture you even if you do."

* * * * *

The climb up the hill was uneventful. The girls were frightened and tense. Ming Kong was last in line, staying back to cover their tracks. Now and then he would run ahead to check they were going the right way, all the while giving words of encouragement. Gunshots sounded in the distance.

Once in the safety of the cave, he signalled Mei Yin to follow him, leaving the girls to settle down. They walked towards the entrance, away from the others. "I have good news from Malacca, your parents are safe. My father was in contact with one of his associates who does business there. I was able to get him to check on them."

She just nodded. Her happiness was unmistakable. It shone in her eyes and the tremor of a smile played on her lips. She was glad he had remembered to look out for them. She thanked him. He squeezed her hands sympathetically and encouragingly

"I should be the one to thank you for looking after Kai Min. My mother would be pleased to know you have coped so well."

They rejoined the others, but the feeling of gratitude and a vague yet disturbing awareness of Ming Kong remained with Mei Yin.

The girls split up into little groups. Some began boiling water and preparing the evening's meal of congee. A strict ration of rice had to be kept, a handful of grains each. Mei Yin and Ming Kong worked happily side by side. They arranged the gunny bags of supplies on makeshift racks to protect them from the damp, and they pushed and heaved the heavy drums of water to one corner.

"Can I do anything else to help?" Mei Yin asked.

"Perhaps later. Once the firing has stopped completely, I will make a quick check of the area to make sure it is safe."

"Can I come with you?"

"No, not today. It's not safe. But in the next few days, I might need your help. We need to collect some vegetables and fruits to supplement our diet. If we eat only rice gruel, we will become ill. I am not sure how long we will have to hide. Around here, there is a kind of fern and a tree fungus, both of which are edible. There might also be some wild fruit trees. You can help me to find and harvest them."

"Fungus, you mean mushrooms? My mother told me never to eat wild mushrooms." She shook her head to emphasise her point, her large brown eyes, half child, and half woman, looked up to his solemnly. He could not help but smile and was rewarded immediately by the two deep dimples that appeared in her cheeks.

"Don't worry, I have eaten them before. Among the things I learned when I went hunting with my father was how to survive in the jungle. We used to hunt with the forest people. *Sakai*, we call them. They were our trackers when we went hunting elephants. They have an uncanny instinct. They know where to go and how to move around in the jungle. Their hearing, sight and sense of smell are unbelievable. They are also wonderful teachers. They know what plants are edible and which ones to use to treat injuries and illnesses. They showed me how to slice through the fern to reach the tender heart, the only edible bit of the plant."

Crouched next to him, listening to his tales of the jungle, Mei Yin became excited at the prospect of learning about and collecting the forest foods. She would have liked to continue the conversation, but the other girls were coming over to join them.

Impulsively, he took her hands and patted them. "We'll talk later. For now, rest. You have been wonderful." Then, reluctantly, he let her hands go.

In those brief moments, Ming Kong had become aware of Mei Yin, not as his sister's friend, not as a potential child bride, but as a young woman. He had always intended to be kind to Mei Yin, thinking that, eventually, he would say no to the arranged marriage. He thought of her as a victim, just like him, of the whole miserable affair. The situation did not seem quite so clear cut now. Away from his mother and other adults, Mei Yin did not seem such a child. In fact, she was a young woman and, he had to admit, a very beautiful one. Then, abruptly, his thoughts returned to Nelly and his promises to her. He stood up. "I have to go now. Don't wait for me, I will be back by nightfall."

*　*　*　*　*

Nelly was sick with worry. She yearned to talk to Ming Kong. She did not know how long she could remain a confidante to Su Hei, without breaking down and revealing her relationship with him. She was also anxious. Two weeks had passed with no news of how he was faring. She could not leave the convent to find out. In the confines of their quarters in the convent, all the women could do was speculate. They wondered how much longer they would be safe. News of the outside world filtered through in bits and bobs. Traders who supplied the convent with provisions came with stories of chaos, rapes, atrocities and hunger from the city.

Occasionally some of the women would be visited by their husbands, sons and relatives. They brought with them news. They were told that large numbers of young men had been rounded up and placed in prison camps. Some were allowed to return to their families after interrogation, others had not been seen since they were taken by the Japanese. What had happened to them. Were they killed, imprisoned or had they become turncoats? The women worried and fretted about their sons.

Clutching her prayer beads, Su Hei prayed aloud, "Please Buddha, keep my son safe. I pray to you Kuan Yin, goddess of mercy.

Keep my son, all the young men, and, of course, the women, safe. I vow to burn incense in your worship for as long as I live."

She turned to Nelly. "I heard the Sisters talking. They say thousands of young Chinese men have been executed. That must be why they have not been seen since capture."

"But why only Chinese men?"

"Mother Superior says the Japanese have targeted the Chinese for harsh treatment. She spoke of someone called Masanobu Tsuji. Have you heard of him? Have any of the other women mentioned his name? She said he fought in China. Apparently, his cruelty there was legendary. He is the one, she said, who led the invasion here."

"But why does he continue this violence against the Chinese even here in Malaya?" Nelly asked again.

Su Hei sighed. Shrugging her shoulders, "Who really knows? I'm only repeating what I have heard."

Their conversation attracted the attention of other women. One by one they joined them. Soon a group had gathered around Su Hei, eager for news. Su Hei was beginning to enjoy herself. Generally ignored, she liked being the centre of attention. She was proud of the information that she had gathered from the nuns. "There is also talk that the Communists have infiltrated the MPAJA."

"Well then, if this is true," interrupted one woman, "you have the answer to Nelly's question. The Japanese target the Chinese in Malaya more than others because they probably think they are facing their old enemy on new ground. All Chinese are suspects!"

This last pronouncement caused outcries of rage and horror.

"You are right. That's probably why they are rounding up the men."

"Yes, I've heard the same. My husband said every young man in our settlement has been taken. Thank God, mine had already left to join the guerrilla fighters."

"You are lucky. My son was taken by the Japanese and is still missing," said another.

"My boys all joined the MPAJA. I have not seen them since the outbreak of war."

"Mine have also joined up, but I am more fortunate. I have seen them twice since. But it has been months now since I received any word from them. I'm worried sick."

"I hope Ming Kong is safe," Nelly said to Su Hei, full of fear.

"I worry too," confided Su Hei. "He said he has enlisted the help of two Malay assistants, who worked with him at The Orient. I told him to be careful, but he doesn't listen. From what I gather, the Japanese are giving the Malays preferential treatment to win their support."

"Yes," said Sow-*mah*, the woman whose sons had been to visit. "One of my sons showed me some leaflets the last time he came. Even the Sisters have seen them. They were full of Japanese slogans on how they want to create an 'Asia for Asians'. They are giving the Malays jobs in the administration left vacant by the British."

"They want to create a greater Indonesia with Malaya as a part of it," explained Su Hei. Su Hei, who had never been interested in politics previously, had become a mine of information about the war by eavesdropping on others. She had got this last piece of information from Sow-*mah* when she was helping her to read the leaflets that her son had given her.

A pale, dumpy woman in her mid-40s edged closer to the front. Ah Toh was new to the convent and not from Sun Chuen. As the months passed, more and more women from other parts of the city had taken refuge there. She was not afraid of Su Hei and this was not the first time that she had cut into her conversation. She crouched down and added in a low rasping voice, close to a whisper, "I have also heard something along those lines. Just before I came here, I heard they have released some of the leaders of the Malay Nationalist movement."

Not to be outdone, Su Hei raised her voice to add, "Even the Indians are faring better than us. The Japanese are exploiting anti-British feeling among the Indians in the British army by giving them hope of independence."

"Talk of independence is nonsense. What they really want is to march into India and replace the British with the help of the Indian soldiers."

Su Hei nodded in agreement, "I hope Ming Kong has placed his trust well in the men he has chosen to help him."

"When the Japanese landed in the north, the Indian soldiers, I have heard, just ran away in fear."

"Are you sure it was fear? Perhaps they were in cahoots with them."

"No, of course not, what a thought! They were most likely just taken by surprise," said another.

"What I don't understand is how the British were defeated so quickly," commented one woman, her expression a mixture of distaste and astonishment. "I never thought I'd live to see British soldiers, hungry, dressed in rags, imprisoned and subjected to such indignity. They were our rulers; they were so well-established. How could they have been forced to give everything up in so short a time?"

Her entire family had been in the service of expatriates for years and had never witnessed a European doing manual labour, let alone dressed in rags. Taken aback by the capture of the British soldiers and with her family forced to flee, she felt let down.

"You are right! I feel as though I've been cooped up here for ages, but, in fact, the Japanese occupation has taken no time at all." Sow-*mah*, counting with her fingers, continued, "The Japanese landed in the north in early December. About a month later they'd got Kuala Lumpur, Malacca and Seremban. By mid-February, Singapore had fallen. It took them less than two and a half months to take over the whole of Malaya."

"How do you know these details?" she was immediately asked.

"From, from . . . I have my source," she answered, annoyed by the challenge. Her sons had warned her about divulging too much. They kept her supplied with news and pamphlets, but told her not to reveal the source of her information. It could jeopardise their operations and cost their lives.

Cornered, she said, "If you don't believe me, ask the Brothers. They say the same. I heard them talking to the Sisters."

"She is right!" A voice rang out, its deep male timbre contrasting sharply with the voices of the women. Everyone turned towards the source.

"Ming Kong! When did you get here? How are you?" Su Hei and Nelly asked almost simultaneously.

Nelly threw her arms round Ming Kong just as his mother stood to embrace him. They collided. Nelly, embarrassed, stepped aside. Su Hei's suspicions were confirmed and her heart sank. But her delight and happiness at finding Ming Kong safe could not be suppressed. She brushed aside other feelings and questions. These could wait.

Ming Kong's face was gaunt with fatigue. There were dark shadows under his eyes and stubble around his chin. But he grinned at their surprise and welcome. "Of course I'm alright. I'm here. Just a bit hungry." Turning to address his attentive audience, he said, "First let me tell you the girls are all safe. They have been very good."

He was instantly barraged with questions from the women, eager for more details.

"I will answer your questions later. Give me a few minutes." He took his mother and Nelly to a far corner of the room. "I came mainly to see how you are. I knew you would be worried. I also came for food. It is getting more and more difficult to find. I had hoped to buy some on the black market, but prices have gone sky high."

"How did you get here?"

"I walked part of the way and found rides for the rest. It was not easy. The Japanese soldiers are everywhere."

"Yes, we know from the delivery men who come to the convent. There is very little transport and petrol is in short supply."

"Well, some ingenious workshops have managed to convert buses to run on fuel made from charcoal. I rode in one for part of the way. I had to avoid being obvious. Most of the time, I wore the cap of a *Haji* to pass as a Malay. I am so dark now that it's not too difficult."

Su Hei blanched.

"Don't worry, Mother. This is not the first time I have travelled in disguise. Look, I cannot stay long. The girls will get worried. They are hungry. We are out of rice and almost everything else."

"Rice is impossible to buy now. You won't be able to get anything here. Nelly was told as much the other day."

"Yes, I am beginning to discover that for myself. Everyone I talked to on the bus said the same." Seeing their worried looks, he reassured them again. "Don't upset yourselves. I'll work something out."

Turning to the other women who were anxiously waiting for news, he said, "You asked why the British were beaten so quickly. The long and short of it is the Japanese had inside information. I heard some of you saying we might not be able to trust the Malays and Indians. You should not jump to conclusions. Do you know who actually provided vital inside information to the Japanese?"

They shook their heads.

"It was a British Indian army captain, a New Zealander! I learned this from one of the senior staff in our company. Not only did he provide information, he also left British supplies for the Japanese to take when the British army retreated. So we'd better be careful before making accusations."

There was a shocked silence. Then out of the gloom came an indignant voice. "The man is right. My nephew told me that many Indians have been executed. They were shot, point blank! He saw it with his own eyes!" Throughout the discussion, the woman had stayed hidden in the corner. A lone Indian lady, she had shrunk from contact with the Chinese women who had been so quick to judge her people. She now stepped forward, comforted that at least one person there would support her. Pulling back the sari that hid her face, she said proudly, "Many of the Indian soldiers were murdered because they refused to give allegiance to the Japanese army when they were captured. Shame on you for telling such lies."

"Yes, but quite a number did!" countered another.

As the women argued, they were joined by the Sisters. A hush fell. Ming Kong continued, "What I don't understand is why they did so little to build up defences here. The naval base in Singapore has a floating dock that is large enough to house the entire British fleet . . ."

Before he could finish, Sow-*mah* blurted out, her voice, harsh and judgmental, "Unfortunately, the fleet was not there." She was not able to contain herself. When her sons last came, they had complained of the lack of support from the British for their guerrilla warfare.

"The British had only two ships in these waters and the Japanese sank both of them," explained one of the Sisters, hoping to calm the squabbling women. "Remember, the British have the Germans to contend with. They are fighting on many fronts, not only in Malaya. We should pray for all those who have lost their lives." Sister Theresa had feared that the discussion might turn ugly. It would not be the first time. There had been similarly heated discussions before, following news from outside.

"What about the air force? Couldn't it have done something?" whispered a woman seated at the back. She had not really meant to be heard, but Ming Kong noticed.

"The British air force could do nothing because it didn't have any safe airfields. The Japanese knew them all."

The plea for prayers from the Sister went unheeded by the women who remained engrossed in their own thoughts. How long could they hide? How long would their loved ones remain safe? The room fell silent as the women contemplated the information they had shared.

Su Hei was not interested in continuing the discussion. What use was talk anyway? She glared at the other women and pointedly turned her back on them. She wanted her son to herself. The women began to move away, their conversation reduced to low murmurs. Any more questions would have to wait. Looking entreatingly at Ming Kong, she said, "It's late. You will not be able to look for rice until tomorrow. There is a curfew. Please stay."

* * * * *

A blanket and some gunny sacks were placed in the corridor. It was to be Ming Kong's bed for the night. Nelly had wanted him on his own, but there was no hope of any privacy. His mother was there and, of course, there were the other women. Ming Kong saw how tired and thin Nelly had become. Fine lines had appeared under her eyes. He felt a growing remorse. He had grown very fond of Mei Yin. "It cannot be love," he said to himself, but he could not stop himself from comparing the two women, two very different women. One was young, vibrant and beautiful. The other was mature, gentle and totally dependent on him.

That evening, immediately after a frugal meal, Su Hei took Ming Kong aside. She did not want to give Nelly a chance to be alone with him.

"Do you have any news of your father?"

"Before coming here I found out from Father's bookkeeper that he is well. Everyone is lying low."

His mother sat down beside Ming Kong. She took his hand and patted it. "Ma-mah wants only the best for you. You are my son and I love you most. So what I am going to ask of you is not for me. I know I have promised there would be no pressure on you to marry Mei Yin, but the war has changed everything. Now that the Japanese are so firmly in control of the country, the girls cannot remain in the jungle. You have to find ways of returning them to their families. Once Mei Yin is back living among us, she will be in danger. You should consider marrying her. The Japanese are forcing single young girls to work in brothels. She would be much safer as your wife.

"Please, this isn't the time," he protested lamely.

"You are the only son. We must try to maintain the family line. We just do not know when the war will end or who will win it. Think about what I am saying. It will make me happy. Don't you like Mei Yin?"

"I do. That's not really the point. I am very fond of Mei Yin, but I'm not sure that what I feel is love. Right at this moment, I am confused. The responsibility of looking after the girls is immense. I would like to focus on just that for the moment. Wait until things settle down. And besides, you have always wanted a big wedding so we could pay our respect to you. It would be impossible in the present situation," he said, hoping to change the course of the discussion. "We would not be able to have much of a tea ceremony."

"*Mo kuan si, mo kuan si.* That's not important," protested Su Hei. "We can always have a second ceremony if need be. I am thinking of Mei Yin's reputation. Everyone knows she is your intended. Living in such close proximity could lead to gossip. She cannot afford that."

A long silence followed. His mother went on, "If you are worried about Nelly, I have a suggestion."

Until then Ming Kong had been staring broodingly at the wall in front of him. He now turned in surprise to his mother.

"Shshsh, nothing has been said, but I'm not stupid. I guessed Nelly must be more than a friend. If you are thinking of marrying her, you should know that she will not be accepted as the official wife just like that. The family would need to know more about her. She is one year older than you, not very important now, but it could be later. Women age faster than men, you know."

"I do not mind that she is older," he said.

"Ah, but do you really know her? During the months we've been together, I have found her evasive about her past. I suspect she has a very complicated, possibly murky, history."

"Who I marry is my business," Ming Kong protested.

"Look, that may well be, but, even if I do not oppose it, your father would."

"What do you want me to do, Mother? I cannot give her up. I owe her so much."

"If I promise to accept her as she is and agree to her remaining in your life, will you marry Mei Yin?"

"How can you do that?"

"Leave it to me."

"You will not hurt her feelings, will you?" Ming Kong beseeched. He hated himself for making this plea. He was giving in, he knew.

But the logic of his mother's argument was unavoidable. He had known from the start that Nelly could never be his official wife. This way Nelly would not be totally out of his life and he would be able to fulfil the letter if not the spirit of his promises to her.

"I will be as gentle as I can," was Su Hei's response.

That very evening, Su Hei made her proposal to Nelly. She explained that she knew of her relationship with her son, that she had grown very fond of her and wished for nothing more than her happiness. While she would not ask for details of Nelly's past, she would ask her whether she could truly consider herself suitable to be the official wife of Ming Kong. She said she would accept her word, but Nelly should be aware that the truth, whatever it may be, would come out sooner or later.

"Although society has changed and we are more progressive these days, when it comes to marriage, there is still one rule for the men and another for women. For a woman to be the official wife, she can only be given or taken once in marriage. She must be a virgin and she must prove it on the wedding night."

Forlornly, Nelly shook her head.

"I shall ask no more. I am fond of you. You have taken good care of me during these months trapped here in the convent. I also appreciate your feelings for my son. This makes me wonder whether you would consider being his second wife? I know it is hard to be second, particularly in love, but think of the alternative. Anyway, I am a second wife. It is not necessarily bad, especially if you have the blessing of your prospective in-laws."

Nelly nodded. There was little she could say.

"Go and tell Ming Kong. Say it is what you want. If you do this, I will make sure you are well cared for. Even if my son loves you, I am afraid he cannot avoid his family responsibilities."

Chapter 15

Ming Kong was in a quandary. He agreed with his mother. When they thought the Japanese occupation would be short-lived, there was every reason to keep the girls hidden. Now, with the increasing likelihood that Japanese military rule could last a few years, even indefinitely, it made sense to return them to their families. The situation was made more urgent because he could not find supplies of rice, not even in the official rice rationing and distribution centres run by the Japanese. He could not smuggle tapioca and sweet potatoes to the hideout; they were too bulky and conspicuous. It was time, Ming Kong decided, for the girls to return home.

Fraught with danger, the process took months. Disguised as boys, they were smuggled back, two at a time to their families. Kai Min and Mei Yin were the last to return.

Su Hei and Nelly also returned to Sun Chuen. Su Hei looked in disbelief at her house. Part of the front porch had collapsed and the beautiful jasmine tree was no longer there. Ah Jee, her hair almost completely grey, came out to greet them. "Second Mistress, I thank the goddess of mercy for keeping you safe." She threw herself on the floor and kowtowed.

Su Hei's eyes filled with tears, "Good, faithful Ah Jee, I have missed you. It is wonderful to be home."

Ah Jee and Nelly worked hard to put the house in order. The two women took to each other instantly. Ah Jee was glad of the help given willingly and without airs by Nelly. "You have to be careful," warned Ah Jee while she scrubbed the floor. "The Japanese have records of the people in each household. We will pass you off as Mistress's eldest daughter. Good job she's not here. Even so, better not tempt fate. Keep to the house as much as possible. Mei Yin is also likely to be here soon."

A week later, Mei Yin, Kai Min and Ming Kong were back home. Not wishing to have her plans upset, Su Hei made immediate arrangements for the wedding. Mei Yin, young and excited over the prospect, felt little of the tension and awkwardness around her. Her only real concern was that she could not talk about it with her mother. Contacting her had always been difficult. Now, with private travel under the surveillance of the Japanese, it was impossible. While she was sad about her mother's absence, she remained oblivious to the rest. She certainly did not notice Nelly's misery.

Su Hei was preoccupied with where and how the wedding ceremony was to proceed. She was the second wife. Under normal circumstances, the wedding tea ceremony should be held in the official home of the groom's father and Suet Ping, the first wife, should be the one to receive the respect and homage of the wedded couple. But, argued Su Hei to herself, these were unusual times and too much traffic between the two residences might attract the attention of the Japanese.

"Go to Father and First Mother," she instructed Ming Kong, "and suggest it might be advisable to have a simple tea ceremony to celebrate the wedding in this house. We will have a proper wedding when things return to normal. First Mother sent Ah Keng to tell us that Father has been ill for some time. I am sure it is from worrying about the business. We should not concern him with details of the wedding. And, with all these problems, I do not imagine First Mother will object. I have already sent Ah Jee as an emissary to gauge their possible reaction. From what she tells me, there does not appear to be much opposition. I rely on you to obtain their formal consent."

Pomp and circumstance, how the wedding was to be organised or who would take pride of place in the ceremonies were the least of Ming Kong's worries. He had already realised his mother's real concern was that she should preside over the events and be honoured. It would help compensate her for being second all her life. He had no objections, providing his father and first mother agreed. He was much more concerned about Nelly and Mei Yin. In one fell swoop, he would have two wives. Having grown up in a polygamous family and witnessed his natural mother's suffering, both imagined and real, he had not intended to follow in the same tradition. He had intended to have lots of girlfriends before finally settling down with just one woman. It was not to be.

Nelly, for her part, felt only pain, sorrow and a sense of *deja vu*, as, once again she found herself swept along by events over which she had little or no control.

* * * * *

Ah Kew came into the bedroom holding a little boy in her arms. She carefully laid him on the bridal bed and held on to his shoulder. She looked anxiously at the clock. A nervous tic played at the corner of her eye. The clock struck. "This is the auspicious time. Roll and play on the bed. Do what you like," she encouraged. Someone giggled. She turned round to the audience that had followed her. "This is to make sure their union will be a fertile one blessed with many male children." She sniffed. "This is the least we can do. Who would have expected the wedding to be celebrated in such a meagre fashion. Come, let's all go to the front of the house to receive the bride."

The little group followed her and assembled at the front porch. "Ah, here she comes."

"Poor thing," one of the group said. "It's not the real thing you know. I mean the bridal journey. The trishaw has only taken her in a circle to symbolise her journey from her old home to her new one. She has no home to come from."

The trishaw with Mei Yin inside came to a halt. Mei Yin in a traditional heavily embroidered, red bridal jacket and long skirt stepped out. The *kua*, previously Su Hei's, sat heavily on her petite frame.

"Come, come. We'll go in and I'll present you to young Master. Don't look up. Just look down demurely at the floor," Ah Kew said sharply when Mei Yin raised her head.

Mei Yin, head bowed as instructed, went first to be presented to Ming Kong.

"Please bow to each other. Good! Good! You must now give homage to the ancestors."

Together they made their way to a makeshift altar, a rough teak plank propped up on two stools. Ah Kew sniffed; her face was red with embarrassment. "The original ancestral altar has been vandalised and . . . this, this is the replacement." Ah Kew could not explain that a lack of resources had made it impossible to replace the original altar, the word "lack" being censored from such an auspicious occasion.

Joss sticks and incense were lit and offered. The ceremony completed, the bride and groom went to Su Hei. Mei Yin knelt and offered tea to her mother-in-law. There were no *longan* or lotus seeds, just a pale insipid brew symbolically sweetened with a pinch of sugar. The absence of Ming Kong's father and first mother and the lack of any family members from the bride's side were remarked upon by guests as they whispered among themselves. But nothing could blight Mei Yin's happiness. Blushing under the scrutiny of the guests, she sought Ming Kong's hand for reassurance. Ah Kew, who had been posted behind Mei Yin to keep an eye on her, intercepted and, with a sharp nudge, whispered fiercely, "You are too bold. You must never show such wanton signs of affection in front of your elders. What can you be thinking?"

Mei Yin withdrew her hand in a flash and, catching the warning glare from her mother-in-law, dropped her gaze, but not before she saw Nelly standing apart at the far end of the room.

The week before, Ah Kew had been assigned the task of preparing Mei Yin for the nuptials. Ah Kew herself was unmarried. The vague and brief instructions she proffered had, if anything, aroused Mei Yin's curiosity. The only substantial advice given to her by Ah Kew, repeated three times to be sure she understood, was she must show "red" on the consummation of the marriage.

"We have prepared a white nightdress for you and white bed sheets. These will have to be presented to your mother-in-law for inspection after the wedding night. The bloodstains will testify to your virginity. *Nai-nai* belongs to the old school and pays particular attention to such things. You will be cast off and disgraced if you fail this test," she warned. "The whole village will know the result because only if your virginity is confirmed will you be able to return to your parents' home on the third day with gifts." She glared at Mei Yin who was grinning broadly from ear to ear. "Don't take this lightly. Long lengths of sugarcane will be hung on the car taking you home, to show that you have kept the sanctity of your body for your husband-to-be. So behave. I see both you and Tai-siew courting by the river and I caution you. Wait."

"But *Nai-nai* said I must stay here because of the war. It will be impossible to go home on the third day," replied Mei Yin.

"Don't be cheeky. If we can't complete this traditional formality, there are other ways of making it known," Ah Kew warned, more than a little irritated at being corrected.

In the end, Mei Yin turned to Nelly for advice. Nelly had been avoiding Mei Yin in the week leading to the wedding. One evening, Mei Yin found her on her own in the backyard feeding two small chickens. They were birds Ah Jee had managed to coax from their neighbour with the promise of half of a bag of sugar that Ming Kong was expecting to buy on the black market. The birds were to provide the main dish for the wedding celebration. Nelly had the job of fattening them up with kitchen scraps.

Mei Yin pleaded with Nelly. "Nelly *Cheh-cheh*, Ah Kew has been telling me all sorts of things to prepare me for my wedding. She speaks in riddles and I don't understand. When I ask, she shuts me up with a reprimand. Please, can you explain?"

"Don't call me *Cheh-cheh*. I know I'm older than you and we will be sisters soon, but I will not be senior to you so just call me Nelly."

She did not want to get involved in any discussion about the wedding, but it was impossible to dislike Mei Yin. After all she had been dropped into this mess just as much as Nelly. Impish and self-willed, traits that had become more obvious since her days in hiding,

Mei Yin made Nelly laugh with her comments and questions even though her heart ached at the thought of the impending marriage. In the end she put aside her own feelings. She remembered her own wedding night. She answered Mei Yin's questions patiently. As dusk drew in, they were still huddled together, whispering and talking. A loud shout from Ah Jee brought their conversation to an abrupt end. Dinner was served.

Clasping her hand to her mouth to stifle her giggles, Mei Yin said, "Once again dinner will consist of boiled tapioca served in beautiful tureens and eaten elegantly with chopsticks; we must pretend they are pieces of meat and fish. In the caves, we ate with our fingers. Tapioca tastes much better if you can lick all the gooey bits off your fingers."

"Shush! Don't let *Nai-nai* hear you. She will be very cross and say you are ungrateful. Ah Jee is reserving our rice for the wedding dinner. You must not let *Nai-nai* see your high spirits. Ah Jee says you have changed and it might not be to her liking," warned Nelly. "Anyway, you might not even get the usual serving of yam tonight. Ah Jee is keeping some back to make dumplings for the wedding. The poor woman is worrying herself sick about putting on a good show. So be kind to her."

Opening her arms wide, Mei Yin jumped up to give Nelly a hug. "Thank you. We will be good friends, I promise." And then, throwing her arms out wide, she said in a loud whisper, "Thank you Ah Jee, I love you too." In fact, at that moment, Mei Yin loved the whole world.

Chapter 16

"Kneel. Don't you dare look me in the eye. Didn't your mother teach you any manners at all. *Mokah kow*, you have obviously not been brought up properly." They were in the sitting room. Su Hei's face was a mask of fury. "When you wish to go out, even with my son, you must ask my permission. Did I not teach you that? So who gave consent for you to go out alone? Your husband has been away for only two days and already you have taken it upon yourself to do as you please."

"*Nai-nai* I am sorry. Please accept this cup of tea. I forgot. It was only to the neighbour's house. I wanted their advice on our new vegetable plot. The plants just do not seem to take."

"Lies, lies you just want to gossip and chat and avoid your fair share of the house work. This is what I think of your apologies." With one sweep of her hand, Su Hei sent the teacup and saucer crashing to the ground.

It was almost eleven months into the marriage and the situation had deteriorated rapidly. Hunger made the task of getting food a continuous preoccupation. Rice was in such short supply that even a willingness to pay exorbitant black-market prices was no guarantee of success. Ming Kong went out every day in search of food supplies. With his father's business near to collapse, getting hold of ready cash to buy the most basic of commodities required all his skill and contacts. He even ventured back to the rubber plantations in the hope of finding villagers he had befriended when working for The Orient. He was convinced they would be able to provide at least some fruits and root crops. This time he had been away for two days. Su Hei, worried about him, took out her frustration on Mei Yin.

"You have brought nothing but bad luck to this family. The health of my husband has declined steadily and my son looks as though he is about to collapse. Eleven months have gone by and still there is no sign of a baby on the horizon. *Ai yah*, Ah Kew is to blame."

"Do not get worked up, *Nai-nai*," Nelly intervened. "It is not really Mei Yin's fault. I am sure Ming Kong will be alright. He gets on well with everyone. Here, let me clear away the broken china before someone gets hurt."

"Not you. I want Mei Yin to clear it up. She dropped it, not you. She has to learn to suffer the consequences of her misbehaviour. She thinks she can do just as she likes because my son favours her. She gets around him to do what she wants. Before he left, he asked me to be kind to her. This must mean she has been complaining about me." She glared at Mei Yin, her face suffused with anger, "Did you?"

"No, no, I did not. I only said I felt very tired and hungry. I asked him if he could get green mangoes. It has been such a long time since I had them."

"Always thinking of yourself. Such a selfish girl. Huh! We don't have rice and you want luxuries. What have I done to deserve such an ungrateful daughter-in-law." Consumed by self-pity, Su Hei's eyes filled with tears as she beat her chest with remorse.

Ah Jee and Nelly helped Su Hei up. Nelly turned and gestured for Mei Yin to make her escape. They were halfway across the room when Ah Jee's nephew rushed in.

"Jee-*mah*, I've just come from Foong Yee. Remember him? Ming Kong's assistant at The Orient. We have news. I'm sorry, it is not good, not good at all. Ming Kong has been taken by the Japanese on his way back home."

"Why?" Mei Yin was the first to ask.

"It's not clear. He was stopped near Kajang on his way back from Seremban. He had caught the bus to Kuala Lumpur from there. It was halted at a military checkpoint. All the passengers had to disembark and have their documents checked. When it was Ming Kong's turn, the guards nodded and ordered him to be taken away. Foong Yee's uncle was on the same bus and saw the whole thing. As soon as Ming Kong had been taken away, the rest of the passengers were allowed back on the bus and no further searches were made. It looks as though they were looking just for him."

"Why, why!" wailed Su Hei.

Mei Yin stood paralysed, her face drained of colour. Then, with a jerk, she bent over, clutching her sides and retched. For a few seconds, the attention of the room shifted to her. Ah Jee rushed forward with her kitchen towel and wiped her face, helping her to a seat.

"Huh! Even at a time like this with her husband in danger, she seeks attention. She must be secretly eating food set aside for her by my poor son. I have long suspected this. So! She is sick, punished for her greed. *Ai yah*, you are bad luck. I am sure my son went in search of things to please you. It's all your fault. I regret ever setting my eyes on you. Ah Kew will pay for misguiding me!"

Ah Jee stepped in. She was used to her mistress's tirades.

"Please, don't get upset or you will have one of your headaches. It is not good for you. What is important is to find out where he is being held and why, and then try to get him released. We will have to tell *Loh-yeh*. Elder Master might have contacts who can help."

Years of service and her loyalty during the hard times had earned Ah Jee a special place in the household. She was treated more like a member of the family than a servant. She gestured to Nelly and Mei Yin to make themselves scarce before their mother-in-law could resume her outburst. Neither of them moved. They were in a state of shock. Both begged to be allowed to see their father-in-law and would have rushed over to his house that very moment. They were refused permission. Instead Ah Jee's nephew was asked to contact him.

"Mistress has a point. It is still dangerous for women to go out, even accompanied, especially with evening approaching. My nephew is the best person to go," persuaded Ah Jee.

Chapter 17

Ming Kong awoke with a start. He blinked, momentarily blinded by the small shaft of bright light that penetrated the gloom of the prison cell. Particles of dust circled and floated in the solitary beam. This was his third day in captivity.

When he had stepped down from the bus onto the platform flanking the military checkpoint, he was confident it was just another routine spot check. His documents were in order and he was carrying only a tiny parcel of food.

The trip to the estate had been a waste of time. The farmers were short of grain themselves and were unwilling to share what little remained. He had tried to contact Ahmed, his foreman and fellow conspirator in the early days of the war, and Ali, his brother, but they were nowhere to be found. People said they were still around, but when he asked for their whereabouts, he always got the same evasive answer.

"*Tak tahu.*" I don't know.

A shopkeeper who used to supply his estate workers did venture a comment. "Ali and Ahmed are rich people now. Good friends of the Japanese. *Sombong*! Very snobbish, we don't see much of them any more." Two days of interrogation had left him in little doubt as to the implication of this statement. The message people had been trying to give him was becoming obvious.

Initially, when he was frog-marched to the military truck and driven to where he was now, no questions were asked. He was just handled roughly. The soldiers had pushed him into his present cell. "Strip! Put these on," was all they said as they flung a pair of dirty shorts to him. Then the door was slammed shut and the key turned.

The cell was dank and dark, its air filled with an overpowering odour of urine and vomit. He could sense the fear and desperation of previous prisoners. With the exception of a raffia mat on the concrete floor, a chair and an old oil can that served as a latrine, it was devoid of furniture. Stumbling to his feet, he hoisted himself onto the chair and tried to recall the events of the previous night.

Japanese men in civilian clothes, accompanied by an army officer, were his first visitors. They started by asking him general questions. At first the questions seemed innocent enough.

"Tell me about your father. What does he do for a living? Give me the names of everyone in your family, explain how they are related, where they live and what they do."

Then suddenly, the mood changed. Leaning forward, the plain-clothed interrogator asked, "You were absent for many months in 1942. Where were you?"

"I was in charge of the rubber plantations in the south. The company I worked for had entrusted them to my care. My duty was reconnaissance of the estates."

Wham, a hand smashed across his face. "I repeat my question. This time be sure to tell me the truth."

Ming Kong felt a trickle of blood roll down one side of his face. Swallowing hard, he repeated his answer.

Wham, another blow to his face. This time someone held him from behind, grasping his hair and wrenching his head back so he could not avoid the full impact of the blow. At the same time, a bright spotlight was turned on. It shone straight into his eyes. He could not see for the glare.

"Listen," his interrogator hissed, "don't tell me half truths. You did spend some time visiting the estates, but you did more than that. Tell me exactly what else you did, where and why."

"I ... I made my rounds of the estates. I tried to persuade the workers to stay on the plantations, and bought and distributed food to them. That meant I had to move about from one area to another."

From the questions, Ming Kong realised they knew his movements and that there had to be an informer. He must stay with the truth as far as they might know it. He tried to second-guess what they wanted to know. Above all he was anxious to keep from them the concealment of the girls and their eventual return to Kuala Lumpur. The Wongs would not have betrayed him. It was most likely to be one or both of his assistants. Desperately, he tried to recall how much each of them might have known. As far as he could remember, he had only used them to keep an eye on the movements of the Japanese soldiers and to search for food. They had never come anywhere near the hideout. He was sure he had not told them about either the cave or the girls. Because of the food, they might have guessed he was hiding people, but it could only be a guess; they would have had nothing to back it up.

"Where did you get the fuel for your vehicle?"

"From the depot in our regional headquarters in Seremban."

"Did you use it only for your work? Did you at any time provide fuel to others?"

"The fuel was for my own use only. I did not provide fuel to others." Blinking under the glare of the light, he kept his face still, his eyes looking unwaveringly straight ahead. He did not look in the direction of the interrogator's voice in case it was interpreted as defiance.

"What about guns?"

A momentary silence; civilians were not allowed to have weapons. All guns had to be surrendered to the Japanese military. Keeping them as he had done was a crime, punishable by flogging, imprisonment or worse. They had him now. If they knew, why had they waited so long? Trying to deflect the question, he answered, "I used to hunt game-birds and occasionally elephant and wild boar. The larger animals are a menace to the estates and farms."

"We have no record of any guns being surrendered by either you or your father. Where are they now?"

He hesitated. Through the glare of the light he saw the shadow of the interrogator's arm. This time the blows came in rapid succession and were as hard as they were quick. His head jolted back with each one. Blood dribbled from the corner of his right eye down to his lips.

It tasted salty and sticky. He felt his eye smart and swell almost immediately. Thoughts flashed through his mind. If he revealed he had stored them in the cave, they would check. Inevitably, questions about what other use had been made of it would follow. Playing for time, he allowed his head to go slack, feigning unconsciousness.

Disgusted, the plain-clothed officer got up, kicked the chair hard and barked out something in Japanese. Ming Kong felt his arms being twisted and bound tightly at the back. Silence followed, then more orders and finally the harsh grinding sound of the key being turned in the lock.

After they left, Ming Kong remained still for some time in case he was being watched. Then he slowly rolled off the chair, his body hitting the ground with a thud. He lay still, going over in his mind the questions he had been asked. There was no hint of any interest in the girls or their whereabouts. Would they be endangered if the Japanese found out that he had hidden them; they were only children. Surely the blame would fall on him not them. Whatever might happen, he vowed he would never reveal their present whereabouts or give their names.

Hours passed. Every muscle and bone ached; he had been given no food and hardly any water for almost 30 hours. The room stank and the still, musty air had become distinctly stale. Drawing up his knees and sliding on his bottom, he edged backwards until he could prop himself up against the wall.

No sooner had Ming Kong sat up than the door was flung open. A soldier came in. "Get up!" he barked. "Follow me!" Ming Kong got to his feet unsteadily. His legs trembled from being cramped for so long and from weakness caused by hunger. He was led past a labyrinth of cells, many occupied. Eyes peeped out through tiny holes in the doors. Sobs and groans echoed along the passageway. Finally he entered a large rectangular room. Bright lights shone from bare bulbs. At one end was a long steel table with an assortment of boxes and tools on it. A smaller wooden table stood on one side. Three men were seated behind it. On the left was the man who had questioned him earlier. Ming Kong was led in front of them and pushed roughly onto a chair. The soldier who had brought him there went back to stand guard at the door joining three others who were already standing there.

Without the glare of the spotlight in his face, Ming Kong was able to look more closely at his earlier interrogator. Still dressed in civilian clothes, he was flanked by men in uniform. He had no doubt that his persecutor was connected with the military. He shared the same military bearing as his two companions. But without the uniform, in scuffed trousers and an open-neck shirt, he somehow looked much more menacing. His eyes were narrow slits, hooded by the thick folds of his eyelids. Ming Kong could feel them boring into him, sizing him up. A fine scar, wax-white, ran from ear to chin on the left side of his face, throwing into relief a surprisingly long nose with a thin bridge and flared nostrils.

The man looked away from Ming Kong and nodded to his companions, picking up a packet of cigarettes as he did so. With deft fingers he dislodged a cigarette and placed it between his lips. His face was disdainful. He began talking softly to his companions, gesturing every now and then in the direction of the prisoner. Occasionally he would grin as if making a joke. His monologue over, the others nodded in apparent agreement before focusing their full attention on Ming Kong.

"Are you ready to cooperate?" To Ming Kong's surprise the first question did not come from the interrogator in civilian clothes but from the officer to his right. He was bald, rotund and with a face that in different circumstances could easily be described as friendly. He looked down at notes in front of him. "According to our information you disappeared for many months from your home only to reappear again towards the end of 1943. You own arms and have not surrendered them. Your father, who also had a large cache of weapons, gave them to you. They too have not been surrendered."

He looked up from his notes, and glared. "You know it is a crime to hold arms. Your father may have given them to you to keep, but they are still registered under his name. If you want, we can call him in for questioning. Let us know what has happened to these arms and we will spare your father this discomfort. He is ill, is he not?"

Numbly, Ming Kong nodded. He was faced with a desperate choice, his father or the girls. "Please leave him out of it. I am responsible. I will tell you as much as I can. But please, can I have some water?" His lips were parched. Even as he spoke he could feel them splitting.

The three men at the table waited while water was poured into a glass. A young soldier brought it to him and poured it into his mouth, spilling most of it down his front. He choked and spluttered.

"Don't keep us waiting," the officer chided.

"No, no, sorry! I hid the guns and ammunition. I hid them in the jungle because I was afraid that looting and chaos would follow the outbreak of war. Some of the guns have been in the family for a long time and are of sentimental value. I did not know then that they would have to be surrendered to the authorities. It was only later when things had settled down that I learned this. By then I could not get to where I had concealed them. I kept quiet because I was afraid of being punished."

"Where are they now? Can you take us to it?"

"I don't know. It has been more than a year. The whole area will have changed. Everything grows so fast in the forest. The paths I hacked out will all be overgrown."

The plain-clothed officer turned to the rotund officer and spoke in English, obviously for the benefit of the prisoner's ears. "In other words, he is refusing to cooperate. If we do not have evidence that the arms are safe, we must assume they have been given to others. For all we know, he might be working for the enemy. We have a dangerous man here. He was missing for months, he had a large cache of arms that he did not surrender and now he is refusing to cooperate. I think there is only one way forward, don't you?"

He spoke in a quiet voice, his manner almost reasonable. The intensity of his gaze and the continuous drumming of his fingers on the table belied this outward calm. The other two officers looked uncomfortable.

"I don't know how the two of you feel," he continued, "but in our unit, we generally deal with such problems with a short sharp dose of bitter medicine. I would suggest caning, 20 strokes will do it."

The rotund officer, obviously the senior of the two, looked askance at the other military officer. The other officer gave an imperceptible shake of his head. The rotund office replied to the plain-clothed interrogator, again in English, "You know Horikoshi-*san*, we have new orders to conduct all affairs by the book. It is part of the policy to re-introduce a civilian administration and encourage local support. We cannot condone whipping without more proof. If this case were to come directly under your unit, which it could easily do if it involves espionage, we would wash our hands of it. You would then be able to proceed as you wish. But are we dealing with espionage here?"

"Leave it to me, Kasahara-*san*," replied Horikoshi, "and I will soon find out."

The two officers stood up, bowed to the speaker, the depth of their obeisance indicating a man of some importance, and left the room. Once they had gone, Horikoshi turned to the soldiers. "Twenty strokes; use your strongest canes and make sure they are split at the end. If he faints, bring him round. He should be awake to enjoy the beating. Call me when he is ready."

The soldiers manhandled Ming Kong to the corner of the room and hauled him up on ropes thrown over a beam. The thin ropes wound around his wrists cut into them. He hung from the beam, his body dangling like a sack, stretched by his own weight, his toes just skimming the ground.

As the guards went about the task, they joked and laughed; the thrashing they were giving him was an everyday event for them, just part of the job. For Ming Kong, each blow caused explosions of pain, sending shock waves along every nerve in his body. He swung under their force. He did not know which was worse, the pain of the split cane biting into his flesh or the struggle to breathe as the weight of his body pulled down against his rib cage. By the sixth stroke, he had passed out, but not for long. Buckets of cold water were thrown over him to bring him back to consciousness. Eventually even this was not enough; he sank into oblivion.

When he came to, he was lying on the floor. His tormentors had moved him to one side. They were sat around the interrogation table enjoying a game of cards, their play interspersed with laughter and expletives. A dense pall of cigarette smoke hung above their heads.

Time passed. Then he heard the sound of approaching footsteps. It was the third officer who had yet to address him. He dismissed the guards before walking over to where Ming Kong was lying. The officer drew up a chair from the table and sat down. In a mixture of Chinese, Malay and English, he spoke softly and urgently. "I am Fujihara. I have very little time so listen carefully. Captain Horikoshi will be back soon. I have received a message from one of your father's friends who knows me. Horikoshi can be put in charge of the interrogation only if you are in league with the Malayan People's Anti-Japanese Army and he has evidence that you have supplied the guns to them. If you can provide him with proof that the guns are intact and un-used, he must pass you back to the military administrative unit to consider any other offences. Under our new policy, Lieutenant Colonel Kasahara would be lenient, I will make sure of that."

"Why should I believe you?" asked Ming Kong.

"Listen to me. Lieutenant Colonel Kasahara's job here is to win over the people of Malaya and to encourage civilian support for our newly established administration. Captain Horikoshi, however, is very different. He was in China before being posted here and is well known for extracting whatever he wants from his prisoners. He is under pressure to show progress against the MPAJA. Their guerrilla tactics and ability to get arms have been a thorn in our side for a long time. Even last night one of our depots was torched. Any Chinese suspected of being an enemy of the state will be tortured to death or until they make a confession. Horikoshi does not mind which comes first. Whipping is only the beginning." Nodding his head towards the long table, he continued, "If you ever have to endure those instruments, you will long for death. I am doing this as a favour to your father and his associates."

Still Ming Kong hesitated. He was uncertain whether it was a trick.

"You do not have much time. Surrender your guns and he will have no grounds for accusing you of giving them to the MPAJA. I can hear him coming." Hurriedly, Fujihara stood up. With one swift sweep of his hand he crashed his chair on to the floor and overturned the table. Then he clenched his fist and drove it into Ming Kong's face.

A week later, Ming Kong was released. Lieutenant Fujihara did indeed have links with his father's business associates. Later, when he went to thank them, they politely brushed aside his gratitude. It had not taken much to persuade Fujihara to help. He could not afford to upset his Chinese contacts. He was heavily involved in the black market for rice and sugar. On his advice, Kasahara set the prisoner free; few questions were asked about the girls. By then, young girls were the least of the concerns of the occupiers as the Allied Forces continued to fight back successfully in the Pacific.

Chapter 18

After the departure of Ah Jee's nephew, Mei Yin sank to her knees, all lifeblood drained out of her arms and legs. She tasted bile, sour and bitter, in her mouth. Her heart pounded so hard and so fast, she thought it might burst. Over and over again, scenes of Ming Kong's capture played through her mind. She feared that her husband might be lost forever. She feared what might be done to him, but she could not show her horror, only Su Hei, it seemed, was entitled to be distressed.

For Mei Yin the days and nights were long and lonely during Ming Kong's absence. The atmosphere in the house was stifling. She could not escape the incessant waspish remarks of her mother-in-law. Every misdeed, accident and sorrow was heaped on her, the cause of all things bad. She felt trapped.

Early that morning, Ah Jee had cautioned Mei Yin. "Keep out of the house. *Nai-nai* is in a bad mood. I'll tell you when it is safe to come in." So Mei Yin had walked up and down the backyard, weeding, watering, trying to revive the newly planted rows of vegetables. She had been there two hours and still no word as to whether it was safe for her to return to the house. Despondent, she sat down on a tree stump. She sobbed quietly, her face cradled in her hands. "Please, please let him come home safely," she whispered over and over to herself.

A flurry of footsteps jolted her from her thoughts. "Good news, good news! Ming Kong will be back today. Father-in-Law and First Mother-in-Law are here. They arrived half an hour ago. Don't cry. It's over. Everything will be alright," cried Nelly, clasping Mei Yin to her. They looked at each other, tears streaming down their faces.

"When? Is he alright? Can I go in now?" Mei Yin asked. Her eyes shone. She jiggled and bounced in Nelly's arms, ready to tear herself away.

"Calm down. I don't know. It is probably best to wait awhile. Ming Kong could arrive any time now. *Nai-nai* will want to have him to herself. She will not wish to share the first moments of his return with us."

They sat down together. Over the past few months, Nelly had gradually assumed the role of elder sister. "Your eyes are swollen from crying. Ming Kong is bound to see. If you present yourself looking like this, *Nai-nai* will certainly say something and there will be more rows."

Mei Yin washed her face, drawing water from the bucket she had been using in the garden. She could not hold back her feelings. "I hate her," she cried. "I hate the way she speaks to me, the way she misinterprets everything I do. She tries so hard to belittle me. I will pay my respect to her because she is my mother-in-law, but I will not curry favour with her. I have finished with that."

After weeks of giving in to her tyrannical mother-in-law, the thought of seeing her husband again revived Mei Yin's spirits. "Once the war is over, I will persuade Ming Kong to leave this house. If I have a son, I don't want her bossing him around like she does Ming Kong."

"Are you . . . ?" Nelly kept her question suspended.

"Yes! I think so. I have missed my period; it is about six weeks late. That's why I spent such a long time with our neighbour the other day. I was asking her for advice. I think I am expecting."

She grinned, a wicked, mischievous grin. "Of course, after the way *Nai-nai* spoke to me, I wasn't going to let her know. Somehow she would turn even this good news into something bad."

"How wonderful! I'm so happy for you." Nelly's heart sank even as she said the words. Ming Kong had been spending more and more time with Mei Yin and it was difficult to contain the hurt and occasional surge of jealousy. But Mei Yin's suffering, especially in the days following Ming Kong's disappearance, touched her. Thrusting aside her own feelings, she reached out to Mei Yin and repeated, "I'm so happy for you."

"I'm a bit nervous and frightened. Nelly, have you had children?"

Startled, Nelly replied, "Why do you ask?"

"It was just that you look so sad every time you see a child pass by and when you hold them in your arms you smother them with kisses and cry. You don't seem to want to let them go. And, even just then, when I told you of my condition, you looked sad and happy at the same time." With the insensitivity of the young, she enquired, "Did yours die?"

Nelly shook her head. "Please don't ask me." Her voice was muffled, she bowed her head. Time had not softened her feelings of guilt and sorrow. Many a time she had found it hard not to rush to a phone and call them, despite her promise to Mary. She had found some solace in speaking to Ah Kuk and learning they were doing well. But following the Occupation, even this contact had been lost. She broke down in tears.

"Don't," said Mei Yin. She planted little kisses on Nelly's cheek and laid her head on Nelly's shoulder.

* * * * *

A commotion came from the direction of the house. Voices shouting Ming Kong's name. Mei Yin and Nelly rushed into the house. They did not enter the drawing room where Su Hei stood next to her husband and his first wife; they didn't dare. Everyone else, including many villagers who had received help from him in the past, had begun pushing forward to greet him until Su Hei's sharp rebuke stopped them in their tracks.

Ming Kong had obviously suffered at the hands of his captors. His eyes, ringed with fatigue, were sunk into their sockets. Both cheekbones stood out prominently, skull-like, exaggerating the hollows of his cheeks. Bruises, the colour of dark plums, ran around the upper eyelids and along one cheek. His smile was a lop-sided grimace; his lower lip still hung swollen, like a boil about to burst.

He embraced his parents. He tried hard not to flinch when they held him. His back was tender and scarred. He disengaged himself and looked around the room. He saw the two women standing at the doorway. Without stopping to speak to anyone, he hastened over to them. He said nothing; he just kissed and hugged them to him.

Su Hei had wanted to exclude the others from the reunion, but Ming Kong's father had insisted that all the well-wishers be allowed to see and greet his son. It was, as he said, a happy occasion to be celebrated. There was little she could do. This did nothing to quell the anger that welled up in her when she saw how quickly her son left her side. She kept her tongue in check. Mei Yin, whose excitement and joy could not be contained, was talking excitedly. It irritated Su Hei. "See how the minx is jumping up and down like a child and throwing her arms around my son in front of everyone," she muttered to herself. Then, noticing a sudden change in the behaviour of the group around him, she wondered, "What has she said? Is she already feeding him lies about me?"

Someone brought a stool for Ming Kong. He sat down gingerly and took off his shirt to reveal his back. Shocked gasps went around the room. People moved in to take a closer look. Murmurs of concern mingled with cries of anger. Ah Soon, the trishaw man, shouted the loudest, cursing the Japanese with such vehemence that mothers clamped hands over their children's ears to shield them from his language. Ah Soon was virtually a retainer of the Ong family, ferrying the children to and fro when the car was not available.

"Thank you, thank you for coming to see my son." Mr Ong had to raise his voice to be heard. "I appreciate your concern. In happier days, I would have invited you to stay for dinner. But, if you don't mind, we would like to have some time alone with him to hear his story and take care of his injuries." Gesturing to Ah Jee's nephew and Foong Yee to stay, he sent for ointment, warm water and bandages. But Nelly and Mei Yin had already got them. They set about treating his wounds.

The extent of Ming Kong's injuries shocked everyone. Not wishing to cause unnecessary worry, his rescuers had said very little to his parents other than the usual palliative, "Don't worry. He's a young man and will soon recover."

Seeing their distress, Ming Kong sought to calm them. "I'm okay. It's painful, but nothing is broken. The wounds look worse than they are. I was lucky, I was helped by one of the Japanese officers. Another round of interrogation would have left me half a man, I'm sure. Thank you Father for getting help. We must thank your friends."

"It's done," came the reply. "We will have to try to get a doctor in to look at your injuries. Doctors are not so easy to find these days. You should rest. First let us all have something to eat. My contacts not only helped to get you released, they gave us some food as well. In the old days, before this mess, I gave them a lot of business, even lent them money. Now, they have repaid me with interest!"

With faltering steps, his father led the way to the dining table. His voice was weak as he continued to speak. "During your detainment, the Japanese commandeered our offices and ransacked our files. Records of business deals, contacts and addresses built up over decades are now lost. Nothing remains but our spirit and the will to rebuild our lives and fortunes again."

There was little Ming Kong could say to comfort his father. Nelly went discreetly with Ah Jee to help with the meal, leaving Mei Yin with Ming Kong. After she had dressed the wounds and helped him to change his shirt, she stayed by his side, holding his hand, happy that he had returned home safely.

The sight of Mei Yin and Ming Kong engaged in deep conversation, enjoying a closeness she had never experienced, with either her husband or son, filled Su Hei with envy. She knew, however, that this was not the time or place to make a scene or rebuke her daughter-in-law. Her husband and his first wife seemed well disposed towards Mei Yin. She needed to tread carefully. She turned to Suet Ping. "Big Sister, I am not someone to criticise for the sake of it, but I made a big mistake in choosing her for our son." Looking in the direction of Mei Yin, she continued. "I relied too much on Ah Kew's reading of the almanac. So far, it has been one calamity after another. I have to watch her like a hawk, a minx without *kakow*. Utter disrespect for her elders."

"Father, Mother, we have good news," Ming Kong called from across the room. "Mei Yin is expecting a baby."

Su Hei's eyes opened wide in astonishment, her jaws slackened and her mouth dropped open. She quickly recovered herself. "Wonderful, wonderful," she proclaimed loudly. "I have always been confident you would bear the Ong family many sons. I was not wrong after all!" She continued with her fulsome praise, ignoring completely what she had been saying only moments earlier.

"Mother, I did not say it is going to be a boy. How can we know? It might be a girl. Girls are just as wonderful. Look at you, look at *Tai-mah* and look at Mei Yin."

"*Choi, choi!*" she exclaimed to ward off bad luck. "Do not say such a thing. Of course it is going to be a boy, my . . . uh . . . our first grandson." She turned to her husband for support. He rewarded her with a grunt.

* * * * *

It was late morning before Ming Kong woke up. The sun was already streaming into the kitchen when he went in and sat down by the kitchen table. Ah Jee was chopping onions. The thumping of the cleaver on the big wooden block echoed around the kitchen, completely drowning out the soft muffle of *bangkuang* leaves being threaded at the other end of the room. Mei Yin was busy weaving a mat, a skill her mother had taught her long ago.

"I'll be with you in a second. I didn't wake you because I thought you should rest," she said. Setting aside the partially woven mat, she got up and went to the stove. "We have made some rice broth for your breakfast and there is *do fo* to go with it. They are from Father-in-Law's friends. It's a real treat after months of boiled sweet potatoes and tapioca." After setting the bowl of steaming hot broth in front of her husband, Mei Yin sat down beside him. "Both your father and first mother left early this morning. They didn't want to wake you to say goodbye."

Ming Kong tucked into his breakfast with relish. "It is good to be back. Where's Nelly?"

"She is with your mother," Ah Jee replied before Mei Yin could speak. "Second Mistress is having one of her migraines. She has left instructions for you to see her after breakfast."

Ignoring this, Ming Kong turned to Mei Yin, "Have you eaten? You should eat well, you know. Have some of this." In the morning light, he could see that she had lost weight.

"She eats almost nothing. All she wants to eat are green mangoes. I do not know how she can eat them, they are so sour. It cannot be good for the baby. But she will not listen to an old lady like me," scolded Ah Jee.

"No, no, that's not true. I do listen. I just can't keep anything down. The only things I seem able to digest are mangoes."

"Plenty of rest, that is what she needs," interrupted Su Hei who walked in at that moment. "Less gallivanting around would do her a world of good. This is what I wanted to speak to you about, my son. It is not good for Mei Yin, or even you in your present state, to be together all the time. You should let her rest for the sake of the baby. You should also rest yourself in order to recover."

She sat down beside them at the table. "I have asked Nelly to prepare a separate room for you."

"Mother, that is absolutely out of the question. I will not have it. If my wife needs a rest from me, she will tell me. We don't need to be ... to be told what to do."

He was spluttering with anger, well aware of what his mother was trying to do. The friction in the household had been evident throughout the previous evening's meal. His mother had made no attempt to hide her dislike of Mei Yin. It had taken all his will-power not to respond in an equally cruel way, but it was his first night back and he wanted a happy reunion. It was only after everyone had gone to bed that, with his arms around his wife, he had learned all that had happened in his absence. "Hold on for a while, we'll leave this place when the time is ripe," he had promised.

"*Ai yah*, what have I done to deserve such sharp words from my own son. *Chang loh poh*. You side only with your wife, I am just saying this for the good of your baby."

"Let us make a pact, Mother. Please be kind to my wife. Do not ... do not force me to choose between you and her."

Su Hei wailed; she beat her chest, lamenting at the unkindness of the gods in giving her such an unfilial son. She blamed it on Mei Yin's bad influence. When Ah Jee and Nelly tried to calm her, she turned on Nelly and gave her a strong shove, "You, you are useless. Why did I take you in?"

Ming Kong was not impressed and showed no sign of relenting. At last she said, "Alright, alright, you have defeated your old and frail mother. I do this for my grandson. I will not raise the subject again. Just don't expect me not to say 'I told you so' when things go sour."

True to her words in the months that followed, she did not interfere ... much. To win Ming Kong, she realised she had to adopt a completely different strategy. This she did by feeding her daughter-in-law, giving her the choicest bits of food available, a happy solution in her eyes because it nourished the unborn child. Mei Yin's life improved noticeably. Ah Kew was again back in favour. She came regularly to see how the pregnancy was progressing, examining the shape of the belly to see if it was a boy.

"See how high she is carrying, see how pointed the belly is and how neat her gait. Without doubt it's a boy."

Encouraged, they began searching for an appropriate name for him. No thought was given to the possibility of a girl. Gradually, even Mei Yin became convinced she was carrying a boy. She looked forward to having a son, which would make her mother-in-law happy. Ming Kong, busy salvaging what remained of his father's business, left the women alone. "So long as they are happy, I am happy," became his credo.

Chapter 19

An Mei was born at five o'clock in the morning, an unearthly hour. From all accounts, she was an ugly child: tiny, wrinkled, yellow and scrawny, with a voice so loud she could awaken the entire household. Mei Yin suffered terrible labour pains that went on for hours. She pushed and panted until her strength nearly failed. Her screams kept everyone on edge throughout the night. Only the support of her mother, who had come from Malacca to be with her, saw her through. Sook Ping had not seen her daughter since her 14th birthday.

Once cleaned, the baby was presented to her paternal grandmother. Su Hei turned away in disgust. "Such an ugly child. Take it away," she hissed. "And don't bother to cook the chicken and special food we have saved. Send them to Kai Min. Her baby is due any time now."

"But what shall we give the mother?" asked Ah Jee. "We should give her some food to nourish her *yang*, to give her energy."

Glaring at Ah Jee, Su Hei replied, "Are you telling me what and what not to do. *Mui Chai* had a child recently. Did she have chicken, wine and ginger? Of course not! She had salted duck egg and rice gruel. She survived. So what's so special about Mei Yin? These are unusual times. We're short of food and the war's not over."

After Ah Jee left, Su Hei sat thinking. The more she thought, the angrier she became. "All my effort and it comes to nothing. The girl should go back to her duties, digging and washing. That is all she is good for. At least we will get something back for the good food we have wasted on her these past months. Her mother must go. I can't stand the woman. Her eyes are always following me accusingly as though I have done something wrong."

Mei Yin, who had expected a boy, was just as disappointed. She had sat enthralled during the last few months, listening to her mother-in-law outline the future of a first-born grandson. "And you, my daughter-in-law, you will receive every comfort during the month of confinement; Ah Jee will give you hot herbal baths and cook you special foods. Pig trotters stewed in black vinegar and chicken braised in rice wine are a must to build up your strength. We'll celebrate with a wonderful dinner when my grandson reaches full moon." Young and impressionable, Mei Yin had believed it all.

As she held her baby who had been so rudely thrust back at her, Mei Yin could not hold back tears of disappointment. She had always been told how beautiful babies were. No one had prepared her for a newborn baby who looked old and wrinkled; with blurry eyes and a nose so bulbous, it looked like a red onion. "A girl, and an ugly one," she had reported to her mother.

"Come, come, stop your tears. It will affect your milk. You will pass your distress onto the baby. You are just being silly. You can try again, you are still so young. You have a whole life ahead of you." Her mother stroked Mei Yin's head as she continued, "The baby is beautiful; just wait and see. In a couple of weeks, you will see things completely differently. See how her little fingers clutch and hold onto yours. Have you thought of a name for her?"

"No," was the despondent reply.

"Then think of one. I will leave for Malacca as soon as Ming Kong returns. Your father needs me. You will have to be strong." Sook Ping made no mention of her sharp exchange of words with her mother-in-law a few hours earlier.

Su Hei had summoned her to the sitting room. In a voice that barely concealed her contempt, she had said, "There is no easy way to say this. You know how things are. Everything is in short supply. I cannot afford to feed another mouth. I have arranged for you to go home." There was no suggestion of regret or apology, just a dismissive nod.

Sook Ping was completely taken aback by the rudeness. She had put aside her hurt at not being informed of Mei Yin's marriage, of being duped and cut-off from her. She had been prepared to let bygones be bygones when, two months ago, Su Hei asked for her help. "*Chen-kah*," she had said then, "Times are hard and we cannot find anyone to care for Mei Yin during the first month of confinement. It would be wonderful if you could come from Malacca to help and, of course, it would make Mei Yin so happy." Such sweet words then, such rudeness now. It was the last straw for Sook Ping. She slammed her palms down on the table. "You have no manners and no heart. You insult my daughter, you insult my family. Who are you to speak to me in this way? What were you before you married into the Ong family? Nothing! I will not have my daughter bullied and insulted by the likes of you. We have our pride. My daughter and grand-daughter will leave with me."

The two women glared at each other, each refusing to give way. Sook Ping stormed out of the room to return to her daughter's bedside. She knew that daughter and child could not leave with her; Ming Kong would never allow it. Her threats were empty. She sighed. At least she had said what she had long wanted to say and had the pleasure of seeing fear in Su Hei's face. If Mei Yin were to leave with her, Su Hei would have to face the wrath of her son as well as of her husband and his first wife.

* * * * *

Rifling through the thick files with one hand and jotting down figures with the other, Ming Kong spoke over his shoulder to Foong Yee. "Please try one more time to phone the house? The baby is due any moment and I want to be there when the time comes. This morning when I tried to call, the line was dead. The phone never works when you need it. You have to try and try, but I just cannot spare the time. I have to finish this before I leave for home."

Foong Yee had been a great help to Ming Kong. In theory, he still worked for The Orient, but, with the company at a complete standstill and its future uncertain, he had volunteered to help Ming Kong sort out the accounts at his father's firm. When Foong Yee arrived at the office that morning, he had found his former boss slumped over the desk fast asleep. Ming Kong had spent the night trying to finish his work so that he could spend some days at home.

There was much more to be done than he had envisaged. Most of the files and accounts were missing and, as a result, he could make little sense of what remained.

"I just don't know what to do," he admitted ruefully. "The company's survival depends on getting the financial records right. We have to be able to collect the outstanding payments from our clients if we are to put it back on its feet once the war is over."

"I don't think we will have to wait much longer. Apparently six months ago the Americans destroyed most of the Japanese fighter planes on the Marianas Islands. Now they are forcing the Japs to retreat in the Philippines. Soon, it will be our turn to force them out."

"We don't have much time to clear up this mess then!" Perhaps the family had been right to ask him to come to the office. He did not want to leave home the previous day, but his mother had insisted. "It is bad luck to be in the birthing chamber. Keep away, keep away."

In the end he had agreed to leave only because everyone assured him it was too early to start worrying. "It is not time yet," they had said. "The first child always takes a long time to come. We will send someone to tell you. Your father's business needs you at this moment and you will only be in the way here. Besides, Mei Yin's mother is taking care of her."

Seated now in the basement of the office block surrounded by piles of files and rubble, he regretted that he had allowed himself to be persuaded.

"The line is still dead," announced Foong Yee. "You will never get a connection. Go home. I will take over. Just tell me what to do. Go on. If nothing is happening at home, you can always come back."

* * * * *

Apart from the ubiquitous presence of the Japanese military, the road was practically deserted as he cycled home. The few civilians who were around scurried along, head down to avoid attention. The eerie calm was completely different from the hustle and bustle of former days when it had been the business centre of the city. Buildings that had once housed great international corporations stood deserted, dirty and dilapidated. Broken windowpanes left the interiors exposed to the elements, blinds flapped in the turbulent breezes of the late afternoon. Many of the buildings had been looted. Potholes pitted the surface of the road. Scrawny dogs foraged furtively amongst the rubbish.

Run-down and neglected though it might be, the city was still far from finished. It was rather a city in waiting, waiting to return to its former glory. Ming Kong could feel it in his bones. Despite the vigilant clampdown on news, most people knew that the Japanese were losing ground. Information was slow to filter through. The defeat of the Japanese in the Marianas six months ago was known only now. When the news first arrived, many doubted its authenticity, believing it to be MPAJA propaganda. Ming Kong did not share these doubts; he believed the tide had turned.

After the first year of the Occupation, his father had suffered a severe nervous breakdown. He managed to pull himself together to work for Ming Kong's release, but the recovery proved short-lived. Within weeks of his son's rescue from the Japanese, he had lost his newfound energy. Ming Kong's first mother entreated Ming Kong to take over the family business and do what he could. He worked hard but doubted whether he would be able to recoup much of what was owed. He would have to be satisfied if he could get together enough capital to restart the business. It was in a bad state. The plantations were completely overgrown after three years of neglect. The Japanese had requisitioned most of the assets and inflation had devalued the rest. It was hard and would get harder, he knew.

Ming Kong had just reached the sharp bend by the bridge near the house when he caught sight of Nelly standing by the road. He came to a halt beside her. A horrible sense of foreboding descended on him as he realised she was waiting for him. "Is anything wrong?" he asked, dreading the reply.

"No, I mean yes. I thought I'd better warn you."

He grabbed her by the hand. "Is it Mei Yin? Is she alright?"

"She is fine, but you have a baby girl," answered Nelly.

"Why but? That's wonderful," he cried, giving her a resounding kiss.

"I knew that's what you would think, but your mother is very upset. She has had a terrible row with Mei Yin's mother who would like to see you before you see your mother. We have to be quiet and meet her at the back door. Mei Yin doesn't know about the quarrel. She is very tired and is resting."

Nelly looked at him, his happiness could not conceal his fatigue.

"You are wonderful, Nelly. I don't know what I'd do without you," he said warmly as he cycled off. Nelly looked with yearning at his departing figure, overwhelmed with the emotion of the moment. She had become, she realised with a heart-rending finality, just a pillar of support to be used, relied on and taken for granted.

* * * * *

Ming Kong left his bicycle by the bamboo grove, skirted around and behind the fence into his neighbour's plot and then clambered through a gaping hole in the fence into his mother's backyard watched by the bemused neighbours.

"Something must be wrong," they decided, seeing Ming Kong take such a devious route home. "All that shouting this morning after Mei Yin's baby was born. Ah Jee is going around with a face like sour plums. When I tried talking to her, she just shook her head and muttered under her breath."

"I heard it's a girl. That is why. There will be trouble," the couple whispered to each other even as they were waving him on.

Ming Kong's meeting with Sook Ping was brief. She told him of the quarrel and her worries that Mei Yin would be ill-treated. "I have to go. I have already out-stayed my welcome and I don't want to add to my daughter's list of wrong-doings by remaining."

She took hold of her son-in-law's hands. "The only way that the three of you can be a family is to get away from this place."

* * * * *

Ming Kong made his way into the kitchen, through the dining room and into the living quarters. He was seething with anger. When he passed his mother's room, he only just managed to control an impulse to march in and have it out with her. He reminded himself that he had to have his priorities right. He moved on to Mei Yin's bedroom.

She was asleep. Beside her bed was a little cot made of *bangkuang* matting. His lips formed into a smile; he recalled the hours Mei Yin had spent making it. Inside it, also asleep, was the baby. The room was quiet except for the soft regular sound of his wife's breathing. She looked pale, her forehead and upper lip were moist with perspiration; strands of hair clung wet against her neck. He sat down on the bed close to the cot. Gently he extended his little finger down into the cot and placed it against his daughter's tightly closed, dimpled fist. The tiny fingers unfurled and closed tightly on the finger. He felt his chest tighten with emotion. In that moment, he fell in love with his daughter.

Mei Yin stirred, woken up by the movement. "You're back," she smiled. "I'm sorry, it's a girl."

"What a silly and terrible thing to say. The baby is so beautiful. I am happy it's a girl." He reached for a towel and began drying her tears. He kissed her and stroked her head. Easing a pillow behind her back, he helped her to sit up. His ministrations were interrupted by a loud cry from the baby.

"She needs her feed. Pass her to me. Mother told me that babies are hungry all the time. Certainly this is one hungry baby. I fed her less than three hours ago."

Handing the baby over, he said, "Your mother has left." Dipping a hand into his pocket, he drew out a small red packet. Inside was a little gold anklet with a tiny bell. "She said this is for the baby when she reaches her first moon."

Mei Yin held the anklet in her palm. "This was my mother's and my grandmother's. It has been passed from generation to generation. I wore it when I was small. My mother said it was useful because she always knew where I was and it kept me out of mischief." Pausing, she glanced out of the window and sighed. "We'll have to find a name for our baby. Do you like the name An Mei? My mother and I discussed it. The name means peace, tranquillity and beauty. Shall I propose it to your mother to see if she approves?"

Su Hei had already entered the room unnoticed. "Huh," she snorted. "You do not have to consult me. Why pretend? I am not important. You have already decided. The child certainly needs a pretty name to make up for its ugliness. If I were you, I'd concentrate on getting another baby. This time, be sure it's a boy."

Before they could reply, she left the room. It was months before Su Hei could bring herself to speak to her daughter-in-law.

* * * * *

Kai Min was sitting in the kitchen with Mei Yin, watching her bottle-feed An Mei. It was quiet in the house, so quiet that the sucking of the baby could be heard. Su Hei was asleep in her room. Ah Jee was taking a break in the backyard. She had both feet up on a stool and her back rested against the cane chair on which she was sat. Kai Min could see that she had nodded off in the heat of the day. As Ah Jee's jaw slackened, her mouth dropped open. She began to snore softly. Her chest rose and fell in a regular rhythm.

"Mei Yin, please try to keep peace with my mother," Kai Min urged. "She is unreasonable, she is old-fashioned. We all agree with you. But the tension is beginning to tell on my brother. When I saw him last, he looked really tired and fed-up. He told me he wants to leave and set up home somewhere else, but his hands are tied. He has obligations to Father who is getting frailer by the minute and, in any case, there are no jobs to be found. After the war, things will change. Until then, try not to rock the boat."

Kai Min was holding her own baby, also a girl who had been born just a week after An Mei. Kai Min had married soon after Mei Yin. Happy and contented in her marriage, she had grown plump.

Her husband, Wong Tek San, a local merchant, was 11 years her senior. Before the war he had built up a large stock of soya beans. After the Japanese invasion he began using them to produce bean curd in his own house, delivering it to the Japanese as well as locals. According to Foong Yee, who had his ear firmly to the ground, his connections might also have contributed to Ming Kong's release by the Japanese.

Ming Kong was not happy about his brother-in-law's business dealings with the Japanese and they had exchanged strong words. Kai Min had been very upset by the argument and sought Mei Yin's help in bringing the two men and their families back together again.

"If Tek San did not sell his *do fu* to the Japanese, someone else would," Mei Yin had said to her husband. "He is not doing wrong. This way, he also helps to feed others. Look, because of him, we are able to get more food than otherwise."

The renewal of Mei Yin's friendship with Kai Min eased Mei Yin's life. Su Hei had been serious when she said Mei Yin should be given rice gruel and nothing else. Su Hei was like a hawk. Anticipating that both Ah Jee and Nelly would disobey orders, she kept all the food under lock and key, and closely monitored the supplies.

A strange turn of events eventually rescued Mei Yin from her plight.

Just a week after An Mei was born, Mei Yin received an urgent message from Kai Min. She was desperate. She had been unable to breast-feed her newborn baby. "Can you please come. I have tried over and over again, but I just do not have enough milk in me and we cannot get hold of any powdered milk. We have combed the entire city and we could not find a single tin."

For four months, Mei Yin breast-fed both her own and Kai Min's daughter. Su Hei's food restrictions were lifted and magically, thanks to Kai Min's husband, food hardly ever seen in the market, including, eventually, powdered milk, became available to the household.

"Won't you try to make peace with Mother? For the sake of my brother, please," repeated Kai Min.

Mei Yin put down the empty bottle, dried An Mei's lips and patted her back until she burped. She took some time to reply and when she did, she offered little hope of a solution. "I have tried so hard, but your mother will not speak or even look at me. Until I have a baby boy, I don't stand a chance of changing her views. I am tired of trying."

With two babies to feed and little sleep at night, Mei Yin found it difficult to do her share of the household chores. Where there had once been three domestic staff, a gardener and a driver, who also helped with the heavier work, there was now only Ah Jee and she was already doing more than most would or could. Nelly's time was taken up almost completely by her mother-in-law. She fetched, carried, listened to Su Hei's complaints and rubbed and massaged her aches. She helped with the washing, but she was not always available to scrub, boil, dry and fold the never-ending pile of nappies several times a day.

"An Mei needs changing about 20 times a day. I have only four nappies," said Mei Yin. "With the heat, she gets nappy rash if she is not changed. Sometimes, I feel at my wits' end."

One of Mei Yin's failures, remarked upon repeatedly by her mother-in-law, was the vegetable plot. Weeds sprouted, nourished by the rain and sun, and choked the seedlings. Su Hei greeted the few leaves that she managed to harvest for the daily meal with derision. "What use is a handful of green leaves? Just a waste of cooking oil. There is not even enough to get caught between my teeth."

Stung by the outburst, Mei Yin had slung An Mei on her back, as she had seen farmers do, and tried to hoe and water the plot under the blazing sun. The baby fretted and cried. Mei Yin became so distressed that she felt like throttling her. She confessed to Kai Min that sometimes she wished she had not had An Mei, who seemed to have brought her nothing but sadness and retribution.

* * * * *

Nelly sat very still, not wishing to disturb An Mei who was fast asleep. The baby had been fretful earlier in the night. Fearful she would disturb the household, Mei Yin had brought her to the kitchen. She had paced up and down to calm her. She had rocked her and sung lullabies, all to no effect. An Mei's face was screwed up, flushed and red in her determination to bawl and protest.

"What's wrong? I have fed, changed and cuddled you. I could shake you," she admonished. Finally, exhausted, she had sought Nelly's help. Thrusting the crying infant at her, she said, "You can have her. I hate her. I can't stop her crying. I am absolutely tired out. Take her away or I will not be responsible for my actions."

In Nelly's arms, the child had calmed down almost immediately. Nelly held her gently and sung her a soft lullaby. Within a short while, An Mei was asleep sucking her thumb.

Mei Yin was astonished at the change. "There, you see, she is better with you, so have her if you want. I am past caring."

The sleeping baby looked like a little angel. Wet lashes lay like fans on her pink cheeks. Suddenly, Mei Yin felt an overwhelming sense of jealousy. She almost snatched her baby back, but she stopped herself. It was far better she decided to take this chance to go back to Ming Kong.

Nelly waited until Mei Yin had left. She kissed An Mei. Whispering softly to her, she said, "I wish you were mine. I would do anything to have you. Your mother is a silly girl not to see what a treasure you are. Never mind. Sleep, my little An Mei, sleep."

Until that moment, Nelly had steadfastly avoided having close contact with the baby. She was afraid that she might reveal her feelings. It was fate, she reasoned, that she should have An Mei.

* * * * *

Nelly was up early the following morning. She brought An Mei into the kitchen and placed her in the little makeshift cot she had made. She had lined a big basket with an old cotton *sarong*. Humming a tune under her breath, she began to prepare a thin gruel for the baby. She took a tiny ladle of rice grains and washed them before putting them into a small pot. Then she added water and placed the pot on the stove. She added a few spinach leaves. She had just taken a small handful of dried anchovies, which she was about to soak to remove the salt, when Mei Yin came in.

Mei Yin lost no time. "I didn't mean what I said last night. I was exhausted. I don't want to give away my baby," she said. "I'm sorry."

Nelly stopped what she was doing for a moment and then carried on with renewed vigour, soaking, squeezing and rinsing the anchovies as though her life depended on it. A lump formed in her throat; she felt her nose fill and prickle. "Of course," she replied. "I didn't believe it for a moment, but if you do need help with An Mei at any time just ask me. I am cooking her food. If you like, I will feed her before I go to *Nai-nai*?"

"Yes, yes please." Placing a finger on her lips, Mei Yin said, almost as an after-thought, "In fact, if you don't mind looking after her for the day, I would like to go with Ming Kong to help sort out some of the rooms in *Loh Yeh's* office. We have so little time together, any excuse to be with him is good enough for me. I am sure *Nai-nai* will not object because I will be put to work, as she puts it."

Nelly nodded her agreement. Mei Yin threw her arms round Nelly. "Thank you! Thank you!"

"*Tai mn tow*," remarked Ah Jee coming into the kitchen with sticks for the stove. Shaking her head, she repeated, "So immature."

As soon as Mei Yin had left, Ah Jee remarked heavily, "Mark my words, soon you will be taking over the care of that baby completely."

"I don't mind."

"Huh! Wait till the baby is thrust on you night after night. Master dotes on the baby and insists that someone goes to her the moment she cries. You will be the one who will have to go in the future. If you do it once, you will be expected to do it always. The young mistress is still a child at heart and like a child she wants to play. *Nai-nai* takes it out on her and then she takes it out on the baby. I do not know where right ends and wrong begins."

"Really it is not a problem for me." Humming again, Nelly busied herself, cooking the food for the baby and preparing her mother-in-law's breakfast.

Chapter 20

The small room was crowded with people. There were many more there than Ming Kong had expected. All the doors and windows were closed; the only light came from a small kerosene lamp hung from a beam. The room was stifling. Ming Kong pushed forward to address the gathering when a buzz of excitement rose. A man, his tee shirt, discoloured with age, sweat and grime, stood up, pre-empting him. The man's eyes sparkled with jubilation. He lifted a hand to get attention, "Okinawa has been invaded by the Americans."

The news was greeted with enthusiasm. "Thank God. It's been exactly 40 months since the Japanese arrived. I have been counting each day," said one man.

"Feels like a lifetime," said another man standing beside him.

"How do you know?" demanded Ming Kong. Even before the speaker could reply, he turned to Foong Yee, "Who is he? I haven't seen him before. Who are all these people?"

He was worried. He had asked Foong Yee to arrange a meeting with a select few of his father's former employees. He wanted to discuss how to restart the business once the war ended. Ming Kong had no doubt the end was near.

"Don't worry," Foong Yee replied. "I invited them." He pointed to the speaker. "He is safe. He's not MPAJA, if that's what you are thinking. The Japanese massacred his entire family, apart from his grandmother who survived after being left for dead. Since then he has been operating his own guerrilla warfare with the support of a few others in a similar position. It's not politics, just revenge. And this is the right time for revenge. Okinawa has gone under. Even as we speak, the Japs are retreating from the Pacific."

"You idiot!" Ming Kong had never lost his temper with Foong Yee before. He was alarmed and angry that his assistant could put his family and others at risk by organising such a meeting under his roof. This was not what he had intended. "I don't like this, Foong Yee. I do not want him or any other of the unfamiliar faces here. The Japanese might be facing defeat elsewhere, but they are still very much in control here. They can be very vicious to anyone who opposes them."

He made no effort to conceal his anger as he spat out his next words. "Don't you realise? Even if he is not from the MPAJA, he will be treated as if he is. All of us would be implicated. In any case, how do you know he is not with the MPAJA?"

"What is wrong with that anyway? Where would the Chinese in Malaya be without the liberation army? In fact, where would the British be without them? It is the British who trained and armed them. I just don't understand you, Ming Kong," Foong Yee retorted. "In any case, what harm is there in letting him tell us about the Japanese defeat? You are blowing it up out of all proportion. We'll be okay. We've been going in and out of here for the past couple of months without any problems. The soldiers are so used to it, they have given up checking on us."

Ming Kong ignored his former assistant. An excited babble had risen following the announcement. He rose to silence them. "I am sorry. This meeting is over. There has been a change of plans. Everyone please leave quietly and discreetly, one at a time. During the coming weeks, I will get in touch, personally, with every one of you who used to work for my father. I would like, in particular, those who have no connection with the family business to leave. You have no place here."

"As for you," he said, turning to Foong Yee, "I don't want to see you here again or anywhere near my family." He turned away, ignoring his assistant's efforts to speak to him, and beckoned the others to follow.

Opening the door carefully, he peered out into the night. It was dark and quiet, apart from the distant barking of dogs. A Japanese soldier stood guard about 150 yards away. He was facing the other buildings. He had stood his rifle on the ground leaning it against his leg. Thin curls of cigarette smoke spiralled from his lips, creating an eerie halo above his head.

"Quick, one at a time. Take different directions and routes."

When the last of the men had vanished into the night, he heaved a sigh of relief. He locked up and made his way to his father and first mother's house. He pushed his bicycle slowly across the bridge, bowing his head in a show of respect to the sentry before cycling slowly away. The sentry did not ask for his curfew pass, a pass his brother-in-law had obtained in return for the help Mei Yin had given to his wife. Ming Kong had gone this way every day for some time; the sentries had got to know him. Even so, by the time he reached his first mother's home, his shirt was wet with sweat and he found himself shivering.

* * * * *

He leaned his bicycle against the porch. Making his way up the steps to the house, he noticed yet again how dilapidated everything had become. The stone steps were chipped; part of the stone balustrade had collapsed and fallen to the ground. The once proud stone lion that guarded the entrance to the house was now a forlorn headless body. Leaves had collected on the verandah where, in his childhood, he had spent so many hours listening to his first mother's stories. With the rain and heat, the leaves had rotted to a carpet of mulch. A malodorous smell of decay rose as he walked over them. There was no one to sweep them away.

"I took so much for granted in the old days. I never considered the upkeep of the place. It will take months to put right," he thought.

Letting himself in, he went in search of *Tai-mah*, his first mother. She was with Ah Keng, her maid, and one of her granddaughters in the second sitting room in the west wing. His step-sisters had moved back to the house bringing their children with them. Both of them had lost their husbands in the war.

"*Tai-mah*." She looked up, saw him and immediately broke into a broad smile. Her normally neat bun, encased in a tortoiseshell with a pin, was askew. Hastily, she tidied her hair and invited him to sit down. "Your little niece has been playing with my hair. She wants to practise hairdressing. It's so boring for the children these days. They can't play in the garden and have to stay indoors all day. So I let them get away with a little nonsense. How is the family, how is An Mei?"

"Well, very well, thank you. An Mei is fine. You don't need to apologise about your hair. I only wish my own mother could be as relaxed as you."

She blushed with pleasure.

"I would like to speak to you before I see Father."

Hearing this, Ah Keng gathered the toddlers together, "Say bye-bye to Uncle, we will go into the kitchen to see if the cat is there. Bye now."

Ming Kong sat down and moved his chair closer to his *tai-mah*. "I have good news. The Americans have invaded Okinawa. Soon the war will be over. Unfortunately, the news on the business is far from good. I need to speak with you first because I am afraid my news could upset Father and make him worse. How is he feeling?"

"He is asleep now. He sleeps badly. He is fretting. He complains of stomach pains. He can't eat and suffers from constant headaches. I am afraid he is not getting any better."

"I have got the office records more or less straight. I've only been able to recover about half the files on our client accounts. The rest have been burnt, lost or vandalised. What remains is still a sizeable amount. If we could call in all this debt and if the currency is not devalued further, we should be able to re-start our business although on a much smaller scale than before. Unfortunately, I doubt whether we'll be able to collect much of the money owed us. Most of our former clients have suffered similar misfortunes to us. Do you know if Father has any cash or assets that could be easily sold to raise cash?"

"I don't know. We have this house and the house in Sun Chuen. We have the rubber and palm oil plantations in Johore and Perak, the tin mines in Selangor and the office block where you have been working and the buildings used to house workers on the estates. He had share holdings, but he kept the certificates in his office safe. I have nothing here, except some jewellery."

"The safe has been blown open. There's nothing left inside. It looks like we have assets, but we do not have the cash to put them back to work. The plantations are overgrown and the workers dispersed. From what I gather, most of the machinery has fallen into disrepair; the trucks and lorries are broken down and rusting. The tin mines are nothing more than gaping holes in the ground. Of course, we could sell some of these holdings to raise cash, but the price of everything is rock bottom at present. Anyway who wants to trade for Japanese currency? It could easily be worthless in a few months' time. Look at Indonesia, you need a cart load of their currency to buy anything at all."

They sat in gloomy silence until Suet Ping murmured, "My jewellery might come in handy for raising cash. I don't think, however, that we should say anything to your father at the moment. Nothing can be done now. It is not as though the war is over. We can only try to get as much as possible sorted out so that we can move quickly when the opportunity arises. We have time."

"Oh, one other thing, *Tai-mah*. I have severed all connections with Foong Yee. He cannot be trusted and I am suspicious about his politics. Don't have anything to do with him, don't see him if he comes here and don't let him get to Father."

* * * * *

Hoots of laughter and shouts of joy rippled through the crowd gathered at Sun Chuen's market square. Men, women, old and young waved, some clapped their hands and stamped their feet, children ran helter-skelter. Bicycle bells rang across the surrounding fields. "The Japs have surrendered! The war is over! Remember this day 15th August 1945 forever!"

In Ming Kong's household, there was a double cause for joy and celebrations. Mei Yin was expecting her second child. Five months into her pregnancy, she found herself reconciled once again with her mother-in-law.

"*Ai yah*, I have prayed hard and long. This time I am sure it will be a boy. Already he is bringing us luck, the war is over and he will be born in a year of peace. I told you *Kah-soh* that if you gave up your baby girl, that *sooi nooi pow*, everything will be alright," Su Hei said. "What use is a bun of misfortune to us?"

In effect An Mei had been given over to Nelly. The possibility that Mei Yin could be carrying a boy meant that nothing must disturb her constitution in case it caused a miscarriage. She was told not to carry anything heavy. That included An Mei. Born in the year of the Monkey, prone to tears, and, according to Ah Kew, destined to be a wilful child, she was to be avoided at all cost.

After the War

Chapter 21

Letter in hand, Ming Kong rushed into the room. "I've got it, I've got the job." He laughed, tossing the document from hand to hand. "With this, we have a chance to wait out this economic crisis. We will leave for Singapore this week."

"Wonderful!" said Mei Yin. She smiled a broad and delighted smile that lit up her whole face.

"What? What do you mean?" asked Su Hei, who until this point had been happily tickling the baby in Mei Yin's arms.

"I mean we are leaving. Mei Yin, Nelly, the children and I."

"What about me?" Su Hei wailed. Turning sharply to glare at Mei Yin, she jabbed her finger at her. "You! It's all your doing. You must have put him up to this."

"Of course she hasn't, Mother! Be reasonable, what choice do we have? It's been a year since the Japanese left and we still cannot make any headway in rebuilding the business. My time is taken up queuing for rice; the ration hardly covers our needs. Meanwhile we have no cash to re-start the business. The plantations are overgrown, the tin mines remain shut. What do you expect me to do?"

"Anything but this," retorted Su Hei.

"Anything? You say anything when you would not sell your jewellery to help raise cash," asked Ming Kong, eyes wide with the incredulous answer his mother had given him.

"What about Wei Han?" Su Hei rushed forward and snatched the baby boy from Mei Yin's arms. "I will not be able to see him." She hugged and kissed the baby and turned her back to Mei Yin.

"It's only for two years. I promise. I'll work hard, save hard and come back. By that time I hope the country's infra-structure will be sufficiently recovered for us to get the plantations and mines back into production." He went over to his mother and said softly and gently, "Come, come. How else can it be done? The salary is good and will reduce the strain we are living under."

* * * * *

Mei Yin was jubilant. "Life is wonderful, life is good," she sang as she crammed clothes and shoes into a bag. "Nelly, isn't it a stroke of luck? Aren't you excited? To leave this place, to have independence," and lowering her voice, "to be free of *Nai-nai*. My heart spills with joy." Running to Nelly, she grabbed her hand and placed it on her own heart. "See how fast my heart beats."

Nelly smiled. "Go on you. Just keep your voice down or you will upset *Nai-nai* even more.

"I don't care, I don't care," sang Mei Yin. She scooped Wei Han from the cot and hummed, "We are leaving, we are leaving. Come, come An Mei, hold my hand and let's march. Left, right, left right and out we go."

* * * * *

It was a lovely bright sunny day when they stepped out of the car and made their way to the long single-storey building.

"Is this it?" whispered Mei Yin staring at the grey, austere building with patches of paintwork peeling off. Her eyes followed the chicken wire fencing that surrounded the house and separated it from the beach and a grove of casuarina trees at the back.

"Yes! What did you expect? This is Changi Beach and this is where the Japs held prisoners of war," said Ming Kong. His face was serious and his jaw set. He did not look at Mei Yin or Nelly. "This will be our home in Singapore. A bit spartan. We have to share a communal kitchen as well as the bathroom with other families. We'll sleep, eat and play in the same room. It's all we can afford." He said this with a finality that broached no questions.

"It will be alright," consoled Nelly. "We'll make do. Won't it be fun to set up from scratch, Mei Yin? We will have fun, won't we An Mei? Let's go in and explore." Holding An Mei's hand she went into the building ahead of Ming Kong and Mei Yin who was carrying Wei Han in her arms.

"Shall we go in?" asked Ming Kong. Mei Yin nodded without enthusiasm. "I meant what I said. Our purpose here is to earn and save as much as we can so that we can go back home with money to help re-build our business. You do understand, don't you? Nelly will guide you. She'll cook and help out with An Mei. You will take care of Wei Han and share the responsibility of managing the household expenses with her."

Mei Yin nodded again.

"Well then," said Ming Kong.

* * * * *

The hawker freewheeled his bicycle into the courtyard and then screeched to a standstill. He jumped nimbly off the seat and with a flourish flipped open the lid of the basket perched on the carrier of the bicycle. "Today, we have a bit of everything, so take your pick."

Mei Yin and Nelly peered into the basket. Fish and chunks of meat were laid on blocks of ice on one side and bundles of green vegetables on the other.

"What about this snapper?" Mei Yin asked. "And some broccoli, green peppers and mushrooms."

Nelly shook her head. "Too expensive." Addressing the hawker, she said, "Just a small amount of your cheapest cut of pork and two cucumbers please."

"No Nelly. Why do we always have the cheapest cut of pork and why cucumber? It's so boring; the same dishes over and over again."

"I know. But cucumbers seem to be cheapest and, well, pork is also cheap. I'll mince it. It will be tender." Seeing Mei Yin's disappointment, she explained. "We have only two tiny stoves in the kitchen we share. With minced pork I need only one stove for all my cooking. This leaves the other free for boiling water for Ming Kong's bath when he gets back from work. I put the rice pot on the stove, then I place the plate of pork on the steaming rice. I close the lid and the steam from the rice cooks the pork. I not only save wood, I save oil too."

Mei Yin wriggled her nose. "I think we deserve a treat just once in a while."

"Come into the house. I have a surprise for you."

Nelly took the bundle of food and hurried indoors. Opening the cupboard, she foraged deep into the shelves and fished out two little books.

"Look what I have here. I got these from our neighbour. He was reading to his children and I asked if I could borrow them. He said he had finished with them and that I could have them for a fraction of the price. Here, you take them. Can you read? Can you remember the English you learnt when you were first with *Nai-nai*?"

Mei Yin smiled. "Hmmm, I'll try. I had only a few months of English tuition and then war broke out. But with these pictures I can give it a go. You are wonderful Nelly!" She took Nelly's face with both hands and gave her a resounding kiss.

Nelly blushed with pleasure. "Go, go and read to them. Enjoy yourselves. I'll prepare these," she said pointing at the meat and vegetable. "If I manage to save something extra, we'll try to get some more books from our neighbour."

* * * * *

Months into their stay, Mei Yin began taking An Mei and Wei Han out on the bus to the city. Nelly steadfastly refused to join them. "No! No I can't. You go," she would say each time Mei Yin tried to persuade her. "Why, why not come with us and get out of this place for a while?" challenged Mei Yin. Exasperated with Nelly for being so uncooperative, she said, "I won't leave you alone until you explain. It's so hard dealing with two children on my own."

"Because, because I lived in Singapore before and when I left Singapore for Malaya, I left my previous life as well. I am afraid that if I go out I might meet people who know me from old." Nelly feared meeting her previous husband as much as she longed to see her two children. But she had promised not to see them. She owed Mary, her husband's first wife, too much to make contact with her children.

"Don't be silly! What can happen with just a bus ride into town. You tell me what you want to do and I'll help you."

"You wouldn't be so sure if you knew who I am dealing with."

"Try me," challenged Mei Yin.

And Nelly told her of her previous life, of Woo Pik Soo, of her two children. "I wish, I wish with all my heart to see them. I don't even know if they are alive."

The next day both women, each holding a child, took the bus to the city. When they got down at the bus stop where Mary Woo's house had been, all they saw was rubble and makeshift huts. Squatters had moved in. Large bulldozers and diggers were busy clearing away the war damage.

Nelly, heart heavy and expecting the worst, went to speak to one of the drivers. "Do you know what happened to the people who used to live here?"

He scratched his head and paused to wipe the sweat from his forehead. He shrugged. "I don't know. Ask her." He pointed to an elderly woman, squatting by the path next to one of the makeshift huts.

Nelly walked over to the lady. "Can you please help me? I have friends who lived in house number 41, over there. Do you know what happened to them?"

"Forty-one," she repeated, gazing at the pile of rubble where the houses had been. "You know, I'm not sure. This area was badly bombed because it was close to the city centre. They might have left before the bombing, but they could just as easily have been caught up by the blitz."

"They had two children, a boy and a girl. Perhaps you knew their servant, Ah Kuk?"

"Ah Kuk, oh why didn't you say? She and I were good friends. We used to go to the market together. That family was one of the lucky ones. They moved out just before the bombing and went to live with a relative in Johore. Ah Kuk came round just the other day. They are back in Singapore and live just two streets away."

"Is . . . is the master of the house still around?"

"No, he died even before the war. A massive heart attack. Good riddance. He was not nice. The children were terrified of him.

"Have you seen the children?"

"Yes, Ah Kuk passes here each day with them. They go to the school over there." She pointed to a building some distance away.

"Thank you, thank you." Nelly's heart began to sing.

Mei Yin and Nelly walked briskly with the children in tow in the direction of the school. Once there they stood outside its gate. Nelly's heart tightened with excitement. She ran her tongue over her lips; they felt like dried coarse sand. Time seemed to pass so slowly. Mei Yin could sense Nelly's tension. She grasped her hand reassuringly and said, "Soon, any time now." Then the school bell rang, its chime, piercing the hot humid air, startled them. They half ran into the school grounds. Children everywhere, some on their own, some with their parents. Suddenly Nelly saw Ah Kuk. She was holding the hands of two children, Chai-chai and Mei-mei! She was walking towards them. Nelly stood paralysed, unsure of her reception. Ah Kuk saw them and stopped. Chai-chai and Mei-mei looked at Nelly. There was not a flicker of recognition.

"Come on Ah Kuk, let's go. Why are we stopping? We want to go home," they said.

Nelly made a sign to Ah Kuk that she understood. She mouthed silently, "Goodbye."

Nelly stood still long after Ah Kuk had left. Her face desolate, her shoulders hunched in defeat. Mei Yin tried to console her. She held Nelly's hand tightly, but she could find no suitable words to say. They walked all the way home without a word. Once indoors, Nelly collapsed. She curled into a ball in the bed. She said and ate nothing that evening. It was the children's complete lack of recognition that broke her.

* * * * *

Two years into their stay in Changi, the family was gathered around the table set in one corner of the room.

"What is this, Mei Yin?" asked Ming Kong indicating the basket of food that she had carried in to show him.

"This, these are all the things you love to eat. Here we have some dried mushrooms, dried prawns, and this," she proudly flourished a can in her hand, "is abalone."

Ming Kong's face changed. "I said that you are to take over the shopping and the household expenses for the week. By that I expect you to buy rice, salted fish, sugar, tea and other essentials. Our mission here is to save money, not spend it on luxuries. Didn't you check how much was in the kitty before spending?"

"No. The shopkeeper says I can pay later. All I want to do is cook the food that Ah Jee taught me before. Nelly hardly cooks anything exciting. All we get is dried cuttlefish with minced pork, pickled radish, salted fish and *fen see* with cucumber. You must be sick and tired of eating dried vermicelli with cucumber surely?"

"I think, perhaps, asking you to manage the housekeeping expenses is not a good idea. I had assumed you would have learned from Nelly. She will take over again. Tell her, Nelly. Explain to her. She doesn't or refuses to understand and I have neither the time nor the inclination to explain. I have too much to do as it is."

Ming Kong was cross. He thought Mei Yin had become too independent, too strong-willed. He recalled their argument over the children's schooling. He fumed. Imagine questioning his decision not to let them attend a Chinese school. "The political situation is just too grave," he had explained when Mei Yin suggested sending An Mei to a Chinese school because it was nearer the house.

"It is only for now. The English school is miles away," Mei Yin had said.

"Yes, but what is the point of a Chinese education? The entire curriculum revolves around China. I warn both of you not to fill my children with ideas of attending Chinese schools. I am proud of my Chinese origin, but we belong here in Malaya. In any case, Chinese schools are not places to be at the moment. You are ignorant of what is happening outside this house. The schools are suspected of having connections with the Malayan Communist Party. Sending the children to a Chinese school, even kindergarten, could be taken to imply that we are in sympathy with China and the Communists."

Mei Yin had retorted, "Most people in Singapore are Chinese. How can you avoid Chinese when everyone speaks it. It doesn't mean we want to go back to China or that we support its politics. In any case, I only suggested it as a temporary measure before they start school properly."

"Be said!" Ming Kong had retorted.

Ming Kong sat, still mulling over these recollections, switching from them to the news he wanted to break to his family when he heard Mei Yin's voice from across the room. "If you say so. Nelly can take over the house-keeping again." She looked defiant and hurt.

Ming Kong got up from his seat, jolted from his thoughts back to the present. "I have to leave for Kuala Lumpur. I had wanted to tell all of you earlier until I got side-tracked," he glared at Mei Yin. "Father is dying. I have to return to Kuala Lumpur. By the time I return, you should be ready to leave Singapore. We are going home."

Chapter 22

In the first few months following their return to Kuala Lumpur, they stayed with Su Hei. Mei Yin was devastated, but she was unable to talk to Ming Kong. He had little time for anything beyond the business of consolidating the estate he had inherited.

"Wait! Please, I have too much on my mind. I can guess what you want to tell me, but nothing can be done for now. We will just have to put up with staying here. I'll speak to you once I have spoken to Tek San. I have arranged to meet him and Kai Min at First Mother's house. Keep this to yourselves."

* * * * *

The ceiling lamp shone dimly down casting a yellow circular glow over the people gathered around the coffee table. At one end of the room, a stand fan whirled. It was a warm and sticky night. Ming Kong sat facing Tek San and Kai Min. Suet Ping sat to one side.

Tek San who had done well during the war continued to prosper after it ended. Taking advantage of low property prices and the easy availability of cheap labour after the war, he had built a chain of small factories producing prepared foods and plimsolls. Ming Kong looked at his brother-in-law and then at his sister. He saw the easy manner in which Tek San sat, arms around the back of Kai Min's chair, his legs stretched out and ankles crossed. A tightness rose in his chest. He just could not forgive Tek San' for his dealings with the Japanese. He looked at Kai Min, his favourite sister, and his heart softened. They were waiting for him to speak. Yet he hesitated. Suddenly he leaned forward, clasped his hands between his knees and looking straight into Kai Min's eyes said, "I am going to sell the house in Sun Chuen."

Kai Min gasped. "You can't do that. Mother will not allow, I mean, like it. It will break her heart. Where will she live?"

"Yes, I know. I have not told her of my decision. I wanted to discuss it with you both first. I'd like to know if you would be interested in buying the house before I put it on the market. If you buy the house, it will be easier for her. The house will stay in the family and you will have made a sound purchase." Ming Kong knew Tek San was looking for a bigger house for his growing family and that Kai Min was attached to the house where she had grown up.

Tek San said nothing. Turning to his wife, he saw her agitation.

"The house is well located. You could probably buy the neighbours out to expand the property. In any case, two of the adjoining plots belong to us and could be included. It is a good investment, one I would have kept if I could," Ming Kong added.

Kai Min interrupted, "But where will Mother go?"

"Here, to First Mother's house, at least initially."

"There is no room," she countered. "She would hate it."

"Yes, there is no room," Suet Ping agreed quickly. "It's impossible."

"I know it will be difficult for you *Tai-mah*, but it will not be forever, I promise. But first lets see whether Tek San wants to buy the house before we think of what follows."

Tek San had kept quiet so far. He agreed with most of what Ming Kong had said. It should be a good investment. Its location was ideal in a city about to expand. Moreover, his wife loved the house. He replied, "I see your point. I will have to think about it."

"Don't take too long. I do not have much time. In fact, I would really like to settle the matter quickly. It is only fair to warn you that I have already received an approach. I have also been given an indication of what might be offered even though I have not spoken to anyone about selling the house."

"Who has approached you?" Tek San was suspicious that it might be a ploy to put pressure on him to buy.

"The Orient. Its old offices are a mess and, rather than try to renovate them, the company would like to cross to this side of the river and start afresh. They have decided that it is more economical to buy new land and build the kind of offices that they want."

"What did they offer?" Tek San asked. He tucked his legs under the chair and leaned forward, his easy stance abandoned, the amused twinkle in his eyes replaced by an alert glint.

"It is not a problem. You don't have to buy it. I'm only thinking of Kai Min and her love for the house and, of course, the pleasure Mother would get from having her daughter own it. She would hate to see the house flattened to make way for an office block. On second thoughts, I probably did not think it through. The price is probably well out of your range. Let's leave it."

"Come on, you know I want to have the house if I can. Tell me."

Ming Kong leaned over and whispered. Tek San's eyes widened, he gasped. Leaning back on his chair, he thought for a while, looked first at his wife and then down at his hands as if counting with his fingers. Finally, he nodded. "Done," he said. "I will buy it."

"Wait a moment. What if The Orient makes a better offer? Will you match it? I will not negotiate with them, but I would be surprised if they do not offer more when I turn them down." Ming Kong's face gave nothing away, he was enjoying Tek San's unease.

"How could you haggle with us. This is not fair," Kai Min protested, shocked to see her brother striking such a hard bargain with her husband.

"Don't interfere, your husband can take care of himself. The money is not for me. I have to think of the others involved, including Mother, and do the best I can. Really, we are not talking so much about the house as the land it sits on. I am sure Tek San knows as well as I do that it is worth much more."

"I would have difficulties bettering the offer by much. My capital is tied up in the factories," said Tek San.

This time Ming Kong sat back. He pondered for a while, then said, "Alright, for Kai Min's sake, I will agree to the price just mentioned plus a share of your factories. The share will reflect the difference between The Orient's final bid and your offer."

Tek San hesitated. This was not a simple deal. He had to think fast.

Seeing the uncertainty on his face, Ming Kong continued, "It's a very reasonable proposal. You don't pay the difference up front in cash; you pay when you draw profits from the factories."

"Can we set a ceiling on the difference?"

"Well, like Kai Min said, we are family. I'll consider it."

Ming Kong was satisfied. Selling to Tek San and Kai Min made it easier for him to tell his mother. More important it would give him the cash he needed to restart the estate he had inherited and a share in Tek San's business, which, if it did well, would allow him to keep on track with the growing economy. Food was good business in a country that had suffered so long from shortages.

* * * * *

Once Tek San and Kai Min had gone, Ming Kong turned to Suet Ping. "*Tai-mah*, I know it will be hard, but I have to ask you to let my mother live here with you once the deal has gone through."

Suet Ping's face blanched. Perhaps blanched is not the right word; even her lips turned grey. Aware that she was about to protest, he continued quickly. "Wait, please let me finish. The west wing of the house could be for her. So, she would not be in your way. My family will occupy the quarters I used to have. I know it is going to be cramped, but it will not be for long. I am thinking of selling the tin mines. With the proceeds, my savings and what is left from the sale of the house in Sun Chuen, I hope to begin salvaging the rubber plantations and to go into property development."

He paused for breath before continuing, "My family will eventually move to one of the new houses I plan to build."

"And your mother? Do you plan to leave her here?"

"If things do not work out for the two of you, I will take her with me," he promised.

There was a long pause before he spoke in a gentle voice, "This is not a good time, but there will never be a good time for what I have to say. You may eventually also have to give up your home; it too might have to be sold. We are strapped for cash. This location on one of the busiest roads in the city makes it a prime site. Obviously I am trying to find a way of raising capital without selling. But, even if I succeed, you must appreciate that the house cannot stay as it is, the only residential property in a road of commercial buildings."

"Then, what will I do?" asked Suet Ping as she gradually realised the full implications of his plans. She had not given any thoughts to her own future believing that the house would always be there for her. Even when the will confirmed that Ming Kong had inherited everything, she assumed the house would be hers in practice.

He put his arms round her shoulders and kissed the top of her head. "I will think of something. I promise I will look after you."

He was sorry. He could not think of any other way out and he did not want to create false hopes. The house was an anomaly in a business district. It would be only a matter of time before the city authorities would put pressure on them to replace it with office buildings or sell out. To comfort her, he said, "All this will probably take years to happen. You don't need to worry, leave that to me."

* * * * *

Mei Yin and Nelly were waiting in the dining room of Suet Ping's house. They had not been party to the discussions that evening. Mei Yin looked very tired. She was almost five months into her third pregnancy. Nelly was also looking worn out. The sudden departure from Singapore, the packing, then unpacking, and settling in at Su Hei's house with its rigid regime had left both women feeling disoriented. Singapore seemed like an old dream.

They looked up in anticipation when Ming Kong entered the room. His face was set and determined. Plagued for weeks by the decisions he must make, he was determined to finish with the stress of giving unwelcome news to everyone. He pointed to the sofa at the far corner of the room, "Let's go over there."

He pulled a chair towards the sofa and sat facing them. "We will be staying here with First Mother." His eyes bored into Mei Yin's. A look of relief came on her face. She dreaded the thought of going back to stay with Su Hei.

"My mother will move here as well."

"Oh no! Why?" cried out Mei Yin who could not hold back her disappointment despite a sharp nudge from Nelly.

"Why?" he glared at her, "because I say so. The house in Sun Chuen will be sold; Tek San is likely to be the buyer. Mother and Ah Jee will occupy the west wing. We will stay here. All of this will probably take some months. I am already negotiating for a piece of land where I plan to build eight bungalows. One of them will be for us. When it is ready we will move there."

Mei Yin burst into tears, they rolled down her cheeks and she rubbed them away with the back of her hands. Since her pregnancy she had become prone to weeping. Ming Kong could not stand her tears. He looked away, but could not disguise his irritation and impatience. "Grow up! We cannot always have what we want."

"Where is the new house going to be?" Nelly asked in an effort to distract Ming Kong's attention from Mei Yin's tears. "Perhaps if we show some interest in his projects he will open up and discuss them more," she thought. His once carefree attitude seemed to have disappeared completely.

"I cannot tell you because I am still negotiating to buy the land. If word were to get out that I am interested, others would try to outbid me."

"How would anyone know?" asked Mei Yin. Recovering from her tears, she also wanted to know where the family would be going.

"Well for a start, you might accidentally tell Kai Min and then she would tell her husband. It has happened before," he replied.

Mei Yin blushed. She had been scolded in the past for repeating conversations. She decided not to press the issue. Instead she comforted herself with the thought that if the arrangement was only temporary, it would not be so bad.

Ming Kong had just one more ordeal left: he had to tell his mother. The following morning, he set off for Sun Chuen. The recriminations during the meeting with his mother were lengthy. Su Hei accused him of a lack of filial respect for not telling her first and claimed that as usual his two wives had not behaved well. No wonder, he thought, as she continued her diatribe, everyone disliked so much the prospect of sharing a home with her.

Chapter 23

"This is the four o'clock news. The State of Emergency will remain in place as the country tackles the growing threat to security posed by the Communist insurgency. Two police stations came under attack yesterday. This brings the number to ten this month. The Government has announced plans to prevent people in villages close to the jungle from supplying food to the insurgents. Starting today, Lieutenant General Templar will oversee the resettlement of the following villages . . ." Ming Kong switched off the radio and went back to his desk, muttering under his breath.

"I do not know when this will end. Such bad luck that after the war has ended we should go into another crisis. It makes work in the plantations very difficult." Seeing his driver hovering in the background, he asked, "Will you come with me to Seremban? I need to check on supplies and see what progress has been made in salvaging the rubber estate. I know it is late, but this is the only time I can go."

"*Minta maaf*! Sorry! Can I be excused? It is already near finishing time. My father is ill and I need to go home," his driver replied.

Ming Kong gave a curt nod and walked out of the office towards his jeep, a half-truck that he used for visits to the countryside. He suspected the driver's excuse was a lie. He was finding it increasingly difficult to get anyone to go out to the estates, except the people who actually worked on them. He could not blame them. If he had a choice, would he risk going to the estates in this weather, he wondered. His mind switched back to his own personal problems. He was weary, so weary. The business was starting to take off. That was exciting. But he was utterly fed up with the juggling act he had to perform to keep peace between the womenfolk at home.

As he drove out of the city through the monsoon rain towards the plantations, he grimaced at the thought of the unpleasant exchanges he'd had recently with both of his mothers. Yesterday Su Hei had complained as soon as she saw him. "Mei Yin never allows Wei Han to come to see me. She keeps him to herself. She stays all day with your first mother and avoids me. She is full of airs. You allowed her too many liberties in Singapore." Then, this morning, his first mother had refused flatly to make any concessions. "If you are asking me to allow Wei Han to be dragged into this tussle between the women of this house, I refuse. I love him too much. He would be ferried to and fro and told different things in the process. It would not work. All it would do is confuse the poor boy. If I was Mei Yin, I would certainly avoid your mother. She has the sharpest and most evil of tongues."

He gritted his teeth. "That was that, but it is by no means the end," he thought, "now, they are fighting over a child who is yet to be born! On who is to name the child! And what support do I get from Mei Yin?"

He turned onto a dirt path on an unmarked strip of land. The land fanned out to join the jungle of the main mountain range to the east and extended to his rubber estate on the west. Indiscriminately cleared by its owners, the land was now covered with a riot of undergrowth, a secondary forest gone wild, ideal cover for insurgents. He stepped on the accelerator, wishing to be out of these dangerous surroundings. The jeep rushed forward through the pelting rain, bouncing on the rough track. Suddenly it jolted to a halt. He cursed. One of the wheels had gone into a huge pothole. The engine stalled as he tried to ease the jeep out of the trap. Creamy red mud flew in all directions as the wheel churned deeper and deeper into the hole. Frustrated, he turned the windscreen wipers to their fastest setting, but they were useless against the downpour; condensation clouded the inside of the windscreen.

As he sat wondering what to do next, a group of four men emerged from the gathering gloom. He gave a sigh of relief when he recognised them as estate workers returning from a day's work. The men were just as relieved when they recognised their boss's truck.

Leaning out of the window, he yelled, "I need your help. I am stuck in a pothole. Get a plank from the back and put it under the back wheel to give the tyre something to grip. *Chepat-lah*!" he shouted above the tumult of the storm. "Quick! It's not safe here!" The men immediately went to work, but it was some time before the wheel finally engaged on the wood and, with a jerk, the jeep lurched forward.

"Get in the back. I'll give you a lift home," he shouted as he revved the engine. The men jumped clear to clamber on board when a shot exploded. Out of the dark shadows emerged half a dozen men, all dressed in jungle fatigues, their rifles trained on the vehicle. "Stop," they ordered. Ming Kong responded by yelling to the men to get on as he gunned the engine and the jeep shot forward.

Everything happened quickly. The men jumped for the back of the jeep. Two got hold of the rails and catapulted into the back. The third managed to get hold of the rails, but he could not swing aboard. The fourth was shot in the leg before he could make a move. More shots followed. The truck accelerated forward. One bullet flew past Ming Kong's right ear and went through the windscreen, shattering the glass to smithereens. Another struck his shoulder. Then, came a loud yell of pain from the back when the man who was still struggling to get on board was shot in the thigh. He clung desperately to the rails. "We can't stop, we have to keep going," Ming Kong yelled through the torn perspex rear window. He did not want to leave the man who'd failed to make the truck, but he had no choice. He drove fast and furiously until he reached the police station in Seremban.

The following month, Ming Kong bought the strip of land bordering the jungle and with the protection of the local Special Constabulary cleared the forest. Having improved the security of his rubber estate, he was able to expand the plantations. He spent less and less time at home.

* * * * *

Mei Yin stared listlessly out of the window, watching the rain pelt against the windowpanes. Big fat drops ran down them making streaks of crystal liquid on the glass. The baby moved in her womb. She placed her hand protectively on her swollen belly. "Nelly, do you think Ming Kong will be back today?" she asked. "Did he tell you where he was going?"

"I don't know. We spoke only briefly before he left. He asked after An Mei and said that she should keep out of Second *Nai-nai's* way. *Yee Nai-nai* called her a *sooi nui pow* and he heard. He warned her never to call An Mei a bun of misfortune again. There was such an ugly scene."

"Did he ask after me?"

Momentarily caught off-guard, Nelly hesitated. It was sufficient for Mei Yin to surmise that he had not. Her face fell and tears brimmed over.

"He was rushed," Nelly said anxious to cover up her mistake. "I am sure that he meant to ask after you. The argument with his mother must have distracted him. But for the argument, he would have come to see you. He knew you were not well and were lying in this morning."

Mei Yin felt a surge of fury. Red heat suffused her face. She turned on Nelly. "Why do you make excuses for him? He should have no need to come to see me. He ought to be here with me. I need him. Since coming back from Singapore, I hardly get any of his time. Yet he opts to stay in the guest room complaining that my fretting at night keeps him awake. How can I not fret with this?" she said pointing to her belly. "I cannot find a comfortable position to sleep and my back aches so." She paused, narrowed her eyes and asked, "He was not with you, was he?"

"No, and you know that," smiled Nelly, amused by Mei Yin's suggestion. "He doesn't sleep with me. You know that from all the time we were in Singapore living cheek by jowl. He is just busy and tired, that's all. Come, put your feet up to relieve your ankles. They look swollen and sore."

"Thank you. I'm sorry for losing my temper and taking it out on you. I am so, so sad. Just when we had grown used to a life of relative freedom, we are back here under such harsh control that I cannot breathe. I'd rather we had not inherited the estate. Ming Kong is so changed. He is short tempered and impatient all the time. Nelly, don't you think he has changed so?"

"We all change." Nelly looked away. A shadow passed over her face. "Look at me. If we are to speak really truthfully, can you really say that he treats me as a wife? A good friend and confidante, an aunty even, but not a wife or lover. So in this at least you are better off. He loves you."

A silence fell between them. Then Nelly spoke. "When the baby is born and Ming Kong completes the construction of the eight bungalows, we'll be moving into one of them. He has promised. We'll return to normal again."

Chapter 24

Mei Yin trailed her fingers lightly on the table and lovingly stroked the back of the new sofa. After two years, their fortunes had changed significantly. They had finally moved to a new home, a large four-bedroom house with separate servant quarters. A wide smile appeared on her face bringing on the dimples in her cheeks.

"At last we have a home of our own. *Tai Nai-nai* is kind and understanding. You know, she has opted to have the bedroom right at the back because she says she does not want to be in the way and Ah Keng will be close at hand. I must confess I feel so relieved that Second *Nai-na*i is not with us any more. I feel guilty thinking this way but I have been so unhappy with her."

"Shhh. She is gone now," said Nelly.

"I'm not giving myself any excuses. I tried so hard. I just gave up trying to please her in the end. So I have this nagging guilt that I am happy because she is no longer around."

"No, you didn't give up on her entirely. You were by her bedside whenever you could be and, at the end, you brought the boys, Wei Han and Wei Hoong, to see her."

"Yes," said Mei Yin remembering. "The boys held their noses because of the terrible smell of the Chinese herbs and ointments that Ah Jee was using to treat her. They were very naughty. Do you remember how the two of them imitated the Taoist priests at the funeral? When the priests leapt over the fires to help Second *Nai-na*i cross over to the other life, they jumped as well. Not everyone approved at that!"

"Yes," smiled Nelly, "but everything is working out. I must admit that even I was beginning to think it might not happen, a house of our own, particularly when Ming Kong sold all eight of those bungalows. I thought perhaps he wouldn't keep his promise after all."

The two women went from room to room surveying their new home, Mei Yin with a child in her arms and Nelly, holding the hands of two children, trailing behind.

* * * * *

They gathered around the coffee table in the family room. The children were in bed. Ming Kong leaned forward, arms resting on his thighs, hands clasped in front of him, his face animated. "What do you think of the idea of doing some work for me, getting involved in the business?"

The women looked at each other, eyes wide and questioning.

"You remember the land and house in Sun Chuen? I sold it to Tek San and to make up the value he gave me a share of his factories. Now he has built a small row of two-storey shop-houses on part of the land. I plan to do something similar on land I own. He has agreed to swap one of the shop-houses in Sun Chuen for one of mine. This way both of us get to diversify into different areas. But, of course, while the shop-house he is offering me is ready, the one I am offering in exchange isn't. So, as a concession, he wants me to sell my holdings in his factories back to him. I always knew that my holding a share of his food business was a sore point with him. He doesn't like me sharing in it. Anyway, I have agreed to sell. I need cash to build on the land and the money from the sale will come in handy."

"What are you planning to do with the shops?" Nelly asked.

"I have several ideas, none of them final. So that is where the two of you come in. I need you to find out what does well in Tek San's shops. See what is happening in the other adjacent shops as well, if you can. I have arranged for both of you to spend some time in Tek San's dried provision store. I want you to watch how people shop, what they like, how the goods are displayed. I also want you to learn how to do the accounts, how to keep track of what is sold and needs to be replaced, even how to keep files and to know what order forms to use. In fact, everything that is needed to run a store."

Mei Yin beamed. "Good! Great! I would love that. When do we start? Will you be with us?" She was bored at home. Her hope that Ming Kong would spend more time at home following their move to the new house had not materialised.

"One thing at a time. We'll work on this. I won't be able to be with you in the new shop because I have so many things going on, not least the new housing project. Tek San or his brother will help you out."

"But can't you . . ." Mei Yin's voice trailed off, her face downcast.

"What about the children?" interrupted Nelly. "Who is going to look after them?

"First Mother. In any case, An Mei will be starting school and Wei Han will be in the kindergarten. Ah Keng and the young maid can take care of Wei Hoong under *Tai-mah*'s supervision. I need both of you to learn and to learn fast."

* * * * *

Mei Yin loved the change. She was good with people and loved talking to the customers, but she hated anything to do with numbers. She could not master bookkeeping; she did not understand how to keep accounts nor was she very interested in learning. "Nelly, you do it, you are better," she would say and go off to do something in the store. She was distracted, enchanted by all that went on around her.

"No Ming Kong, I am sorry to say, Mei Yin is not learning as fast as I had thought she would," reported Tek San. "She is completely disorganised. She will take an item from one shelf and put it down on another. Or she gets into a conversation with a customer in the middle of doing something and then forgets to finish afterwards. I just don't understand how Mei Yin, so quick and intelligent otherwise, is so easily distracted."

"What about Nelly?"

Tek San nodded. "Yes, she is much better," he admitted reluctantly. Until she came to work in the shop, he had had little

contact with Nelly. He considered her an upstart, a second wife. Like
Kai Min, his allegiance was with Mei Yin. "She is certainly better
than Mei Yin at keeping the books."

"In that case, I will have to rely on Nelly to manage the store. I
don't believe in relying on outside help. Small stores fare better when
they are supervised by a member of the family."

* * * * *

The store was an Aladdin's cave. It sold practically everything–fresh
vegetables, frozen foods, dried provisions, stationery, toiletries–all
under one roof, a marked contrast to the open markets that people
normally used. On the first day of its opening, long queues formed
outside the store.

"This is really convenient, being able to buy everything under
one roof," commented a customer. "It is like the Cold Storage that
the Westerners go to."

"No it is better. The Cold Storage sells mainly imported canned
and frozen foods that foreigners cannot find in this country. This
store sells foreign goods and local products, fresh and dried."

"Yes, and so modern! A woman manager!" exclaimed another.

Mei Yin was not pleased at Nelly's appointment. At first, she was
not very upset. She did not like the day-to-day work of keeping
accounts and inventories. Moreover, she was distracted by Ming
Kong's sudden interest in teaching her how to drive. He taught her
every day and she would regale the household with the hardship she
had to endure under his tutelage. "He shouted at me all the time.
Stupid! You nearly killed the guy! Use your brakes, change the gear,
keep both hands on the wheel. I would have had a nervous
breakdown if I were a weak woman," she concluded. Her eyes
sparkled. She enjoyed the tutoring and took all comments with good
humour. Above all, the lessons gave her time alone with Ming Kong.

She passed her driving test the first time. Ming Kong's praise was
fulsome and she shone with pride. He said, "You can now help with

the business. I know you don't enjoy managing the store. But you can help towards it. Would you deliver Nelly's meals to her when you do the school rounds? She comes home late. An Mei can go to her in the office and do her homework in the store. This way, you will have mainly the boys to care for."

Mei Yin could not say no, but her stony silence said it all.

With Nelly managing the store and calm prevailing at home, Ming Kong threw himself into his building projects and the plantations. He was always busy; acquiring land and organising the finance of property projects. Life for Mei Yin became a routine of ferrying the children to and from school and ferrying meals for Nelly.

"There," she plunked the brightly coloured tiffin carrier on Nelly's desk. "There! Fish in the first container, meat in the one below and the vegetables and rice at the bottom. All piping hot. Hope they meet with your approval!" She glared. "I am quite fed up with carting this to you every day. I feel like your hand-maid."

"Then don't," replied Nelly. "I can always fetch something from the coffee shop next door."

"What and risk Ming Kong finding out! I know which side my bread is buttered. You are management now." With that she left.

An Mei's Recollections

Chapter 25

"**A**n Mei!" I looked up, surprised to see Mother in my classroom. The school bell had rung to signal the end of the school day only seconds earlier. I knew something was wrong. Two bright spots burned on her cheeks and strands of hair had fallen across her cheeks. She looked harassed and upset.

"Why are you taking so long?" she asked, highly agitated. Snatching my satchel, she marched me out of the classroom walking past the teacher without a word. Parents were not normally allowed in the classroom, but Mother appeared preoccupied and completely oblivious to the surprised look on my teacher's face. "We must hurry," she announced. "We are not going home immediately. I'm going to Aunty Jeanie's place first, your friend Karen's mother. Come on, quick." She tugged at my hand. "Why are you so slow? Jeanie is waiting."

We hurried, elbowed past parents, teachers and children mingling at the gate, and went straight to where Aunty Jeanie was waiting in her car. "Follow me," she instructed. We got into our car and followed.

"Aren't we going to have lunch?" I asked, "I'm hungry." In fact, I was very hungry. Breakfast seemed such a long time ago. Mother turned right round, I was on the back seat, and gave me a murderous look. I slid lower into the seat. Before she could reprimand me, a loud honk sounded from an oncoming car, followed by a loud screech of tires. Mother braked very hard and the car came to a juddering halt.

Within seconds, a man's face was staring threateningly through the windows of the car. He banged first on Mother's window and then on the bonnet, his face ugly with rage. "Are you blind? Didn't you see the traffic lights?" he shouted as he tried to wrench open our car door.

Mother just collapsed onto the steering wheel. She had done what Father was always accusing her of doing, not looking where she was going. Meantime, Aunt Jeanie had stopped her car and rushed back. In her best pleading voice she said, *"Minta maaf enchik,* sorry, sorry, but the lady is not feeling well."

After much debate and haggling, the incident passed without further ado. Aunty Jeanie pressed some money into the man's hand, apologising profusely all the while. When he had left, she said in English, "Too big for his boots. He thinks he is very grand. They all like that now, think they own the road. Cheapskate!"

She tapped Mother on her shoulders, "Pull yourself together and follow my car." She then looked severely at me. I had virtually disappeared into my seat by then, quivering with fear. "Don't make your mother angry," she wagged her finger at me before striding back to her car. Her determined walk made her sway left and right. I did not like Aunty Jeanie.

When we arrived at her house, I was sent off to the kitchen to find some food. Mother and Aunty Jeanie stayed in the living room. No one told me what I should do and Karen was not around. She was three years my senior so I was not her friend as Mother had inferred earlier. The cook gave me a bowl of noodles. Clutching the dish, I returned to the living room. Mother and Aunty Jeanie did not look up, they were in deep conversation. Mother's eyes were puffy and red. I sat down on a pouf and ate silently, all the while listening to what they were saying.

"Listen to me," Aunty Jeanie said in Chinese. "I saw them together. They were in the goldsmith shop. He was definitely buying her jewellery. If not, why were they there? I could have slapped her for you. So slimy, like a snake. Now and then, she would touch his arms, lean forward and smile. I could see from the way she was dressed and made up that she was a *loh kooi*. A prostitute definitely."

Mother sobbed.

"Ai yah," Aunty Jeanie continued, "if I were you, I wouldn't cry. I would have it out with him. Give him a piece of your mind. Give him an ultimatum: either she goes or you will, just tell him that." She was getting worked up by her own talk, her language became increasingly intemperate. "And when you leave him, take him for all he's got. I would if I were you." She turned, saw me and said loudly in her style of English, "Why you here listening to adult talk. Go!" She omitted to tell me where. I simply left the room and stood behind the door where I could still hear everything. I was not sure who or what they were talking about. I was just worried by Mother's tears.

Mother looked up. "What did she look like? Was she pretty?"

"Not pretty, not like you," Aunty Jeanie comforted, "just a *how poh*, a loose woman, dressed to kill. How many times do I have to say it; you just cannot trust a man. They are like putty in the hands of such women, all useless. They can't say no. Remember what I say. Make him pay."

* * * * *

That evening when Mother brought me to the store, she stopped to talk to Aunty Nelly. They had a long conversation, heads together. I did not dare ask about dinner, even though they talked and talked well past my dinnertime. My stomach rumbled with hunger. The food in the tiffin carrier was getting cold.

It was good to see them together. They had grown apart. Aunty was completely engrossed with the store and me; Mother with Wei Han and Wei Hoong. Sometimes, they even argued because of us, each taking the side of their charges.

Aunty looked pained as she listened to what Mother had learned from Aunty Jeanie. She put her arm around Mother's shoulder and stroked her head with her other hand. "Let's hope it is not true. People often see what they wish to see. I don't think you should say anything to Ming Kong without making absolutely sure. Even then, it might not be a good idea to rush headlong into a confrontation. You and he are too strong-headed. He will never give in."

Mother was not convinced. She shook off Aunty's hands impatiently. "What do you know? It's easier for you, he relies on you for help in the business. What am I? I'm a driver. I look after his kids. What is worse, I think I am expecting again. Why, why," she sobbed. "I cannot bear the thought of him being with another woman."

"We cannot really be sure that he has another woman," comforted Aunty Nelly, trying to convince herself as much as Mother that it was not true. Seeing me, she beckoned me to her. "Come, give your mother a hug and kiss, then have your dinner."

Turning back to Mother, she continued, "We have to think this through carefully, Mei Yin. Think of the children, especially now that you are expecting another. Oh dear, what a mess. I know who would be able to find out if it is true, Tek San. He would not tell us, but if you persuade Kai Min, she would drag the truth out of him."

* * * * *

We gathered in the sitting room. Aunty Kai Min, hands on her hips, feet spaced wide apart, glared at her husband. "I am asking you again. Is it true that my brother is seeing another woman?"

Having put her children to bed in my brother's bedroom, she had marched Uncle Tek San into the sitting room, sat him down and begun her interrogation. Uncle feared his wife's temper. Like my father, she could be fearsome. She had always been fond of my mother.

"Come on. I do not have all night. Or would you prefer I ask him myself?" she demanded.

"No, of course not. You would only come to blows. I just don't think we should get involved."

"In other words, you are saying yes. Who is this woman?"

"I don't know!"

"In that case, speak to me only when you do. I am taking the children away on holiday."

"For goodness sake, why get involved? You will only cause more trouble." He reached out to her, but she shrugged off his hands and turned away from him. He knew that sooner or later, she would wear him down. "Okay! Okay! Promise you will not confront him and I will tell you what I know."

She did not bother to reply. Her eyes bored into his.

"I don't know if anything can be done; he is already deeply involved. The woman is, well, a sort of secretary. She works for one of Ming Kong's business associates. Don't ask me how it started, but, from what I hear, Ming Kong sees her a lot."

"What do you mean by sort of . . . is she or isn't she a secretary?"

Sheepishly, he explained, "I heard she was his associate's mistress and that she passes herself off as a secretary. So, she is a sort of secretary."

Stamping her feet with rage, Aunty Kai Min raised her voice, "You stupid man. *Chon, chon, chon!*" she repeated in Chinese in emphasis. "You mean you have known all this and yet you chose to keep it from us. You are as bad as him." She gave him a hard shove. "Imagine, when we were young, he always vowed he would not behave like our father, that he had learned from the pain Mother suffered. Now look at him, the minute he has a few cents he does exactly what the other men in the family have done." Turning the full force of her anger on her husband, she shouted, "How can you look at Mei Yin and her children and not feel guilty at letting this go so far?"

"I am not your brother's keeper," he protested.

"And what about you? Are you keeping any secrets from me? If I catch you . . ." she left the threat unsaid.

* * * * *

Aunty Kai Min beckoned me into the car as I came out of the school gates. Mother was sat at the wheel beside her. "Come An Mei, get into the back of the car. You are a big girl now. You can learn from this. Your mum needs us. Let's go. First, to your father's office."

Minutes later we were parked outside the building where father had his office. We sat in the car waiting. It was hot outside. At first, we had wound the windows halfway down. Then we wound them up again. The exhaust fumes, noise and dust, combined with the fetid smell of the monsoon drains, made it almost impossible to breathe. Undecided which was worse, the heat building up inside the car or the conditions outside, we went on alternately winding the windows up and down.

Aunty Kai Min drummed her fingers on the dashboard, impatience brewing up to unbridled rage. Goaded by Aunty Jeanie to take firm action and supported by Aunty Kai Min, Mother had been raring for a fight with Father. But seated in the stifling car, faced with the immediate prospect of such a confrontation, her face was pale. He had not been home for a week. Telephone calls to his office and messages went unanswered. Frustrated, she had gone to First Grandmother for help, only to be disappointed. First Grandmother did not want to be involved.

"Mei Yin," she had said. "You must take some responsibility for the situation. Ming Kong works very hard. When he comes home, you are often out. Stay home more and don't fight with him. Your friends are leading you astray." On learning our plans to confront Father, she added a further warning. "Don't march into his office and make a scene, if you hope to salvage something out of the marriage."

So there we were, parked outside Father's office, waiting for him.

The minutes passed. A Malay traffic policeman had walked over to us twice and asked us to move on. In response, we had driven at snail's pace to another spot, waited for him to move away and then driven round the block back to our original parking place. The third time the policeman approached, Aunty Kai Min felt some explanation was needed if they were to retain his good will. She explained in Malay that my mother was expecting a baby and was waiting for her errant husband. She needed money for food for the children. "Please let us wait here." Seeing Mother's distraught face, he wavered, before saying in a half-hearted, stern voice and indicating with his five fingers, *"Lima minit sahaja!"*

Five minutes turned into almost an hour. "Say what you like, this Malay officer is very kind."

"There he is," cried Mother as Father walked out of the building and got into his car.

"Follow him," ordered Aunty Kai Min. We followed his car out of Ampang Road into China town, past the Chan See Shu Yuen temple and into Loke Yew Road. Then the car turned into a side road, slowed and came to a halt. He got out of the car and went into a corner double-storey house.

"What should we do?" Mother asked, turning to Aunty Kai Min for guidance. "Shall we knock on the door? I can't stand waiting here, imagining what is going on in there."

"Do you want me to go with you?" Aunty Kai Min asked hesitantly. She had promised her husband that she would not get involved in a direct confrontation with her brother. "Nelly should be here. She is letting us do all the dirty work. It affects her too."

Mother replied, "I know. She said she can't leave the store. Your brother is a cunning man, he has tied us up in his business, making us do all the work while he does what he likes. And, I have to say, that stupid woman Nelly is completely devoted and loyal to him. Stay here. I will go alone. Tek San will be cross if you get involved."

Mother's spirits, which had flagged during the long wait, were up once more. She was ready to tackle Father. She got out of the car, marched to the house and knocked loudly. A servant dressed in black and white opened the door and, after a moment's hesitation, withdrew presumably to call her mistress. The door was left open. Mother entered. Minutes passed, we heard loud voices. They got louder. One voice was definitely Father's, another was Mother's and a third voice was that of another woman, strident and shrill.

Unable to contain her curiosity and fearing for Mother, Aunty Kai Min shouted over her shoulder to me, "Wait here!" She clambered out of the car and ran to the house. I saw her shove open the front door. Through the gap I saw Father pushing Mother away. A woman, dressed in a slinky dress, stood behind him, shouting and gesturing. In a flash, Father stepped forward with raised hands and I saw Mother reeling from a hefty slap he had landed on her face. Aunty Kai Min stepped straight up to the woman and slapped her hard. Absolute silence followed, before the woman let out a loud wail, all signs of her sneer had been wiped from her face. Aunty Kai Min rushed to Mother and helped her up and out of the house. When she reached the door, she wheeled around to face Father, "You deserve her if that is the sort of woman you want. Not pretty, not even young. Just available! You don't deserve Mei Yin. Even Mother, for all her prejudices, would agree if she were alive today."

* * * * *

Against all her principles, Aunty Nelly closed the store as soon as she saw the state of Mother and accompanied us home. A dark weal ran down one side of Mother's face and there was a little cut on her lip. Her eyes were swollen. Aunty Kai Min was livid with anger and Aunty, ever the pacifist, was trying to calm things down.

"Leave him," advised Aunty Kai Min. "We will understand; we are on your side. I could have killed that woman. What can he see in her? He tells us he likes women to be pure and simple, and what did he get for himself? A witch with 'I am available' written all over her. She was flaunting herself, even during the quarrel. Yuk! I have lost all respect for him, he is a swine, a . . ."

Aunty stopped her. "Shush, the children are here."

We had milled around Mother. Alarmed, Wei Hoong burst into tears, Wei Han followed suit, then me. I am not sure we understood fully why we were crying, just that Mother was sobbing and Aunty had tears in her eyes.

"Why did the witch write on her face?" Wei Hoong asked. "Was it because she isn't allowed to write on the walls?" He had received a sharp smack from First Grandmother when he wrote on her wall.

"No, no, Aunty Kai Min did not mean it that way," explained Aunty Nelly. "Go and play," she coaxed.

No one moved. We were not interested in play, something serious had happened. Fear, anger and bewilderment welled up in me as I recalled the scene I had witnessed. Suddenly a cuddle from Mother became essential and I moved towards her. Mother placed her arm around me and then beckoned the boys to come to her. "What would happen to them if I left?" she asked.

"Yes, think of that," advised Aunty. "Don't rush into things. After all we've been through to help him become wealthy, to leave is just to admit defeat and let her win."

"Yes, well said, Nelly," boomed Uncle Tek San as he entered the room. The room had become full of people; First Grandmother, Ah Keng, Aunty Kai Min's maids and children had all joined us. He looked apologetically at his wife, "I'm sorry. I had to bring the children. They were looking for you. I could not leave them at home. Ming Kong rushed over; he told me everything. He's sorry, but too proud to say."

"Too proud? What about Mei Yin's pride? What pride has he left her, hitting her in front of his slut?" shouted Aunty Kai Min.

Mother sobbed, we sobbed, aunty sobbed and even First Grandmother had to wipe tears from her eyes.

Uncle Tek San nodded in agreement. "I'm really sorry. I am not making any excuses for him. What we have to deal with now is what is best for Mei Yin and the children."

* * * * *

It was a beautiful sunny day, in sharp contrast to the previous evening when it had rained non-stop. Droplets of water still clung to the dark waxy leaves of the chiku tree in the front garden. In the strong morning sun, they sparkled and twinkled against the background of green. We were just about to leave for school. Mother had unlocked the car and we were scrambling in when Wei Han shouted, "Father is back!"

We turned in the direction of his finger and saw Father striding towards us. He had left his car on the road. Almost at the same time, Uncle Tek San drove up, blocking our exit. I could see the panic in Mother's eyes; Aunty caught hold of her elbow, "If he is sorry, be kind and try to make a fresh start. Think of the children."

This had been Mother's main concern throughout a restless night. Irritated, she retorted, "As if I don't know. I've thought of nothing else. It's easy for you to advise."

Hurt, Aunty's eyes filled with tears. I had heard her crying the previous night. Everyone seemed to assume she would not be affected by Father's infidelity. They had forgotten that she was Father's second wife. She was the dependable aunt, Father's right arm. It was only in her late 60s that she finally admitted when questioned and pestered by me that she had never stopped loving Father. Her denial of any feelings of jealousy was her way of dealing with her own pride.

Wei Hoong and Wei Han wriggled out of the car and rushed to Father. They threw their arms round him. I hung back sheepishly waiting for my turn.

Uncle Tek San interrupted, "I came by on the off-chance that I might be of help. I am free this morning. I would be happy to take Nelly to the store and drop the children off at their schools."

Father looked at Mother beseechingly. She looked away, fiddled with the car keys, then nodded her agreement.

* * * * *

Things seemed to return to normal after that morning. Father came home regularly. Mother's pregnancy progressed. Once she grew bigger, she stopped driving us to school. Aunty took the boys by taxi to school. I went to the same school as my three cousins, all girls, so it was arranged that I should go with them.

I threw myself into my studies. I also read whatever I could lay my hands on. I received little guidance. My school, an Anglican missionary school, did not have a library and, aside from textbooks, I do not recall being recommended any other book to read. Aunty Nelly's special treat was to buy me three books every month. On those special Saturdays, we would leave the store and walk to a bookshop two streets away. There I would browse and make my choice.

Schooling in an Anglican school was, on reflection, a strange experience. We said the Lord's Prayers and sang hymns each morning. We studied English history, English literature, religious knowledge (the Bible); even the mathematics had an English slant. We counted in pounds, shillings and pence. Outside school, we conversed in Chinese and Malay, prayed to our ancestors, used Malayan dollars and cents, and ate rice, steamed gingered fish, soya-sauced pork, *sambal* and curry. And yet we accepted such absurd anomalies as normal. We were taught not to question.

Life was very pleasant. The family was united once more. At least twice a month, Father would take us to either Port Dickson, a seaside resort to the south of Kuala Lumpur, or to the waterfalls in Ulu Klang. They were wonderful days.

At early dawn, before the sun rose, we would wake up, wash and change into our day clothes. We would stop on the way to our destination for a breakfast of steamed buns, stuffed with roast pork, and lots of hot coffee, brewed black and heavily laced with condensed milk. We loved the condensed milk. When the adults were not looking, we would slurp the last remains at the bottom of the cup, using our spoons, even our fingers.

We had a little bungalow in Port Dickson. Painted white and blue, it was small, compact and very basic. It boasted one bathroom, one toilet, a kitchen with two kerosene stoves and a tiny cupboard, three bedrooms and a living room. It stood on concrete pillars. Father stored a little boat with an outboard motor in the space beneath.

My brothers and I spent most days on the beach watched over by Aunty or Mother, sometimes both. Dressed in *sarongs* tied up high on their chests, they would show us how to scrape sand and find little clams. The clams were special treats, which we would take home for dinner. Sometimes we would bring little pots of water that had been used to rinse rice grains before they were cooked. Sprinkling 'rice water' on the sand immediately attracted little marine worms, which popped out the moment it touched the ground. Wei Han and Wei Hoong loved catching these squirmy worms. I did not.

The sea was warm, but we were not allowed to swim unless Father was with us. Mother and Aunty could not swim. When they tried, their *sarongs* would billow up covering their faces, attracting loud squeals of laughter from us.

Ulu Klang was very different. The water, straight from the waterfall, was ice cold and very, very clear. There was no sand at the bottom of the fall, just smooth round pebbles. Swimming was limited to a small pool some distance from the waterfall. The current was too strong in most parts of the river for swimming, but the pool provided an oasis of relatively calm deep water, the colour of dark green moss. Under Father's instruction, his jungle guide made us a bamboo raft which we used to good effect, letting the torrents of water carry us down river until we reached the pool. Dragging the raft back to the start was a different matter. It was hard and sometimes painful work. We had to thread our way along the side of the river and brave the leeches lurking there. Father would use the smouldering tip of a cigarette to burn and dislodge them from our bare feet and legs.

Delicious food, and an abundance of it, was very much part of the joy of our sojourns at the waterfall. Cooking stoves were left hidden in the bushes and retrieved on arrival. We brought with us fresh vegetables, meat, fish, prawns and chicken to cook on them. We harvested wild rambutans, a fruit similar to the lychee but with a softer, thicker skin and stubby follicles. We had a wonderful time. Mother said the waterfall and surrounding forest reminded her of being with Father during the Japanese occupation. They were happy days, full of laughter and play. Then, almost imperceptibly, our life began to change yet again.

Chapter 26

The banner rippled gently in the breeze. On it was emblazed 'MERDEKA, 31 AUGUST 1957'. *"Merdeka! Merdeka!"* People shouted, punching their fists into the air. The chanting of "independence, independence" reached a fevered pitch. People clapped, they swayed, they cheered. Then a hushed silence fell over the crowd. The Prime Minister had come on to the stage to give his speech.

More clapping then the music struck. It was our turn to perform. The school had been preparing us for months to dance a colourful multi-cultural dance: we wove streams of soft silks, clicked our heels to the tinkling of brass bells and wore Malay, Chinese and Indian costumes to demonstrate the unity of the different ethnic groups. It was well over an hour before the ceremony ended.

Mother had arranged to pick me up after the celebrations. I was to wait for her at the nearby Chin Woo building. Parking, she said, would be impossible near the stadium where the event was held. She was right.

I pushed through the crowd, squeezed between the cars, trishaws and bicycles parked outside the stadium and walked rapidly downhill towards Chin Woo. Mother did not like to be kept waiting. Pregnant for a fifth time, her patience had become shorter in recent months. Ignoring the flags and banners, and the shouts of schoolmates to join them, I hastened on. Now in my early teens, Father was even more strict with me than before. Contact with friends out of school hours was only allowed with his permission. All after-school activities had to be vetted and approved by him.

I found Mother waiting in the car. The windows were wound down. She was fanning herself with the sandalwood fan Father had brought her from Hong Kong. He was away a lot. Business was good.

The mini market in Sun Chuen was now just one of three he had acquired. By far the biggest expansion in his business, however, centred on property development. The appetite for houses seemed insatiable as the country prospered and rubber and tin prices boomed. In contrast to the strict economies of the early post-war years, the household finances had become quite relaxed. By then we had moved once again, this time to a substantially bigger house.

"Where is Wei Han?" I asked the minute I got into the car. He was supposed to meet us after his school practice at the stadium.

"He is with his friends and will find his own way home. Probably his friend's parents will give him a lift back."

"Why is he allowed to go wherever he wants and I'm not even allowed to visit a school friend?" I protested.

Mother stopped the car, turned and glared at me. "Because your father says so. If you want to know more, you should ask Aunty Nelly, I am not consulted on such matters." She could not stop herself from making hurtful remarks about Aunty. The relationship between them had deteriorated once again.

Aunty's success in managing the first mini market had resulted in her managing the other two stores as well. Mother, however, had been left to continue in her dual role of housewife and driver. She was bitter and took it out on Aunty and inevitably, me. "I hate having to cart you around. I have to be in the sun and in the car most of the day. I fail to understand myself why your father will not allow you to go anywhere alone. Believe me, it's not my decision."

She started the car again and slowly inched her way through the milling crowd. "I'm not going straight home, I have to pick up some cosmetics from Aunty Jeanie." Mother had recently taken to wearing make-up and had renewed her friendship with Aunty Jeanie against the advice of First Grandmother.

"You know, An Mei, a woman needs to look beautiful and feel beautiful. Aunty Jeanie is going to show me how." Glancing at herself in the rear view mirror, which she had adjusted to become a looking glass, she continued, "I used to have such beautiful skin."

"You do look pretty," I protested. "Anyway, Aunty says that beauty is only skin deep. It is more important to study hard and have a career. She says this will ensure a woman's independence."

I had said the wrong thing. As quick as lightning, Mother's mood changed. "Stop quoting your aunty to me. What does she know? She hasn't had much schooling. I was the one who studied. My mother wanted me to pursue a career. Study hard she would say. And I did. I could have gone to university, but for the war. What has it got me? Nothing. So don't believe everything you are told."

She was not finished. Her voice went up a notch higher. "Nelly may have what she calls a career, but it's not from studying, more like by buttering up your father. She is filling your head with nonsense."

Glancing at me, she grinned. "You are looking more and more like Nelly. You have nothing of me, certainly not my nose or eyes. Be careful, they say people take after those who care for them."

* * * * *

Aunty Jeanie lived in Kenny Hill. Within easy reach of the Lake Gardens, the town centre, the Selangor Club and the municipal hall, the hill was a mass of greenery interspersed here and there with large whitewashed houses. Copses of tall *angsana* trees lined the roads. Many of the houses were split-level and built into the hill. You parked the car on the top floor and descended to the main parts of the house.

Most of the houses were occupied by expatriates who held senior posts in foreign companies. Only a handful of Malayans lived there. Aunty Jeanie had moved to Kenny Hill with her new partner after she split up with her husband. Mother was impressed and, in one of her more amiable moods, confided in me that he was a *Datuk*, a title equivalent to the British 'Sir'. "He is very important in the government," she had added, as if by way of explanation.

I was worried about the detour. Father did not like Aunty Jeanie. I was afraid he would find out about Mother's continued contact with her and even worse, she was using collecting me as an opportunity to meet.

"Will we be long?" I asked anxiously. "Father might decide to come home early. He hates it if we are not there waiting for him."

"He is away at some meeting. If he does return home unexpectedly, you must not tell him we visited Aunty Jeanie. Understand? Promise?" demanded Mother. "I won't be long. Your father doesn't approve of Jeanie, but she is just moving with the times and faring better than most women. Do not judge."

The minute Aunty Jeanie appeared at the door, Mother forgot her promise not to be late. "You look so beautiful-*lah*," gushed Aunty Jeanie. "I don't know how I can make you more beautiful-*man*, but I will try. Leave it to me." Turning to me, she remarked, "Is this An Mei? Couldn't recognise you-*lah*. Big girl, so fat! You give her too much food, Mei Yin." Pinching my cheeks in a playful manner, she said the usual, "Go to the kitchen and get yourself a drink. Your mother and I very busy."

The exaggerated way she added *lah* and *man* to her words so as to make them sound more Malayan really irritated me. I left them to their talk and went to the kitchen. Aunty Nelly was right; Mother was so gullible.

Drink in hand, I wandered out to the garden, a large rolling expanse of green that sloped down to a little creek at the bottom. Bright red cannas competed with pink hibiscus all along one border. I wandered over to the bed of deep blood-red spider orchids and buried my nose into their bouquet. No one was around except for the gardener who was listlessly sharpening a scythe.

After walking around for a while, I got bored and decided to go in search of Mother. They were still in conversation or rather Aunty Jeanie was still talking, pausing only to dip brushes into pots of cosmetics. Mother had her face turned towards Aunty Jeanie, eyes closed and lips pursed. I watched, fascinated, as she changed into someone else, someone with big smouldering eyes, glossy lips and high cheekbones. Aunty Jeanie, I had to concede, was good. Mother looked even more beautiful. Her skin, tanned a golden brown, took on a luminous quality.

Triumphantly, Aunty Jeanie turned to me, "See how beautiful your mother is. I don't know why your father looks at anyone else."

My return reminded Mother of the time. "I must rush. It would be just like him to come home early on one of the rare occasions I pick up the courage to visit you. He doesn't like me to go out. I hardly get to go anywhere. He rarely includes me in his business dinners; I'm afraid we're heading back to the situation we had a few years back." Tears began welling up in Mother's eyes.

Slipping her arms around Mother's shoulder, Aunty Jeanie clucked and tutted. "*Shoo, shoo*, pull yourself together. You will spoil your beautiful face. You are young and have the whole world before you. I know all about business dinners. I went through them with my previous husband. You have two choices. Either strike out on your own and find someone else, as I have done, or stay put and try to win him back. Either way it takes courage."

She took hold of Mother's shoulders. Her voice was serious as she switched back to speaking Chinese. "The problem is you have four children with a fifth on the way. That makes leaving very difficult. I had only one child and that was difficult enough. If you opt to fight for your man, make sure you keep not only your face beautiful but your body as well. Do a bit of family planning. You are barely 30 years old. Take a rest from having children."

Mother was quiet for most of the journey home. It was not until we were almost there that she broke the silence. "An Mei, you heard what Aunty Jeanie said. What should I do?" At such times, Mother treated me almost like an adult. I had guessed from the conversation and Mother's sadness that something was not right and it was linked to Father's absences from home.

"You are not leaving us, are you Mother?" I asked anxiously. "Please speak to Aunty Nelly or Aunty Kai Min. I know you say that Aunty Nelly takes Father's side; it's not true. She always speaks well of you." My heart was pounding; the alarm and bewilderment tied my stomach in knots; just like when Father and Mother had quarrelled violently a few years back. I wanted to say more about Aunty Nelly, but I was afraid it would just make things worse.

"I cannot get Kai Min involved again," Mother replied. "The last time, your father nearly broke off relations with her. It wouldn't be fair. Nelly might be able to do something though."

Aunty Nelly and Mother rarely saw each other except in passing. The few contacts they did have usually concerned we children.

Mother mulled over my suggestion and brought the car to a stop in a lay-by. "Well, I have nothing to lose. I shall try to speak to her. We'll do it now. I will go to her office. That way, I will have an excuse for being late. We will be stuck in a traffic jam anyway."

It was testament to Mother's desperation that she went to talk to Aunty that day.

* * * * *

Aunty Nelly's face lit up when she saw me, but clouded over the moment she saw Mother. She hurried over. "Is everything okay? You have arrived just in time for a cup of tea. Or would you prefer Ovaltine? I was just going to call the coffee shop." The coffee shop was two doors away and Aunty had taken to ordering her meals and drinks from there instead of having them delivered from home.

"Anything!" was Mother's distracted reply. "Leave us, An Mei, so I can talk with Aunty?"

"Let her stay. She's a big girl and has a right to know what is happening."

"It's about Ming Kong." Mother paused, uncertain how to proceed. They both looked uncomfortable.

"Mother is leaving us," I blurted out. "Aunty, please tell her that she has to stay."

"No one is leaving," Aunty replied. "Hush, come here and sit next to me." She put an arm around me and turned to Mother. "You would be silly to even think about it, especially in your condition.

We talked about this the last time Ming Kong went astray." She paused. "I was expecting this to happen. It is a repeat of before. The late nights and frequent trips."

"What should we do? I cannot bear another scene like the last one," said Mother.

"Scenes will not solve anything. He has changed; wealth and the company he keeps have altered him. All those people fawning over him have made him conceited. He doesn't even talk to *Tai Nai-nai* now."

"You have not answered my question," Mother said, exasperated, "what should I do?"

"It depends. Do you still love him?" asked Aunty. I wriggled uncomfortably waiting for Mother's reply.

She nodded.

"Then, fight for him. Ming Kong may be very clever in business, but he is weak when it comes to women. He needs to be flattered. So flatter him. You used to go hunting with him until the children came along. Go with him again. Put your cooking skills to use, reach his heart by feeding his appetite. Give up some of the time you spend with the children. Get some extra help in the house. We can afford it."

I suspected from the uncharacteristic rush of words that Aunty Nelly must have spent some time thinking about the problem and had just been waiting for a chance to talk. She was not finished. "I can only do what I am doing now. You have a much better chance to win back his love. When I met Ming Kong, I never thought being one year older would be an obstacle. I was wrong. I am 41 You are still young."

Mother looked doubtful.

"We have been through so much with Ming Kong," said Aunty encouragingly, "I hate to see anyone else benefiting at our expense. Take courage, you will win if you try."

Mei Yin

Chapter 27

The sound of boots squelching in soggy mud was interrupted by the barking of dogs followed by rapid gunshots. An acrid smell of cordite filled the air. The men watched the snipe flutter and fall with a thud onto a bund between two paddy fields. Then, shouts of jubilation.

"Good shot," shouted Wing Lok. He turned to the boy standing behind him, and said in Malay, *"Ambil!"* indicating the bird with his hand. The boy ran quickly to the dead snipe, picked it up and ran its head expertly into the bird hanger, alongside a dozen or so other birds.

"You've got quite a bag of birds now," Wing Lok exclaimed. "Would you like to call it a day? Shirley is waiting in the car for us." A broad jovial smile broke in his face. "You should get to know her better. Quite a girl!" His eyes, though half-closed, were as sharp as an eagle's as he watched Ming Kong's reaction.

Wing Lok was one of Ming Kong's new business associates. Short and podgy, his face affected a perpetual affable, almost simple, smile. Behind this apparently benign expression lay a very ambitious man.

Wing Lok had been courting Ming Kong for months, hoping to get the building contract for his next housing project. He had learned that Ming Kong had had some kind of disagreement with the contractor who had worked with him for nearly a decade. Sharp words had been exchanged. Wing Lok had expected Ming Kong to replace the contractor, but he kept him on. Ming Kong had explained that he could not get rid of someone who had been loyal to him over so many years and had contributed to his success. Wing Lok did not comment; he continued to bide his time.

Almost on cue, Shirley came onto the scene. Bored with the heat and mosquitoes, she had decided that enough was enough. She would not wait any longer. What was so exciting about shooting birds, she asked herself, that grown men would endure these awful conditions for hours on end.

This was her second shooting trip with them. Wing Lok had promised her rich rewards if she could interest Ming Kong and help swing a business deal. So far, nothing had happened. They had dined and danced; she had gone with them on business trips. Ming Kong was always flatteringly attentive, but nothing more. She knew Wing Lok was getting impatient. She could not afford to annoy him. She owed him too much money. Addicted to *mahjong*, she had played for ever-higher stakes in the hope of wiping out her debts, only to end up with even greater losses.

Gingerly she approached the men. She had hitched up the bottoms of her trouser suit to avoid the mud, but could not prevent her high-heeled shoes from sinking into the soil. The narrow shafts of the heels became trapped. Cursing under her breath, she masked her annoyance with a smile. "Hey, you there, help! I can't move."

Ming Kong rushed to her aid.

"I think I have twisted my ankle. Can you help me back to the car?" Placing an arm around his shoulder, she leaned heavily against him as he half carried her to the car. He set her down gently on the back seat of the car with her legs dangling through the open door.

Crouching down, he felt her ankle and calf, "Does this hurt?"

"It feels quite sore. I don't want to spoil your shooting, but I think I should go home. Perhaps one of you strong men could stay with me, at least until the doctor arrives," Shirley appealed, looking beseechingly at the two men.

"I'm sorry," Wing Lok replied, "I have a previous engagement. Ming Kong might be able to help." Turning to Ming Kong, he asked, "Can you give her a hand?"

"Of course, but it would be better to go straight to the hospital, just in case it's serious. I don't think anything is broken, but I am not a doctor."

"No, not the hospital," Shirley said. "The A & E unit is awful; if you are not ill when you arrive, you soon will be waiting there. I will not be able to cope with it. Waiting at home with a friend would make the pain much more bearable. Can't anyone spare a little time for me?" she asked looking straight at Ming Kong. Her ankle did really hurt and she was beginning to feel a little sorry for herself.

Ming Kong looked embarrassed. "Of course. I just need to call my wife and tell her I'll be late. I promised her that I would go straight back after the shoot."

"That's settled then. You can call her from my house," said Shirley.

Ming Kong got into the driving seat. Wing Lok sat beside him. Ming Kong said softly, "I hope Mei Yin will not mind. This is the third time in a week that I have broken my promise to be home early. She's expecting again and can get quite ratty with me. Are you sure you cannot help out and stay with Shirley instead?"

"You'll be alright," comforted Wing Lok. "My wife never complains about my irregular hours. Men, she realises, have great responsibilities. They cannot be expected to succeed if they are kept on a tight rein. She is wonderful. As you know we have three kids. Never once did she expect me to be at her beck and call. Your wife, I bet, will be just as understanding." He paused, glancing at Ming Kong.

Ming Kong said nothing.

* * * * *

It was two o'clock in the morning. Mei Yin was huddled under the bedclothes. She had turned up the air-conditioning because it was very warm. Now after four hours with the air-conditioner running full blast, she was beginning to feel cold. She rubbed the calves of her legs and lowered her body to a half-reclining position, tucking pillows under her for support. Her back ached.

Nelly had spent most of the evening with her after the children had gone to bed. Ming Kong had phoned to say he would be late. He was vague and in a hurry. She was troubled by his vagueness, but tried to dismiss her suspicions. Try as she did, however, she could not get rid of them. Again! Every night for the past month! She was convinced that he was with someone else. Tortured by her thoughts, she could not settle down.

"I wish," she had said to Nelly, "I could be like you, with the strength to put bad thoughts aside. Perhaps, I should go to a Buddhist temple and pray, leave it to karma, and accept whatever happens as inevitable. But I just can't do it."

"Everyone is different. There's no point in trying to be what you are not. Having said that, and at the risk of sounding long-winded, I advise you not to fight Ming Kong. You will only succeed in alienating him just when you really want to regain his affections. Rest now. Think of the baby."

Now, alone in the dark, her thoughts were in a muddle. "Think of the baby, that's all people say. It will be at least five months before I am back to normal. By then, I will have lost him. Please God, let him come home to me."

She fretted, switching from one train of thought to another without arriving at any sensible solution. "Perhaps I should try to leave it to fate. If fate is to be my guide, I would say this; if he does not return tonight, I will interpret this as fate telling me to take drastic action." Tossing and turning, she eventually fell into a troubled sleep.

* * * * *

Morning came. Mei Yin struggled into a sitting position half-blinded by the bright rays of sunshine that came through the half-drawn curtains. Nausea immediately overwhelmed her.

It was Saturday and the children had come into her room with An Mei as usual to chatter and play before breakfast. The younger boys loved to hide under the sheets and challenge her to guess who was who. Normally welcomed the play was just too much for her. "Please leave Mummy for a while. I don't feel well. An Mei, take them away." Then, clutching her stomach, she rushed to the bathroom and retched.

Hastily she cleaned up, sponging her face with a small towel, rinsing her mouth. Staring at the pale reflection that looked back at her from the mirror, she was shocked by her appearance. Fatigue and the restless night had left her eyes ringed with dark shadows, exaggerating the pallor of her skin. "No wonder he has lost interest in me," she mused aloud.

"Stop tormenting yourself in front of that mirror," scolded Nelly. She had just come into the room with tea for her. "You look fine. Eat something; you hardly touched your food last night. I know it's difficult, but try. Come down to breakfast. The boys will like that. They were scared out of their wits when you shooed them away."

"I have to go out." Mei Yin went to the wardrobe and at random took out some clothes, which she hastily put on. Seeing the look of alarm on Nelly's face, she said, "Don't worry, I'll be back. Just hold the fort for me." Then, with a sudden impulse, she threw her arms around Nelly. Hugging her tightly, she whispered, "And thank you."

* * * * *

Mei Yin manoeuvred the car into the narrow lane and parked a few yards from the gate. She waited. Using a newspaper to shield her face, she slid lower into the seat, but the steering wheel dug into her swollen belly. Wriggling back into an upright position, she hiked the paper high and waited stoically. Minutes passed. The clanging of a wrought-iron gate opening was followed by the sound of a car starting. She peeped and saw Jeanie's husband getting into the car. Within minutes of his departure, she was ringing the door bell.

"Jeanie, it's me, Mei Yin," she called.

The door opened and Jeanie beckoned her in. "I've sent the maid to the market. We are completely alone. Have you thought about what we discussed?"

Mei Yin nodded. "I am ready. Let's go before I lose courage."

"If you're sure. There's no going back once we're there."

"I am sure. Really, there's no alternative."

"Wait here. I will get my handbag and leave a message for the maid. I do not expect the *Datuk* to be back home until late this evening. He has a meeting at UMNO headquarters and they usually go on for some time."

Soon the two women were in Mei Yin's car heading north out of Kuala Lumpur. When they had left the city behind, both of them heaved a sigh of relief.

"I was a bit tense just now. I was so worried we might see someone we know," Jeanie confided as she removed the shawl she had wound round her head. "Saturday is not a good day. Weekdays are better. You know the men are out of the way in their offices. And, if you keep clear of the main shopping areas, you can avoid most of the women you know." She turned to look directly at Mei Yin. "I am doing this for you, Mei Yin, so don't tell on me whatever happens. Promise?"

"I promise. I'm grateful, you know that. Tell me where to go."

"Just keep driving. I will tell you when to turn off. The woman we are looking for lives in a settlement just beyond Batu Caves so slow down once we reach the mountains."

They spoke little, each engrossed in their own thoughts. About 50 minutes into the journey, Jeanie spotted the towering limestone cliffs. She pointed to a steep and long flight of steps carved into the mountainside. "Have you climbed those?" she asked. "I once went up there with Indian friends to pray in the Hindu temple during the *Thaipusam* festival. We had a wonderful day. I cannot do it any more though: I am going to be a Moslem."

Jeanie was anxious to know what Mei Yin thought about her decision. Changing religion was no small matter. She looked at her friend hoping to gauge her reaction from her face and was shocked to find her white-faced and shivering. Mei Yin was holding on to the steering wheel so tightly her knuckles were red; her eyes were wild and staring. All thoughts of herself vanished. "You look like death, Mei Yin! Do you want to stop for a drink? Look at the sweat on your forehead. Are you running a temperature?"

"I'm alright. It's just nerves, just silly nerves."

"The woman is good. My friends have used her with amazing results. Look, see those batik cloths hanging out there in front of the houses with the Batik and Handicraft Factory sign. Go on about 100 yards and then turn left. The house is behind a grove of *langsat* trees. Slow down, slow down! We will churn up dust and the people in the factory will not like that."

Mei Yin, in her excitement had stepped on the accelerator instead of slowing down. She immediately switched her foot to the brake pedal. The car came to a halt and stalled. She had forgotten to use the clutch. "I'm sorry. I am so nervous."

"Nothing to worry about!" Jeanie replied, feigning a calm she did not feel. "Come on. Leave the car here. No one will try to steal it."

They walked towards the house. Jeanie poked her head through the door, which had been left open, calling out in Malay, "*Mak cik!* Aunty! Are you in? We are here!" A voice from inside invited them to enter and make themselves at home.

They sat down on a rattan sofa. The room, which was quite small, had a strange array of knick-knacks; colourful vases, little figurines including, somewhat incongruously, one of an English shepherd girl, plastic flowers and paper kites. In the middle of the ceiling hung a fan. Dark verges of dust had collected on its blades. A strip of fluorescent lighting, also with a patina of dust, hung askew above the window frame. Jeanie could see dead insects clinging all along the tube. She wrinkled her nose, lifted her bottom from the sofa and started dusting the seat. She was unaware of the woman who had entered the room and was watching her with amusement.

The woman laughed aloud, showing teeth stained bright orange from chewing betel nuts, "*Tak kotor!* Not dirty! *Dudok, dudok!*," she ordered gesturing to Jeanie to sit down again.

Mak cik was enormous in girth. A loose top hung untidily over a *sarong* tied around her waist. Her buttocks jiggled as she waddled barefoot towards them. A malodorous wave preceded her, a combination of ginger, turmeric, betel nut and the root galangal, acrid and pungent. She sat down in an armchair opposite them. "I got your message this morning so I know roughly why you are here. But tell me again. I want to hear it from you." Leaning over, she squeezed Mei Yin's knee, "Your secrets are safe with me." She smiled, her eyes, the colour of dark currants, twinkled in apparent good humour.

Mei Yin looked at Jeanie and, receiving a look of encouragement, began, "I have come to you for help on two counts. The first concerns my husband. I think he has another woman. I would like your help to win him back. The second is this," she pointed to her belly. Pale faced, she forced the words out, "I am four months pregnant. I don't want the baby."

"Hmm, let's take the first request. Your story is common enough; I myself have had this problem. I solved mine as I hope to solve yours."

She leaned forward again, this time bringing her face close to Mei Yin. She felt giddy as the odour of betel nut enveloped her.

"To help, I need some personal belongings: hair from your husband's head, an item of his clothing, your hair, an item of your clothing and personal belongings of the third party. All of them must be clearly identified for obvious reasons."

"Do I have to pull the hair out of his head?" asked Mei Yin alarmed. She leaned back to escape the acrid odour. But *Mak chik* moved closer and whispered, her face almost touching Mei Yin's. "No, no, just take hair from his hair brush. Be sure it is his and not someone else's. This is not something to trifle with."

"I don't want to harm anyone," protested Mei Yin. "Will harm come to my husband or the other woman or me?"

"You cannot be weak and frightened when you decide on this course of action. No harm will come to either you or your husband, of course. In fact, both of you will be safe from harm. But for the woman, this third party. Huh! What do you think all this is about? It stands to reason doesn't it? If she does not get your man, this will be harm enough."

A look of annoyance appeared on her face and the tone of her voice hardened. "Shall we get on with it? I am not interested if you are not. Please don't waste my time," she said crossly.

Jeanie also looked cross and impatient. "What has come over you Mei Yin? We came all this way. We have talked for hours about what needs to be done."

Mei Yin looked up, straightened her shoulders and said, "Yes, yes, please go ahead. I will bring you what you want."

Mak cik was all smiles again. "Don't worry. You are in good hands. This woman has put a charm on your husband. It can only be counteracted by equally strong magic. Bring the items along and leave the rest to me. I will pray for you." She placed her hands on Mei Yin's head and with eyes tightly closed, she mumbled under her breath.

Suddenly, *Mak cik* opened her eyes wide and stared hard at Mei Yin. "On the second request, I see difficulties. It will not be easy to lose this baby. Your life might be put in danger."

"Please, we have to try. I have to be free to win my husband back," Mei Yin pleaded. "I know it is wrong, but I cannot go through months of pregnancy, watching him tire of me as I grow big and ungainly. A few more months and I will lose him forever. I do not want to live without him."

"*Adoi, sayang!*" said the woman. She nodded to reaffirm that she was sympathetic to Mei Yin's dilemma. She agreed to help. So saying she left the room and returned with a bottle, no higher than six inches, filled with a dense greenish liquid. "Take this potion at home. You must finish all of it," she said. "You'll feel cramping pains. I warn you they will be severe, they could be strong enough to make you scream out loud. Also you will bleed. Make sure you do not leave any evidence behind. Have someone you trust with you. You will need looking after."

She turned to Jeanie, "Bear witness, I have warned your friend of the consequences. I don't want you coming back and blaming me. She is not in her early months of pregnancy. There will be danger.

Don't involve me if something goes wrong. I will deny all knowledge of the affair and I will lay a deadly curse on anyone who dares to try to involve me."

They were dismayed, shocked as the implications sank in.

"I don't have to give you this. You don't have to take it. You could go to a doctor and have it done."

"No, my husband would never allow it. This has to be done without his knowledge."

"Just take it," whispered Jeanie in Chinese so that *Mak chik* would not understand. "Take the potion home and think about it. If you decide against taking it, you can just dump it. I think it is safer to accept the potion even if you decide not to use it. We must not make her angry. We should leave. I feel uncomfortable."

* * * * *

Nelly was worried. She had not seen Mei Yin since she left in a hurry that morning. Ming Kong had come home briefly to bathe and change. He exchanged a few words with the children and left, grumbling that Mei Yin would have to explain her absence.

"She complains when I am not at home. When I do come home, she is not here. How many times have I said no one should go out without my permission. That means you (nodding towards Nelly), you (An Mei) and all of you here. It also includes your mother. When she returns, tell her what I have said just in case she has forgotten!" With that, he snatched up his jacket to leave.

"Aren't you going to wait for Mother?" asked An Mei.

He stopped mid-stride. "Are you questioning me; answering back?"

Nelly stepped forward, "No, of course not. She is just concerned. Mei Yin was very worried when you did not return. I am sure she went in search of you." Turning to An Mei, she said, "Say sorry to your father."

"I didn't do anything. I only asked because I don't understand why Father says he wants to see Mother, but won't wait for her," An

Mei replied. Then, undeterred, she followed her original question with yet another one. "Anyway, how can we ask you for permission when you are hardly ever at home?"

Ming Kong was shocked by his daughter's questioning. Once more he turned around to face her. He glared at her and, as if this might not be enough, jabbed a finger in remonstration. "I will talk to you later. I'm in a hurry. You had better thank God that I am. Nelly, see that she stays home. You are to blame for spoiling the girl." With this, he left.

"He is changing so rapidly I hardly know him," Nelly murmured to herself. Turning to An Mei she said, "Go to your room and write a note of apology to your father. You were very rude. You know he will not stand for any cheek. Even if you are right, there is still a proper time to say things. That was not the time. It is also something for adults to sort out. You should not interfere. Go and do as I say, then come back down for dinner."

* * * * *

The minute she arrived home, Mei Yin went straight to the study. Nelly would be there. She could see light seeping from under the door. She went in. Nelly had fallen asleep in the armchair. Her legs were splayed out in front of her, her head lolled to one side and her mouth hung open. She looked tired even in sleep. The room was dark except for the solitary table lamp next to the armchair; it lit up a patch of the floor, a circular shining patch.

"Nelly, wake up, I need your help." Mei Yin shook Nelly gently.

She awoke with a start. "Gosh, you gave me a fright. Where have you been? We were worried sick. Ming Kong came home. He wasn't pleased to find that you had gone out without telling him."

"Yes, I expected that. Did he say where he was going and when he would be back?"

"No, he doesn't tell me any more. He was in a hurry. Sit down. You look pale, are you alright?" Nelly placed her palm on Mei Yin's forehead. "You feel really clammy. You should go to bed. You must have been on your feet all day. I will bring you a drink. "

'No, I'm okay, just a bit tired. Don't get up, I don't want a drink. Just hear me out. I need your help." Mei Yin paused, "I went to see a *bomoh* today."

"What? What on earth made you do that? I don't believe in their magic and you should keep clear of them."

"I am going to have an abortion. I don't want the baby. I cannot go to a doctor for help so I've got a potion here which I am going to take. She warned me it will cause severe pain and someone must be with me, just in case. I have no one to turn to, only you. Please do this for me."

"Don't do it. It is too dangerous. You could die. I cannot be responsible," replied Nelly in anguish.

"I am going to take it whatever the consequence. I am desperate. The only difference is whether you will be at hand to help or not. Please Nelly, please help me. I am going to my room now. I will slip into my pyjamas and then I am going to take the potion. Stay with me. I might not be able to do it alone. I need you, please, please say you will help."

"What will Ming Kong say? What should I tell the children?"

"Tell them I have a tummy upset; tell Ming Kong I miscarried, that I ate something which did not agree with me, or that I fell, anything except that I went to a *bomoh*. He must not know I deliberately sought an abortion."

* * * * *

The long corridor smelled of disinfectant. Two benches were set haphazardly against the wall. A white enamel spittoon stood in the space between them. One bench was occupied by a Sikh, who was laid full length on it with the skirt of his *dhoti* tucked between his legs. He was snoring, breathing with great snorting gasps. Periodically the noise would stop to be followed by a grunt and the loud sound of

SWEET OFFERINGS

air being blown out. The sound of his stentorian breathing was broken occasionally by other noises, the sounds of people moaning in pain and distress. The Sikh remained oblivious to everything. He had been there waiting for his relative for almost 24 hours and was tired beyond care or concern for his personal dignity.

Ming Kong looked at him with envy, mesmerised by the heaving chest, envious of his sleep. He too had been up all night waiting, but there was little news of Mei Yin. Nurses and doctors hurried past. Every time he asked, they brushed him aside. "You must be patient; we do not know; it's a near miss; you have to wait; she is in a critical condition." He ran his hand through his hair in frustration. "Why can't they explain more?" His eyes were puffy, his shirt wet with sweat.

He sat on the bench, head bowed low, hands clasped between his legs, drained of energy and emotion. His legs felt weak. He could smell the sweat on his body, a stale salty odour. Nelly's words kept going through his head. "Mei Yin was asking for you throughout her pain. Even when she realised she had lost the baby, her first words were, where is Ming Kong. We could not find you. Where were you?"

He hung his head. He was with Shirley.

He had returned home from his assignation, oblivious to the trauma gripping his family. He had worked out a strategy to fend off questions concerning his whereabouts. He believed the best defence was attack. So he was prepared to launch into a tirade about Mei Yin's failure to tell him of her whereabouts and of An Mei's rudeness. When he entered the house, however, he could see something was seriously wrong. The children looked terrified and upset. An Mei was sobbing; Wei Han, Wei Hoong and Wei Shu had red running noses and tears still clung to Wei Shu's eye lashes. As soon as he saw his father, the little boy blurted, "Mummy dead, Mummy dead," and immediately started howling. The others followed suit.

No amount of consoling by Nelly and their grandmother could quieten them. They were sure that their mother was dead. They had seen her carried out, motionless and white, on a stretcher. The ambulance had taken her away. Nelly was stricken. She was unprepared for the pain and the loss of blood that Mei Yin suffered. She had expected some blood loss, but not a haemorrhage. Luckily, she had the telephone numbers ready at hand. The family doctor, Dr Murugesau, was contacted, then the ambulance. The commotion had woken up the whole family. She had tried to clean up. The bed was soaked with blood. She shifted Mei Yin to one side of the bed and sponged her face, rubbing tiger balm on her temples in an attempt to revive her and ease her pain.

"Have I lost the baby? I'm so sorry for all this. I want Ming Kong. Look after my children," Mei Yin said over and over, as she slipped in and out of consciousness. Nelly comforted her and tried to ease the pain. She blamed herself for not stopping Mei Yin. She was overwhelmed by a combination of guilt and compassion.

* * * * *

The hospital corridor stirred to life at the first flush of dawn. Hospital staff arrived in neat white uniforms. A woman marched in pushing a trolley loaded with mops and pails; she poured disinfectant over the floor's already saturated surface. Dressed incongruously in a white uniform top and a colourful *sarong*, she chatted as she cleaned. She did not bother to watch what she was doing; down went the mop into the pail and out it came dripping with water. She banged it down on the floor, splashing water everywhere, including onto Ming Kong's trousers. He muttered in annoyance. Outside the hospital entrance, hawkers had set up their stalls.

The activity all around Ming Kong stirred him into action. "Surely by now they will let me see Mei Yin or, at least, have some news about her." He walked resolutely to the reception desk.

A new staff nurse was now on duty replacing the one who had dealt with him so curtly a few hours earlier. He asked for Mei Yin.

She nodded, checked a sheet of paper, "She still hasn't come around from the anaesthetic."

"Is she alright?"

"Yes, providing there are no further complications. The doctor will come to check on her in a few minutes. He will be able to tell you more. You can see her, but you must not stay long. She needs to rest. She is in Ward 19."

He thanked her and half ran in search of Ward 19. He found it, a long dormitory lying parallel to another one, separated from it by a strip of grass with a bed of marigolds. The hospital consisted of a series of long, single-storey, wood-plank buildings. He walked briskly until he found her bed. A partition shielded it from the others. He peered round the screen. "I must move her to a private ward," was his first thought as he saw her pale face. She was on a drip. A nurse was busy monitoring her blood pressure. She motioned him in.

"How is she?"

The nurse smiled, "I think she will be alright. She will feel drowsy when she wakes up. She has lost a lot of blood and, as you probably know, the baby as well. She will feel very low. Doctor will tell you more. He should be around any minute. Please sit here quietly and wait for him. Don't wake her up."

Ming Kong sat down on a metal chair beside the bed. He could feel a prickling sensation in his nose. A profound sadness came over him. Why, oh why, he asked himself, did he get himself into situations where he hurt the ones he loved. He despised his father for the pain he had caused his mother; he could not understand his infidelities and had vowed never to be like him. Yet he was his father through and through. Putting an end to his affair with Shirley would, he had no doubt, be the right thing to do as far as his family was concerned. Looking at Mei Yin's pale face, he could not believe he could love anyone other than her. Unfortunately, there was a complication. Shirley had announced she was expecting his baby. The news had taken him by surprise; she had assured him she took precautions and that he need not worry.

There was a small movement. Mei Yin gave a low moan. Her eyes were still closed, but he could detect movements behind her eyelids. He half stood to lean over her, waiting for her to open her eyes. "Mei Yin," he said softly. "I'm here, how are you feeling?"

Mei Yin opened her eyes. They were full of pain and regret. Numbly, she nodded her head, unable to speak. He took both her hands and brought them to his lips. He held them there. Neither of them made any attempt to speak. She did not wish to know where he had been, it was enough that he was with her now. The silence was only broken when the nurse eased the partition open and announced the doctor had arrived to see the patient.

The doctor was tall, six feet at least, and very slim. He introduced himself as Dr Yang. "I attended your wife last night. Could you leave us? I need to examine her. Wait outside. I will not be long. I'll speak to you afterwards." He asked the nurse to take Ming Kong away.

Ming Kong took an instant, unreasonable, dislike to the doctor. "Is he always so abrupt with the relatives of patients?" he asked the nurse.

"Not normally," she replied. "He must be tired. He was up most of the night. He is a good obstetrician and gynaecologist. He is highly thought of in the hospital. Your wife is in very good hands."

* * * * *

Dr Yang finished his examination. Removing the stethoscope from his ears, he smiled encouragingly. Sitting down on the chair that Ming Kong had vacated, he drew closer to the bed.

"Would you like to tell me how you came to be in this state?" he asked gently. Mei Yin did not reply. He did not hurry her, but sat patiently waiting. Only after some minutes when no response came did he say, softly and sympathetically, "I have to know, Mrs Ong. It was not an accident that caused the loss of the baby. There was extensive damage to the womb. We had to remove . . . I don't want to go into details; it would upset you. However, I will have to explain to your husband."

Mei Yin bit her lip and turned her face away. "He will kill me if he knew I deliberately got rid of the baby," she whispered. Turning to face the doctor, she continued in the same soft whisper, "No one is to blame but me. I made the decision. I cannot explain to you why. It was not something I did lightly. I could see no other way out." Mei Yin sobbed.

"Mrs Ong, please don't cry. I believe you, I really do believe you. I am not here to judge, just to help. Knowing helps me explain to your husband in a way least harmful for everyone. Knowing helps to guide me on what is best for you."

Mei Yin interrupted, "I took a concoction. Please do not ask me where I got it."

"Did anyone make you take it? This could be a police matter."

"No, no, it was entirely my own doing."

"Rest now. Think only of getting well. I will do my best to smooth things over. One day, I hope you will trust me enough to tell me more." Dr Yang patted her arm and went in search of Ming Kong. From his patient's delirious rambling the previous night, he had surmised that all was not well with her marriage.

* * * * *

Mei Yin made a slow but steady recovery. Dr Yang visited her every day to check on her progress. Gradually she confided in him. True to his word, he was not judgmental; he allowed her to pour out all her feelings and emotions. On the fifth day she was allowed to leave hospital. That morning he paid Mei Yin a final visit.

"You look much better. Take it very easy." He handed her his card. "Please call if you need help or want someone to talk to."

Chapter 28

Home. It was as if she had never been away. Yet things could never be the same. Mei Yin felt different, numb, as though something had died in her, as indeed it had. The children greeted her warmly, even exuberantly. The boys were keen to tell her everything they had done; An Mei was attentive bringing her tea and fussing over her. Nelly was contrite, still blaming herself for what had happened. Ming Kong made a point of being home every day. He had cancelled all his engagements except for a few he could not set aside. Her mother-in-law was kind.

Mei Yin was touched yet something in her remained cold, detached. The anger, anguish and fear of losing Ming Kong that had pushed her to the edge of sanity seemed to have disappeared. All that remained was emptiness, a cold calmness that enveloped her entire being, stifling her emotions.

Gradually she resumed her daily duties. After three months, she was accompanying the children to and from school. She did not drive, she found it too taxing. A driver had been employed. Mei Yin was determined to return to normal life and to get out of the house whenever she could. The children were the only element in her life capable of arousing emotion. She was glad of Ming Kong's presence at home. When signs of his impatience returned and he began to stay out late again, she no longer fretted. It was, as Nelly said so often, "What to do? Never mind, leave it to fate."

One morning, after she had left the children at school, she asked the driver to make a detour to the Lake Gardens. She had arranged to meet Jeanie. She had not seen her since that fateful day. They had spoken on the phone, but meeting her was difficult. Ming Kong said he knew intuitively that Jeanie was involved somehow.

Mei Yin arrived early. She brought peanuts and bananas to feed the monkeys and while away the time. The Lake Gardens abounded with monkeys. Sometimes a whole troop would arrive to beg for food, the mother and her young all vying for the fruits and nuts. She left the driver and walked towards one of the bamboo groves that dotted the park. Seeking shade, she sat on a bench under the arching stems. She looked at her watch. Jeanie should be along soon; it was nearly ten o'clock and her husband would have left for the morning parliamentary session. Jeanie had promised to come to meet her straight after dropping him off at the parliament building.

Desultorily, she scattered peanuts for the monkeys. Jeanie, she thought, was not very bright, but she was all heart. Even though she had what Nelly described as irritating ways, she had her interests at heart and made her laugh. Sighing, she said aloud to the monkeys, "I need to laugh!"

"And so you should," a man's voice said.

Mei Yin started, unaware that she had company. Looking up, she exclaimed with relief, "Dr Yang, I didn't see you. What a coincidence."

"It is. Please call me Jung. This is the last place I would expect to see you. I come here to read and walk on days when my hospital duties are in the afternoon." Looking at her more closely, "You look well, Mrs Ong. Are you taking it easy?"

"If I am to call you Jung, you must call me Mei Yin. I have not really thanked you properly for keeping my secret and taking such good care of me. I am truly very grateful."

"Not at all, it was my pleasure. Would you like to join me for a coffee? I would love to learn how you have been coping. I was on my way to the little gazebo over there to get a drink." He pointed to a gazebo set under a nearby bamboo grove. It housed a little coffee bar with tables and chairs arranged around it.

Before she could reply a loud voice cooed from some 20 yards. "*Ai yah*, Mei Yin, I thought we were supposed to meet on the other side of the lake," Jeanie called in English. "I waited there so long, you know; so hot! Look at my blouse, all wet with sweat! I would still have been there if I hadn't spotted your driver. *Alah mak!* He was smoking! Right next to your parked car. I thought you said Ming

Kong does not allow smoking." She looked breathless. Her *baju kurong*, a traditional Malay ensemble of a tunic worn over an ankle-length skirt, clung to her. Since her engagement, she favoured the more conservative Moslem attire over the Chinese *cheongsam* with its tight bodice and side slits that revealed the legs. "So hot," she complained again as she came to a halt in front of Mei Yin.

She waited to be introduced. When no introduction was forthcoming, she pretended to become aware of Jung Yang for the first time. Beaming, she said, "Sorry-*lah*. I didn't realise you had company. Sorry to disturb. Don't mind me, carry on."

Not showing any signs of being sorry or embarrassed at being obviously nosy, she stretched out her hand and introduced herself. "You, friend of Mei Yin?" she asked, eying Jung up and down. Turning to Mei Yin, "Nice looking man, why you so secretive and not tell me", she whispered.

Embarrassed, Mei Yin explained softly in Chinese, "He is my doctor. It is a coincidence that he is here."

"Please excuse me. I will be here again tomorrow," Jung said, realising Mei Yin had a prior engagement. "I can talk to you then if you are around." Taking his leave of the ladies, he walked away.

Jeanie waited until he had gone. "Why you not mention him?" Her curiosity was killing her. "Is he special friend?" Not convinced that it was a chance meeting, she became serious, switching to Chinese, "You are not keeping anything from an old friend, are you?" She looked keenly at Mei Yin. "It will not do to make friends with that young man. Your husband will not like it. He does not even want you to have women friends. He does not behave himself and will believe others are the same. Mark my words." She nodded in the direction of the driver, "Be careful, he might tell."

"I told you. He was my doctor when I was in hospital. I did not come here to discuss this; I came to see you. We've not been in touch since that day."

Jeanie looked contrite, "Yes, yes, I'm sorry. How are you?" She switched back to English to cover up her embarrassment. "I called many times, but everyone so slippery. Not this, not that, not here, not there. *Alah mak!* Frustration! So eventually I gave up. Your Nelly does not like me; she thinks I misled you. She is right. I should never have taken you there and let you risk your life. My maid promised me you would be okay. She insisted it was commonly practised, always successfully, in the village. 'Don't worry-*lah*, madam,' she told me. I sacked her after that. She don't worry."

"It's over," consoled Mei Yin. "I am okay. The trouble is I feel so dead inside."

They walked, stepping around the flower beds, heads close in conversation.

"Is Ming Kong treating you better. Has he told you anything?" Jeanie asked, switching back to Chinese. She was troubled. Blaming herself for Mei Yin's near brush with death, she was not sure if she should tell her anything more about Ming Kong's affairs. She had learned a lot from gossip. It could make matters worse. On the other hand, she felt disloyal keeping vital matters from her friend. After all Mei Yin had been through, she deserved better, Jeanie thought to herself. So she listened with bated breath for Mei Yin's answer, for a clue as to broach the matter.

"He is more attentive than before, but he has started returning home late again. Business, he says. I don't care so much now. In fact, I don't feel anything much."

"I care for the children, of course," she continued, "but even there, I feel a change in me. I can now step back and look at myself critically. I know I have been guilty of favouring the boys. We are brainwashed to put boys first and I have carried on in the same tradition. I realise that I have not been a proper mother to my daughter. Nelly is more a mother to her than me. And, to make matters worse, I have blamed Nelly for everything. Yet, the two of them have been wonderful, supporting me throughout. An Mei listens to my grief; I have never listened to hers." Her voice broke. "As for Ming Kong, I need time. Time to think it over. I need some direction to my life."

Jeanie kept quiet, still unsure what to do. She was taken aback by Mei Yin's remarks about An Mei. She had taken Mei Yin's side believing Nelly to be a bad influence on her friend's daughter and she had taken every opportunity to criticise them as well. She felt sorry. "Perhaps I should not open my big mouth at all," she thought.

"That's enough about me. What about your news? Has a date been set for your wedding?"

Jeanie brightened up and nodded. "Yes, next month, only two weeks and two days to go. I hope you will come. Bring the whole family. It will be an all-day affair, a proper Malay wedding. I am so excited! Second time strike lucky. The *Datuk* is a wonderful man. I am fortunate to have a second chance, *insha Allah*. Look, I have adopted the Malay dress. It pleases him so much." Lowering her voice, she confided, "The only thing I have not quite given up is going to the Buddhist temple. Don't tell anyone. I have become a Moslem, but every now and then when I pass a temple, I feel guilty. So I light a joss stick. Old habits die hard-*lah*. My old mother is always getting at me for becoming a Moslem. 'Why you not filial,' she asks, if I do not pray to the ancestor's tablets when I visit her. She says that in my next life I will be an insect. So, I think that to pray to all gods is safer, just in case. Better safe than sorry. I am not doing anything bad, am I?"

Mei Yin laughed. "No, you are just being you. You've not changed."

* * * * *

Against all instincts and Jeanie's advice, Mei Yin went to the Lake Garden the following day to meet Jung. She reasoned it was, at the very least, the polite thing to do, considering all the help he had given her. Just one coffee and that would be it, she promised herself.

Time passed very quickly that morning. Jung was a good listener. He was also entertaining when he regaled her with little comic episodes from the hospital and his student days. "And there I was, scalpel in hand, sweat pouring down my face. My professor gave me a look and said, 'If you are not going to make that incision, we'll call it a day.' Nervously I put the tip of my scalpel on the abdomen and plunged it in. My knees buckled and the next thing I knew my nose was buried in the cadaver. I had fainted across it!"

"It can't be true. You are pulling my leg," Mei Yin laughed. It was a long time since she had enjoyed genuine, uninhibited laughter. It was wonderful to talk about ordinary daily things, to listen and to be listened to. She had never had a conversation of any length with any man other than her husband.

"I would love to speak English well," she told him. "I started learning when we were in Singapore, but I never did it properly. I pick up new words from my children and husband, but I know I don't speak it correctly. I speak like Jeanie, the friend you met here yesterday. If I could speak well perhaps my husband would take me to his business functions. He says they are not for me because I would not understand what was going on."

Even as she spoke, Mei Yin knew that improving her English would not make any difference. *Why am I lying to myself? I am saying it in the hope that Jung will offer to teach me.* She blushed, ashamed at her own deceit. And, sure enough, he did. They arranged to meet in the Lake Gardens at the gazebo with the coffee shop. Mei Yin tried to retract, but her heart talked her into agreeing. She had not enjoyed herself or laughed so much for many a day. Surely, she reasoned, it could not be wrong to want to learn, to laugh and be happy. It was all in the open. What harm could come from such a thing.

* * * * *

"Ah Keng, stop Mei Yin. Ask her to come to me; I'd like to speak to her," said Suet Ping. Mei Yin was just about to accompany the children to school and was on the verge of leaving. Instead she retraced her steps.

"Yes, *Nai-nai*, you want to see me."

"Why have you been out of the house so long after taking the children to school these past weeks? Yesterday Ming Kong left for work later than usual. He noticed that you had not returned. He asked. I could not explain and you know how it is, he got quite upset." Her mother-in-law sighed. "I have no wish to interfere, but servants talk. Ah Keng told me the driver has been hinting that you are meeting some man in a park. You must know that once this gets back to your husband, he will be very angry. Why are you meeting this man? Does Ming Kong know?"

Mei Yin could find no easy answer to the unusually direct questioning of Suet Ping. In the euphoria of finding a companion she could talk to and learn from, Mei Yin had deceived herself into thinking that others would see the meetings for the innocent occasions they were. It was an outrageous delusion, the more so because, in her heart, she knew people would think in the way that Jeanie had warned.

"I have always tried to be fair and to make up for the hardship you suffered at the hands of Su Hei. If you are misbehaving, then you have misplaced my trust. Have you misplaced my trust?"

Mei Yin stared numbly at her mother-in-law.

"*Suen-lah, suen-lah*. I don't want to be involved. In any case, I won't be here much longer. I am thinking of entering a Buddhist nunnery. I would like to devote myself to prayer, meditation and abstinence. I have been contemplating this for some time. I have been here too long. Ming Kong has been so curt in recent months and now this! Ah Keng wants to go with me. I have asked her to stay, otherwise you will have to find someone new to manage the household."

Stricken, Mei Yin broke her silence. "Please don't go. I have done nothing wrong. I'm only meeting the doctor who looked after me in the hospital. He's teaching me English. That's all. The only wrong I have committed is not to ask Ming Kong for approval. I am so sorry. I didn't ask because I was afraid that he would not agree."

"Why then do you do it?"

"I feel so lonely with nothing to do. At least in the old house, I had a routine of a sort. Now, other than accompanying the children to school, I have nothing to do. Maids take care of the housework, gardeners tend to the garden, drivers fetch and carry. I just sit around, waiting and waiting for Ming Kong."

But nothing she said could make her mother-in-law change her mind. "I understand," Suet Ping said, "but I'm too old to get embroiled in the ups and downs of you young people. I will try to make it clear to Ming Kong that my decision has nothing to do with you." And with a tenderness that touched Mei Yin, she clasped her face in both hands and kissed her forehead.

That evening when Nelly came home, Mei Yin confided in her. "It's all my fault. *Tai Nai-nai* has been so kind to me and all I've done is bring her trouble. Ming Kong, Ah Keng told me, has been very abrupt with her. Accused her of conniving with me to keep secrets from him. I have been silly. Nothing I do is right."

"You must try to persuade *Nai-nai* to stay," said Nelly, her face full of dismay. She took Mei Yin's hand and made as if to march her to their mother-in-law's room.

"I tried, I did, but she is adamant," cried Mei Yin.

"I wish I had known what was going on, I would have warned you. You are a silly goose sometimes. Don't you know that despite all the social changes in recent years, the one sacrosanct rule is still respect and love for a parent. To have *Tai Nai-nai* move out and stay in an old folks' home in a Buddhist nunnery will cause Ming Kong a great loss of face. It is almost universally taken for granted that a good son is one who takes care of his parents. *Tai Nai-nai*'s leaving can only mean for some people that Ming Kong is not a good son. Can't you see the gossip this will cause?"

Nelly shook her head in despair. "And on top of all this, the secret meetings with Dr Yang and in a place well known as a lovers' rendezvous! I really do not know how all this will end, Mei Yin. Why, why didn't you talk to me? Studying English could be something to explore. But this . . . this secrecy. No matter how innocent . . ." She sighed. "I really don't know what to say. Has *Tai Nai-nai* told Ming Kong of her decision?"

Mei Yin shook her head.

Ming Kong

Chapter 29

Large tracts of the land had been cleared. Workmen were busy laying foundations for houses and erecting a pylon for the electrical supply. Ming Kong looked around with satisfaction. He loved the hustle and bustle, the men and women busy building something for the future, the heat, even the dirt churned up by the excavators. Dust filled the air. He could feel it settling on his arms and face. All around him was land, a vast expanse of it, all his, and cleared like a drawing board on which he would place his mark.

The economy was growing rapidly. He was determined to keep pace with it. He had bought the land some years before when no one wanted it. Outside Kuala Lumpur, it was, in the words of his friends, "in the sticks" with a handful of wooden houses scattered among the remnants of old tin mines. Large muddy lakes left from dredging the ore were all that remained of the mines. "No one," continued his critics, "has heard of Petaling Jaya. You are foolish even to consider it."

Ming Kong disagreed. "Mark my words, this will be a growth area. People who do not want to live in the crowded centre of Kuala Lumpur will opt to move out and travel daily to the city. And this will be the ideal suburb from which to commute." What he did not reveal was that he had learned a highway was planned from the city to this area. More importantly, he knew that applications were already underway for factories to be built in what would become a satellite town once the highway was completed.

"Factories," he confided to Wing Lok, "employ people ranging from those slaving on the assembly lines to the top management.

The executives might be happy to commute from palatial homes in Kuala Lumpur, but the workers will want cheaper accommodation. This is the time to go into low-cost housing and shops to provide for these people. I could use a couple of shops myself and bring my mini market outlets here."

Pointing to the expanse of muddy water at the foot of the gentle hill housing his development, he said, " See over there, we should also get the architect to see what can be done with the lakes. A floating restaurant on one of them might be the answer. After we have cleared the lake and stocked it with fish and planted water lilies, it will look very different."

Wing Lok had by this time become one of Ming Kong's main contractors, responsible for over half of his housing projects. He was good at his job and Ming Kong thought very highly of him. He delivered and kept to schedule. A major problem in the construction business was to find good workers and keep them. With the housing boom, competition for labour was high. It was Wing Lok who came up with a solution: employ more women. Women had become a common sight on building sites carrying loads of bricks or cement in baskets, one on each end of a bamboo pole, which they balanced across their shoulders. Women were cheaper and more reliable in many ways.

Ming Kong was aghast initially. "I know they are cheaper to employ, but I have qualms about sending them up the bamboo scaffolding with loads of bricks."

Wing Lok had brushed aside his unease. "Look at it objectively", he explained to him. "You are really doing the women a favour by giving them an opportunity to work. They are not forced to do it. It is their choice. Don't worry. These women are both strong and agile. They are much better, in fact, than the men at climbing up the scaffolding."

Now, standing next to Ming Kong, he waved expansively at the female coolies. With their hoods pulled far forward to protect their faces from the strong sunlight and coolie hats balanced on their heads for additional protection, they all looked alike, marching back and forth like an anonymous army of industrious ants.

Ming Kong turned and walked briskly back to his car, absorbed in thought. "I need to look at one more site and then I am finished. I have to attend to matters at home."

"Trouble at home still?" queried Wing Lok. "I thought Shirley mentioned she was expecting you this evening." He pretended not to know that Ming Kong had not told Mei Yin about Shirley. He had heard this from Shirley herself. She had railed against Ming Kong for not keeping his promise to tell his family about her.

"Brave Shirley," he said, "I hear she has lost a baby too. She is bearing up well, never complains. I've known her since she was little. She was a bright little button then, always cheerful, never letting things get her down and, above all, loyal. Difficult to find such a woman these days."

Ming Kong shrugged. "No, I have to go home early today. I will call Shirley to tell her. She will understand."

When he'd learned that Shirley was pregnant, he had promised her that he would arrange with his family for her to become the third wife. Surely, he had reasoned to himself, Mei Yin would not mind, having been through a similar situation. Although she was his first wife, she had in reality come after Nelly. Circumstances had changed from the early days of casual flirtation with Shirley; he could not let her down. Then, Mei Yin had had the miscarriage. He was contrite. For weeks, he'd blamed himself for his neglect of her, wondering whether his affair with Shirley might have contributed somehow to the awful event.

Memories of better and happier days made him wish he had never embarked on the affair. He could not bring himself to tell Mei Yin about Shirley and was determined to stop seeing her. He offered Shirley money, future security and a house. She had refused everything. Instead, she had sobbed, cried and clung to him. A couple of weeks later, she too lost the baby. Now, he was in limbo between the two women.

Keeping his thoughts to himself, unaware of how much Wing Lok knew, he got into his new Chevrolet. With Wing Lok at his side, he drove to another building project to oversee its final completion.

* * * * *

Cushions were scattered everywhere. Bits of kapok stuffing stuck out through torn fabric. A vase lay broken, its water spilt on the carpet; flowers lay limp beside the shards of broken glass. The room looked as though a tornado had passed through it. Shirley hollered in rage, "Damn, damn, damn! He promised to be here this evening. Instead, he has gone back to his wife. I told you. I should have taken the money, the house and all he offered and called it a day. But no, you persuaded me to hold on. For what? He's just keeping me on a string."

Without waiting for Wing Lok's reply, she yelled for her servant, "Ah Kum, come and clear this up. Quick! Are you blind? Can't you see the mess? Do you want me to hurt myself treading on bits of glass?" she scolded, venting her frustration on the hapless maid.

Wing Lok interceded. "Hang on. I thought you were the one who opted to take the longer view. You said it would bring bigger gains than a quick settlement. Anyway it's a good job you opted to get rid of the baby. It was not Ming . . ."

Shirley glared at him, gesturing with her eyes the maid's presence. "Are you mad?" she hissed. Instructing Ah Kum again to clear up the mess, she beckoned Wing Lok to go into the den. Once inside, she slammed the door and turned on him with fury. "What do you mean by that gaffe? Do you want her to report it to Ming Kong or gossip and speculate? You have as much at stake as me. So keep your big mouth shut and put your brains to better use by making sure Ming Kong does the right thing by me."

"Well, all I can say is you are not suffering unduly. It is a very lucrative string, as I can see," retorted Wing Lok, pointing to the house and its furnishing. "Look, I have not been inactive in your cause. I have found out from talking to one of his drivers that Ming

Kong has trouble at home. That's why he is not here. Apparently, Mei Yin has been meeting a man in the Lake Garden. Nothing untoward, according to the driver; they meet in the open, laugh and talk a lot. But Ming Kong will not like it. We have just to sit back, gauge the situation and capitalise on it at the right moment. Control that temper of yours; he might be putty when you are soft and gentle, but, let me tell you, he did not get rich by being soft."

Shirley listened intently, digesting this latest piece of information, her mind already busy mapping out ways of using it to her advantage. "Good! That's really good. I agree with you. The more we can find out the better." She smiled with glee and purred, changing her tone to honeyed sweetness. "Don't worry about my temper. I never show it when Ming Kong is around. I know my trump card is not to be like a wife. I give him what he cannot get at home. I'm sorry for biting your head off just then. The long wait is getting to me. I cannot ask you to stay for dinner, the staff will gossip. I will make sure, however, that another contract comes your way."

* * * * *

Ming Kong did not go straight home. Instead, he went to see Nelly at the store. He wanted to find out what she knew. He had seen little of her other than brief encounters at home just before leaving for work. Almost all the management and administration of his chain of mini markets was in her hands. She was adept, loyal and he trusted her. Opening her office door unannounced, he saw her bent over some office ledgers, absorbed in her work. For a couple of minutes, he stood there looking. He saw Nelly through fresh eyes, observing how plump she had grown. He saw the strands of grey hair escaping from the tight knot of hair she wore, so different from the Nelly who had once set his heart pulsing in anticipation of meeting her.

He coughed and she looked up, her face breaking into a smile. "How long have you been there? I didn't hear you come in. I was so wrapped up in this," she indicated the file before her. "This account is giving me a headache; he's one of our oldest clients. Recently, he has been late with his payments. I would hate to do anything drastic; he's been with us such a long time."

Without waiting for a reply, she got up and poured him a cup of tea from a flask next to her table. Despite the success of the business, her office was still a little cubby hole, filled with ledgers and filing cabinets. She maintained the tradition of keeping a flask of Chinese tea handy and even plates, bowls and cutlery for the occasional meal she had with An Mei when she visited.

"Tired?" she gazed up at him. He did not reply, still unsure how to pose his question. He knew she and Mei Yin were close. He sat down.

"Trouble?" she asked.

"Yes, trouble. Perhaps you already know something and would like to tell me before I speak to Mei Yin. She is so withdrawn. It makes me impatient. Her tears only make it worse because she cries silently to herself. I hate that. It drives me wild. So I am trying to understand what is wrong before I go home."

She had guessed something was brewing the minute she saw him. She steeled herself and played for time. "What do you mean?"

"Does the name Dr Jung Yang mean anything or ring any bell?"

"Oh, Dr Yang, Mei Yin's doctor. She tells me she's learning English from him. She is doing well and is practising with the children at home." Her voice was light, but her heart missed a beat.

"Learning English in Lake Garden? Does she think I am stupid?" he asked in disbelief, working himself up. "Why can't she find a proper teacher? Why him and, if it is to be him, why doesn't he come to the house?"

"You know why. She's afraid of exactly this kind of reaction. If anything improper was going on, it would not be out in the open and with the driver there," said Nelly. "Look, Mei Yin is under a lot of strain. She always tends to be impulsive. She probably thinks nothing of learning English in a park because she is doing nothing wrong. Have some faith in her."

Wishing to change the subject and prevent him finding out himself, she said, "Your mother says she's going into a nunnery for her remaining days. We've tried to persuade her not to, but she's adamant."

"Why?" was his startled response.

"Have you spoken to her roughly?" asked Nelly, pretending not to know.

"Yes, but she should know by now that I was just in a bad mood. It's all because of Mei Yin. I didn't mean anything by it."

"Perhaps she is tired of having to second guess whether or not you mean what you say. She is old. Go home. Speak gently to her and dissuade her."

He let out a huge sigh, running his hands through his hair, "I do not really want to go home, at least not now," he admitted. "There is always some problem or other. I have had such a busy day at work. I need some peace. Anyway, what's the use of going home? I cannot get near Mei Yin these days. She seems to have lost interest in everything, including me."

He sat thinking. As he mulled over what he had just said, he became angry again. He cursed aloud and shouted, slamming his fist down on the arm of the chair, "And yet, she has interest enough to arrange regular meetings with another man. No, Nelly, for a moment I thought you might have a point. I am sure there is more to this than meets the eye. I cannot see a guy with so much to do giving up time to teach another man's wife English. Unless, that is, he is getting something in return!" He jumped up and, pointing a finger at her, cried, "And you, stop trying to make it sound as though I am to blame!"

Putting her hand on his arm to calm him, she said gently, "You are, in a way. Mei Yin has lost her baby. She has gone through a traumatic operation. Her hormones are all upset; she's bound to be depressed. And you're not helping by being away from home so much. Why not devote more time to her, take her out, show her you care."

"Who gave you this newfangled idea about hormones, what do you know? Has this doctor been filling your head with bloody nonsense as well. I thought I could trust you. You surprise me, Nelly."

Nelly bowed her head, bit her lip and replied, "It is not bloody nonsense. If you cared, you would at least try to understand."

The rage and jealousy he had bottled up during the day tore through him. He kicked the chair over. "Nelly, I am disappointed in you for not knowing right from wrong. I don't go home because there is nothing for me there, just a bunch of neurotic women. I am tired, sick to my stomach of all of you." Pushing her aside, he strode out through the door, past a small group of on-lookers who had gathered outside the office, and on into the streets.

Nelly ran after him, but he was already in his car and away by the time she reached the street. Shaken, she rushed back to the office, ignoring the stares of customers and staff. The scene revived dreadful memories. She phoned Mei Yin to warn her and explain that her attempt to help seemed to have done more harm than good. "Ming Kong has just left. I am not sure if he is heading home. He said not, but he might be. I don't know! I'm so sorry. Try to talk to him. I've never seen him so angry. It might be a good idea to put the children to bed to avoid them getting involved." She hesitated and changed her mind. "On second thoughts, perhaps you should have them with you for protection. Oh dear, I can't think clearly. I am coming home."

* * * * *

Mei Yin put down the phone. A cold calmness descended on her. How could she feel this way in the face of what was likely to come, she wondered. It was almost as though she welcomed the approaching confrontation.

She gathered the children together and asked them to be good and to play quietly upstairs. Taking her daughter aside, she explained, "Your father is very angry and upset. He is on his way home to have a serious talk with me. I do not want any of you around; it is an adult matter. Please help Mummy by looking after the boys."

"Will you be alright, Mummy?" asked An Mei anxiously. "Will you both fight?"

"I'll be alright. I have done nothing wrong," replied Mei Yin, giving her daughter a hug. She could not say more. The younger ones were already impatient to get on with their play. Wei Han was reluctant to leave with the others. "No, Mummy, I want to stay downstairs. I have not seen Father for days and I want to speak to him. I want to ask if he will buy me a new bicycle and let me go camping with my friends."

"This is definitely not a good time to ask. Go with An Mei, she will explain. I can hear his car in the driveway." Wei Han could be stubborn. Suddenly, her feeling of calmness was replaced by sheer panic. "Please, Wei Han, do as you are told and go, immediately!"

Sensing something was seriously wrong, he left, but not without a show of defiance. He closed the door behind him so hard the shelf lining the adjacent wall shook sending books crashing to the floor.

Mei Yin prepared herself. She sat facing the door. Her heart pounded. Where was that calmness she had felt only moments earlier, she wondered. Clutching the hem of her blouse, she twisted it into a tight coil. Her hands were clammy. Her knees felt weak and she clung to the back of the chair for support. She longed for those early days in Singapore when, away from her mother-in-law, she had questioned and bantered with Ming Kong. His patience had diminished as his wealth grew. It was, as he put it, such a waste of his and her time to question his decisions. He was always right. His orders on how she should run her life ran in haphazard order through her mind. "Don't you go anywhere without consulting with me, not to friends, to relatives or even on shopping trips! And never alone. Take your children with you. Do you understand?"

And she had failed in all. How could she explain herself? Her meetings with Jeanie, the one person he was dead set against. Meeting men had never been specifically mentioned, perhaps because it was not something to be even contemplated. She looked around wildly in the room as though she was seeking help. "My occasional lapses, meeting Jeanie," she thought, "are nothing compared to this. As Nelly said, it looks bad even though it is innocent."

* * * * *

Mei Yin heard Ah Keng open the front door, his voice asking for her, then his approaching footsteps. Another door slammed and then he was there standing in front of her, his face flushed with anger. Her thoughts dissolved into a crazy patchwork of inconsequential reflections. "Why have his thick eyebrows grown long like Kuan Koong, the warrior god," she wondered. She had not noticed before.

Taken aback by her wild-eyed stare, Ming Kong shouted, "Why are you staring like that, don't you recognise me?"

She silently moved her lips.

"What have you got to say for yourself? How many times have I told you not to go out on your own?" Without waiting for an answer, he continued, "How many times have I caught you meeting up with that woman. Yes, don't bother to lie, I know. I know all about your friendship with Jeanie. I told you I do not like her, but you kept on meeting. I have tried to be patient. I let it be and said nothing. Now, I have to find out from my staff that you have been meeting a man, and in Lake Garden of all places. You have made me a laughing stock."

Mei Yin tried to speak again but no words came. Tears pooled in her eyes and streamed down her face, her breakdown was complete.

Seeing her cry enraged Ming Kong even more. To him, her tears and silence were an admission of guilt. He was convinced she was having an affair. Bits of what Wing Lok had said, comments that seemed irrelevant, now flashed through his mind falling neatly into place and supporting his suspicion. He brought his hand up, swung it back in a wide arc. Slap! And again, slap!

Mei Yin reeled with the impact of the blows. He could not stop himself once he started. Jealousy ate into him. She tried to defend herself, holding up her arms to protect her face. He pushed her back and she fell.

Ah Keng was the first to reach the room followed by An Mei and Wei Han. Hearing the commotion, they had run down the stairs.

Charging to the aid of their mother, they tugged and pulled their father away. Spent, he collapsed into the armchair, watching while Ah Keng and An Mei helped Mei Yin to her feet. Her cheeks were a bright livid red, her eyelids already swelling and her neck bruised.

Still Ming Kong looked on, his body slumped, his rage dissipated. Then slowly he began to cry tears of self-pity that he could be so betrayed, so fooled by his wife.

* * * * *

Ming Kong could not cope with the situation: Mei Yin's battered face, the horror in the children's eyes, the accusing look of Nelly who had now arrived, the sadness and silent tears of First Mother who had also come to the room, attracted by the uproar. He got up and left.

Arriving at Shirley's was like reaching a sanctuary. The contrast with his own home had never been so great. The air smelt fresh, fragrant and exotic, redolent with Shirley's perfume. It was quiet except for the background tinkling of piano music from the record player.

"Tired?" she asked, guiding him to the sofa before kneeling to remove his shoes. She brought him a drink, frosted and cool, and mopped his eyebrow with a warm, scented towel.

"Yes, I've had a rough day."

"Wing Lok said you had to rush home because of some trouble. Are the children okay?" she asked with an air of innocence.

"Yes, they are alright. It had nothing to do with the children." He hesitated, uncertain whether he should continue. A niggling loyalty to his wife stopped him from saying more. "I do not wish to talk about it now. I just want to rest."

She snuggled up closer to him and, stroking his arm, whispered softly, "Then rest."

An Mei's Recollections

Chapter 30

Long after everyone was asleep, I was still tossing and turning. I pulled up my sheets, pummelled my pillows, even tried sleeping on my front. When that did not work, I changed position to lie head down at the foot of the bed. It was all useless. I could not settle down.

Over and over again, I re-lived the moments when I saw Father beat Mother. Anger and frustration welled up in me. I wished I had not obeyed Mother's order to stay in my room and had come down earlier. I could have done something more to prevent him from hurting her. I wish, I wish, I wish. And why did he do it? I asked over and over again. I tried to enlist Wei Han's support to press for an explanation. His reaction was to lock himself in his room. Later, I tried to go to him again to talk and seek solace, but his bedroom door was still locked. I could hear him sobbing inside.

After Father left, we helped Mother to bed. Aunty sponged her injuries. Little was said. There was a tacit agreement not to discuss the matter in front of us. I felt shut out by this conspiracy, this secret they shared. I called my father names, but Aunty took me aside and silenced me. "Shooh, it's better not to take sides, An Mei. Do not get involved in the affairs of adults. Your mother needs all the love and support you can give her. Focus on that."

Yet how could I avoid taking sides? "Is it because Father is seeing another woman again?" I asked, recalling what had happened some years back. "Mother was beginning to look so much better; she was taking an interest in things again and then he has to come along and spoil it all. It's so unfair," I cried. "Bloody idiot, bloody fool, shit, bastard . . ." In my anger, I shouted all the words we had been told never to use, as though shouting them would help erase the frustration and anger I felt.

"Stop that or go to your room," Aunty commanded.

At that moment, I hated even her. In fact, I hated all of them and their conspiracy of silence. I went to my room and banged the door shut. If they did not want to tell me, I did not want to know.

The night progressed and silence enveloped the house. I could not bear the loneliness of my thoughts. I crept out of my bed, tiptoed past my aunt's bed (I still shared a room with her) and stole into Mother's room. She was huddled on one side of the enormous bed. I did not have to ask if she was asleep. I knew she was not. I could hear her muffled sobs. I ran over, put my arms around her and hugged her close. Her cheeks were as wet as mine. I have never felt so close to my mother as on that evening.

She lifted the blanket and I crept into her bed. Minutes passed; then she told me what had happened, why Father was angry, blaming herself for being foolish.

Her vitality and love of life were ebbing away. Self-doubt and in-security were taking over. Mother was no longer the spirited person she had once been. I almost wished I could argue with her as we did before to revive her spirit. I empathised with her. I understood how she felt; the longing for freedom, to be able to meet people, socialise and to talk because the same stringent rules were applied to me as well. "It's unfair," I whispered. "Father never tells us where he goes. Why is there one rule for him, one for the boys and one for us."

I did not share Aunty's views that I should conform to these rules; I obeyed them only because there was no alternative. At least, not then, but I had great plans for the future: I would study hard, I would be successful, I would be rich and then I would have the independence to make my own decisions. These aspirations kept me going. Poor Mother had none of these goals. Every decision she had taken in those past few months now seemed to her to have been seriously flawed.

"I don't know what will happen next," she confessed.
"It will be alright, he will forget."

*****

At first, life did seem to return to normal. We went to school as usual, although Mother no longer accompanied us. Aunty Nelly went to her office every day. We saw little of Father, he was home one moment, out the next. No one felt at ease when he was around. I felt to be friendly towards him would be disloyal to Mother; to ignore him, Aunty had warned, would be to take sides. So, most times, I opted to run downstairs, greet him as brightly as I could and then retreat back to my room. I threw myself into my studies.

My little brothers, however, remained more or less oblivious to the situation. It had been decided that what they did not know could not harm them. Wei Han, however, was moody and withdrawn. Whenever I tried to speak to him about the discord between Father and Mother, he would say he did not wish to know or talk about it. I suspect he had some inkling of what was the cause or at least thought he knew. He must have heard a biased account because he was very distant with Mother. Several times I caught him looking at her questioningly, even disdainfully.

Mother's bruises were healing slowly, but they were still obvious enough to prevent her from going out in public. She did not see a doctor. It would have been an embarrassment for the family. Ah Keng resorted to brewing evil-smelling herbs, which she bought from a Chinese herbal store, and applying the resulting balm to the bruises. Aunty would stay late into the night talking to Mother. She also had her own remedies. Once I saw her rolling a warm boiled egg over the bruises. Grandmother was also sympathetic although she could do little other than offer words of comfort and prayer.

Then late one afternoon, it must have been about nine days after the day of the beating, we returned home to find Mother gone. "Gone! Where, why, when?" we asked. There was panic. Aunty was at home, eyes red and swollen. She just stood there wringing her hands and blabbering incoherently. Something awful must have happened; she was never home during a working day, not even when she was ill. Her office was her sanctuary. We rushed from room to room, searching for Mother. In her bedroom, we found the cupboards and drawers thrown open and large black bin bags filled with Mother's belongings stood on the floor.

"Is Mother dead?" I screamed at my aunt. I did not understand why else my dependable, solid aunty would be sobbing the way she was. She shook her head vehemently. I ran to Grandmother's room and found her praying. "What's the matter?" I cried. Getting no sense from them, I turned to Ah Keng. "What has happened?"

Haltingly, she explained. "Your father . . . he . . . he ordered your mother to leave. He told her to go back to Malacca. He said that he did not want her around so that he could think more rationally as to what he should do. He then left. But he must have arranged it all because the driver just came and literally bundled your mother into a car and drove off. He gave her no time to pack."

"Didn't anyone intervene? Did no one go to Mother's help?"

"Your Aunty Nelly was not here, she was in the shop. *Tai Nai-nai* tried. She went after your father when he was leaving the room, but your father closed his ears to any reasoning. He just shouted. You should have seen him. He was like a crazy man. He accused your mother of having a lover and said he no longer trusted her."

I stared at them, incredulous at the cruel and presumptuous actions of my father. So there was no discussion. Mother had no choice. The servants were instructed to pack her clothes and personal effects to be sent on to her. Fury welled up in me. I choked back my tears. "How could you let Mother's things be put in bin bags?" I yelled at Aunty. "How could you? You have left her with no dignity. Where is the help you promised her?"

"They were your father's instructions. I had no part in it. By the time Ah Keng told me and I had rushed back, your mother had gone and the servants were packing her things. Don't look at me like that"

"Why do we always have to do as Father instructs? Can't we decide for ourselves what is right or wrong. I hate you. I hate you." I vented my anger on my aunty, but in my heart I knew that, like me and like Mother, she could not have prevented what had happened.

Hoarse and exhausted, I sat down. The servants had long since left the room. Ah Keng was looking after Wei Hoong and Wei Shu. Wei Han had bolted out of the house. Aunty Nelly and I were alone. "I think we should call Aunty Kai Min and Uncle Tek San," I suggested.

"Yes! Uncle Tek San will probably know what has brought this about. He has his ears firmly tuned to the grapevine. I have heard things as well," she volunteered hesitantly, without expanding further. Although I was 15, she still thought of me as a child.

"What things?" Without waiting for an answer, I knew there would not be one. I picked up the phone and called Aunty Kai Min. We had not seen her and Uncle Tek San for a long time. They had become distanced from Father. He felt that his sister had interfered with his household, offering unsolicited advice. He considered her a bad influence on Mother. However, I remembered Aunty Kai Min's kindness to Mother and how she and Uncle Tek San had helped bring my parents back together the last time. I waited, clutching the phone tightly, willing them to be at home. Finally, someone picked up the phone, I asked for Aunty Kai Min. She came to the phone and listened quietly to what I told her. When I had finished, I was breathless. My words had come tumbling out without structure, sequence and, possibly, sense.

"Stay there. We'll be with you shortly." Within the hour she arrived with Uncle Tek San.

* * * * *

Her first words were, "Is your father in?" We shook our heads and took the two of them through to the family room. With age, Aunty Kai Min had come to resemble Father, the same square jaw, heavy eyebrows and sharp eyes that could be as warm and charming as they could be deadly. She sat down and without any preliminaries began unfolding her plan of action. I felt I was in the presence of an army general.

"What we need to do is to get in touch with your mother to tell her she has our love and support. It will be easiest for me to contact her. I will drive down to Malacca tomorrow. Next, we have to find out what has brought this on. Does anyone have any idea?" She scrutinised each of us in turn.

"Ming Kong has this preposterous idea that Mei Yin is having an affair," said Aunty.

"Strange. In the natural course of events, knowing my brother," reasoned Aunty Kai Min aloud, "this would certainly provoke him to shout and rage. I am surprised that he resorted to such violence as well."

"Remember the last time? Well he did slap Mei Yin even then," said Aunty Nelly. "That is why I have always cautioned Mei Yin not to fight with him."

"Yes that was then and I think he hit Mei Yin because he thought she was going to launch herself at the other woman. This time, he came back home to ask Mei Yin to explain herself. Why then did he not let her do so?" Aunty Kai Min paused, her face still registering disbelief. She shrugged and continued, "Well, in any case, say his temper has gone worse, I would still have thought that if he had really wanted to drive Mei Yin away, he would have done so there and then. He is hot-headed and yet you say he has waited for over a week before taking any action." She shook her head. "Something is not right. It is not like him. He does not harbour malice. Someone is pushing him to do this." She turned to her husband, eyebrows raised quizzically, "Do you know anything we don't?"

Uncle Tek San looked up somewhat furtively; I could see his ears had turned a bright red. "Remember the . . . the last time?" he stammered, "I thought we agreed to keep out of his affairs? So, if I hear rumours, I try to keep out of it."

She glared at him. "What rumours?"

"I heard he has a girlfriend, mistress, whatever you want to call it. This time, apparently, it is more serious than before. He has set up a home for her."

"And you kept your mouth shut and did not tell us! We will talk about this later. For now I want you to find out more. Can you do it?"

"No! Why don't you do it, ask the servants? They probably know more than us. They meet with other maids and are privy to all sorts of confidential information. You should start there. I'm not as clever as you. So you do it," he repeated sullenly. Uncle Tek San was clearly peeved. He was uncomfortable and did not relish being told off in front of us. Over the years, he had become increasingly cowed by his wife, but he had no intention of being made a scapegoat. "Why get angry with me? It's your stupid brother who can't keep his pants up. What has that to do with me?"

Finding out from the servants was not as difficult as they had anticipated. Once Ah Keng was asked, a whole string of information came out.

"I give the Master's driver his breakfast," she explained, "and he takes me to the market and back. He tells me bits of this and that. He learns a lot from other drivers when they meet at the food stalls. When the boss is lunching with business associates or friends at the big restaurants, he ambles over to the stalls to have a smoke and a chat." Not wishing to create problems for the driver by giving the impression that he was skiving, she added quickly, "Where else would he be able to eat but these stalls. Rich people eat inside, poor people eat outside."

"He said Mr Wing Lok's driver had been asking him a lot of questions, especially about Mistress Mei Yin. He seemed uncommonly interested in knowing what she did, who her friends were and where she went. I told him he was *bodoh*, stupid to tell so much. He doesn't seem to know whose hand feeds him. *Ai yah*, what to do? You cannot trust these Malay drivers!"

"What else has he told you?" asked Aunty Kai Min, ignoring Ah Keng's comments. Ah Keng was known for her prejudices.

"He told me he is not as *bodoh* as I think. He claims he has wheedled important information out of the other driver. He says Master has a mistress."

"What else?" asked Aunty Kai Min.

"Yes, what else. What about the other maids, even you?" asked Aunty Nelly. "Have you heard anything?"

"Not much," she replied.

"And has anyone been asking you questions?"

Ah Keng became uneasy. Twisting the hem of her tunic, she replied. "Well, it might not be important. You know *Tai Nai-nai* is preparing to go into a nunnery. I've been going to the Tzu Yeh temple to pray and make offerings on her behalf. She cannot make the journey. I met this young girl. She was ever so friendly and helpful. She offered to help carry my baskets. I thought her a very pious young woman. When I pray, she prays. Every time I kneel before the altar, I see her there as well. I have never seen anyone doing so many *kowtow* so often and so fervently, such a good girl. Don't get many young people doing that these days, you know."

Ah Keng was digressing. Aunty Nelly gently returned her to the matter in hand, "Don't worry about her piety. What did she say?"

"Well, general things. She seemed very interested in weddings, especially in this family." Looking at me, she said, "She wanted to know how your father and mother got married. I thought perhaps she is going to get married and wants to know more about the ceremonies. I thought nothing of it at the time, but she just kept coming back to the subject. How are they arranged? It just went on and on. I don't know if this is significant. Recently, I've not seen her at the temple." There was more to tell, but she kept it to herself. She was afraid she would be scolded for saying too much to strangers.

Aunty Kai Min looked at Aunty Nelly and said, "I am not sure what to make of this. It seems strange, but I cannot put my finger on it. Perhaps I am becoming paranoid, too suspicious."

* * * * *

After Aunty Kai Min left, we clung to each other for comfort. We were happy that she would make sure Mother was well and pass on our messages of love. Aunty Nelly did not return to office; she stayed with us all day. She cuddled, kissed and comforted. After a while, Wei Shu and Wei Hoong fell asleep. They were exhausted by all the emotion of the day. For my part, it is difficult even now to describe how I felt. Physically, I was spent and I couldn't muster any coherent thoughts. I was angry one minute, sad the next.

Father came home early that day. We rushed downstairs. We were hoping to hear him say that it had all been a mistake. We waited, five pairs of accusing eyes, eyes that were swollen and red. We were to be disappointed. All he did was smile, open his arms and say, "What a greeting!" He looked anxious. It was awkward. I could not stand it and, when my younger brothers broke into tears again, I marched them upstairs. It was an act of defiance, which I would not have dared contemplate on a normal day. But it was not a normal day. Not for me, not for any of us. How dare he smile as though nothing had happened. I choked with fury.

We locked ourselves in my room, but not for long. Wei Han knocked and we opened the door. "Father says we should talk. He wants us in the family room."

"What family? What family do we have without Mother? Why pretend? And why are you carrying messages for Father?" I cried.

"Stop that, An Mei, that is enough!" said Father. I did not hear him coming up to my room, he had obviously heard me. His face was ashen, his early conciliatory tone completely gone. "I know what I am doing," he said sternly. Then, with effort, he softened his voice, "If you feel more comfortable here, we can talk in this room." He walked to one of the beds and sat down.

Wei Shu, my youngest brother, broke rank and ran to Father and clambered on to his knees. I stared at the floor not wanting to witness this treachery.

Clearing his throat, Father began. "I know this is hard for you. It is hard for us all. I am very sad too. Unfortunately, there are things grown-ups have to do, things that children cannot be expected to understand. It is best for all of us that your mother goes back to Malacca to stay with her mother. Trust me."

"I am not a child!" I retorted. "It is not best for me and it is not best for them," pointing at my brothers. "It might be best for you," I pressed on. "Why did you send Mother away? Is it because you want to marry someone else?"

"An Mei! Do not push your luck. Who has been filling your ears with this nonsense?" He looked past me straight at Aunty Nelly who was standing in the background. For once, she was not her usual deferential self and stood defiant.

"Don't look at me. People gossip. The children have ears. Is it true? You owe it to them, and for that matter to me as well as Mei Yin, to explain yourself."

"You know why I have sent her away. I have already explained to Mother. I do not want the children to know to protect their feelings," he replied softly, astonished at this outburst.

"Are you sure that's the reason? If it is, you have no real cause for concern. What you said to *Tai Nai-nai* is just not true."

"Are you going to marry someone else?" I persisted.

"No, no, of course not," he replied all the time looking at Aunty Nelly. Her eyes were brimming with tears.

"I know, though, that you will need someone to care for you." Keeping his eyes on Aunty, willing her not to interrupt, he continued, "I have asked a friend to come to stay, temporarily, to help me look after you. If you like her, she could remain longer. She is a wonderful, kind woman. You will like her."

A sob escaped from Aunty.

I shouted, "No! We don't need her. We have Aunty Nelly and we want Mother back."

"Mummy, Mummy," cried Wei Shu, scrambling off his knees to run to me.

"How could you? So soon! Mei Yin's bed is not even cold!" said Aunty reproachfully. It was, she told me later that evening, as though she did not count. He seemed to have totally forgotten that she was family, his second wife, at least in name, and loved all of us and had helped to looked after us.

"Will you stop! I know what's best for this family. I have made up my mind. I would like all of you," he paused to look at each of us in turn, "to give this a chance. I will have to think further about your mother's situation. I do not want to discuss it now. Let us all behave sensibly and go down for dinner."

It was a dinner never to be forgotten. Each mouthful choked me. I cried and sobbed into my bowl. I cannot recall Aunty being at the table.

Intrigues

Chapter 31

Humming a tune, Shirley walked into the breakfast room. She sat down at the table and poured herself a cup of coffee. Nursing the cup, she flicked through the newspaper that Ah Kum, the young maid, had placed in front of her. "Hmm, nothing much on. I will be going out later this morning. If Master calls, tell him I am with Mrs Lim," she instructed Ah Kum, who was busy dusting around pots of bamboo standing by the window. "You do not have to say anything more to him. I will be back round about five o'clock in good time for his return."

Shirley paused to be sure she had her maid's full attention, "Make sure Ah Hing prepares a good dinner. Master likes his food piping hot. If she can get skate, it would be good. He likes it in a chillied tamarind sauce with slices of fresh pineapple. If she cooks this *Nyonya* dish, tell her to stay with that theme. She tends to put together a mixture of dishes that do not go with each other. You know what I want, I will leave it to you."

"I will tell Ah Hing now before you leave, just in case she has some other suggestions," replied Ah Kum, wiping her hands on a towel tucked into one side of her tunic. Ah Kum had worked for Shirley since she was 15 and knew all her pet hates and loves. The cook, Ah Hing, had been recruited only a couple of months ago after the mistress moved into this big house. Already friction had arisen between the two of them. The cook was a more senior member of staff than a housemaid, but Shirley liked to give instructions through Ah Kum. The cook disliked this intensely. Ah Kum realised that life

would be better if she had both women on her side so she tried hard
to smooth the way, particularly by making cook feel important.

Shirley looked up, nodded and smiled. "Good! You are learning
fast, a real diplomat. You did well getting the information from
Master's servant. Mind, not a word to anyone, especially Master. You
are sure she had no idea who you were?"

Ah Kum nodded. "Yes! She's a chatterbox, likes to show off her
knowledge. I just coaxed her on, she didn't take much persuading."

"Well then, go to Ah Hing and do what you need to do. I'll see
you get an extra bonus this New Year."

Pleased that everything had gone smoothly, Shirley picked up
the phone and called Wing Lok.

"Any news?" she asked as soon as he answered.

"What about?" he replied. He sounded vague, even disinterested.

"You know what about. Has Ming Kong mentioned anything
more about his wife or family?"

"No, nothing. He is troubled and moody. Goes around with a
long face. He feels guilty about sending her away. Of course, the
children and that woman Nelly are playing on it. Apparently, he had
a rough time with them last night."

"Hmm, as I expected. They need careful handling. You must
strengthen his resolve in case it falters. Tell him he will lose face if he
changes his mind and has her back. Remind him it would be bad for
the children if gossip about her affair spreads. Say that it will be all
over the school. Remind him how cruel school children can be. I've
been hinting at this. It might not go down well if I were to be more
forceful and direct. It would be more convincing coming from you."

"Yes, yes, I have been saying all this. You don't have to tell me
what to do. I made sure that everyone important in town knew
about Mei Yin's meetings with this young doctor. What do you
think drove him to kick her out?" Wing Lok blustered, irritated with
her instructions. "I have put him on to that lawyer we spoke about
earlier. The lawyer took some convincing to take on the job of
helping make a strong case for annulling his marriage. But as I see it,

those old-fashioned ceremonial weddings might have been okay in the past, but not in this day and age. More important, no attempt was made after the war to make things legal. Of course, she can kick up a fuss and, if she has enough money, hire a lawyer to make things difficult. The lawyer says she will have grounds. I doubt that will happen. She is a weak, ignorant woman."

"Good! I knew I could rely on you." Shirley was pleased.

"Yes, you would not be where you are without me. Just remember that. By the way, keep your mouth shut and do not make even oblique suggestions. Just pretend not to know anything and keep your temper under wraps," he cautioned. "Do not call me unless absolutely necessary. He could be with me and we would not want him to know we are on such close terms," he sniggered.

Shirley was offended. She held back, however, reminding herself that she would have to get rid of him eventually. Aloud, she said, "You're right, of course."

Chapter 32

Kai Min settled back in the car seat and turned to look at her husband. They had driven for nearly three hours without saying a word. When they had returned home after leaving Mei Yin's children, they had had a blazing row. She had accused him of keeping important information from her. In the heat of the argument, she even suggested that he may have had a hand in causing Mei Yin's situation.

He had denied this vehemently. "Mei Yin is like a sister to me. Of course, I did not want such a thing to happen. Do not blame me every time your brother goes astray. Look at your father and his father before him. It is in their blood. Thank God the girls in your family do not behave in the same way. Not that the two of you are so different otherwise. Look at your temper. You should have some sympathy for me."

Now as they journeyed in silence, Kai Min thought again of what Tek San had said. "I must change my ways," she thought, "otherwise I could also lose my husband to someone else." Impulsively, she leaned over, caught hold of his hand and mouthed, "Sorry."

Tek San smiled, shrugged his shoulders, "I don't know what to do with you. You are a fierce little devil, a real *chilly padi*." Patting her hand, he said, "Let's forget last night. We were upset. We should concentrate on helping Mei Yin and the children."

"Have you found out anything at all from your friends?"

"Not really. I have not had much time. The woman's name is Shirley. Ming Kong has bought a house for her. Very little is known about her origins. I have heard she is fond of gambling. I doubt Ming Kong knows that. A besotted man rarely believes anything bad of the one he is enamoured with even if you wave the evidence in front of his nose."

The car swung into a dirt road. A wake of dust was stirred up as the wheels bit into dry, baked soil. Within minutes the windscreen was coated with an orange-red film.

"We are near Mei Yin's mother's house," Tek San announced. "A few hundred yards and we'll be there."

"Wait, can we stop for a minute to discuss what we are going to say?" Kai Min asked.

Tek San pulled the car over to the side of the road. Drumming his fingers on the wheel, he said, "It goes without saying, we should try to bring Mei Yin and your brother back together. How we set about doing it needs to be discussed. It will be very difficult. He is very stubborn. We also need to find out if he has provided for her. If he hasn't, we must see how we can help. For me that would be the easiest part. What about you? Do you have a plan?"

She shook her head. "I agree we should try to get them back together again. It won't happen overnight though. Meantime, what about the children? I feel very sorry for them. They are completely cut off from their mother. I am sure she will ask our help to see them. I have no idea how we can manage it."

"That part, I leave to you." Tek San was not going to get involved in what he considered woman's work. Instead, he continued, unsure how his wife would respond, "I have an idea. What if I were to involve Mei Yin in our business?"

"What do you mean?"

"I have not thought it through so don't hold me to it. For a long time, we've been trying to expand our food department. Kuala Lumpur is getting expensive. There is too much competition. Malacca is still a rather sleepy place and relatively cheap. It might offer better opportunities, especially now that the government is trying to improve the tourist trade in Malacca."

"So?"

"It would be worth seeing whether we could set up a business here. If we can, Mei Yin might be able to help. Both she and her mother know their way around. I just want you to know what I am thinking. You know, to make sure you don't object before I open my mouth." He grinned. "I don't want you to be jealous."

Taken back, Kai Min stared at him, uncertain. She punched him playfully. "Why should I be jealous? In any case, Mei Yin may not be in Malacca long enough to be involved in your business."

* * * * *

The car turned into another, even smaller dirt road. They had arrived. The house was just as Kai Min remembered. She had visited it once before when she gave her sister-in-law a lift there on her way south to Singapore. The house had looked drab then, but it was even worse now. Some of the roof tiles were cracked and quite a few were missing. Corrugated strips of metal had been anchored here and there with bricks to keep out the rain. The paint on the walls had long been spoiled by the driving monsoon rains.

"I find it strange that Ming Kong has done nothing to make this place more comfortable for his in-laws," remarked Tek San.

"It's because Mei Yin's mother is proud. She doesn't want to ask and he has been too busy to consider such things. Mei Yin has been sending her money when she can. I don't think he has visited for years. It was always Mei Yin's mother who came to us. I suppose my mother is to blame. She set a trend and we never thought to change it."

They climbed the wooden steps to the front door and called, "Mei Yin, are you there?"

Slow footsteps and a tapping sound could be heard coming towards them. It was overtaken by quicker, surer footsteps. A voice called out, "Kai Min? Is it really you?" Mei Yin stood in front of them, her face a mixture of relief and hope. "Did Ming Kong send you? The children? Are they with you?" She looked past them. Seeing no one was with there, her face fell.

Her mother soon joined her. Sook Ping walked with a slow shuffle, one foot dragging after the other. Time had not been kind to her. She leaned heavily on a walking stick. She lifted a gnarled and swollen hand and patted her daughter's shoulders to comfort her. "Come in, come in, take a seat," she said, motioning them to enter.

They sat down on wooden stools set around a table. In its middle stood a rattan box. Lined with a padding of assorted cotton cloth, it served as a tea cozy, keeping the tea warm throughout the day. Mei Yin lifted its lid and took out the china teapot that was nestling there. Carefully, she took out four small teacups from the box, set them on the table and poured out the tea.

Kai Min did not know how to begin. She reached out for Mei Yin's hands. "The children are fine, really they are. I saw them only yesterday. They miss you. They all send their love. Look, they have drawn a card for you. An Mei and Nelly are looking after them.

"And Ming Kong?"

"I have not seen Ming Kong, I thought it best to speak to you first, but I gather he is none too happy."

Mei Yin nodded. She did not speak for fear it would cause a fresh round of sobbing.

Kai Min sighed, "I'm sorry. I blame myself for not keeping in closer touch with you. What a mess!" She paused, feeling awkward and uncertain. "I'm here to help, but I need to hear from you that Ming Kong's accusations are false."

Mei Yin did not reply.

"Tell me everything, please," begged Kai Min.

"Kai Min!" reproached Tek San. "How can you ask? How could you doubt Mei Yin?" Embarrassed he looked guiltily at Sook Ping.

"I am not doubting. I just want to hear it from Mei Yin." Kai Min turned round to glare at Tek San. In that brief instant, angry at being contradicted, she forgot her resolve to be kind to her husband and reverted to her usual form. "Look, we need to work with a clean slate, have the facts as they really are, before we can make our case. The more we know, the better. All we know, so far, are bits and pieces from different sources. If I start on the wrong foot because I do not know all the facts, it could easily make matters worse."

"Tell her, Mei Yin," said her mother.

An Mei's Recollections

Chapter 33

"This is Shirley. She's here to look after you," Father announced. We were gathered in the family room, Wei Han, Wei Hoong, Wei Shu and me. We stood in a line. Father had told us that morning he had a surprise for us. That we were to be neat and tidy for when he came home in the afternoon. "Yippee! Mother must be coming back," I had thought, optimistically. I rushed around bossing my brothers, telling them that they had to be good, to bathe and dress neatly, that it was likely Mother would be back. By lunch time, I was convinced Mother was coming home. I had also convinced my brothers.

Now this! I stood frozen. We had never believed he would bring her here; we felt sure that our strong reaction when he first suggested bringing a friend home to look after us had worked. My brothers looked at me accusingly.

"How dare he?" I thought. I felt my face flush.

Father looked at each of us and me in particular. "I expect you to treat Shirley with respect. I have made her promise to report any bad behaviour to me. I trust I am making myself clear."

Leaving Shirley to fuss over my little brothers, he walked over to me. "I do not want to see that expression on your face when I am speaking to you." He took me by the shoulders and lowered his head until we were face to face. "Do you understand? I have had enough of this over the past few weeks." Then, softening his voice, "I don't know what has come over you. I am only trying to do my best for all of you. Give Shirley a chance. She is a lovely lady. You may not think so, but it is kind of her to offer to help. We will talk about your mother another day. It's too soon and too painful for everyone at present. And I can see you are not in the right mood."

He smiled and clasped me to him. The smile, the hug, made me believe for a moment that things would be fine. The spell was shattered a moment later by a sharp call from across the room.

"Come and see, Ming Kong. So clever!" Shirley exclaimed, clapping her hands.

Wei Shu was grinning his toothless grin, eyes crinkled up, pointing and reading the alphabets she was holding up. Happy to be praised, he rushed around picking up more pieces of alphabet, reading and then throwing them down, his little sturdy legs busy as he ran to and fro. Wei Hoong, not to be outdone, brought out his school books to show her his work. Even Wei Han seemed reconciled, sitting by himself, trying out a pen he had been given. Father went over to join them. I was left standing alone.

Shirley walked over to me. "So you're An Mei!"

I stared at her. She touched her hair self-consciously.

"Would you like to go shopping with me? Give me a chance to get to know you better."

I wavered. She smiled. I saw no warmth in her eyes. They were as hard as flint. I shook my head. "I have my exams soon."

"Don't worry about exams. Girls don't have to take them seriously, you know. Take time off. The best thing to do is to enjoy yourself. There are some nice boutiques that have just what I think would suit you. Come with me. Tomorrow?" She cocked her head, her smile persuasive.

I shook my head. She was saying the opposite of what Aunty Nelly taught me. Girls have to put in more effort to achieve. That was what I intended to do. I did not like her.

"Well, if you change your mind." She left me to join the others. I could see she was not pleased.

My little brothers were happy to be with Father and were flattered by the praise she lavished on them. A box of chocolates also helped. We were never allowed to eat chocolates before dinner and here was Wei

Shu taking his fill, his lips a dark stain of rich brown. I wanted to go to my room, but I did not want to attract attention. So I just sat on my own, my heart heavy, a lump in my throat. I tried not to sniffle.

"Go to your room, if you wish to behave like that." Father had noticed. I ran out to my room, longing for the return of Aunty Nelly.

* * * * *

Mother had been gone over a year. We had not seen her, but we kept in secret contact through Aunty Kai Min. Mother spoke to me a few times on the phone. I was not able to call her; calls to Malacca had to go through the operator. Father would have found out. Mother called instead when we knew it would be safe. Aunty Nelly also kept in touch by letter. I could not read them because they were in Chinese. Aunty Nelly would read them to me in bed at night.

Everything had to be done in secret. Mother sent her letters to the shopkeeper next door to our store. I could not tell Wei Shu and Wei Hoong about them because they were likely to let the secret out. Wei Han was still angry with Mother. He said it was all her fault. He would not talk about her.

"Why, Wei Han? Mummy loves you best." I was shocked.

"No, she doesn't. She did once. Since she went to hospital it has been you and her cooped up in the bedroom talking. I was not included. You turned her against me!"

He was jealous! I had no idea. Wei Han had always been Mother's favourite; she loved all the boys, but Wei Han most of all. As for me, it was only lately that Mother had shown any interest. He was, I thought, extremely silly.

I lay in bed staring at the ceiling, listening to the chatter and laughter downstairs. I looked around my room. I loved it, every square familiar inch; my desk and bookshelves by the window; my potted plants; my bed with its colourful batik quilt. How strange that everything still looked so normal when my life had been turned upside down.

I dozed off, exhausted, only to be woken by Ah Keng. "An Mei," she whispered. "they've all gone for ice cream at the new A & W Snack Bar. Your brothers will probably be full when they get back; they won't want dinner. I've brought a drink. Aunty Nelly will be back soon. Will you wait for her or would you like to eat now?"

I had eaten almost nothing during lunch. I was hungry. "Can I eat in my room, this once?"

"Just this time," she replied. She fussed around the table. She looked ill at ease. I could see she was steeling herself to say something. "An Mei, I am leaving to join your grandmother at the temple. I am staying just long enough to pass on my duties to the new Madam's maid. New Madam is bringing her own maids tomorrow."

"Not you as well. Don't leave. Please, please, we'll have no one."

"Shh, shh. I will visit often. I cannot leave your grandmother on her own. She is too old. Anyway, your Aunty Nelly is here."

"Yes, but she cannot take time off from her office. Father will not allow it. He thinks we are cared for now by this woman. If she brings her staff here, I won't be able to speak to Mother at all. They will intercept the calls and report them to Father."

"Oh dear, oh dear! I will bring some food up. You will feel better after you have eaten," she said. Sighing heavily, she muttered to herself, "*Ai yah! ham kah luen sai loong*, the whole family is in turmoil. What to do? What to do?"

I sat in darkness after she left. Aunty Nelly would, must, know what to do. She was my rock. I loved her dearly and trusted her completely. Did she know Father had brought this Shirley home?

Huddled under my bedclothes, I waited until Ah Keng's footsteps approached the door once again.

"Come, come, get up. I have brought you food. You had best eat it while it is hot. No point starving yourself. It will not help," she said, carrying in a tray.

My stomach rumbled with hunger. I got up and went over to my desk where she had placed the tray. A hot fragrant steam wafted up to my nostrils. It was wanton noodles. I gulped, sat down and ate.

Ah Keng waited until I had finished eating before coming up to my room to tell me that Aunty Nelly was back. "Wipe your tears An Mei. Don't upset Aunty Nelly. She is already very unhappy," she advised as she straightened my bed. "I have to get your mother's room ready."

"For what?"

Ah Keng stood still for a few seconds as if considering what her answer should be. "I am telling you this to prepare you. Please try not to get upset. Your father has instructed that the new Madam be given that room."

My response must have been a wail, I cannot remember. She came over and rested her hands on my shoulders. "I am telling you," she repeated, "so you will not be surprised when you see her there. You are a big girl. Just bear it for a few more years. Study hard. Your mother wouldn't like to see your studies disrupted because of this."

I could not bear it. One bad thing after another. I pushed the bowl away, guilty that I could eat in the midst of all this. I wanted to get away, escape from all this misery. I ran blindly out of the room only to crash into Aunty Nelly. "Steady, steady," she said as she hugged me. That night, we talked till the early hours of the morning. No immediate solution came out of our discussion, only a resolve to direct our energies to better ourselves and the hope that Mother would eventually return.

* * * * *

"She has taken the news very badly," said Father. It was the day following his introduction of Shirley. I stood outside the family room straining to hear what he was saying to her. I had been summoned downstairs by Father. I stood quietly by the door.

"I am a bit surprised at her reaction. I had hoped it would be easier but . . . " his voice trailed off for a second before he resumed resolutely, "I am troubled, to say the least, but we must give her time. These are big changes; the children need time to get to know you."

"I will do anything for you. You know that," she replied. "Even if it is against my better judgment. An Mei is very difficult. She has a sharp tongue and . . ." Shirley sighed, leaving the sentence unfinished.

"What? Has she been rude?"

"No, no, forget it. She is young and upset because of her mother. I will bring her around. I need your support to do it though."

I walked in. Father was sitting on the settee; Shirley was perched on an armrest at his side. He looked tired.

"So, here you are."

I nodded.

"Do you not address your elders? Where are your manners?"

"I do not know what to call her."

"For the moment call her Shirley-*sum*."

I was shocked! So soon! The word *sum* means aunty. It is often used by children to address their father's secondary wives. In Chinese, Aunty Nelly would be "Nelly-*sum*." We called Kai Min, my father's sister, *koo-mah*. Both *sum* and *koo-mah* translate into English as aunty, but there is obviously a big difference in how the words are used. By making us call Shirley the way we called Aunty Nelly, Father was making clear her position in the household.

"I would like you, for my sake as much as your own, to behave well and make me proud of you. Shirley will be moving into the house. Grandmother has left and Ah Keng too." He frowned. "I must say I am surprised that Ah Keng left without saying goodbye. I thought she would have waited until I had got back here. I wanted to give her something extra for everything that she has done over the years. Well, never mind. We have new staff now and Shirley will manage them."

"Why can't Aunty Nelly stay at home during the day?" I asked.

"She's needed in the office. I don't wish to discuss the matter until you are ready to be sensible. I want you to come down for dinner and to behave. You are the eldest, you should set a good example."

I left the room, but I waited outside hoping to speak to Father alone when he came out. I could hear them faintly.

"An Mei is very attached to Nelly," Shirley said. "And you know, Nelly has not been very friendly. You saw how she greeted me when we went to see her in the office. As long as she's around, I don't think I have any chance of winning An Mei over. I would love to look after her, but I cannot do it if she continues to reject me."

"Nelly has been looking after An Mei since a baby. There is a strong bond between them. I wouldn't want to break it. You cannot expect Nelly, who is a member of my immediate family, to behave differently," he replied wearily.

"Yes, of course, but it's going to be hard. My position is not helped by uncertainty. If we were to marry properly, if they knew I am to be their mother, they might accept me. This . . . this position that I have is just untenable . . . moving me into your house as another *sum* gives me no status. I would like us to marry properly in the eyes of the law."

"I am not sure if it can be done. I know Wing Lok's lawyer says my marriage to Mei Yin can be annulled, but I have consulted another lawyer and the case is not as clearcut as he suggests. I don't wish to sue for divorce on grounds of adultery as so far I have not been able to get tangible proof. Until I can find a more amenable way, I am still bound to Mei Yin. And what about Nelly? I owe her too. Let's leave things as they are until I have sorted out the legalities of this mess."

Soft murmuring followed. I could not hear them. Then I heard him say, "Come on, let's get some fresh air."

I tiptoed and ran up to my room. It did not look as though speaking to Father would be of much use!

* * * * *

The noise of doors banging shut, followed by a starting car, echoed through the house. I waited. Once the car had left, I ran downstairs to the kitchen. Ah Keng's sudden departure without saying goodbye seemed very strange. Earlier she had said she would stay till late afternoon to say her farewells. "Don't worry, I'll be here. You can not get rid of me so easily," she had joked to lighten our gloom.

The kitchen was a large, square, sunny room. Attached to it was a little kitchenette. Equipped with charcoal stoves, big woks and clay curry pots, this was where the real cooking took place. It was Mother who had suggested cooking there rather than in the main kitchen with its furniture and fitted cupboards. It would not do, she had said, to have charcoal fires, hot oil and cauldrons of steaming broth in such a beautiful new kitchen.

I could find no one in either the kitchen or the kitchenette. Where were the new maids Ah Keng had mentioned? I went out to the back of the kitchen. This part of the house was normally off-limits for us. Father had told us not to intrude. This was the servants' domain. But since Mother had left I had often visited Ah Keng for solace. Here in the evening, after the day's work, Ah Keng would sit on a wooden stool, roll a cigarette and have a quiet smoke. I would talk to her then. It was also where she chatted with the driver and gave him his meals when he was in town.

I was not surprised, therefore, to find the driver having a cup of coffee there. It was Father's driver, not the one who usually drove us to school. Father must have been driving when he left with Shirley. With the driver were two women who I had never seen before. They were talking excitedly.

"Lucky boss-lady sent her away. It was very embarrassing for me to meet her here. She recognised me immediately. *Ai yah*, she said, aren't you the girl in the temple who asked me so many questions. I didn't know what to say. I expected this, you know," the younger of the two women said. "I didn't want to come so early. I thought I might meet her. I said to boss, 'let Ah Hing go to take over from Ah Keng,' but he insisted. Boss-lady could not say no."

I stepped closer. They heard me and turned to look. When the driver saw me, he muttered in Malay, "The boss's daughter." He looked away, uneasy.

"Where is Ah Keng? Has she really left without saying good-bye?" I asked.

"Don't know," they replied, shrugging their shoulders.

Tides of Change: 1961

Chapter 34

Mei Yin replaced the phone and looked forlornly around her. She was in a largish room. In one corner, a group of women were busy preparing a pastry mix for moon-cakes. Next to them, another table was presided over by four women. They kneaded, rolled and cut; their hands moved deftly and swiftly to fill the pastry. Several young girls moved in and out of the room carrying trays of prepared cakes to the next room where the ovens were. Laughter and chatter filled the room. Most of the noise came from the farthest end of the room where the fillings were prepared: sweet black bean paste and salted egg yolks; ground lotus seeds, dried fruits, preserved flowers and crushed rock sugar; and plain red bean sprinkled with sesame. The women vied and competed to produce the best filling. They were promised an extra bonus if the cakes sold well.

Tek San referred jokingly to the room as the 'four seasons kitchen'. It was where special confectioneries were produced for the different festive seasons. For the spring (Lunar) festival, it would churn out biscuits made of thin coconut-cream batter. Cooked between round metal plates over hot charcoal and rolled into wafer-thin leaves, the women called them 'love letters', a labour of love because the heat from the hot plates burned their hands. *Lin-koh*, a sticky cake made from rice flour and black molasses, also featured prominently in the Lunar festival. To serve them, dried cakes of *lin-koh* had to be sliced and re-steamed until soft and then eaten with freshly grated coconut. Alternatively, the cakes were sandwiched between slices of yam, dipped in batter and served fried, crisped on the outside and soft in the centre. Both ways of preparing the cakes symbolised the earth coming back to life and the start of the planting season.

Sook Ping had initially opposed making *lin-koh*. "There's too much work for such an uncertain market." But Tek San made light of her opposition. "Don't worry, we will not rely only on them. There are enough festive seasons to keep this kitchen busy all the year round. We have the Dragon Boat festival on the fifth day of the fifth lunar month. We will be busy preparing *choong* then. And, don't forget, we have the full moon festival on the 15th of the eighth lunar month. He would have gone on to illustrate the long list of cakes that would be churned out, but the women protested, "Stop, no more, we believe you!"

More than 18 months had passed since Tek San and Kai Min had driven to Malacca in search of Mei Yin. After the meeting they had discussed long and hard how best to help her. Giving money would not do, they concluded. Mei Yin's mother had always refused hand-outs. In the end, Tek San's idea of expanding his food business to Malacca, combined with Sook Ping and Mei Yin's experience in making cakes, gave rise to the idea of a pastry kitchen.

To start with, they had to find suitable premises, a job Tek San took on. When none could be found within budget, they bought a bungalow and converted it. Then came the recruitment of staff and planning the production line, a task given to Mei Yin and her mother.

The two women scoured the neighbourhood in search of people with differing expertise in cake making. In Malacca, amongst the *Nyonya* families, practically every household could boast a culinary skill of one kind or another. In one case, almost all the adult women of the family, mother, daughter, daughter-in-law and cousin, were recruited. Mei Yin worked out the quantities of ingredients to be purchased and the cakes to be produced, and the cost and prices. Finding suppliers and sales outlets was not a problem. They were readily available through Tek San's existing businesses. Nelly advised and liaised from a distance.

"How is Mei Yin?" Kai Min asked Sook Ping during a quick visit to the pastry kitchen a month after it was launched.

Sook Ping shook her head. "Not too good. She is fine during the day. Look at her now as she dashes around the kitchen. She works like a person driven. The work has been good for her. She confessed to me that it was the first time she had made use of the little she had learned at school. Come nightfall, however, she is a different person. She sleeps very little. She has been pacing the room night after night and I hear her tossing and turning in bed. Some nights she sits by the phone biting her fingers to stop herself from calling the children."

* * * * *

Mei Yin walked over to her mother who was busy helping out with the preparation of the bean paste. "A bit more sugar is needed," she was saying to one of the women. "Remember? When we made the trial batch, we agreed that the filling needed to be sweeter. I reckon we need to increase the sugar by about a tenth. This means we need two *katties* of sugar for this amount of bean paste. You must measure the ingredients and be consistent. No more a pinch of this and a drop of that! It won't work when you are making such large quantities."

She smiled to take the edge off her words. It had proved difficult to persuade the women to follow a recipe. They all wanted to do it their own way; they claimed to have managed for years without measuring and did not need to start now. Fortunately, after some initial resentment, they agreed to follow instructions. The hands-on approach of Sook Ping and Mei Yin won them over. Now, they merely winked and grinned in response to Sook Ping's gentle chiding.

"Yes-*lah*, boss-lady! No problem," they would reply cheekily.

Wiping her hands on the large makeshift apron tied round her waist, she turned to her daughter. "What is wrong?"

"Kai Min just phoned. Can we talk in the office?"

"Yes, of course." Aware that the women had stopped work to stare, Sook Ping asked them to carry on without her. "When this is finished, prepare the next batch. Remember, measure!" she instructed, with a big smile. "I'll be back in a minute."

They walked over to the little cubicle that passed for an office. Inside the office, boxes of stationary and files were still unpacked. Pushing them aside, they sat down.

Sook Ping rubbed her back and legs. They had been troubling her all day. Mei Yin went to her mother and gently massaged her back and neck. "Does this help?"

"Mmm, nice. So what did Kai Min say?"

"Not good news. She has made no progress at all with Ming Kong. She has been unable to see or speak to the children now that he has this woman in the house. When she phones, there seems always to be something or other to prevent the maids from passing on the call or having the children come to the phone. She finds it hard to go to the house in case the woman is there. She said her palms itch to slap her. You know how hot-tempered Kai Min is?"

"What about Nelly? Can she help?"

"Only when she is at home to receive Kai Min's calls and pass them to the children. Nelly is having a very hard time. There is almost open warfare between the two women."

"Can't Kai Min try to talk to Ming Kong directly and persuade him to let us see the children? Surely he cannot say no all the time?" asked Sook Ping. "You've not seen them for two years."

"Tek San is still working on this. He says Ming Kong will agree only if I accept a divorce, something about signing a document declaring that I am not his wife and will not make any claims on him. He is worried Tek San will help me get a lawyer to contest him."

"But I thought your marriage is considered worthless because it was not officially registered?"

"I thought so too, but, according to Tek San, a good lawyer could make a convincing case for it. Of course, he doesn't want it to come to this. It would mean laundering dirty linen in public, not good for Ming Kong or the children. We must remember that Kai Min is Ming Kong's sister. This makes it difficult for them to help." Mei Yin sat down and continued in a small voice, "I don't understand what is legally right and wrong. All I want is my children. I don't want his money. He is worried that if I have access to the children, I'll turn them against him. I suppose he'd rather they suffer."

"Perhaps we should risk going to Kuala Lumpur to see what can be done," her mother suggested. "Let's think about it this evening. We should get on with the cakes now." Hugging Mei Yin to her, she comforted, "Have courage. Something good must come out of this. I believe that right is on our side. Eventually we will win."

"Yes, I will go. In fact I want to go. I am not afraid of meeting him. I am ready to do battle." Mei Yin's eyes flashed as she spoke. Her colour heightened and for a moment, the spirited Mei Yin of old surfaced.

Sook Ping studied her daughter. She had seen her spirit eroded over the years, reaching its lowest ebb after the loss of the baby. Mei Yin had been almost a zombie then. Perhaps, at last, her fire and determination were returning.

Chapter 35

The last vanload of cartons and boxes had been stored. Nelly checked the items against her list, signed the delivery sheet, and returned to her office where Tek San was waiting. Since taking over the management of the mini stores, Nelly's responsibilities had grown. He had been amazed by her application and ability to learn. When she first started, Tek San had been sceptical of her ability to run a store. Now, she was running a chain of them almost single-handedly, overseeing the accounts, sorting out staff problems, and checking and monitoring the inventories.

He recalled her words when they had learned that a huge supermarket was going to be built in Kuala Lumpur. They had met to discuss how their stores would be affected.

"People come to us for competitive prices and good service," she had said. "With the entry of larger supermarkets into the business, we will face greater competition. I have no doubt about that. But, if we can maintain the variety of goods on offer and price them competitively, we will continue to have a niche, especially if we are not competing in the same neighbourhood."

She had been right. Her business acumen had proved itself over and over again, thought Tek San. He looked at her as she rushed in, hair awry, spectacles perched on her nose, eyes squinting. She was breathing heavily from the effort of rushing about. She had put on weight. "Probably too many hastily eaten bowls of noodles," he thought, smiling wryly.

"Sorry, I am a bit behind. Did you get a cup of tea?" Her voice was off-hand and curt. Tek San looked at her in surprise because her normally long-winded entreaty to take tea was unusually brief. Before he could answer, she launched into a tirade. "Her Majesty turned up here today. She poked her nose into everything. Said she should have a closer involvement in the stores. She marched in without so much as a greeting!" Bringing a hand up to her throat in emphasis, Nelly continued, "I have had enough of this woman! She really is the limit, but when I try to talk to Ming Kong, he just shrugs me off."

"He is very unhappy."

"He brought it on himself. I have no sympathy. I mean, both Mei Yin and I have worked hard, supporting him through thick and thin. But when the good times came to stay, he changed. I know Mei Yin can be thoughtless at times. She married him so young! What does he expect? He kept her at home, stopped her from improving herself!"

Tek San stared at Nelly in amazement. He had never seen her with her hackles up. She had always been loyal to his brother-in-law, always making excuses for him. Something must have happened. He waited, his expression encouraging her to continue.

"I am here only because of the children. Last night An Mei said that stupid woman told her there was no point in studying. That no provisions would be made to see her through university."

"What? I have never heard Ming Kong say that."

"She could have made it up to taunt An Mei. But I would not be surprised if this isn't what she is planning. She slapped Wei Hoong so viciously, the whole of one side of his face became inflamed. And all because he had allegedly been opening the fridge one too many times. A reprimand I can understand, but a slap that hard? It's completely uncalled for."

She kept busy with her hands, trying to control her emotions. She stacked the pile of papers in front of her and fussed with pencils and pens. After several arrangements, none of which seem to satisfy her, she gave up. "What can we do, I mean what can we really do to get out of this mess? Every time I talk to Mei Yin, I hear her cry; the same thing happens when I speak to An Mei. Ming Kong is unapproachable. Even the boys are feeling it as this woman . . ."

"Call her by her name," interrupted Tek San.

"As I was saying, this woman, this Shirley, is beginning to show her true colours." Nelly gave Tek San a withering look. Over the past few years, the relationship between the two of them had become one of equals. His original picture of her when she was young as a *femme fatale*, he had come to realise, was mistaken. Now he had only respect for her.

"I finally cornered Ming Kong. We spoke at length," Tek San told her. "He did not say it, but I have the feeling that he is beginning to regret his actions. He is missing Mei Yin, more than he lets on. Unfortunately, his pride and suspicious mind won't allow him to admit, even to himself, that he was wrong."

"Is he no longer enamoured with this wom… uh…uh … Shirley? If he isn't, why is she still with us?"

"I think he is and he isn't. Anyway, from what I hear, she is none too happy either. Being in the main house, surrounded by children, is not her idea of fun. Cramps her style. Some of the bad vibes must be passing on to him. Just last night we met someone at the Tai Tong restaurant who knew her. They play *mahjong* with her. They told us that she complains that she has to hurry home to mind what she calls 'a bunch of ungrateful brats'. Apparently she doesn't like having to cut short her *mahjong* when before she could stay as long as she liked."

He waited a few seconds to let his words sink in before adding, "She is also getting seriously into debt."

"Serve her right!" said Nelly. She lowered her voice. "Keep this to yourself. A couple of days ago, I found her maid, Ah Kum, in tears. She had been sacked. Shirley accused her of being too lenient with the children. We could not speak in the house so I arranged for her to come here to the shop. I learned the whole story, of how she wheedled information from Ah Keng, *Nai-nai*'s maid, how Shirley used it to persuade Ming Kong to get rid of Mei Yin. How Shirley abetted and supported his suspicion of Mei Yin. In Ah Kum's words, *kah yeem, kah choh*, at every turn Shirley had added salt and vinegar to the situation!"

Grim-faced, Nelly continued, "I also gained another important bit of information from Ah Kum. Before Shirley moved in with us, she had a frequent visitor at her other house. Wing Lok!"

"Wing Lok? Are you sure?"

Nelly nodded. "That is what she said. Do you know what the connection is between them? Can you find out?"

"You did well getting all this from Ah Kum." Tek San was astonished at the change in Nelly. Mei Yin's departure and the unceremonious way in which Ming Kong had brought Shirley into the family must have been the cause. She was no longer self-effacing and deferential to the point where, at times, she appeared colourless. He wondered if his brother-in-law realised how much he depended on her for this side of his business and what would happen if she left. In fact, he wondered if Nelly owned any share of his brother-in-law's stores. Probably not, he kept his wives on such a tight financial rein. Funny that! Ming Kong was not succeeding as well with his mistress.

Ignorant of Tek San's thoughts, Nelly continued, "It was luck really. She was remorseful about what she had done, especially after she got to know the children and grew fond of them."

* * * * *

Shirley was exasperated. Things had not gone as smoothly. She had welcomed the move to the main house. She took it as a statement of Ming Kong's intentions. Confident it would be followed by a proposal of marriage, she had swung into the role of mother with some enthusiasm. The two younger boys were easy to handle. Boxes of sweets and chocolates, a few toys and trips to the A & W for one of the new soft ice creams and they were happy. The older children, Wei Han and especially An Mei, were different. Wei Han was distantly polite, but not hostile. She felt she might win him over with time. The girl, however, was hostile and impossible! No amount of gifts and cajoling would persuade her to relent. Her father called her stubborn, an apt description. Shirley loathed the sight of her.

By the second year the situation had become intolerable. The presence of the children wore down Shirley's patience. It was difficult to play the seductive siren with so many eyes on her. Ming Kong looked sheepish when she made any intimate advance in front of them. Her daily fix of *mahjong* had become a hastily-snatched unsatisfactory hour or so while the children were at school. She even had to miss the races because of school holidays.

She had thought her presence in the main house would so demoralise Nelly that she would leave. Wing Lok had assured her that Nelly was a *chui fan poh*, a kitchen maid good only for cooking rice and would be no competition. "Don't worry! A fat thing like that, you can make mince meat of her." Yet, Nelly was still around. In fact, she seemed to be around even more. She was coming home early most days.

"A fat thing she might be and hardly a sight for sore eyes," thought Shirley, "but she still exerts influence over Ming Kong." No matter the slights and the insults Shirley delivered when Ming Kong was not around, Nelly clung on doggedly. Her face stony, she looked through Shirley as though she did not exist.

Tense, Shirley paced up and down the room. Pausing mid-stride, she went to the dressing table, opened a drawer and searched for the packet of cigarettes she had hidden there. Taking a cigarette, she was about to light up, when she stopped. She recalled the last time she had smoked in the house and changed her mind. "Shit! I can't even smoke in my own bedroom!"

Ming Kong disliked cigarettes as much as he disliked and disapproved of alcohol. She had seen him warn the children against it. The last time she had smoked in her bedroom, An Mei rushed in sniffing exaggeratedly. "Is anyone smoking?" she had asked innocently although she could hardly have missed seeing the cigarette between Shirley's lips.

Then there was the other evening when she almost had a fight with An Mei. Anxious to get Ming Kong to herself, she had introduced the idea that the children should eat separately and earlier. "This is how they do it in the West so that parents can have some time to themselves," she explained to the children. They were appalled.

"I want to eat with Father, we always eat with him," Wei Shu said.

Wei Hoong joined in the chorus. "Yes, I say the same. This is the only time we see Father. Everyone at my school eats with their parents."

"And I am not a child!" An Mei added for good measure; she was 16 going on 17.

"I prefer to eat with Father as well," said Wei Han. "We are a family; we eat together, always." He stressed 'always'.

An Mei looked at him gratefully.

Losing patience, Shirley pointed to the door. "No, I have spoken. Go! All of you go to the kitchen. I have asked Ah Hing to lay a table there for you."

They rushed out. For a second, Shirley thought she had won. The smile was quickly wiped from her face when she heard them running upstairs. They had gone to their rooms, instead.

"Good! Starve, for all I care," she muttered.

That was not to be the end of the affair. Cook came in and asked where Nelly was going to eat. "Is she to eat in the kitchen as well? You said I'm to lay a table for only two in the dining room."

"Yes, of course! She likes to be with the children, let her be with them. Go, do not bother me!"

She stamped her foot in fury as cook left, "Gosh, all idiots!" she shouted after her, unable to contain herself.

"Who are these idiots?" asked Ming Kong, coming through the door. "Where is everyone?"

Shirley swung around, taken aback. She had not expected him so early. It was only six o'clock. Stepping forward, she put her arms around his neck and kissed him. He responded half-heartedly, he seemed preoccupied. "Can you call the children?"

"Oh, don't ask me. They are completely out of control."

Ming Kong looked at her quizzically. "Why do you say that?"

"Because I cannot get them to do anything. I asked them to eat early this evening, in case you came home late, and they bolted out of the room."

"Oh, good job they haven't eaten. I came home early to take all of you out for dinner. I have been thinking; I should do this more often. More like a family. I have been neglecting them."

"How could you?" complained Shirley, "I was really looking forward to an evening with just the two of us. Can't we go out without them?"

"We have been out alone five out of the past seven evenings. Surely you don't mind?" he retorted, astonished. "I have asked Nelly to come home early to join us as well."

Shirley's jaw dropped with incredulity and her lips, a slash of bright red, parted letting out a loud protest. "Don't you care about me any more? I wanted to talk to you alone . . . about us. I don't want Nelly around. She is the main cause of my problems, she is why the children behave so badly. I will lose what little credibility I have if you reward their bad behaviour by taking them out for a treat!"

Ming Kong was embarrassed by her display. He put his arms around her, "How was I to know you might be having a spot of trouble with them this evening? Anyway, running to their rooms is not such a big crime, is it? They are children!"

He brushed away a strand of hair that had fallen across her face. "Please don't criticise Nelly. She has been through thick and thin with me. I cannot do what you have asked. I have thought it over. To send her packing is out of the question."

He disengaged himself from her and moved away. Then a sudden surge of irritation rose in him. He was angry with Shirley's dramatic outburst. Why was she so unreasonable when it came to the children? He looked around the room. There were no traces of warmth in it. Mei Yin used to have cushions of all hues and shapes thrown on the sofa for the children to cuddle and lie on. They used to sit on the cushions, placing them as close to his feet as possible. In fact, they would compete for the spot nearest to him. Most days now, he found himself staring at pinched, pale faces. He had hoped Shirley would fill the void left by Mei Yin. It didn't seem to be working out that way.

Shirley was clever enough to know she could not win with Ming Kong in his present mood. She put on a tremulous smile and said softly, "Let's not talk about Nelly just now. You are right about the children. I'm sorry. It is just that I find it difficult to cope with them when they . . . gang up on me. You are right. Let's all go out this evening and make a fresh start."

* * * * *

Nelly gathered up her bag and locked the drawers of her desk before popping her head into the adjacent office. "Maan-*sook*, I have to leave early. Please lock up and make sure everything is secure. I will see you tomorrow. Give your wife my best wishes. Would you also give this to her from me?" she asked, handing him a carton.

Maan-*sook* had been with Nelly since she first took over the management of the store. He smiled when he saw what it was. "Thank you, she still has two bottles left from the last batch you gave her. She was making them last; she will be very happy. Now I will be able to persuade her to use them." Clutching the carton, which contained six bottles of Brand's Essence of Chicken, he beamed. "Yes, my wife will be very pleased. She believes this is very nutritious and gives her the *yang* she needs. She still feels poorly."

"You must make sure she sees the doctor," was Nelly's parting comment as she walked briskly out of the shop.

Her mind went back over the day's events. After Tek San left, she had spoken to Mei Yin on the phone. It had become a daily routine for Nelly to go to the shopkeeper next door to use his phone and collect any letters from Mei Yin.

The shopkeeper lived with his family above the shop. Over the years, they had developed a strong bond with Nelly. She had helped him through a bad patch in his business and they were grateful. It was nothing much in financial terms. Nelly had little by way of savings of her own. She had helped by allowing him to store goods and valuables in her warehouse when his debtors came to call in his debt. She had also been generous in her gifts of provisions to the family.

It was clear to Nelly that things were coming to a head. Mei Yin had told her she was coming to Kuala Lumpur to see the children, no matter what. It had been months since she had been able to speak to them on the phone and two years since she had seen them.

Having sat on the fence for two years, hoping things would work out, Nelly decided she was wrong. They were getting nowhere. She had thought that she needed to keep on the right side of Ming Kong in order to stay on and watch over the children. "I have to have a thick skin and take whatever comes. Otherwise, who will look after them if I leave as well," she had said to Mei Yin. "I cannot be seen to be involved." This too had not worked out the way she had hoped.

Now on her way home, she wondered what lay in store this evening. He had rung and said, "Come home early."

* * * * *

The dinner at the Szechuan Restaurant in Bukit Bintang Road was not a success. Ming Kong had chosen the restaurant because the family used to go there. The children loved the restaurant's spicy dishes; Ming Kong himself was partial to its sizzling platter of eels steeped in sesame oil. What also made it his obvious choice for the evening were the nearby food stalls. When the children were little, they would have the main meal in the restaurant and then adjourn to the food stalls for desserts! The children loved to eat sesame buns, stuffed with red beans and taken straight from the cauldron of hot oil, and iced soya bean curd with lashings of syrup. Ming Kong maintained that even the most important business tycoon ate there. "They ate here when they were poor and, after they prospered, they continued to do so. I am no different."

The minute they stepped into the restaurant, things began to go wrong. "Good evening. Welcome, welcome. We have not seen you here for a long time. How is first Mrs Ong? And how are you, *Yee Tai-tai* ?" the head waiter asked Nelly, showing them to the table.

The silence that followed his greetings made little impression on him, he was too busy arranging the chairs and seating. Fussing over them, he pulled a chair out for Shirley several seats away from Ming Kong. He sat Nelly, as his wife, next to Ming Kong. Seeing the expression on Shirley's face and anticipating that she would say something unpleasant, Ming Kong said, "Sit down. What does it matter where we sit. It is a round table. For goodness sake!" He was becoming exasperated with Shirley's quick temper. He had not noticed until recently how quickly she became upset. "Must be the pressure of being settled with a new family," he thought, forgiving her instantly.

Conversation flitted across the table. The children tucked in.

"So have you got your results," Nelly asked Wei Hoong.

A big grin broke on Wei Hoong's face. "I got a star. The teacher has put my project on the notice board."

"Good, and you Wei Han?"

Nelly asked, the children answered. Soon Ming Kong joined in the revelry. The children's laughter rang across the table. It was not the sort of dinner Shirley enjoyed. Seated some distance from Ming Kong, she fumed that he had not intervened to introduce her as his wife. She smarted at being ignored. Amidst the chatter and happy banter, she grew steadily more resentful. "I might as well have stayed at home," she thought. She disliked the easy way Ming Kong spoke to Nelly and strained to hear their conversation. Finally, unable to contain herself any longer, she got up and said loudly, "This din is giving me a headache, I'm going to the bathroom." She stormed out.

Minutes passed. Ming Kong grew distracted. He did not like the way Shirley had flounced out of the room. After a while, when she did not return, Ming Kong asked An Mei to look for her. Wei Shu wanted to follow so An Mei took him along with her.

They found Shirley in the ladies' room. She was pacing the floor, pausing every now and then to draw deeply on the cigarette she held between two fingers. Startled by them, she threw the cigarette down, ground it with her heel and went to the sink to wash her hands.

"Have you come to spy on me?"

"No. Father sent us to ask you to come back to the table," An Mei replied.

Shirley took her time, fixing her hair, re-applying her make-up, ignoring the two children. Still they waited. "Idiots!" she muttered. When she had finished, she sprayed perfume on herself. She was just about to reprimand An Mei for staring when Wei Shu reached over to put his hands under the running tap to wash them. He sprayed water all over the front of her dress.

It was the last straw for Shirley. Furious, she turned and gave him a resounding slap across the face. An Mei darted forward, pushing past her. Without another word, she took her brother away. Marching back to the table, An Mei's face was a bright red while Wei Shu was in tears. Within seconds, Shirley arrived, anxious that she should be the first to tell Ming Kong her side of the story, of Wei Shu's misbehaviour.

Ming Kong took one look and realised something unpleasant had happened. Not wanting to have a scene in public, he turned to Nelly and said, "Settle the bill. I will take Shirley home. The driver can wait for you and the children."

* * * * *

Once in his car, Shirley burst into tears. "Surely now you can see how they treat me. Nelly is behind it. They exclude me from everything. I cannot take their rudeness. Wei Shu deliberately splashed water all over me. Look! I am wet through," she said, pointing to the wet patches on her dress. "And, do you know what your daughter did? She pushed me. Something must be done to control her. She is wild. She was going to hit me!"

Ming Kong sighed. "I am sure she would not do that. You could have joined in the conversation. I did not see anyone stopping you." He felt tired and frustrated. What he had hoped would be a happy evening had turned sour.

"You always take their side," she wept. "If they knew that I am to be their mother, if I had any real position at all, it would make such a difference. But I . . . I am nobody."

* * * * *

Ming Kong got out of bed and stole out of the bedroom. He had been awake the past hour listening to Shirley's deep breathing. The tempestuous outburst was followed by protestations of love and then lovemaking. That bit was good, he conceded, the rest was unbearable.

Once downstairs, he unlocked the sliding door and stepped out onto the terrace, He settled down in a cane chair. The night was warm and humid, a sharp contrast to the cold air-conditioned bedroom. It was a full moon; its light shone pale silver across the lawn. Dark shadows moved, mirroring the leaves and tree branches swaying in the breeze. All was quiet except for the natural sounds of the night. He needed to think.

Events over the past two years or so had been like a tidal wave he could not stop. He blamed it all on Mei Yin. He had not been a model husband, he knew, but to think that she had cheated on him! He could hardly bring himself to think about it. She had made him a laughing stock! All his friends agreed that he had done the right thing by telling her to go. Having done that, he had to face the consequences. How to care for the children! He could not let Nelly leave her work to stay at home. She virtually managed all that side of his business. He depended on her.

When Shirley had said she was keen to help, he accepted. She now insisted that she read his invitation to move into the main house as a proposal of marriage! How could he possibly marry her? There was still Mei Yin. What about Nelly? And the children? He had given her what he thought was the best he could, a place in the household just like Nelly's but Shirley obviously expected and wanted more.

When he first got involved with Shirley, it was just fun. Wing Lok had described her as understanding. Later, the affair took a more serious turn, but surely she knew that he could never marry her, not in the way she wished, not officially. Obviously, he had not made it sufficiently clear. So the accusations and counter accusations went to and fro. She accused him of misleading her. Why did he set up a second house with her; why did he invite her to live with him when his wife left? Why did he ask the children to call her *sum*? He replied that he had bought her a house to appease her and as a demonstration of his affection. She, herself, had offered to help with the children. And how else could the children address her when they were sharing the same room. They had to maintain a modicum of respectability. Now, even Wing Lok was saying he had given the impression that he wished to marry her. Had he, he wondered.

The warm night air clung to him. He began to perspire and his pyjamas clung to him. He remained seated there, silent, thinking and brooding.

Chapter 36

They arranged to meet in the old corner coffee shop a few blocks away from the offices of Harrisons and Crossfield in the old commercial area of Kuala Lumpur close by the River Klang. It was a shabby place. The floor was yellow with grime, grease and years of neglect. In its hey-day, before the housing boom had replaced the two-storey Chinese shop-houses with multi-storey glass and steel complexes, this coffee shop was popular. Now, few people came. The owner was unwilling to spend any money on the building; he was just biding his time, waiting for an offer he could not refuse. He expected his shop and the others alongside to be bought eventually by a developer. They would be knocked down and replaced by a modern edifice, testimony to the growing prosperity of the city.

Mei Yin sat down at one of the round marble-topped tables. She placed her travel bag carefully on the chair next to her. She was first to arrive. A waiter shuffled towards her, he wore green rubber flip-flops. A dirty cloth, once white, now almost brown, was tied carelessly around his waist.

"What do you want to drink?" he asked with a complete absence of the customary politeness of his profession.

"Coffee please."

Minutes later, the waiter returned carrying a cup of coffee, some of which had spilled over into the saucer. It was a hot black brew, sweetened with a huge slug of condensed milk. The milk formed a thick creamy sediment in the bottom of the cup. As Mei Yin stirred the coffee, its colour turned from a smoky black to velvety brown. Just like the colour of the River Klang, she thought irrelevantly. Then again, perhaps it was not so irrelevant; it reminded her of her first outing there with Ming Kong. He had brought her on his motor-bike to the river, just minutes' walk away. Holding hands, they had walked by the river. They were so in love. Her problem then was her mother-in-law. She had thought there could never be a greater difficulty. What a fool she had been! When they had reached the bridge that spanned the river between Batu Road and Ampang Road, they had headed for this coffee shop. Everything tasted like nectar that day. Now, as she slowly sipped the coffee, its heat scalded her tongue and its bitter aroma quickly brought her back to the present.

She felt a hand on her shoulder. She looked up. Nelly! Followed almost immediately by Kai Min and Tek San. Nelly and Mei Yin looked at each other, unable to speak. Decorum prevented them from embracing in public. Both of them could see the damage that the past few years had wrought. When everyone was seated, they busied themselves ordering refreshments, anything to get rid of the waiter.

"Why did you choose this place?" Nelly asked Tek San, making small talk as she struggled to control her emotions, not wanting to break down and possibly spoil everything.

"I thought it would be the least likely place to meet Ming Kong or anyone who might know either him or us," replied Tek San. "Anyway I like the coffee here. I am not particularly fond of the instant coffee they serve these days in the trendy places. This is the kind of coffee, l like." He pointed to Mei Yin's cup. "But we are not here to discuss coffee. Come on, Nelly, you were always pestering me about Mei Yin, asking me how she is. Well, here she is, why don't you ask her yourself?"

Mei Yin's mouth quivered. Nelly looked away. Both fought for control. Even the normally voluble Kai Min was quiet.

The awkward silence added to the charged atmosphere.

"Mei Yin," Nelly finally began, "how ... how have ... " Nelly had so much to say and ask that she could not find the right words.

Mei Yin nodded vigorously and swallowed hard. "I'm okay, really, just a little anxious. Let's not talk about me. When can I see the children? Do they know I am coming?"

"Soon," Nelly replied, "we will pick them up from school this afternoon. We've been lucky. There has been a spot of trouble between Shirley and Ming Kong. She has gone back to her own place for a few days. I persuaded Ming Kong to let me take two days off, leaving Maan-*sook* in charge. That's why I asked you to come immediately. I have told only An Mei, not the boys, just in case they spill the beans. The younger ones are petrified of Shirley." Reaching for Mei Yin's hands, she smiled, "They will be so happy to see you."

"I'm nervous," admitted Mei Yin. "What about Ming Kong? Can I see him? He cannot ignore me forever. This morning before I left Malacca, I received yet another letter from his solicitor. He is prepared to settle a substantial sum on me if I give up all rights to the children, including access. Why no access? Does he think I will harm them? I cannot believe he could be so cruel." The tears she had managed to stifle brimmed over to roll down her cheeks.

"I can no longer vouch for what goes on in his head. He is cruel." Nelly said. "Cruel, spoilt and self-willed, and we have helped to make him like that. We aided and abetted our mothers-in-law in this."

Mei Yin's tears were attracting attention. A few more people had come in; it was lunchtime. Several were casting furtive glances at them, straining to hear. A little boy, his lips ringed with drinking chocolate, slid off his stool and toddled over to them. "Why you cry?" he asked. His mother, embarrassed, rushed forward and led him away.

"Let's go somewhere else," said Tek San. He paid up and they walked to his car which was parked a few yards away. Once in the car, he took up the question of Mei Yin's wish to see Ming Kong. "We have talked it over and we can't see how we might do it . . . I mean arrange a meeting with Ming Kong." He looked sheepish. He could see the disappointment on Mei Yin's face.

While the three of them had agreed that they should help Mei Yin to see the children, persuading Ming Kong to see Mei Yin was another matter. He would realise immediately that they had been secretly in contact with her against his wishes. There would be a terrible row. He might even ask Nelly to leave. Their belief that the children would be better off if Nelly stayed had never faltered. A similar argument applied to Kai Min and Tek San. If he discovered they were also involved, Ming Kong might not let them see the children anymore.

"Take heart, we don't have only bad news. We have made some encouraging progress in finding out why Ming Kong has behaved the way he has," Kai Min said. "There is some sort of connection between Wing Lok and Shirley. Tek San is trying to find out more. We think it could help. I am not sure how, but I suspect there is more to this woman than meets the eye."

"At least you can see the children and spend time with them this afternoon," Nelly comforted. "Let us take one step at a time."

"And," chipped in Tek San, "I'm working on Ming Kong to bring him around. His tiff with Shirley might make him more amenable."

"Come on, let's go or we will be late," suggested Kai Min. "Tek San has to return to his office so I will drive you both to the school. It will be a tight squeeze, but it is better than using two cars. This way we can do without a driver. You can't trust anyone nowadays."

As soon as Kai Min started the car, Nelly leaned over and whispered in Mei Yin's ear. "About a week or so ago, Doctor Jung came to the house, An Mei told me. It was lucky she opened the door, otherwise there would have been even more problems. Do you know why he called?"

Mei Yin shook her head.

* * * * *

"You had better reconsider your decision and return to the main house." Wing Lok glared at Shirley with barely disguised disdain. "If you don't, I can guarantee you won't have a chance of regaining his trust and, for want of a better word, favour."

He had received an urgent phone call from Shirley. She explained she was fed up and had told Ming Kong she needed time on her own to think. "I am back in my own house. That should make him sit up and not take me for granted. I will have his proposal yet," she boasted.

Within minutes, Wing Lok was at her door. He told her in no uncertain terms that she was wrong. "Don't think he is stupid. He is not going to capitulate to such demands. Softly, softly is the approach that wins with him." Ignoring her expression of disbelief, Wing Lok continued. "Look, he's attracted to you because of sex. Face facts. He is not, I repeat, not in love with you. He has brought you more and more into his life because he thinks he owes you. He's like that. Make him feel guilty, make him feel you depend on him, make him feel indebted to you, that will work. Try driving a hard bargain and you are as good as lost."

Lowering his voice to a menacing growl, he said crudely, "If I were you, I'd rush back to the house this very minute. Eat shit if needs be. Don't forget, you're badly in debt again. You need your meal ticket. Forget about Nelly. We were mistaken in thinking that she is an easy target. He owes her too much to cast her aside."

Wing Lok had grown tired of Shirley. She was in the habit of being rude and spiteful when she felt certain of Ming Kong. She'd insulted him once too often. It is time, he thought, to show her where she would be without him. "Mei Yin was an easy target, only because we could make him believe she was having an affair. And we put the heat on by telling everyone. From what I see, he still has a soft spot for her. I can tell. I watch his face when he speaks of her. So don't get too full of yourself. Look at you. The effects of all that secret smoking and drinking, if I am to believe the servants, are beginning to show."

* * * * *

The children were standing together outside the school's main gate. Mei Yin saw them. Her children. Their lovely, lovely faces lit up by broad smiles. "Mummy!" they called. She rushed to them, hugged each of the smaller ones in turn, savouring the feel of their bodies on hers, smelling their sweet, sweet breath. She turned to Wei Han and An Mei.

"Can I have a kiss?" she asked them. An Mei ran to her mother and showered kisses on her. Mei Yin held on to An Mei's hand and turn to Wei Han. "Wei Han?" she asked. He went to her hesitantly. The blame that he had laid on his mother for the break-up of the family had gradually shifted over the years. When his father brought Shirley home, he had reluctantly realised that he might have misdirected his anger. Yet he had resisted his mother's entreaties to speak to him on the phone. Now, seeing her face to face, he felt as if a load had been taken off his mind. His initial truculence gave way to a smile. He went into her arms and sobbed. For the first time in many months, he spoke freely, breaking out of the shell of toughness he had created as a protection from hurt.

All the children were sworn to silence about the meeting. "You don't need to worry about mine," explained Kai Min. "We don't see Ming Kong as a family. No invitation since you left."

"Are you coming back, Mummy?" asked Wei Shu.

"Yes, of course she is . . . eventually," Nelly interjected when she saw Mei Yin's face. It was difficult for Mei Yin to explain to the younger boys what had happened. Predicting what might happen in the future was even more difficult. She did not know herself.

All the way to the school, the two women had asked Mei Yin about her feelings. "Do you still love Ming Kong?" asked Kai Min. "That is the crux of the matter! It will influence what course of action we take."

Mei Yin looked wistfully into the distance. Her voice dropped to a regretful whisper, "I do. He was everything to me for so long that living without him these past years has been hell. Don't ask me why I do. How can I explain it?" Mei Yin clenched her fist and placed it against her heart. She looked down at her hands, clasping and unclasping them. "Yet, I know I have changed. I don't think I can go back to a life of just waiting for him, hanging on to his every word. Working and earning a living have given me a new lease of life. Surely, there is more to life than just sitting at home, waiting for him?" She looked from Nelly to Kai Min, trying to will them to understand.

"No, I don't think I can go back to him on those terms of compliance, even if he wants me back."

"Well, to be with the children, you have to go back to Ming Kong somehow, perhaps on any terms. He will never give the children up. Three boys to you? What if you remarry? I'm sorry to be so cruel, but I don't want you to build false hope."

"I think Kai Min is right. You might have to eat humble pie and seek a reconciliation. *Tai Nai-nai* will be supportive; she will be very happy for this to happen," said Nelly.

"But I have done nothing wrong!" Mei Yin protested.

"We have to make him realise that. Your silence, the gossip that suddenly sprang up in town, yes, don't shake your head," admonished Kai Min, "that is what happened. Everyone was talking about your meetings with this doctor. Your explanation that he was teaching you English sounded like a really tall story to the rumour-mongers."

"Do you think the doctor would speak to Ming Kong," asked Nelly. "His reputation is as much involved as yours."

* * * * *

Shirley stepped into the hallway of the house and was instantly struck by the silence. The only sound came from the impact of her high-heels as she made her way down the hallway. "Strange, where is everyone," she wondered. It was late afternoon and the children should be back from school." The two younger ones generally had a nap after lunch. By now, however, they would be making themselves a nuisance. "So where can they all be." She swept into the kitchen. Ah Hing was sat at the table peeling and slicing shallots. Her eyes were streaming with the tears caused by their spicy fumes.

"Where is everyone?"

"No one is at home. We didn't expect you back today."

"Huh! Playing hooky are they? I shall have to tell their father."

"No, no, the children are not out on their own. *Yee Tai-tai*, second mistress, is with them. She called. Said they will be late. She left instructions to prepare noodles in hot tamarind fish broth for this evening."

Ah Hing swept the finely sliced shallots into a bowl with one swoop of her knife and proceeded to seed a pile of fresh chillies. Her hands moved quickly and skilfully, splitting the pods and tossing away the bits inside. She was happy in the main house and was fond of the children, especially Wei Shu, whom she called 'little master'.

"I must say *Yee Tai-tai* is very thoughtful," she continued in anticipation of Shirley's objection to noodles for dinner. "She was worried they might be late home and did not want me to spend time cooking something that might spoil. That's why she suggested a dish that can be served at any time by just re-heating."

Shirley could not believe her ears. "You had better watch what you say. Remember, you work for me! One more remark like that and you are out!"

She stomped out of the kitchen. Within minutes, she was back. "Where are the other maids? The place looks a mess! How many times have I said that I want my drawers and cupboards tidied every day?"

"It's the new maid's day off. The other one, who was brought in to replace Ah Kum, handed in her notice this morning and left. She has found a job in a factory. It is getting difficult to find people to do housework. Young girls prefer the regular hours of factory work. Gives them a social life and, they say, better pay."

"What! Why did you let the new maid take today off? You should have told her to take her leave another day."

"Please, do not take it out on me. The new one might not be coming back. She complained. Said she does not know which of the dresses you threw on the floor were for washing and which had to be folded away. These young people do not work like us old folk. She too wants to work in a factory. Who knows? She might be looking for a job this very moment."

Ah Hing looked at Shirley. The maid had complained bitterly of the mess and had brought Ah Hing upstairs to witness it. Clothes and shoes were strewn everywhere, on the floor, on the bed, on the chairs. Shirley had packed in a hurry. The new maid pointed to the garments, "If one item is not in its allotted place, she will bite your head off. She has even tweaked my ear."

Ah Hing got up from the table and went to the sink with her bowls of shallots and chillies. She had never liked Shirley and suffered her sharp tongue because she needed the job. How many people would stand her tirades day in and day out, she wondered.

* * * * *

Ming Kong had returned home late. Mysteriously, everyone seemed in a convivial mood. Must be because Nelly had spent the day at home with them, he thought. What surprised him most, however, was Shirley. Her unexpected return, warm greeting and genial mood reminded him of the Shirley he knew of old. "Not a word of complaint tonight," he thought. "So her day away was sufficient to bring her to her senses."

Now in the bedroom, lying on his front on the bed, the stereo piping out soft music, he began to relax and respond to her ministrations.

Shirley could be wonderful when she wanted to be. Placing a hot, scented towel on the back of his neck, she kneaded his shoulders. Skilfully she applied pressure to the muscles between his shoulder blades until the knots of tension yielded. He could feel his body responding to her touch, to her proximity. Slowly, using her thumbs and the heel of her palms, she kneaded and worked her way down the entire length of his back to the base of his spine and to his buttocks. She worked long and steadily. Strong firm strokes were followed by deep pulsating kneading until he felt himself drifting, his body heavy and relaxed. It was only the light feathery touch of finger tips and nails stroking his back, the tingling sensation and the expectation of what was to follow that woke him up. Turning over, he pulled her into his arms.

Chapter 37

Shirley turned up the air conditioner to its maximum. It was hot sitting in the car. She was waiting for Wei Hoong and Wei Shu outside their school. "Don't worry about them," she had told the driver. "Just collect the other two. I will bring the boys from school." She wondered whether it would be worthwhile, "If it isn't, I'll give Wing Lok an earful. I don't know why I should be fetching them. The noise and dust! What's keeping them? The bell rang ages ago."

When she had told Wing Lok about the other evening, how the children looked relaxed and happy and how Nelly had taken them out for the whole day, he was immediately on his guard. "Something is not right. That woman never takes a day off. I wonder what they did together that could make them so happy. Such a sudden change. Long miserable faces to bright happy ones. Hmm . . . You have to get it out of the younger boys. Ask them where they went. In any case you should do more of what Nelly did that day; put yourself out to win their affection. Perhaps take them out after school. That's what you were supposed to do in the first place, win their affection!"

From a distance, she could see the two boys running towards the school gate. Clad in white shirts, white shorts, white socks and white canvas shoes, they looked remarkably alike, separated only by their height; Wei Hoong was some three inches taller. She got out of the car and in an uncustomary motion, opened her arms wide as though to receive them with a hug. They stopped, stared at her and looked around for the driver. Reluctantly, they approached her, eyes cast down, and greeted her politely.

"I've come to take you home, get in. We're going to stop for a burger on the way." She knew that they were crazy about hamburgers and Curly Q fries. Ah Hing had complained to her that the children rejected her food and asked for a hamburger. "How can people like burgers?" she had asked, her eyes wide in disbelief. "*Soh-soh!* Such a bad beefy smell, and no ginger to get rid of it!" She had shuddered as she emptied the carefully prepared dish of braised pork and mushrooms into the dog's bowl. "Such waste!"

The offer to buy them a burger took the boys by surprise. They just stared. To say yes could be disloyal to their mother, but to say no! In their mind's eye, burgers appeared before them, piled high with meat, sliced cheese and tomato ketchup. Hunger gnawed. They nodded reluctantly.

Shirley smiled, ushered them into the car and drove to the nearest A & W snack bar. Seated on the high stools in front of the tall tables, the boys sipped chocolate milk shakes as they waited for the burgers and fries to arrive. Shirley soon had them chatting happily about their friends and school. The food arrived and they tucked in. She sat patiently, toying with a black coffee, waiting for them to finish. "Should I or should I not," she debated with herself. "Why not," she decided, "best to take the bull by the horns."

Leaning closer, she took a napkin and wiped the boys' mouths, patting their faces. "You are such good boys. I am sorry for having been angry with you. I should have realised that both of you were not really naughty, just unhappy, missing your mummy."

The boys looked at each other. Wei Shu's mouth slackened and bits of bread fell from it. Wei Hoong gave him a quick nudge.

"You do miss your mummy, don't you?" she asked, sensing immediately that she had stumbled onto something.

Both boys shook their heads, guilt written all over their faces. Alarm bells rang in her head. "You must do. You haven't seen her for ages. When was the last time you saw her?" she asked casually.

Still they shook their heads. Wei Shu started to whimper and his brother held on tightly to his hand. By then they had dropped what remained of their burgers.

"You'd better tell me. You know your father has said that you are not to see her. I will tell on you if you don't tell me the truth." They looked petrified. "Come on, tell. I will keep your secret," she coaxed, giving her brightest smile, hoping the change in tactic would persuade them. Wei Shu's whimpers turned to howls. Wei Hoong put on a brave face.

Shirley settled the bill. She was getting impatient. She wanted to scream at them. Once in the car, she rounded on Wei Shu. Taking him by his shoulders, she shook him, "Stop howling! When was your mother here?"

* * * * *

Shirley said nothing for a week. She went about calmly, devoting all her energies to making Ming Kong happy. She flirted, massaged, smiled and ministered to him. She had his favourite meals prepared. When he was at home, she played the loving mother to his children. Not a single sharp word escaped her lips. Wing Lok told her that her best weapon was to charm Ming Kong until he ate out of her hand; the rest would follow. And it did.

When the children, frightened and confused, told Nelly they had broken their promise and Shirley knew of the meeting with their mother, Nelly was alarmed. The alarm gave way to anger when she saw the state of Wei Shu's face. His ear was swollen from the slap he had received. Wei Hoong's arms were bruised from being pinched. "I'll tell your father when he comes home this evening."

"No please don't tell Father," they begged. "She promised she would not tell on us if we kept quiet. Father will be very angry with us if you tell him. We will not be able to see Mummy anymore." So for one whole week, they had waited with bated breath for a sign that their father knew. Uncertain, apprehensive, they did not know how to respond to Shirley's friendly overtures when their father was at home. They were quiet, tongue-tied and awkward. Ming Kong interpreted this as surliness. He enlisted Nelly's help.

"Try talking some sense into the children. Shirley is doing her best and they spurn her. It hurts her. She wants to be nice. She doesn't complain, but I can see she is hurt. Try, they will listen to you."

For a few seconds, Nelly could not find her voice. Then she snapped, "I cannot help her. Ask her to try kindness, ask her not to slap them around. Maybe that will help." She could not keep the sarcasm from her voice. He was absolutely blind, only seeing what he wanted to see, she thought.

"How could you talk like that?" he cried, astonished by the outburst. "What lies are you trying to tell me. I've never seen her behave in any other way than with the best intention. Go, I have no intention of listening to such malice."

Ming Kong was troubled. Could Shirley be right? Was Nelly turning the children against her?

Eight days on from that fatal day, Shirley came out with the proposal to send the children to boarding school abroad. It would be good for them. They would be with other children who were also separated from their parents. Their mother's absence would not seem so singularly their plight. They would learn to be independent and they would get an education that would benefit them for life.

Wing Lok threw his weight behind her suggestion. "If they stay in Malaya, they will have to learn Malay. It's going to be the first language of the country, in line with the new thinking that language is the soul of the nation, *bahasa jiwa bangsa.*"

"What use is Malay outside of Malaya and Indonesia? Far better to study English. We should send the children abroad," Shirley argued.

It was not an unfamiliar argument. Ming Kong had heard it from many of his Chinese friends and associates. They saw the policy to make Malay the main medium of instruction as a further erosion of their culture. In fact, they said that anyone with money should send their children to be educated abroad. Australia or England, they thought, were the two best destinations.

"It is most important that boys have a chance to do well. I would send all mine if I could," said one of his associates.

When he told Nelly, she protested, "No, surely not all the boys and not all at once. The two younger ones are too small. Families send their children overseas for further education, not when they are just in primary and lower secondary schools. They are too young," she repeated.

When Ming Kong pressed his case, she reluctantly conceded that Wei Han might wish to go. "But ask him how he feels. And, if you are sending Wei Han, think also of An Mei, I know she wants to go to university. She will be completing her A-levels soon."

His mother, too, expressed doubts. "If you send them when they are too young, they might not be able to cope. If they do and they stay for 10 to 12 years of their formative life, they may never want to come back. Then they will lose all of their cultural heritage. What is more, who will take over the business that you have built up?"

* * * * *

The businessmen met for a lunch of dim sum at the restaurant in the Federal Hotel. The hotel, one of the earliest modern luxury hotels in the city, was a symbol of Chinese success and entrepreneurship in post-independence Malaya.

As soon as Ming Kong and Wing Lok were seated, others joined them at their table. Waiters hurried over to expand the table of four into a round table for ten. They lifted the extension flaps and covered them with freshly starched white tablecloths. Waitresses, dressed in tight-fitting *cheongsams*, hurried over and arranged fresh crockery and chopsticks. A bowl, a plate, a silver chopstick rest, a pair of ivory chopsticks and china soup spoons were placed in front of each diner.

"*Chang-sik, chang-sik.*" Ming Kong invited his guests to eat, gesturing to the dishes with his chopsticks. "The food will get cold."

The *dim sum* dishes in little bamboo caskets and sweet braised and roasted meats came in rapid succession. There was little talk. Only when they had finished eating would the conversation switch from comments on the food to the serious business that had brought them together. Ming Kong signalled to a waitress that they had finished and she could clear the table. "We would like to have some fresh fruits; papayas, lychee and melon will do. And, Miss, please will you put all the uneaten meat and vegetables into a box for me?" Turning to his friends, unabashed, "They make the best *chop-suey*! Boil them in tamarind, pickled mustard green and pig trotters, it's a dish fit for a king! My mother taught me, waste not, want not."

Everyone nodded in agreement.

"You are right; waste not, want not," said an old gentleman. "All of us who had to work hard to build up our fortunes have this motto. My old woman will not buy a new pair of shoes until she wears out the old pair." The man laughed, revealing teeth stained with tobacco; the gold fillings that lined his back teeth glinted in the light as he threw his head back in a raucous laugh. "Not like my mistress," he added. He slapped his thigh and brought his hands up. They were old and gnarled from years of hard work. He had been a business associate of Ming Kong's father. He started life buying and selling scrap metal. Now, he owned a chain of businesses.

"What I don't understand," he continued, "is why you have adopted such a philosophy. Didn't your father leave you with a lot? Most people in your place would just spend and spend."

"Yes and no. I had to work pretty hard to salvage things after the war. But let us talk more seriously." He was not put off by the old man's direct comments. His contact over the years with his father's friends had taught him that most of the older folk were like the old man. They were not the sort of people you took to the Selangor Club, he thought, remembering his first introduction to it. The Club, which had previously allowed only English members, opened to locals after Malaya's independence. Such a conversation, he knew, would be considered vulgar.

"Have you heard any more about the Government's economic policy?" he asked, provoking a chorus of comment.

"Yes! It's getting worse. They are going to strengthen their policy to remove the differences in wealth between the ethnic groups. More and more to the Malays, that is what it really amounts to."

"Rumour has it that companies will have to allocate a certain proportion of jobs and posts to Malays. The same apparently applies to business licences, even for taxis. Is this true? If it is, you could be affected, Ming Kong. Rules might be introduced to ensure that a proportion of new houses have to be sold to them."

"I do not mind who buys my houses as long as they can pay," replied Ming Kong.

"Lucky you! I wish it were that easy for me. I find it really difficult to do business now," said one of the men.

"I must say I am less bothered about these policies than their proposal to form a larger political entity, Malaysia. I haven't done too badly financially," said the man seated next to Ming Kong.

"I agree. When our Prime Minister first put forward the idea of bringing Malaya, Singapore and the North Borneo states together, I thought it was a whim. But he's serious. And, it looks like he has the support of Britain. It's very worrying. Already Indonesia is protesting and is up in arms against us," said the old man. "You know, I am not sure if Singapore is all that keen to become part of this Malaysia."

"Singapore has to be in. It relies on peninsula Malaya for a lot of things, even water!"

"I wouldn't bet on it," responded the old man.

"Well, if Singapore does not join, the ethnic balance will worsen for the Chinese population in Malaya."

"Don't worry. Nothing might come of it. The whole thing is uncertain. They are arguing over everything. Sabah and Sarawak might be willing, but Brunei? I doubt it would join. Why should it hand over its oil wealth to us?"

"That's why I told you the other day, Ming Kong, to send your children abroad. There is too much political and economic uncertainty here," Wing Lok finally chimed in. The apprehension building up around the table offered an opportune moment to push his case. "Let them have a good education so you can be proud of them. You can afford it. Don't listen to your mother. She's old-fashioned. Look at him," he indicated a man dressed in a western suit sitting two tables away. "He's western-educated, he came back. If you learn only Malay, you are stuck here. You never know what might happen in the future. A good education opens up the world."

"Yes, I agree," said another. "Even the Malays are sending their children abroad!"

* * * * *

The months that followed saw a flurry of political activity as the country prepared for the formation of Malaysia. The date set was 31 August 1963. Tension was high in the region. President Sukarno of Indonesia was against the formation of Malaysia and spoke of a state of *Konfrontasi*. Armed attacks were launched against Malaya and across the land frontiers of North Borneo and Sarawak. In the Philippines too, President Marcos expressed anxiety over its formation and, in particular, the proposed changes in North Borneo close to its frontier. Talks between the various interested parties continued to falter. The United Nations was brought in to ensure that the heads of state carried with them the wishes of the people. A revised date, 16 September 1963, was set for its formation.

Ming Kong was busy. Now convinced that, in the midst of such political and economic uncertainties, the best course of action was to send the boys abroad, he searched for schools in England. He consulted the British Council, he tried the British High Commission, he spoke to friends with children abroad. He toyed with the idea of Australia. "It's nearer to Malaya," he said to Shirley and Nelly. "It will be easier for them to come home during holidays."

Nelly was keen, Shirley objected.

"I need guidance," he confessed to Wing Lok. "No one in my family has ever been abroad to study. University education was not so important in the past. In fact, I would have refused to go even if my own father had suggested it. Then, there were opportunities here for anyone who worked hard. But now. Well, things have changed."

With an exasperated sigh, he jabbed his finger at the sheet of paper in front of him. "Look at this list of schools. I have no idea which would be best for the boys. How do they expect me to choose? Also, some of the schools have such strange requirements. I have been told that children from so-called upper class homes are preferred. Do I qualify? I am from an old family, but I don't have a title, nor have any of my forebears been to one of these schools."

Finally, with the help of the British Council and with much encouragement from Wing Lok, applications for places for all three boys were sent.

He said to Nelly, "I hope it is not too late; the school year in Great Britain starts in early September."

"What about An Mei? She is clever. Doesn't she deserve a chance as well?" she asked. Seeing his reluctance, she added, "It would be useful. She could keep an eye on her brothers. Even so, I still think that you could wait for a couple of years before sending the two smaller boys. They are so young! They are frightened. Wei Shu has been wetting his bed these past few nights. Please, can't you leave him here with me?"

"No, no. He has to go. The more I hear of what is happening, the more I worry. I just hope that this *Konfrontasi* is not going to continue and turn into a full-scale war. I worry when I see armoured vehicles rolling by. It seems like only yesterday that we finished with the Emergency. Even my business is suffering."

"And An Mei?" asked Nelly again.

"Let me think about it," was his response.

* * * * *

"If I had a daughter as pretty as yours, I would not send her overseas," was Wing Lok's comment when Ming Kong discussed sending An Mei away to university.

"Boys are different. The more girlfriends they have, the better. Girls! We might be westernised, but, deep down, we are still the same. I am a man of the world, but, if I had a son, I would oppose his marrying a girl who had a reputation for going around. I tell you, it will be difficult to monitor what she does if she goes away."

Wing Lok shook his head. "My friend's daughter came home for holiday after eight months in England. And you know what? He was disgusted. She arrived wearing make-up, her eyes ringed black, lips red, and a mini-skirt that came up this high!" he chortled, pointing to his thigh. "Her mother had a fit."

They were having a drink at the Selangor Club. It was just after five in the afternoon. They had driven there with Shirley. The wide verandah was laid out with tables and chairs for afternoon tea. The place was filling up. Waiters in starched white uniforms, bearing trays of tea, delicately cut sandwiches and slices of fruit cake, mingled with those carrying gin and tonic, whisky and soda and little plates of roasted peanuts. From their table they looked over the *padang*, a large expanse of neatly clipped lawn. A cricket match had started.

"Look at them." Wing Lok pointed to the players. "Not one Chinese among them. The Indians have taken more to this game than any other race."

"That's because the British made cricket popular in India. What's fashionable there still influences Indians here. Anyway, the Chinese are not interested in games, only gambling ones," concluded Ming Kong.

Shirley did not like the drift of the conversation. Gambling was not a subject she cared to discuss. In any case, she had wanted to interrupt Wing Lok when he suggested that An Mei should not be sent to England. Why did he say that, she wondered. His original plan had been for them to get rid of all the children. She was the one who had thought sending An Mei to a British university would be a waste of money. Apparently, he had changed his mind.

She looked at Wing Lok, trying to catch his eye. He looked away. She took her chance, "I have been thinking about Wing Lok's comments. We don't need to make an immediate decision on An Mei. She's only just sitting her A-levels. The results will come out at the end of the year, too late for the start of the academic year in Britain.

I would suggest sending her to the local university. Its first term starts early next year. The timing is just right. Then, if it doesn't work out, you still have time to apply to a British university for next autumn."

She smiled encouragingly. "Now we've settled the boys' schools, there is not that much urgency. We have been stressed out these past few months, chasing after people, filling in forms. We deserve a rest."

"Anyway," she continued, "An Mei's education is not as important. It's not as if a girl has to be so successful. All she really needs is to earn some pocket money. Marrying well is more important."

Ming Kong raised one eyebrow and grimaced. "I don't think either my daughter or Nelly would agree with you on that. You are right in one respect, though. We have time, there's no great rush."

Shirley, glad that she had succeeded in sowing the seeds of her intended fate for An Mei, smiled. In fact, the more she thought about it, the better she liked the idea. If she played her cards well, she could persuade him to send her to board at the local university. It would get her out of the way. It was a pity similar arrangements could not be made for the boys. It would save a lot of money!

* * * * *

Nelly had taken the afternoon off, leaving the shop in the hands of Maan-*sook*. She did not tell Ming Kong. He was away in Singapore. She had learned of his trip the previous day when she phoned his office. His secretary said he would be away for two days. The minute she knew this, she decided to call Mei Yin to arrange for her to come up from Malacca. She had been inconsolable since Nelly informed her that the boys would be leaving for England. She had wanted to come up immediately to see them. But no meeting could be arranged. Their movements were monitored and spied upon at every turn. Now they had a chance.

Nelly's hands felt clammy as she held the phone, waiting for Mei Yin to answer. She was excited and apprehensive. So much had happened since they last met.

As soon as she heard Mei Yin's voice, she went straight to the point. "I am taking the children to see *Tai Nai-nai*. We plan to go see her immediately after I have picked them up from school. So we should reach the temple around two o'clock. Could you be there earlier? It is important that you get there before us. I have to use the driver. He must not see you and put two and two together. Once inside the temple, you will be safe. He is a Moslem and will not step into a Buddhist house of prayer. I will meet you in the temple after seeing *Tai Nai-nai*. Her lodgings are in the adjacent building."

"Do you think I could see her? I would like to pay my respects to her as well."

"Let's see. It might not be a good idea. If Ming Kong finds out, he'll not take kindly to it. He will accuse her of taking sides and, according to Ah Keng, she doesn't want to get involved in family squabbles. She devotes all her time to prayers. But wait at the temple and I'll ask her. I know how fond you are of her."

* * * * *

The car made its way through Chinatown past the Central Market and eventually turned into the quiet alley and the tiny Szu Yeh temple. They stepped out of the car and were immediately hit by the heavy aroma of incense that hung thickly in the air. The contrast with the fumes and odours of the congested market they had just left behind had Wei Shu sneezing. Ah Keng was waiting at the entrance.

Speaking in Malay, Nelly told the driver to go for his tea and return at half past four. She pressed some notes into his hands. Grinning, he lifted his hand in salute and drove off. He was glad to get away. He did not like the area.

Nelly and the children made their way to Ah Keng.

"My, how all of you have grown," exclaimed Ah Keng, her face wreathed in smiles. "Look at you, An Mei. A proper little lady now; and the boys! They are inches taller. Come along, your grandmother has been expecting you the whole morning. I've not seen her so happy for a long time."

Walking ahead, Ah Keng led them to a building next to the temple. They took off their shoes and padded bare-foot into the building. There were no sounds other than the soft chant of prayers coming from somewhere in the back. Wide-eyed, the children looked awed, uncertain. They had never been there before, or to any other temple for that matter. The boys went to a Catholic school while Anglican Missionaries ran An Mei's school. Religion was something they associated with older people; prayers were what you said in assembly at the start of the school day.

"We must be very quiet," whispered Ah Keng, "they are just finishing afternoon prayers. Your grandmother will be ready to see you soon."

Turning to Nelly, she said, "She has lost a lot of weight. I am not sure that the fasting and a strict vegetarian diet are good for her health. She insists that a vegetarian diet cleanses the soul, a way of paying penance."

"Is she well otherwise?"

"She coughs a lot, a dry hacking cough that leaves her heaving for breath. The conditions here are not good, but she will not listen to me. *Ai yah*, what can I do? I'm only a servant." Her lips trembled with emotion.

"Don't say that; you mean much more to her. And you mean a lot to us as well."

Ah Keng had become gaunt and thin. Nelly wondered how she might persuade the two old ladies to come back home. "The children didn't get a chance to say goodbye when you left. They miss you."

"I was forced to leave quickly by the new mistress. And after that I didn't dare come to all of you. I was so ashamed of what I had done." Then Ah Keng told Nelly the entire story, including how she had inadvertently caused problems for Mei Yin. "It's my big mouth. I'm sorry."

"We know all about it. Ah Kum told us, so do not worry. We do not blame you."

They waited in silence. The boys fidgeted. The clock ticked on the wall, a slow, ponderous sound.

Finally, Ah Keng announced, "I think we can go in now. I hear footsteps and voices. They must have finished their prayers."

A nun came out and invited them into the back rooms. Clad in a white cotton tunic with a mandarin collar, her head was clean-shaven; the only evidence of her hair was a shadow of blue on her scalp. She led the way through a corridor with a warren of small cubicles on one side. The air was filled with a sweetish odour reminiscent of age. It reminded Nelly of paper that had yellowed with time, of dried flowers gathering dust. It was a stale, sad, oily smell. Their guide stopped in front of one of the tiny rooms, the door was open. Inside sat an old lady, small and almost bent double. Nelly could hardly recognise her mother-in-law. Ong Suet Ping, who had been larger than life in her youth and prone to putting on weight, sat on a hard bed. A thin ghost of a woman, only her smile was the same.

The children hesitated; she beckoned with her hands, her smile and joy in seeing them were obvious. Without warning, the ice broke. "*Tai-mah-mah*," they echoed as they quickly moved into her welcoming arms. They had so much to tell her; this grandmother with whom they had spent so many happy hours listening to ancient Chinese stories. Nelly wanted to remain by the door to let the children spend time with her before going into the room, but the nun motioned her to step outside.

Gently, she said, "Your mother-in-law is growing weak. I fear she has not much longer to live. Perhaps you should be thinking of arrangements for the future, should this happen. It's good that her grandchildren came to see her. Could you tell her son and daughters of her condition? I'm sure they would wish to visit as well."

* * * * *

Mei Yin looked at her watch. It was late. What could be keeping them? Wandering around the tiny temple had taken her a matter of minutes. The temple, one of the oldest in the city, had been built in the late 1800s under the auspices of Yap Ah Loy. He was a key figure in the founding of Kuala Lumpur and the appointed head of the Chinese Clan. Its once rich aura of red and gold decoration was almost gone. In its place were walls darkened by the smoke from burning incense and smouldering joss sticks. The religious scrolls and wall hangings had been faded by sunlight and discoloured by the fumes. Flecks of dust floated and danced in the sunlight that filtered through the windows.

Mei Yin looked on as people drifted in to offer their prayers. Candles sizzled, oozing molten wax. People knelt, touched the floor with their foreheads, hands in supplication offering incense. The chanting was interrupted intermittently by the sound of a brass gong. Mei Yin walked to a little table where a woman was seated. The table was placed near a side door that led to the dark interior of the temple.

The woman smiled. "Pick one of these and I will read you your future," she pointed to a tin packed full of sticks with painted calligraphy and numbers.

Mei Yin backed away, afraid. "No, no thank you." Her near death following her encounter with the *bomoh*-lady had removed any wish to associate with soothsayers, no matter how benign they might be. She walked to the main door and looked out. No sign of them. Someone tapped her on the shoulder, she turned. It was Ah Keng.

"Come, *Tai Nai-nai* wants to see you. It's all right. The children told her you are here. Follow me."

An Mei's Recollections

Chapter 38

Fifth October 1963. My brothers had left for England a month ago. Everyone had cried. Wei Shu had clung to Aunty Nelly, not wanting to leave. Even Father's eyes had been wet. He'd kept repeating to himself it was for their good.

I was sat at my desk. My eyes were blurry. I was tired. I had been studying hard, burning the midnight oil, hoping to get the best results possible. "Aim high," said Aunty Nelly, "perhaps you will get a scholarship or, at least, persuade your father to send you abroad as well."

I knew the odds of gaining a scholarship to study abroad were stacked against me. Even the teachers had their doubts. "It is not because we think you would not do well," they said, "but scholarships are incredibly difficult to . . ." They left the sentence unfinished.

Aunty Jeanie was more forthright. I had not seen her since Mother left, but one day, while waiting at the school gate for our car, I saw her drive by. I put up my hand and waved, then checked myself; Aunty Jeanie was not a friend of mine. She saw me immediately and stopped her car. She put her head out of the window and said loudly, "Hi, how are you?" She looked pleased to see me. "I'm so sorry, all this business about your mother. Not true, you know. What-*lah!* I was with her when she met this doctor, all innocent, *tak ada apa apa*, nothing whatever. I should know. I'm your mother's best friend. They damn liars, *bohong*, all of them."

As usual Aunty Jeanie switched between Malay and English. I stifled a grin. It was strange that I found it funny now when in the past I had been so annoyed at her for mixing her English with Malay.

It was good to speak to her, someone who was loyal to Mother and spoke well of her. I was fed up with the continuous innuendo from Shirley. Aunty Jeanie asked me about myself. I told her of my plans to win a scholarship. She stopped me mid-sentence. "Excuse me, don't get angry like you do. Always you like this, when I say something you don't like. Don't waste time dreaming, girl. Very difficult for you to get scholarship. I've got to speak the truth. You are not Malay. If you are, well you might have a better chance. Sorry."

I was dismayed. If I did not get a scholarship, then I would not be able to study abroad. Shirley would see to that. With my brothers gone and Aunty Nelly at work, life was unbearable at home. Nothing I did was right. Shirley taunted and teased. She threatened to tell Father of our meeting with Mother and Aunty's role in it. "I know you're still in touch with your mother. I can stop it any time I want." So we were forced to tolerate her nonsense.

A car horn sounded. The driver had arrived. I said impulsively, "Mother would love to talk to you. I am sure she would. Here is her telephone number, take it." I pressed into her out-stretched hand a piece of paper with Mother's telephone number on it and hurried to my car. But not before I heard her say that she would come to see me again, the day after. "Tell your driver school will end late."

* * * * *

The next day, I was waiting for her. Nudging my heavy school bag with my feet to one side of a tree trunk, I sat down on the gnarled, knobbly roots. They were enormous, irregular humps that fanned out like the tentacles of a giant octopus. An army of black ants was heading down the trunk towards me. Good job I saw them; these kind of ants have a well-deserved reputation for vicious bites. I shifted to the next knot of root, made sure I was in the shade, sat down and rummaged in my bag. Half-past one was not a good time to be in the sun.

"I had better revise. She might be late," I thought. Opening my history book, I started reading. The A-level exams for history covered ancient Greece and Rome. I was soon completely immersed in the Greco-Persian Wars of the 5th Century BC. I did not hear Aunty Jeanie until she was standing next to me.

"So hard-working. You really good girl, your mother say so," Aunty Jeanie said in her Malayan English. "Come, let's take a drive. I'll bring you back here. What time your driver come?"

I told her. We went to her car. "What you reading?" she asked.

"Ancient history."

"Good, important my husband say. Very important we know our roots. You learning about Hang Tuah?"

"No," I laughed. Hang Tuah was a famous 16th Century Malay warrior, whose thoughts and deeds have had a profound influence on the Malay heritage. "I'm studying ancient Greek and Roman history. By ancient, I mean really ancient, before Christ was born."

Peeved, she chided, "Don't laugh. What use is that to us. More important you learn Malay history. With all this talk about new education policy I thought syllabus changed already. I'll ask *Datuk* why students still studying ancient Roman history. *Gila*! Mad! I tell him the policy . . . is *rojak!*"

I giggled. *Rojak* is a local salad, a wide-ranging mixture of various roots, sprouts, bean curd and fruits, salty, sweet and spicy hot. She looked at me, one eye cocked, and grinned. Slapping her hands on her *sarong*, she laughed, "You find it funny? Me too."

Suddenly serious, she said, "I spoke to your mother on the phone yesterday and then to Nelly."

I sat up. "And?" I asked.

"Your mother is well. Both are worried about you. You're set on going overseas, they say. Your Aunty Nelly wishes that for you too. But, like I said yesterday, it will be difficult if your father doesn't support you. I don't wish to be cruel. I hear about government policies every day. The chances of a scholarship are slim. Try hard, but don't feel bitter if you don't get one."

She spoke in Chinese this time. There was no trace of the comical mishmash of English and Malay words she favoured; her tone was serious, no inflection, no jokiness. A different Aunty Jeanie from the one I had known and ridiculed in the past.

Without giving me a chance to protest, she continued, "There's no harm in studying in the University of Malaya. It has a good reputation. Never mind what others may say. It is important to learn about our roots. People laugh at the policy to switch to Malay, but if you wish to live and work here, you should learn the national language. It's not an unreasonable thing to ask. I'm not saying you should give up English. It is too important an international language . . ."

She broke off, looked beyond me suddenly distracted, and told the driver to stop. She got out of the car and, without another word, walked to a road-side stall. I could see her gesticulating, pointing to the little copper caskets sitting on the stoves. The vendor grinned, nodded and took out a piece of newspaper, laid a banana leaf in its fold, and promptly fished out thick pancakes from the copper caskets. Laying them on the leaf, he doled out large spoonfuls of roasted ground nuts and syrup and drizzled these onto the pancakes. Armed with the parcel of pancakes she returned to the car and placed it on my lap. "Eat. You must be hungry. You've missed lunch."

I ate. She talked. I had never seen her like this before. I was impressed by the change in her.

"As I was saying, if you stay at home, you will be able to keep an eye on the family; your mother and Nelly need you at home. Your father too, although he may not realise it. Otherwise, Shirley will take over completely. Also, look at it this way. She thinks she's making you miserable by stopping you from going overseas, she will get little joy from her tactics if it turns out to be something you wish to do yourself. Go with the wind," she advised.

"Will it really help Mother and Aunty if I stay and study here?"

"Definitely. If you are abroad, you'll be worrying about them anyway. You are their link, binding them and giving them strength. Without you, they will have lost a purpose in life. If I were you, I would definitely stay here, but make sure your father doesn't send you to board at the University."

I was awed by my responsibility. I had no idea that I played such an important part in the lives and happiness of the two people I cared for most in the world. I chewed in silence, the pancake did not taste the same. It had become a cloying mass that stuck in my throat.

* * * * *

I waited for dinner to be over, impatient to talk to Aunty Nelly. It was a tortuous affair. Four of us were sat at the table: Father, Shirley, Aunty and me. Conversation was strained. Aunty and Shirley said virtually nothing to each other. Father looked tired. I had not noticed the bags under his eyes before, crescent-shaped and dark with fatigue. Aunty told me he was having business problems.

"What problems?" I had asked.

"Don't worry," she said as usual. "There is nothing you can do."

With Father distracted and Shirley and Aunty not on speaking terms, all conversation was directed at me. It was not conversation that Shirley really wanted. Rather, she used me as a sounding board to report my misdeeds. "The driver said you stayed late at school." My heart fluttered. I cast Father a surreptitious look, but he was wrapped up in his own thoughts and did not hear. I was not allowed to stay after school unless he approved.

I mumbled, "I had to talk to a teacher about career prospects." My ears felt hot and I looked at Aunty for help.

Shirley was not yet ready to let go. "Are you sure? He said he saw you speaking to a woman."

I stuttered. Aunty came to my rescue, "That would be your friend's mother asking after your mum, wouldn't it?"

Shirley gave her a murderous look. Picking up a spoon, she reached for the plate of *choy sam*. She took a large portion of the mustard greens and heaped it on my plate. "This is good for you. Will help get rid of those pimples on your face," she smirked.

I hated *choy sam!* Its bitter taste filled me with revulsion. I told myself I could eat it. I did not want a fuss. Otherwise, she would bring up some other misdeed of mine to attract Father's attention. I was conscious of Shirley watching me expectantly. My reaction was no different from in the past. My eyes watered and I gagged.

Aunty leaned over, took the vegetables from my plate and said quietly, "I'll eat them. Go and wash your face."

I stood up and left for the bathroom, but I heard their sharp exchange. Shirley accused Aunty of spoiling me. Aunty accused her of baiting me deliberately. Father just sat there. When I returned, he had left. It was as though he had not heard a single word.

* * * * *

The words became a blur, row upon row of black wavy lines, shimmering and dancing out of focus. I bent closer to the book. Still the words would not register. Carefully, I placed the book-mark on the page and closed the book. I rubbed my eyes. I was tired. I needed spectacles.

I felt tense, waiting for Aunty Nelly to come up to our bedroom, wanting to tell her about my meeting with Aunty Jeanie and to discuss her advice. Usually, she would come upstairs soon after me. But there was no sign of her. Where could she be?

I made a desultory attempt to get back to my book. I could not concentrate. I tiptoed out of the bedroom. I could hear music coming from Father's bedroom at the end of the landing. Shirley was speaking. Excited shrills of laughter punctuated her words and clashed with the background music. I listened. Father was not with her, I was sure. It was a one-sided conversation. She must be on the phone. I went to the top of the staircase and looked down. No one was about. I went down and made my way to the family room.

The lights were on and I could hear the television. The television was a new acquisition. Until we bought it, I had only seen them in magazines. Father had reluctantly bought one after much pressure from Shirley. She had insisted television was the latest thing and we must have one. Lucille Ball was saying something to Desi Arnaz. The volume was so loud, it almost drowned the two voices engaged in deep conversation in the room. I moved towards the room, then stopped. I could hear Aunty comforting Father. Over and over, she said, "Don't worry."

It was not a time to intrude. I went back to my room to wait. She would tell me. If she didn't, I would ask her. I feared something must be seriously amiss. I had not seen Father so distracted before.

* * * * *

I was awake at the first ray of sunlight. I struggled to a sitting position and reached over to wake Aunty Nelly. I must have fallen asleep while waiting for her the previous night. If we were to talk, it had to be now. In an hour's time, I would be off to school.

She sat up with a start, then reached for her specs. "You were sleeping so soundly last night, I didn't have the heart to wake you up," she explained, stifling a yawn.

"You were very late. What were you discussing?"

"Your father was telling me his business problems. It is rather complicated and will take time to explain; I will keep it for this evening. Tell me your news instead.

I told her about Jeanie. She listened quietly. After I had finished, she said, "There is some sense in what she says, but I don't want you to sacrifice yourself. I have some savings and I've asked Uncle Tek San for a loan. If you want to study overseas, you can. You should think of yourself first."

I shook my head. Last night, waiting for her to come upstairs, I had already decided. If I went against Father's decision, if he knew that I went with the help of Uncle Tek San and Aunty Nelly, I would just be creating problems for them. Aunty Jeanie was right; there was more than one way to excel.

A Change in Fortunes

Chapter 39

Ming Kong steered the Sunbeam Talbot convertible into the building site and skidded to a halt by an idle Caterpillar digger. Thick clay soil clung to the wheels of the car. The blue metallic sheen of its bonnet was barely discernible beneath a film of dust. He had taken over from the driver who had sat white-knuckled at his side. Ming Kong needed to drive to clear his head after the long session with his lawyer. He had driven hard and fast on the new highway; he had the hood down, testing the car's speed, letting off steam, taking a detour before returning to the site. Handing the car keys back to the driver, he asked him to park further away from the dirt and grime, saying, apologetically, that the car would need a wash before it was returned to Shirley. It was Shirley's car, his present to her two months ago. Two months before the fiasco.

A group of workers were huddled under the zinc roof of a makeshift hut. Some were squatted on their haunches, smoking. Others were just standing idle. They looked at him, nervously, unsure what to do. As he walked towards the site office, some of them began to move slowly back to where the foundations of the houses were to be built. Others remained as they were, knowing that no work would be done until Wing Lok said so. He was their boss.

This was phase VII of Ming Kong's housing projects in Kuala Lumpur and Petaling Jaya. After the first four phases, he had come to rely increasingly on Wing Lok. He was not just his contractor, he also helped with the administration. Based on Wing Lok's projected work schedules and costings, Ming Kong took care of the rest.

Until recently, things had gone like clockwork. Any differences between projected and actual costs or between scheduled and actual completion dates were minor, well within the contingencies allowed for in the plans. All this changed, however, with the decision to move into Singapore, a decision triggered by political events. Indonesia's military skirmish with the newly-formed Malaysia troubled Ming Kong as did the breakdown of talks between the Prime Minister, Tunku Abdul Rahman, President Sukarno of Indonesia and President Macagapal of the Philippines. Continuous talk of policies to redistribute wealth, of special privileges for Malays, and hints that Singapore might separate from Malaysia added to his unease. His friends advised him to spread his risk geographically. And he did.

When he began operations in Singapore, he handed over most of the financial administration in Kuala Lumpur to Wing Lok. Shirley was pleased. "We can spend more time away on these business trips," she had said. At first things seemed to work well. Then the rot set in. He sighed as he made his way up the steps to the site office. He might have given Wing Lok too much to do. If so, why didn't he say, why had he kept saying everything was on schedule when it was not!

He pushed open the door and went in. An ice-cold blast from the air conditioning hit him. Wing Lok was there with three other men. They were hunched around a table, each holding a hand of cards! Startled, the three men got up and left immediately. The look on Ming Kong's face was sufficient to send them away. Not Wing Lok, he stood his ground. "Let's not say anything we might regret."

Holding his tongue, Ming Kong sat down. The two men stared at each other. Neither spoke. Minutes ticked by, the only the sound was the clattering of the over-worked air conditioner. Wing Lok was the first to break the silence. "It's not what it seems."

"What is it then?" Ming Kong could feel his temper rising. "You said the applications were sent on time and that the delays were caused by the authorities not replying to them. I've been in touch with all of them." He slammed a sheaf of letters down on the table in front of Wing Lok. "None of them, not one, has received our requests for permits. As a result, all our building work is suspended because the permits have not been released. Yet, you initiated the loan, signed up workers, hired equipment. Why?"

Wing Lok shrugged. "If you're not happy with the way I run things, you should be around to do it yourself. Don't blame me. I have too much to do."

"Yes, so much that you have time to gamble during office hours. Remember you offered to take on more responsibilities. The letters were ready to be sent. You just didn't send them. Now you want to blame others for your negligence."

Ming Kong cursed himself for being deceived so easily. The problems came in dribs and drabs, nothing major at first. When asked, Wing Lok would say, "All these new policies, no one knows who should be doing what, the left hand doesn't know what the right hand is doing. These government officers are all useless."

He would tell Ming Kong to leave it to him; in the past he had always managed to sort them out. This time, however, they had snowballed until virtually all work schedules were not being met. The banks called Ming Kong to alert him that the overdraft facilities were being drawn to their limit. The architects called to complain that they had not been paid. Meantime, the prices of building materials soared well above the projected costs.

It was Ming Kong's discussion with Nelly that had finally alerted him to the need to take over directly and to talk to the authorities himself. "They've always responded quickly before; they were always helpful in the past, weren't they?" she had said. "It's odd they should all change. Some perhaps, but all? If it's a policy directive, you should find out for yourself."

Reflecting on her suggestion, Ming Kong blamed himself for his stupidity. Why hadn't he thought of it himself. It was, he acknowledged, because he trusted Wing Lok completely, so much so that he had let him handle the company's finances, something that previously he would never have done with anyone except Nelly. He'd been blind!

Wing Lok's manner changed even as Ming Kong considered what to do. In a deadly voice, he warned, "If you do not like what I'm doing, terminate my contract. You will find that you owe me a great deal of money. I doubt whether, in your present circumstances, you will be able to settle the debt. Check with your lawyers."

Ming Kong had done just that. He knew he was in dire financial straits. With a delay of eight to twelve months and the two projects suspended, the very existence of his company was threatened.

It would cost him a lot to end Wing Lok's contract. Unless, of course, he could prove fraud and deliberate mismanagement. It would need much more evidence than delays in sending letters, blame for which Wing Lok could easily pass on to others.

* * * * *

Ming Kong arrived home early. He did not recognise the girl who opened the door. There had been a steady stream of new maids. Stepping inside, he was again reminded of the changes at home. Once it had been warm with the voices and laughter of his children, now a cold silence greeted him. An empty stillness on a stifling, muggy day.

"Is nobody home? The Mistress?" he asked. He was anxious to talk to Shirley.

"No, she has been out since this morning," the new maid replied as she closed the door behind him.

"An Mei?" he asked, turning round to face her.

"She's upstairs studying."

Good, he thought. Shirley's absence would give him a chance to talk with her. Nelly had told him about An Mei's anxiety over her exams. He made his way to the staircase. He was about to go up when he heard a car turn into the drive followed shortly by the sound of Shirley's voice. She was shouting for Ah Hing to carry in her shopping. There was no point now in trying to talk to An Mei. He would do it later, after he had sorted things out with Shirley. As he returned to the drawing room, he recalled the bank statement he had received. Three full pages. He was in the red again.

Ah Hing staggered in with parcels and bags full of shopping. Shirley followed. "Put them down by the sofa, be careful, you clumsy woman!" She was so engrossed in chastising Ah Hing, she failed to see Ming Kong standing there observing the scene. She flopped down on the sofa, pulled her shoes off, tossed them aside and was about to ask Ah Hing for a drink when she noticed him. "You are back early."

He did not reply. His eyes went from parcel to parcel.

Seeing his grim face, she asked, "Is something wrong? Not my car, I hope. You've not done anything to it, have you? It was such a nuisance having to use the other car. We should get rid of it and get a new one." She had reluctantly relinquished use of the Sunbeam that morning, agreeing only because Ming Kong's own car had spluttered and stalled, and he was late for his meeting.

He sat down opposite her, his hands clasped in front of him. "It is difficult to buy anything new at the moment," he said. Pointing at the bags strewn on the floor, he continued, "We have to curb our spending. You must cut back on your shopping. The bank has been in touch again. This is the third time in recent months."

Shirley smiled, hoping to coax him out of his mood. "Come on, these are only little things. What is money for?" She got up and sat on the arm of his chair. Kissing him on his head, she started rubbing his back, her fingers digging deep into the tight knots of his neck. "You're so tense, don't take it out on me, it's not my fault you are in a foul mood."

"I'm serious," he said. "Our finances are in a bad way."

She stopped. "Are you really serious?" she asked in disbelief. Every one of her gambling mates had assured her she had hit on a *kum san*, a gold hill. She recalled the fuss they had made of her as they toasted to her success.

"As serious as I can be," he affirmed. "We have problems with our turnover. So I want you to cut down on your shopping and reduce the household staff. And I want you to do it immediately!"

"If you want to cut down on expenses, you should reduce the money you spend on the children's education," Shirley retorted, conveniently forgetting it was her who had wanted them sent away.

She ran to her room and locked herself in. Ming Kong ran after her. He banged on the door in frustration. "Open up! Be reasonable. We have to talk."

"Go away," she wailed.

"No! You listen and listen carefully. We cannot sustain any more debts. I am facing a financial crisis, no thanks to Wing Lok. You hear me? Great losses, not just tens of thousands but hundreds of thousands, perhaps even more. So no more spending! You hear?"

Leaning heavily behind the door, Shirley panted. She tried to collect her thoughts. She could not believe things were so serious. Wing Lok would have told her. Only the other day he had assured her their plans were on course. It must just be a ploy to stop her spending.

* * * * *

They met in a small cafe, choosing a secluded table, hidden behind a big pot of ferns. It was dark inside; a tinted glass window cut out the bright sunlight. The air conditioning was on full. Someone came in, leaving the front door wide open. A swoosh of hot humid air rushed in and the glass table top turned damp. Shirley shivered. She did not like the look on Wing Lok's face.

"Is it true about Ming Kong's money problems?" she asked.

"Yes," he replied. Wing Lok was enjoying himself. He was not going to give her any information until she begged for it. Their relationship had always been balanced on a tight rope of mutual dislike and greed, now he allowed his dislike of her to show. He had little further need for her, except in one area. She, however, needed him more. Getting her to co-operate would not be easy, he was sure of that. So he sat back and waited, feigning indifference.

"Why didn't you mention it before?" she asked crossly. "We are supposed to be partners."

"I do not report to you," he sneered.

She waited, but he said nothing more. He seemed engrossed in the piped music, nodding and tapping his fingers in time to the beat. Impatient, she said, "I'm not playing your little games. If you want to let me know, then do so. Otherwise, I've better things to do." She got up and reached for her bag.

"Sit down." He grabbed her wrist and pushed her roughly back into her seat. "If you so want to know, then yes! Yes! Yes! Yes! Ming Kong is in big financial trouble. While you were enjoying yourselves in Singapore, building work here in Kuala Lumpur came to a standstill. The money has run out. Ming Kong is now trying to blame me. So I challenged him to sack me. Huh! That is if he can afford to have a battle with me. It'll cost him! Don't think for a moment he can get off easily."

Shirley listened in horror. White-faced, she let out a hiss, "Then, then there is nothing for me. So my getting rid of the children overseas is for nothing, just another strain on our money."

"I'm afraid that's it. I would not put it past Ming Kong to ask you to return the house he bought you, he's so desperate for cash."

"Bastard! Never! He'd better not even think about it, the shit!" She then turned on Wing Lok, accusing him of treachery. "You swine! You kept all this from me."

"Be careful. We're in public. You don't wish to show your origins, do you?" he warned, his voice low and menacing.

Continuing, he beamed with triumph. "I hold the key to his future; whether he can come out of this crisis depends on me. If he does not survive financially, your *kum san* is gone, kaput! If, however, I do not press to be paid and manage to get the building work more or less back on schedule, half if not most of his problems will be over."

"How could you do that? Why would you help?"

"Don't you worry about how, that's my business. But as to why, huh! It is not for love of him, nor you. I want something that he has. Do you want to know what it is?" He was amused by Shirley's confusion.

"An Mei, she is what I want." He leaned back on his chair and patted his stomach in satisfaction. There! He had said it out loud at last.

Incredulous, she asked whether he had taken leave of his senses. "*Teen*," she said. "*Gila!*" She repeated in Malay, her lips curled in disdain.

"No, *teen* I am not. I have watched her grow up into a beautiful young woman. Why did you think I singled her out as the only child he should keep here?"

"He'll never agree. And Nelly and An Mei herself will make sure of that!"

"Then, I leave it to you to persuade him, to bring him around to my way of thinking."

* * * * *

Long after Shirley had left, Wing Lok remained seated. He ordered another coffee. Nursing his drink, he reflected on the events of the past few months. It was pure impulse that caused him to take a completely different route from the one he had originally mapped out with Shirley. He was glad he took it. This was what life was about, he thought, grabbing your chance.

It was a meeting with another contractor, a friend, that set him thinking. Innocent words, delivered without malice. If he wanted to, the man had boasted, he could make or break the property tycoon he was working for just by not pulling his weight. "All I have to do," he had said, "is to adopt a *tidak apa* don't care attitude and work *perlahan-perlahan* slowly-slowly, and it would all end in chaos. Not that I would do it. That old man treats me well, like a son."

Wing Lok had no such qualms. Ming Kong's venture into Singapore gave him the opportunity that he was waiting for. Ming Kong was a careful, diligent boss. He went over everything with a fine-toothed comb, questioning and even reworking project schedules. As long as he was around, it would be impossible to play hooky. With Ming Kong away in Singapore, the field was left wide open for him to set his plan in motion. I have to thank that idiot, Shirley, he admitted to himself. Unwittingly she had helped by enticing Ming Kong to stay away a little longer each time. In less than a year, the extras he had pocketed from contracting building materials had given him more than enough not to press for payment should he choose.

He chuckled, satisfied with his work. "I am in a win-win situation. If he chooses to take a hard line and end my contract, he has to pay me a large settlement. If he chooses a softer approach and agrees to my proposal for An Mei, I will become a member of the family!"

Chapter 40

The last of the women had left. Mei Yin took one final look at the register to make sure all the names had been ticked. "You cannot take the risk of anyone, no matter the reason, remaining in the factory," Tek San had admonished. A month before, one of the women had stayed back. The day before that, she had been badly beaten by her husband and had hidden in the factory kitchen, hoping to make it her temporary home. Her husband had found out and, in the middle of the night, smashed his way in. Fortunately the neighbours were alerted and called the police. In such situations, Tek San advised, it was far better to help the woman by reporting the violence to the police. "What if he had set fire to the factory or killed her?" Since then, she had been extra careful.

Satisfied everyone had gone, she locked the front door and went back inside the factory. She checked once more that all was in order: the stoves and ovens had been switched off; the windows were closed; and the kitchen was ready for the next day. It was quiet now. The women made such a din while they worked, swapping news, gossip and salacious stories, often accompanied by waves of laughter.

Leaving by the back door, she padlocked the gate and went to her car. It had been a busy day. The business was in full operation. The long-awaited biscuit section was now open. Sales were brisk. Both Tek San and Nelly had helped by stocking the new lines of cakes and pastries in their food outlets. She was grateful for their support. Thinking of what had been achieved filled her with pride. She felt that familiar prickling sensation in her nose.

"Mummy, I don't know why I am so mixed up," she would say to Sook Ping, "I'm happy and sad at the same time; I feel guilty about feeling any happiness at all."

That at times she felt almost happy was undeniable. She had

made something of herself. She could not, however, shake off the deep aching sadness of being separated from her children. She felt a familiar weight in her chest. She straightened her shoulders. This was not an evening to be thinking sad thoughts. She was late. She started the engine of the little delivery van and drove out on to the main road. She was not going home. She was meeting Jeanie.

* * * * *

They had arranged to meet at St Paul's Hill by the gate of the fortress, *A Famosa*. From there it was a short drive to the old quarter of Malacca town where Jeanie wanted to be later that evening. Mei Yin arrived first, parked the van and walked towards the gate, *Porta de Santiaga*. The setting sun cast a red glow over the ruins of the fort. The worst of the day's heat was almost over. A cool sea-breeze was gaining strength, bending the spindly trunks of the coconut palms and whipping their fronds into a dancing frenzy.

Stepping over the stones and débris at the gateway, she saw a group of tourists gathered around a guide. "This," he was saying, "is all that remains of the fortress. Built by the Portuguese in the early 1500s, it was later taken over by the Dutch who rebuilt it in 1670. When the British came, they ordered the fort to be destroyed; only the gate, *Porta de Santiaga*, was left."

The group moved on. Mei Yin stood surveying the scene. Hawkers were preparing to leave: brightly-coloured kites and paper machés were carefully packed into cardboard boxes; and sliced pineapples, papayas, water chestnuts and coconut which had been laid out on blocks of ice were being carefully stored in insulated boxes. Even as the hawkers were completing this daily chore, the glow of the evening sky disappeared as the sun set over the sea.

Mei Yin began to fret. "I hope she arrives soon. I don't want to be waiting here on my own."

As if on cue, Jeanie's voice floated across the car park, "Sorry, sorry, I'm late. I couldn't get away. The *Datuk* invited some of his friends for refreshments at the hotel. I could not leave without at least saying hello. Then, one thing led to another. Anyway, here I am." She opened her arms out wide. "It's so good to see you."

Mei Yin swallowed hard, hesitated and went into Jeanie's arms.

"You are too thin, all bones," said Jeanie. She placed her hands on Mei Yin's shoulders and held her at arms' length to have a better look. Her eyes, concerned and anxious, belied her light-hearted words. "Terrible! No meat on you, like a *kampong* chicken. What-*lah*! Eat more. We might as well make a start now." She led the way to her car.

"There is a restaurant I wanted to see again. It was my favourite when I was a little girl," Jeanie explained. "You didn't know that I also came from Malacca, did you?"

Mei Yin shook her head, still speechless as she adjusted herself to Jeanie's tendency to switch from one topic to another. "She is like a machine gun panning from side to side in full rapid fire," Nelly had remarked once.

Jeanie continued to reminisce. "Very few people do. I have kept it a secret from most people."

"What, even from me?"

"Sorry, what can I say! When I first went to Kuala Lumpur all those years ago, I had little wish to be associated with such a backward place. I was ashamed. Now! Now I don't care. I will tell you about it another day. We shouldn't stand here chatting, it's getting late. Let's drive in my car to the restaurant. I will ask my driver to follow us in your van. We can talk on the way."

* * * * *

They went to the *Restoran Nyonya*, a small eatery run by a woman, some 40 years old. Her appearance left you in no doubt about the reason for its name. She wore *Nyonya* clothes. They remained untouched by the changes in fashion and fads that had begun to colour even the traditional Malay *sarong kebaya*. Her blouse was of a peachy transparent material with seams of heavy embroidery running round the entire hemline and up the twin front panels. The panels were held together by three gold broaches. Beneath was a tight corset, a hallmark of modesty that was somewhat incongruous alongside the flirtatious top. The cotton *sarong*, brown and decorated with twining tropical flowers, was wrapped tightly round her ample hips and secured by a heavy silver belt. On her feet she wore beaded slippers, a matching peachy shade.

She took their orders, then turned to leave, her bottom straining tight against the *sarong*. The twin mounds of her buttocks jiggled and bounced, pushing against its soft fabric. When she was some distance away, Jeanie broke into giggles. "My mother used to wear that. So sexy yet so old-fashioned. We don't see much of the *Nyonya* dress in Kuala Lumpur." Looking down at her own costume, a long loose tunic blouse reaching the knee over a loose tailored *sarong*, she grimaced. "This is what Moslem women in the capital city wear now. We've been hit by conservatism in dress. When the rest of society is reaching for the mini skirt, we are covering up. We might need to wear veils next."

Mei Yin nodded, but she was not really paying much attention. She kept thinking of their conversation on the way to the restaurant, her mind going through in detail each and every thing that Jeanie had related. She was anxious to continue the conversation, she had a host of questions.

Jeanie had been busy after their phone conversation some months back. Convinced that Ming Kong's misunderstanding could be removed if the doctor, Jung Yang, cleared the air, she had gone back to the hospital in search of him. He was not there. Eventually, she tracked him down to Singapore.

"Jeanie," Mei Yin interrupted, "you still haven't told me about Dr Yang."

"Sorry, I got carried away. It's just that I am tired of wearing the same style all the time. In my position, you see, I have to be prim and proper. So this is the result," pointing at her own dress.

"Jeanie," Mei Yin cried, exasperated. "Tell me. Tell me! What did he say?"

"Such a nice man! He was very concerned. He said you should have told him."

"What else? Did he agree to clear the air? It's a bit awkward, I know, especially when there is nothing really to clear. If he tries to explain to Ming Kong, it is as though he has something to hide." Mei Yin placed both hands on her red and anguished face. "I was so ashamed at that time. I couldn't bring myself to get his help. I felt it reflected on me to be so distrusted by my husband. Anyway I had no time. Ming Kong bundled me out of Kuala Lumpur."

"It's not easy for Dr Yang to help. He has something to hide. That is why he left for Singapore. Poor guy."

"You're not making sense Jeanie, what has he to hide?" Mei Yin was getting even more exasperated.

"Ah, the food has arrived. Look, fish head curry! And chicken *kapitan*, my favourite. I've not had real *Nyonya* cooking since I moved to KL. People say Penang's *Nyonya* cooking is the best. But for me, nothing beats a good *Nyonya* dish in Malacca. Smell, just smell it . . . mmm . . . coconut cream, turmeric and galangal. Eat, eat!"

Mei Yin put a restraining hand on Jeanie, stopping her as she reached towards the curries. "Tell me first, please."

Jeanie put her chopsticks down and turned serious. "I know, I know what I'm supposed to do. Can't you see that I am playing for time because I don't know how to say it."

Mei Yin had never known Jeanie to be lost for words before.

"He agreed to help; only he's worried, worried about the actions that Ming Kong might take. He does not want any publicity, anyone looking too closely into his affairs." Lowering her voice, and looking around, Jeanie whispered, "He says he does not like women in that way, you know . . . I mean not, uh, sexually. He is very fond of women and respects them and in particular he wants to help you. He likes, even loves you, but not, you know, uh . . . uh."

Mei Yin's eyes widened in disbelief.

"There, I told you. I expected you to react this way, mouth open and all," Jeanie said, crossly. "Of course, if he tells Ming Kong, your innocence will certainly be proven. The problem is, his kind of behaviour is not legal under Moslem law. The question is, would it get him, a non-believer, into trouble if he tells anyone? Whatever happens, though, his reputation and standing in the medical world could be affected. What if Ming Kong were to expose him? The scandal of it, especially in his line of work. A gynaecologist!"

Mei Yin interjected. "No, he can't take the risk. I would not want him to make such a sacrifice. He was already very trusting to tell you."

"He didn't tell me willingly. I put him under duress, pushed him, and went on and on about your plight. He must have felt he had to explain. I felt so sorry for him. He looked sick, his face was practically green! *Sayang*! Such a pity! A good-looking man like that."

"How did it all end?"

"He said he will try to speak to Ming Kong, but he may not tell all. He's chewing on this, how to help without implicating himself. We must wait to hear from him."

She picked up her chopsticks. "Now, can I eat?"

Mei Yin hardly touched her food. She was immersed in thought. Then out of the blue, Jeanie asked. "You think he's like that because he is so disgusted at looking at women's private parts . . . not very nice! *Chi lak kak*! Bad luck!" Mei Yin laughed. It was impossible to remain serious with Jeanie.

Chapter 41

Ming Kong looked across the expanse of polished wood. He could smell the polish, a resonance of teak oil. There were five people, including himself, seated around the table: his solicitor, the bank manager and two other banking associates. Everyone was avoiding his eye. All seemed preoccupied with the papers in front of them. The manager cleared his throat and began. He spoke about the long association of the bank with Ming Kong and his father before him, and how sorry he was about the problems Ming Kong faced. He then referred to Ming Kong's financial position, giving details of the overdraft. His voice droned on and on.

Ming Kong felt an overwhelming sense of fatigue. He was losing touch with reality, his head woozy from sleepless nights and the continuous juggling with his finances. He drifted off in his own thoughts.

He could still see the photographs that Tek San had placed in front of him, one after another, their black and white grainy images forever imprinted on his mind. The pictures of Shirley and Wing Lok together and the familiarity between them. Worst of all was the taped telephone conversation between the two. All documented, all irrefutable from a detective that Tek San had employed. He remembered with shame and humility his response when Tek San had first tried to warn him about Shirley. "Don't you dare drag Shirley into this and badmouth her. She might have her weaknesses, but never this. She would never betray me. You have to give me proof." So the evidence was laid before him.

The ugly events that followed tumbled one after another through his mind. He broke into a sweat, just recalling. Wing Lok's insolence when he tried to terminate his contract. "You can't get rid of me so easily," Wing Kong had sneered. "This is what you owe me." He had waved a wad of papers in Ming Kong's face. "And I want it now plus interest. And don't think I'll hand over the administration and building without a fight. Remember the papers you signed so unwittingly in your hurry to leave with Shirley."

Anger had gushed through Ming Kong's veins, anger so strong that he found it difficult not to hurl himself at Wing Lok and wipe out the look of contempt and spite on his face. Ming Kong had been holding on to the back of a chair, pressing it hard in an attempt to release his fury when Wing Lok said, "You can help yourself out of your difficulty and I'll forgive all your accusations. All I want is An Mei and I'll . . ." Before he could finish the chair crashed to the side and Ming Kong landed such a punch on Wing Lok's face that he reeled and fell backwards.

Events after that just spiralled out of control, gaining impetus with every twist and turn of events. The battle between the lawyers. The arrangement of further overdrafts to pay off Wing Lok. The restarting of building work and the delays caused by deliberate sabotage. Building materials went missing and vital documents were lost. His legal battle with Wing Lok was costly. With each increase in his overdraft, he fell deeper into debt. Then, as if things could not be much worse, the housing boom petered out because of political and economic uncertainties as a result of anti-Chinese riots in Indonesia.

Ming Kong felt someone nudging him. It was his lawyer. All eyes were on him. The banker was summing up. He steeled himself and smiled, re-connecting with the group. He took a sip of water and put on what his father called his poker face. The banker was addressing him. "I'm sorry. We cannot extend your overdraft facilities unless the existing debts are settled. I'm afraid we have to call in the debt and repossess the land you gave as collateral." He paused. "I can give you just one more month to make the repayment. After that, I am afraid, we will have to act."

Ming Kong had anticipated this outcome. He had discussed it long and hard with Nelly the night before. He could not let them take over the land; he had to complete the building work. Once he had sold the houses, his liquidity problems would be over or at least most of them. "The unrest in the country is bound to be settled. Indonesia cannot continue its confrontation forever."

Nelly, who did not entirely share his optimism, was nevertheless encouraging. "Let's hope this month's summit of the three leaders in Tokyo is successful. Now that the Americans are also pushing for a settlement, perhaps..." She left her sentence unfinished. She was not really confident that the issues could be resolved so quickly. President Kennedy had cut off military aid to Indonesia in September 1963, but the Indonesians remained defiant. In early 1964, President Sukarno told the Americans in a public rally, "Go to hell with your aid."

"They must, Nelly, I'm banking on it. I need to borrow against the shop-houses and stores, to settle my debt and keep the land."

Now sat in front of the bankers and lawyers, Ming Kong replied, offering them yet another slice of his business as security. His lawyers brought out the papers. The mood in the meeting room lightened. Smiles all round. The bankers agreed to look at the proposal. The date for the next meeting was set. Handshakes, an exchange of solicitous enquiries as to the health and well-being of the family, and the meeting was over. Another reprieve.

*****

"For the moment, at least, we should be alright," Ming Kong told his sister and brother-in-law. Nelly, An Mei and he were at their home.

It was the first time he had visited them for many years. It was to be a quiet celebratory dinner, a reconciliation between the two families, and a recognition of An Mei's success in her A-levels. The headmistress said she had done them proud. He too was proud. "At least in one area things have turned out well. Although it is through no thanks to me," he reflected sadly.

Kai Min led her brother out to the verandah. "Dinner will be ready in half an hour's time. Let's leave the children to catch up." They sat companionably on the iron swing. Kai Min sensed his sadness. He was subdued and contrite. He had earlier confessed to Tek San that he missed his wife, but he had said nothing to Kai Min. So she waited. She knew she had to let him take the initiative. His unwillingness to be pushed had been the main source of friction between them. When at last he spoke, she remained silent as he unburdened himself.

Then she told him, "We've never believed the stories about Mei Yin. Now we have heard from the doctor with whom she was alleged to be having an affair. There is no way he could have been involved with her, except as a friend. He's not interested in women in that way."

Jung Yang had contacted Nelly who, in turn, told Kai Min. It was agreed that Kai Min should tell her brother about Jung Yang. They thought it would be less incriminating and less confrontational.

Ming Kong buried his head in his hands unable to speak. Minutes ticked by. Kai Min could see dinner was ready. The children were hovering around the French window, the maid was gesturing for them to go to the table. Tek San and Nelly were shooing them to silence. Ming Kong appeared not to notice, he was completely lost in thought.

He lifted his head and looked at his sister. "Do you think she will take me back?"

"I don't know. You will have to ask her."

* * * * *

Mei Yin stood at the table, arms immersed up to the elbow in flour. A patch of white had landed on her cheek. She brushed her face with the back of her hand. "Could you pour the oil into the centre for me?" she asked her assistant. Intent on her job, she concentrated on drawing the mound of flour into the pool of oil. Then, sensing that someone was watching her, she looked up. And there he was. Standing by the door, looking at her.

Mei Yin blushed, looked down again, and continued mixing the flour and oil, talking to her helper, explaining how to rub in the flour

and breadcrumbs, kneading and rolling. She did not hurry, she
needed time to collect herself after the shock of seeing him. It had
been so long since she had seen Ming Kong.

Aware of the eyes on her, she tried to keep her voice light. "There,
you take over now. Just feel the crumbs as they pass through your
fingers. They should feel light. Add a tiny drop of ice water. Yes,
that's it. It should bind nicely. When you knead, use the base of your
hands, push lightly forward and then pull it back until the dough
feels pliable. Try again." She kept her entire attention on her helper.

Only when she was satisfied that the process was complete, did
she turn to the curious women around her and instruct them to carry
on. "I'll be in the office."

The women simpered. "Must be a boyfriend."

No, more likely to be her husband. Heard her talking to her
mother. They said that he might turn up this week. Didn't you
notice how tense she's been?"

Mei Yin could hear their whispers and imagine their covert looks
as she strode towards Ming Kong. She felt her ears grow hot; worse
still her heart was beating so hard, she swore she could hear it thump.
She kept her pace, eyes fixed on a distant object. Then she was next
to him. Her legs felt as though they were about to give way at the
knees. She walked past him and into the office. She invited him in
and offered him a seat. She sat down facing him across the desk. It
was vital to keep that distance between them.

She spoke first. "Why are you here?"

"To see you." He looked keenly at her. She looked the same, the
same oval face, the wide almond eyes and the shiny, long black hair
tied back carelessly with a band. But somehow she was different. If
she was nervous, he could not see it. Her demeanour had little in
common with the Mei Yin of old. Suddenly he was not confident.

Mei Yin did not reply. She kept her gaze steady. Searching for
the right response, she felt a surge of anger. It drove away all vestiges
of her earlier fear and apprehension. How dare he come and sit
calmly in front of her after years of warding her off. How dare he!

He could sense her change of mood; it was evident in her eyes. They shone fire, the brown pupils a molten lava of changing light. "I know what you're thinking. I'm so, so sorry for all the wrongs. Will you forgive me?"

"That is too much to ask at this point," was her flat response. She felt cold, her arms were covered by little pin-pricks of goose bumps. Still the anger remained. "Do you deserve forgiveness?"

He was not prepared for such a question. He knew it would not be easy. Going to Mei Yin, eating humble pie would never be easy. What he had hoped for was some warmth, something, perhaps a chink in her armour, that he could reach through. Now he was here, he could detect none. First, the cold indifference as she kept him waiting, now this hard, fiery stare. He shook his head. "No, but that does not stop me from hoping you will."

She needed time. Nelly and Kai Min had warned her of his plan to visit. She had spent sleepless nights preparing what to say to him. Now, she was tongue-tied. Through the glass panes of the office window, she could see the women had stopped working; they were all looking at them.

"I cannot talk with you here. Can't you see it is disrupting everyone's work?" she asked fiercely.

"Shall I come back later?"

"No, not here. Go to my mother's house. She's not well. I have to be back to see to her."

"Will six be alright? Can I bring Mother anything?"

She shook her head in reply. Before he could say anything more, she was on her way back to the kitchen without so much as a backward glance. His heart sank.

* * * * *

Ming Kong drove a short distance away and then veered down a dirt track to the edge of a rubber plantation. A signpost said FELDA (Federal Land Development Authority) Estate. Lines and lines of small rubber saplings criss-crossed the area to the left of him, their thin trunks contrasting with the bigger, more solid mature rubber trees to the right. He could see a cluster of new brick buildings, the houses of the farmers, further on down the track. He stopped the car engine and rested his elbows on the steering wheel.

He sat thinking. Should he go early to see if Sook Ping would help? She had always seemed to have a soft spot for him. Certainly, he did not deserve it. He felt uncomfortable after learning that she had been unwell. He did not want to trouble her, but he was desperate for support. He knew Mei Yin placed great store on what her mother said. He decided to try. He started the engine, turned the car around and returned to the main road. He had about two hours to make his case before Mei Yin's return. There was no time to waste.

* * * * *

The countryside had changed little since his last visit to Malacca. If anything, some parts of it had deteriorated. The paddy fields were overgrown with weeds. Here and there, the bunds separating the plots had been breached, allowing water to run off the land. Pavements of hard mud, riven with a mosaic of cracks, had formed where the soil had dried out. Where rice was still being cultivated, small patches of paddy were growing, the panicles almost bare, a poor omen in a country striving to grow all the rice its population needed. A woman in a *sarong* was bent over weeding, each movement a slow desperate act set against the fecund growth of the unwanted intruders.

What a contrast with the FELDA plantation he had just left. He was familiar with the scheme, having tried unsuccessfully to win the contract for the very houses he had seen. If he had succeeded in the bid, he would have had to clear the land, plant the rubber trees and then divide the plantation into three or four hectare plots for allocation to Malay settlers; transforming them in effect into a new rural rich. "No wonder," he thought, "paddy farmers don't want to farm unless they receive more support as well. The pursuit of equality creating inequality... Just like me, causing havoc to the lives of those I love."

He turned into the track that led to Sook Ping's house. He slowed down to take in the surroundings. Kai Min had warned him about the desperate state of the house. Nevertheless, he was totally unprepared for what he saw. If anything, the steps leading up to the house looked in a worst state than she had described, with sharp splinters jutting out of the damaged woodwork. From the earliest days of their marriage, Mei Yin had never approached him for money for her family. He assumed they could manage. He never bothered to ask. He sighed, how could he have been so insensitive?

Ming Kong got out of the car and climbed the steps. Even before he could knock on the door, Sook Ping opened it. Her face showed little signs of surprise; she merely nodded and invited him in. She walked with great difficulty, limping despite the support of the walking stick. When he attempted to help her, she waved him away. "I'm fine, please sit down."

He sat waiting as his mother-in-law slowly negotiated her way towards a seat. He had a sudden urge to go to her assistance, to help wipe out years of neglect, but he remained where he was. How could he do anything now, when he had shown so little interest before. He had not even known of her ill-health. His whole effort had been focused on reviving the family's fortune and amassing more wealth. It would seem grossly insincere to fuss now. He looked at the stark room. The sunshine that poured in merely highlighted its shabbiness. The cane armchair he occupied had bits of rattan worn almost to shreds. Little tendrils of the cane had unwound and hung from its base like a dishevelled fringe. The floral pattern on the cushions was faded to a dull dusty blue.

Sook Ping finally settled down on the chair facing him. A fine sheen of perspiration had formed on her forehead and above her lips, accentuating the pallor of her skin. She took some time to recover her breath sufficiently to speak.

"I am afraid I cannot offer you tea. I have difficulty managing pots and cups," she explained.

"So how do you manage on your own?"

"My neighbour comes in. She brings me lunch and checks everything is okay. The pain comes and goes. Some days, I'm fine, other days I'm just a mass of aches." She shrugged, "Comes with old age. Not really a problem, just inconvenient."

Ming Kong did not know how to broach the subject he had driven in such a hurry to discuss. He could sense her uncertainty. Finally, she asked, "Does Mei Yin know you are here?"

"Yes and no. I went to see her at her work, but it was difficult to speak with all those busybodies around. She agreed to meet me here at six. I came early because I wanted to speak with you first. When you opened the door, I thought that Mei Yin had warned you to expect me."

"No, she didn't call, but somehow, I thought you might come today. We heard from Kai Min that you were planning to come. So when I heard a car, which was certainly not our little van, I assumed it must be you." She paused for him to speak, then prompted him, "Well, why do you want to speak with me after all this time?"

He told her everything. He did not spare himself. He said he wanted to atone, have Mei Yin back, but he was afraid she did not feel the same.

Sook Ping sat impassively. She watched this strong, clever man pour out his heart, saw his tears and sincere regret. She had loved him like a son, entrusted him with her daughter against all odds and despite misgivings, only to see him fail her time and time again because of his weakness for women. Yet, she knew her daughter's loneliness, her secret tears at night when the hustle and bustle of work no longer occupied her mind. Sook Ping believed in the sanctity of marriage and its importance for the children.

"I will try to help if Mei Yin asks me for my views. That's all I will do. I am not going to persuade her.

An Mei's Recollections

Chapter 42

The Great Hall was packed. Parents, siblings, relatives, friends and fellow graduates jostled to find seats. They sat cheek by jowl. The low buzz of conversation in the main body of the hall was punctuated by shrills of excited laughter and barely contained excitement from the back of the stage where the first batch of graduates assembled. They were waiting to be called.

It was 1967. We were waiting for Convocation to begin. It was a great day for the University of Malaya. Established in 1949, the University had moved from its original site in Singapore to Kuala Lumpur in 1963. We were only the second batch of graduate students to have spent all three years of our course on the same campus.

I was in the queue backstage. We had been waiting for three-quarters of an hour for the ceremony to begin. The guests had to be seated, a seemingly endless task. There was much scraping of chairs. People stood up to let others pass, then sat down, only to get up again to let still more people pasts. Under-graduates from the first and second years were acting as ushers. I could hardly recognise them. They were solemn and smart in their best suits, very different from their usual crumpled tee-shirts, scruffy jeans or skirts.

I stood on tiptoe and craned my neck. I was looking for my parents and Aunty Nelly. I saw a hand wave. Aunty Nelly had seen me. There they were. Father, Mother and Aunty Nelly walking down the aisle, making their way to their seats. I smiled, waved back and swallowed hard. Somehow the three of them looked complete together. Father in his long-sleeved batik shirt, Mother slender and petite in her *sarong kebaya*, and Aunty, comfortably dressed in a loose shift with a low Mandarin collar.

Mother did not live with us. Not really. The first two years, following my father's Father's visit to Malacca, she visited every weekend. At first, she stayed with Aunty Kai Min and only later with us. On weekdays, she stayed with Grandmother in Malacca, still taking care of the pastry business. She said the weekends suited her best because Aunty Nelly and I were both at home, but I suspected she needed us as a buffer from Father. And, of course, the pastry business was going from strength to strength. She was running it single-handed since the deterioration in Grandmother's health.

The first few months of this arrangement were strained and awkward. Kuala Lumpur was alive with gossip about our family. Most people approved of the reconciliation, but some doubted Mother's story: a doubt that was a powerful source of gossip. Others pointed an accusing finger at Father and laughed at his failures. Everyone, it seemed, had something to say. People would go back in detail over the events that had torn our family apart. Even campus life had not protected me from rumour and speculation. Students would stop talking when I approached; others openly asked me how I felt. Mother avoided meeting people. It was hard. I kept my time on the campus to a minimum, confining myself to obligatory lectures and tutorials. I studied hard, but mainly at home.

Then, after almost a year, the whispers and gossip suddenly ceased. It was as though they had never been. A demise brought on by exhaustion, Aunty Nelly had concluded. For us, it was like sunshine and calm after the turbulence of a monsoon.

Father's business was back on track. Under Aunty Nelly, the stores continued to be the bulwark of his business. Father repaid Uncle Tek San for the help he had given Mother. By my third year at the university, all of the mini-markets had sections selling Mother's pastries and supplying them to the many hotels springing up in Kuala Lumpur.

Father had done his utmost to persuade Mother to return for good. She declined. We could see that she was torn and undecided.

She was worried in particular about Grandmother's poor health. Now Grandmother was no longer with us, she had passed away two months ago, well maybe . . . My thoughts drifted. A hush fell over the hall. Then applause. Someone behind was pushing me. "Wake up, stop day dreaming. We'll be called soon. The Vice Chancellor has finished his speech."

* * * * *

The ceremony over, I rushed through the lobby of the Great Hall and out into the scorching sun. Hundreds of people were milling around. Some posed for photographs. Smiles mingled with tears, chatter with laughter. It was difficult to see who was who. Further away, near the car park, the traffic congestion was building up. There were cars reversing, cars slowly edging forward, cars trying to make U-turns. The notices banning the use of horns within the university grounds were ignored. Tempers frayed.

We had arranged to meet at the side entrance to the hall away from the administrative buildings. "Stand by the fish pond," Father had suggested. I made my way there.

"An Mei," shouted Aunty Nelly, rushing towards me. She folded me in her arms. "We're so proud of you." Father and Mother followed. They were holding hands, something I had not seen for years. They clasped me, including Nelly, in their embrace.

"You did very well." Father's eyes were twinkling, the creases round them deepened as his mouth stretched into a seemingly endless smile. Mother looked as though she was about to burst with pride. She said little, her kisses said it all.

* * * * *

A celebratory dinner party was planned for the evening. Uncle Tek San, Aunty Kai Min and my cousins would all be there. Aunty Jeanie and her husband, though not family, were also coming.

Flowers and cards were everywhere. My brothers had sent their congratulations. They were still abroad. Wei Han was in his second year at Cambridge University studying engineering. My other two brothers, Wei Hoong and Wei Shu, were at Repton School in the English midlands. Wei Han and Wei Hoong had both adapted to their new life in England with ease, but Wei Shu had a hard time at first, but helped by his brothers, he too eventually settled down. When they came back for the summer vacation, we used to arrange holidays in Malacca with Mother and Grandmother. Under the direction of Father, the old house in Malacca had taken on a new lease of life. Modern plumbing, bathrooms and toilets were installed. The kitchen was extended and re-equipped. The roof was repaired and the walls painted. Yet it still remained essentially the same, retaining its graceful blend of traditional Malay and Minangkabau architecture.

As soon as we stepped into the cool hallway, Father took hold of my hand and said, "We've good news." We moved into the drawing room and sat on the settee. Aunty Nelly was excited. She caught hold of my hand and held it tightly. Mother looked at me anxiously. Father began. "An Mei, we have good news."

"You already said. I'm dying to know what it is."

Aunty Nelly began, "You see An Mei, they..."

"Let me tell her, Nelly," interrupted Father. He was clearly keen to get something off his chest. "Your mother has agreed to... marry me... again!" He turned a bright red, as bright a red as Mother's ears were pink. "I mean we were always married, but we are going to do it properly," he added lamely. "I mean we've always been married properly, but we are going to register the marriage."

I was confused. "What about Aunty Nelly?" Even with my limited knowledge, I knew he could not have a registered marriage and still have a second wife. Would Aunty have to leave us? What's happening? Aunty did not look the least bit concerned. She held my hand even tighter, her dimpled cheeks still puckered in a smile. "Never mind, never mind," she said. "Listen to your father."

"Well, you see," he said, his embarrassment evident, "Nelly was my second wife, but actually she's not, I mean she's not been my wife for a long time. In fact, the marriage never really took place."

"Let me help explain in a different way," interrupted Aunty Nelly. "What your father is proposing will not change anything with respect to my relationship with you or anyone in the family. Your father and mother will be married in the modern way by registering their marriage. Their first marriage was ceremonial, the way it was done before the war. The more important, practical change, that no one has thought to mention, is your mother is coming home. She will be living here."

I turned to look at Mother.

"Yes, I am coming home," Mother confirmed. She looked at Aunty, "You're sure about this, Nelly? You don't mind?"

"Mind, why would I mind an arrangement that makes everyone happy and settled?"

"What will I call you?" I asked her.

"Just as you have always done: Aunty. As for friends, they will probably continue to address me the way they have always done. If some still call me Mrs Ong, I will not bother to correct them. It makes no difference to me. You won't mind, will you Mei Yin?"

"No, of course not," Mother laughed. "After all these years, I don't care about gossip. People will have to accept us as we are. We are, for all practical purposes, sisters."

"Yes, we'll be a family again," concluded Father.

* * * * *

In July 1967, Mother married Father at the registry office in Kuala Lumpur. My brothers flew over from England to attend the simple ceremony. Mother was 40 years old, my father had just turned 50. Aunty Nelly was 51. In early September, I left with my brothers for the UK. They continued with their existing course and I began a postgraduate degree in political science at Oxford University.

Epilogue:
Letters to An Mei

I folded the letters. Drawing my legs up on the broad window sill where I was sitting, I pushed my face against the window pane. My warm breath made a tiny blur of condensation on the cool glass against my forehead.

It was late spring in Oxford, almost summer. The daffodils were long over. Their dying leaves formed droopy clumps underneath the trees. Everywhere else fresh flowers bloomed. It was England at its best, awash with colour and the scent of flowers. The lilac tree, flushed with blossoms, each a plume of dense purple, vied with the large silken petals of the peonies. In a week, possibly less, they too would be replaced by pale creamy Philadelphus flowers redolent with orange perfume. It was a time of change.

Until this moment, I had not expected to see another spring in England. I was completing my postgraduate degree and I planned to return home to Malaysia in three months' time. It was not to be. My parents had decided to start life afresh in a new country. It was hard for them, especially Father who had seen so many ups and downs in his business, and whose roots in Malaysia went back to its earliest days. It was hard for me. I was born and bred there. I unfolded the letters to read them again. I would have to give my brothers the news.

* * * * *

23 May 1969

Dearest An Mei,

We will be coming to see you and the boys within a few months. We will let you know precisely when once we have finalised arrangements. It could take time. There are so many things to settle.
We plan to leave Malaysia for good. I am not certain where we will settle eventually, but for now we intend to spend some months in the UK. Who knows? Perhaps life will be better for us in England. We will have to see. I will let your mother explain. I expect you will have been following the terrible events here in the British media. You hear so much more about what is happening over here than we do.

Take care. All our love,

Father

* * * * *

23 May 1969

My Dearest Daughter,

I am sending this letter with your father's short message. Please forgive him if he seems distracted. He is very upset. We all are. He asked me to explain his sudden decision to leave Malaysia, which must come, I am sure, as a shock to you. It is not easy. This must be the fifth time I have tried unsuccessfully to explain. So I am going to tell you instead what has led up to our decision.
We were taking a weekend break at the bungalow in Port Dickson. It was a beautiful day. Father went to the market in the morning. You know how he just loves to buy food. At the market he arranged for Fatty, remember the fat man who cooks noodles (you

*used to play with his daughter), to come over in the evening to cook a
slap-up meal. That way we would be free to watch the election
campaign and follow the results as they were announced on the
television.*

*It promised to be exciting what with the new political parties. The
ruling Alliance Party was expected to get a good fight from them. For
once we had debates in the run-up to the election and it caught
everyone's imagination. You would not have believed it. Thousands
turned out at rallies to hear the opposition speak. They reckon that
about 10,000 people were at one rally in KL. Imagine, 10,000
people! We had never seen anything like it. They demanded racial
equality, an end to Malay privileges, and a commitment to equality
in education.*

*You can imagine, just being able to air these grievances was
exciting. We felt so optimistic with so many wanting to reduce the
divisions between the races and build a truly multiracial,
multicultural nation. But the whole thing turned ugly when the
results started to come in on 11 May.*

*The Alliance won, but with a reduced majority. Their share of
the popular vote fell to less than half. The new parties, we learned
later, took to the streets the following day to celebrate their gains. This
provoked anger and the situation quickly got out of hand. Violence
broke out. In Port Dickson, we knew nothing of the fighting because it
was not mentioned on the radio or television. All we knew were the
election results as they were reported.*

*On 13 May, we set out to drive back to KL. Suddenly, we saw
convoys of army trucks with soldiers, armed to the teeth, heading in
the same direction. We were stopped and told to drive to the nearest
police station. We ended up in a car park with a lot of other cars. The
army ordered us to stay in our cars.*

*Our first thought was that the Indonesians had invaded. We were
told nothing. There was nothing on the radio. After a while, some of
the people tried to leave their cars, but the soldiers told them to stay
where they were, unless they wanted to be shot. It was terrifying!*

Towards evening, the families of policemen came over and we were allowed to leave our cars and go with them. We were escorted to the home of one of the policemen. His wife, Cik Fawziah, fed us well. Bless her, she was so kind. Only then did we learn that the whole thing had nothing to do with an Indonesian attack. It was because of an outbreak of racial violence in KL.

We were not allowed to leave for home until the following day. The journey was horrible. We saw houses burning, some totally destroyed. We were told later that they were mainly Chinese homes. Why? Why? Even now I cannot believe the terrible things that happened, not when I think about the kindness we received from Cik Fawziah.

The whole country is now under a State of Emergency and we have to stay in the house. We have been told that the curfew will be lifted for a few hours tomorrow when we hope to post these letters to you. I am not sure if the postal service will be working. We still don't know what is really happening. We have no newspapers and the television provides very little news.

Tomorrow morning, Father and Aunty Nelly will go to look at our shops. Father fears the worst. We have spent many sleepless nights discussing what to do. I do not know if your father will change his mind about leaving. He loves the country so much. I only hope his decision, whatever it may be, will be the right one. So for the moment, keep this to yourself. We don't want you to say anything to the boys until we are absolutely sure.

I have to stop now. I will write again when we have more news. Aunty Nelly sends her love.

Love and miss you.

Mummy

* * * * *

29 May 1969

Dearest An Mei,

I went with Aunty Nelly to look at our shops. It was the first time the curfew has been lifted. The roads were practically empty, but there were road blocks and soldiers everywhere. Most people seem to have stayed home although I would have thought that many of them must be running short of supplies by now. They are probably waiting to see what happens to those of us who have taken the chance to go out!

Two of the shops have been badly damaged, one is completely gutted. Someone must have torched it. They have been looted so nothing remains to be salvaged. The others are more or less intact although I do not know for how long. There is still sporadic fighting, despite the curfew. It is frightening to discover so much mindless hatred.

I am now more determined than ever to leave. My heart bleeds. I never imagined that I would ever feel the need to take such a step.

Take care of yourself. Could you look out for accommodation and let us know what is available? Once again, I leave your mother to give you the details.

Love,

Father

* * * * *

29 May 1969

Dear An Mei,

Just a short note from Aunty Nelly and me. She is standing next to me blowing kisses. Thank God, I continued to study English during my *time in Malacca. Nelly says that you must teach her when we come to England.*

As you will have seen from your father's letter, we are definitely coming. It might take some time. A lot depends on how long it takes to unwind the business, immigration rules and so on. Father is a broken man. He has worked so hard to rebuild everything and it will be difficult to sell up in the present situation without big losses. Needless to say, we are already having to make economies. So when you are looking for a suitable place for us, think small!

Aunty Jeanie has been very helpful. It was her husband who made it possible for your father to visit the shops. So strange that there should be such good friendships and such hatred at the same time. Aunty Jeanie is sure the madness will pass. But last night, after hearing the chants and the prayers, I am not so sure. We climbed to the top floor and saw gangs of young men with white bandanas around their heads wielding parangs! It was frightening.

Don't worry about us. Aunty Nelly has brought back some tinned food from the shops that were left alone. We are growing bean sprouts in the cupboards and I have sown some pak choy in place of the African Daisies! We still do not know how long the curfews will last, but we are well supplied for now. Look after yourself. Please share our news with the boys and tell them we will write soon.

Much love and kisses,

Mother and Aunty Nelly

* * * * *

I got down from my window seat, folded the letters and reached for the phone, but he stopped me. "You can't stay here in England. You have to come back with me to Malaysia. We have to build a life together. The country needs us more than ever. We have to tell our parents about us," said Hussein.

★★★★★ "An ambitious novel, populated by intriguing characters brought vividly to life. A thought provoking book that is hard to put down."

June Hargreaves *(from review in BAFUNCS Newsletter No.56, September 2009)*

★★★★★ "This book has a strong storyline and well-drawn characters. It held me as it drew me into a very different world from my own. It taught me about a period of history and a part of the world about which I knew little. I cared about the characters and the book left me wanting to know more."

Sylvia Mills *(from review submitted to www.amazon.co.uk)*

★★★★★ "The reader is taken on a roller coaster of emotions in this dynastic saga set against a period of tremendous social and political change."

Arthur Antony *(from review submitted to www.amazon.co.uk)*

★★★★★ "The book takes you under the skin of the characters as the family saga unfolds. A very enjoyable read - I liked the references to Malaysian food too!"

H. Harkness *(from review submitted to www.Amazon.co.uk)*

★★★★★ "I took this book on holiday and found that I just couldn't put it down even though the pool looked so tempting! The story flows beautifully and you warm to the main characters. Looking forward to the sequel!"

Gil Healy *(submitted to www.sweet-offerings.co.uk)*

★★★★★ "Excellent first novel. I found it hard to put it down. The descriptions of the market and the setting of the scene at the beginning were wonderful. This story held my attention from start to finish. I would really recommend it."

Edie Radford *(submitted to www.sweet-offerings.co.uk)*

★★★★★ "Chan Ling Yap's book keeps you turning the pages in excited anticipation to the very end. A most impressive first novel."

Margaret Paterson *(submitted to www.sweet-offerings.co.uk)*

★★★★★ "Just loved this book from start to finish - the characters come alive and the reader becomes totally involved in their lives. A book that is impossible to put down, can't wait for the sequel."

Anna Odin *(submitted to www.sweet-offerings.co.uk)*